Bound

by

Kate Sparkes

Dedication

For my parents, Steve and Wendy Lowden, who taught me to love books

And for Andre Sparkes, who continues to encourage my addiction.

Chapter One

Aren

The barmaid didn't offer her name to me as she would have to any other unfamiliar man who entered the tavern, but it was there at the front of her mind. Florence, though she preferred to be called Peggy. I could have dug deeper into her thoughts and memories to find out why, but it didn't matter. She didn't matter. She was just another loose end I was going to have to tie up at the end of the night, another irritation in a long chain of them.

The wooden clock on the wall read half-past eleven as I moved toward a table in a dark corner, trying not to draw the attention of the half-dozen border guards who were preparing to leave. I wished only to be left alone, to get the information I needed and move on. The hood of my cloak blocked my peripheral vision, but I kept it up to cover the shoulder-length hair that would identify my status as an outsider in this strange land.

A red-haired brute bumped my shoulder as he slipped into his heavy coat, and he cursed at me. His friends laughed. They'd have been more cautious if they'd understood what I was.

For the sake of my mission, I allowed them to leave unharmed.

Peggy knew what I was. Every time she glanced in my direction, her thoughts jumped to the preserved dragon head in the back room. She pushed the thoughts away, refusing to make the connection. It was an attitude I was familiar with. The people in this country, Darmid, feared magic. They'd spent centuries destroying every form of it within their borders, protecting themselves from a threat they didn't understand.

Few things irritated me more than willful ignorance. I needed to get home to Tyrea before I snapped and strangled one of these people who so reminded me of spooked cattle.

The barmaid ignored me as the seconds and minutes ticked audibly by on the intricate monstrosity mounted behind the bar. Her anxiety grew, pushing out of her in high, fluttering waves that I ignored. I breathed slowly and deeply, focusing my magic on the area outside of the inn, staying aware. All was quiet. Peggy and I were alone.

She jumped as a tiny door on the clock popped open and a bright red bird popped out, tweeting an off-key tune that did nothing to lighten the atmosphere. It pulled her out of her anxious stupor, and she turned to me.

"Drink?" she squeaked.

I shook my head, and she went back to sharing her attention between the door and the clock.

"We're closing soon," she said a few minutes later. "Do you…" she hesitated, torn between emotion and professionalism. "Do you need a room?"

"No. Only a few more minutes, and I'll be on my way."

She nodded, but made no move to begin closing up.

The door flew open, blown back by a gust of wind and rain. A slender man entered, wearing a black coat matching those of the men who had left earlier. He struggled to pull the door shut behind him. The hat he wore low over his eyes had done little to keep his face dry, and his thick mustache dripped rainwater down the front of his already-soaked garments.

He nodded to the barmaid and removed his hat as he passed. "The usual," he muttered.

He turned his head from side to side as though sniffing for danger, paused as he caught sight of me, then hesitated for a moment before sliding onto the bench across the table from me.

I took a moment to reach outside of the building again with my mind. He had followed my instructions, and had come alone.

Drops of water from the hem of his coat made dull tapping noises as they hit the grimy floor, out of time with the clock. He knocked his fingers on the table and pretended he wasn't afraid, but his thoughts pressed out of him, propelled by uncontrolled emotion. Fear, dread, a touch of excitement. Seeing a person so exposed repulsed me, and once again I longed for this assignment to be finished.

So finish it, I thought.

"You are Jude Winnick?" I asked him, dropping my voice to a pitch and volume that grabbed his attention but left the barmaid unable to listen in.

She interrupted us, leaving the safety of her post long enough to deposit a cup of sharp-scented spirits in front of my companion. She ignored the droplets that sprayed the table as she retreated.

He drank deeply, then wiped his mustache on the sleeve of his coat. "I am."

"Your brother is Myles Winnick, the magic hunter?"

"Might be. Might not be." His words were confident, but his voice trembled. "I know who you are, Aren Tiernal. I know who *your* brother is. I could turn you in."

Half-brother. Even as I worked to gain Severn's favor, I couldn't help but distance myself from him in my mind. "Is that why you answered my message, why you came here tonight? Are you going to place me under arrest?" I allowed myself a small, humorless smile and leaned forward, catching his gaze with my own. "No one knows you're here."

He licked his lips and took another long drink, then signaled to the barmaid to bring more. She looked away.

Winnick cleared his throat. "What do you want?"

"Your brother has been a busy man lately."

Winnick snorted. "Well, he's good at what he does. He sniffs out people like you better than a fox after rats."

"I'm looking for a magic-user born in your country. Any one would do, but your brother is killing them off. It's inconvenient."

"Not for us, it isn't."

"It could be."

Another attempt to drain the dregs from his cup, and

a scowl. "Why don't you talk to Myles about it? He's the magic hunter. I'm just the muscle."

I leaned back and rested my hands on the table. "Your brother is well-protected, and I don't think he'd be interested in speaking to me. But you—you could get close to him. Pass on a message. I heard a rumor that he's captured another Sorcerer. Perhaps he'd be interested in letting me take that person with me. Far less messy for your people than trying and executing him."

The drink must have been strong. Winnick's inhibitions were lessening after just one serving, his confidence growing. He pushed the cup too far to the side of the table, and it clattered to the floor. "And help you Tyreans? Not bloody likely. Why do you want him for, anyway? As I hear it, your country's just lousy with people like you. What do you want with ours?"

"That's not your concern." *Nor is it mine*, I added to myself. My brother Severn, regent of Tyrea, had ordered me to bring him a magic-user from Darmid, and to make sure no one in our own country saw me do it. I didn't care what happened to them after delivery. I just wanted to find one so I could leave this magic-barren land behind and return home for a reprieve from the manipulation and the killing.

I wasn't eager to see Severn again, but some things couldn't be avoided.

Winnick grinned, revealing several gaps in his yellow teeth. "What if I told you we'd just executed that one this morning? That he died bitching and moaning about his innocence, how he couldn't help having magic?"

I clenched my hands into fists under the table, but held my temper in check even as my pulse quickened. "I would be displeased if I heard that. Is your brother tracking anyone else right now?"

"I don't know."

But he did know. Had I not been able to read his thoughts with magic, the shift in his eyes and the nervous twitch of his wrist would have given him away.

"Look at me." He obeyed, and in an instant I was past his almost non-existent defenses, probing his thoughts. "Where?" He felt me in his mind, and tried to push the name of the town away, but I caught it. *Widow's Well.*

"How uplifting," I whispered as I released him.

He collapsed back against the booth and tried to pull his thoughts together. "You're a monster," he gasped.

"I wouldn't have to be if you'd cooperate."

"I'll never help you." He shuddered, then pushed his short hair back from his brow. "My brother will hear of this, and his superiors, and theirs."

"I'm terrified." I glanced at the barmaid. She stood straight and still, jaw clenched as she listened, looking anywhere but at us. At least her ignorance and fear were working in my favor.

"Are we done?" he asked. His right hand slipped under the table.

"Don't." I spoke sharply enough that the barmaid risked a glance in our direction. "This won't end well for you if you attack me."

He didn't listen. The hunting knife gleamed dully in the lamplight as he raised it and held it tight in his trembling fist. I gritted my teeth. *I should have taken that drink.*

Winnick stood and adjusted his grip on the knife's bone handle. "I don't think you mean for this to end well for me either way. I know about you people, and where your power comes from." He blinked and looked around. "I shouldn't have come. Making a deal with the bloody devil himself, that's what this was."

I stood, reached slowly into my pocket and produced a heavy gold coin, which I set on the table. "So you're not interested in a reward for the information you've so generously shared?"

His eyes widened, and he swallowed hard. His left hand reached for the coin, but he pulled back. In that moment of unguarded distraction I forced my way deep into his mind, past thoughts, memories and desires. He tried to close himself off, but it was too late.

I had all of the information I was going to get from him. I decided I would alter his memory and let him go. After all, Severn wanted this done quietly. I could be done with Winnick in a matter of moments and go on to search elsewhere for a magic-user.

Memories flooded Winnick's mind. Images of people he had helped his brother hunt down. Men, mostly, and hardly any with significant power. A few might have been classed as Sorcerers if they'd had the education and opportunity required to develop their talents, but not one had been given the chance. I saw them hanged. I saw a young woman screaming as the hunter and his men dragged her away from her crying children as her neighbors looked on and did nothing. And I saw this man and his brother laughing over their victories in this very tavern. My breath caught in my throat as rage finally overtook me.

Winnick bared his teeth in a mad grin. "You see that?" he whispered.

He tried to back away. I didn't let him, and his eyes widened as he understood the extent of my control over him. His knife clattered to the floor, though he tried to hold onto it. His thoughts turned to pleading, his emotions to fear and desperation as he tried to anticipate how I would hurt him.

A low moan escaped his throat, and behind him the barmaid clapped both hands over her mouth. I ignored her. She wouldn't remember any of this once I was through with her, and neither would Winnick. Not until he had to. Not until the suggestion I planted in his mind was ready to become action.

To hell with subtlety.

I leaned closer, and whispered to him what he was going to do.

Chapter Two

Rowan

Another day halfway done.

Another morning working at the library, with the smells of the old paper and new ink, with adventure and romance and tragedy. A few more hours of listening to Mr. Woorswith reminiscing with his cronies about the wonders and horrors they'd seen when they traveled to Tyrea in their youth. I'd lurked in the shadows behind the historical reference shelf, wishing I could see it all for myself, just once. Not much chance of a good Darmish girl like me doing anything of the sort, but I enjoyed eavesdropping on the old men's tall tales. They got me through long shifts and distracted me on days when the headaches tormented me. Today it hadn't been enough, and I'd asked to leave before lunch.

I slipped out the front door of the library and reached into my bag as I descended the stone steps to the street. The book of fairy tales that I carried felt heavier than it had any right to. *No reason to feel guilty about it,* I reminded myself. True, I was technically not allowed to access materials in the restricted section, and no one—not visiting scholars, not curious magic hunters—was allowed to remove a book about magic from the building. But no one would know. They'd never caught me before.

My boots scuffed over the dirty cobblestone streets, kicking up dust that swirled in the autumn breeze and settled into a thin layer on the bottom of my skirt. A sudden gust blew my auburn hair into my eyes, and I tied it in a thick knot at the back of my head. Not fashionable, but there was no one nearby I felt like impressing. My mother would have told me to lift my face to the world, to take pride in myself, and for goodness sakes just *smile* a little. But she wasn't there to bother me about it, and I could hardly be bothered to care on my own.

A bright ray of sunlight broke through the clouds overhead, and the dull headache that had been building all morning pressed harder at the back of my skull. The world swam in front of me, and I paused to take a few deep breaths. *You'll be home soon,* I told myself, and closed my eyes against the light. *Just get home, make some heartleaf tea for the pain, go to bed, everything will be fine. Nineteen years of this hasn't killed you yet.*

A clattering noise interrupted my thoughts. Hoof beats on stone, faster than they should have been. I opened my eyes, but the pain made everything slow. By the time I lifted my head and struggled to understand exactly what was happening, they were almost on top of me. Four horses with uniformed riders wearing the king's blue and gold, armed but not armored, completely out of place in the town of Lowdell.

What's the rush, boys? The thought passed slowly through my thick mind. One of them yelled. I tried to step out of the street, but something wasn't working. My legs wouldn't respond. I closed my eyes again.

Someone grabbed my arm and yanked me away, spinning me out of the road as the horses thundered past. It hurt my shoulder, but that hardly registered over the pain in my head, which screamed to life as my head snapped sideways. I pressed my hands to my face and leaned into my rescuer.

When I opened my eyes a few seconds later, my older brother Ashe stood looking down the street where the riders had disappeared. He ran his fingers through his short blond hair and frowned. "Didn't even look back."

"Must have been late for something." I slumped onto one of the crates that the grocer had left stacked outside of her store.

"Too late to do any good, that's for sure." Ashe scratched at the arm of his blue messenger's uniform and bent to pick up the papers he'd dropped when he pulled me out of the road. "You all right, Ro?"

"Same old thing," I said, and tried to smile. "Just need to get home to bed."

He frowned. "I'll walk you." I started to object, but he held up a hand to stop me. "I know, it's not my fault you're incompetent. Still, I'd feel sort of bad about it if something happened to you. I just have to post these on the way."

I stuck my tongue out at him.

He grinned and offered a hand to help me up. "Come on."

Three more soldiers on white horses trotted down Main Street as we waited to cross, their expressions grim and their gazes forward.

"Seems strange, doesn't it?" I asked Ashe.

He didn't answer.

The notice boards in the center of town kept us informed of all the important things. Posters for community events, help-wanted notices, and advertisements for matchmaking and snow-clearing services overflowed from four sides. The fifth was reserved for birth announcements, but there was rarely anything to post there, and nothing until a baby was at least six months old. On a really exciting day we might find a new reminder about the dangers of magic and the proper procedures for reporting a magical creature or plant if we saw one—or, God forbid, a person using it.

"What's this?" I took a heavy, cream-colored page from Ashe before he hung it.

"Read it for yourself."

Bold, scarlet letters stretched across the top of the paper. "Notice: Every able-bodied man over the age of sixteen is required to volunteer for security patrols as part of a province-wide initiative…" I glanced up at Ashe. "This is ridiculous."

He snorted. "I know. How is it volunteering if we're required to do it, right?"

"Not quite what I meant." I scanned the rest of the notice. "They don't even say why, do they?"

"Same as it's always been. The threat's just escalated since the Tyrean king disappeared. His son doesn't seem willing to let us be." Ashe took the paper from me and tacked it up high, partially covering a list of banned flora.

"It doesn't bother you at all?"

"Nah. It's never as bad as they make it out to be."

I wouldn't have taken the news so calmly if it had been my name being added to that list. Mother would have said that was typical. I've never liked being forced to do anything.

The pain was receding to its usual dull ache, but I leaned on Ashe's arm when he offered it, and we started toward our parents' house. I still had trouble thinking of it as home. My parents sent me to live with my Uncle Ches and Aunt Victoria when I was six years old. Their home, called Stone Ridge, was a half-day's journey from Lowdell, and my parents had hoped that life far from the city would be good for my health. I'd been back in town for a few years, but I still felt like a visitor in my parents' house and an outsider in town.

"There's no point worrying about it," Ashe continued, mistaking my silence for concern. "Folks have been talking about the possibility of Tyrea invading for ages, probably since our people settled here. But there have never been any large-scale attacks on any of the border towns, nor so much as a hint of their navy on our waters for as long as I can remember. Besides, even if something did happen, I doubt we would be the primary target."

Though Lowdell seemed like a bustling city to me, it was tiny compared to other places in Darmid. Ardare, the capital city, would be far more valuable to the Tyreans than our port town.

"The Tyreans probably wouldn't even remember to

tell us if they did take over," I said. "We'd just wake up one morning and the dragons would be back."

Ashe made a sour face. "Don't even joke about it. The dragons wouldn't be the worst thing to show up, either. I'd rather deal with one of them than with a person using magic."

We walked in silence for a few minutes. I breathed the ocean air as we left the protection of the town's buildings and followed the road through fields of long grass that stretched down to the bay. The smell of salt water and seaweed calmed me and cleared my mind like nothing else.

I slowed as we got closer to our parents' house. I rarely had a chance to speak to my brother alone, and our conversation brought up questions that were more pressing than my pain. Instead of saying goodbye, I leaned against the fence.

"Ashe, have you ever met a Tyrean? Or anyone else who used magic?"

"Never have, never want to," he said, with a firm shake of his head. "You haven't, have you?"

"No," I said. *Not really*. During my first years with my aunt and uncle, a family of Wanderers from beyond the mountains had come by a few times, selling wares. They seemed nice enough. I'd never tell Ashe, though. Most people considered the Wanderers harmless, and they'd never seemed magical to me. Still, their visits to Stone Ridge were a well-kept secret. We were a good family, and did not associate with anyone connected to magic or Tyrea.

Remembering the Wanderers and their disappearance troubled me, and I spoke without thinking. "If you've never seen magic, then how do you know it's bad?"

Ashe gave me a sharp look. "Same way you know a fish has gone bad just from the smell. You don't need to taste it to know it'll make you sick. You haven't been thinking about that again, have you?"

"No," I lied. I'd been thinking about it less in recent years, and I'd mostly accepted that real life had nothing in common with magic as I'd imagined it when I was a child. Still, I felt out of tune with the rest of the people in town, like I had too many questions that no one else seemed inclined to ask. Ashe was the only one I trusted not to shun me for them, and to answer me honestly.

"But no one will talk about it," I continued, hating the slight whine that crept into my voice, "and the old stories—"

"Were written in a very different time and place," Ashe finished for me.

"I don't need a history lesson." My uncle was a well-known historian, and he'd given me as complete an education as anyone could in our country. Hundreds of years ago, our ancestors overthrew rulers who wielded magic, who used it to enslave their countrymen. Our people rose up and killed the Sorcerers, then fled to this land at the Western edge of the mountains. Our magic hunters had been ridding the land of every trace of magic ever since— and every memory of it, including my beloved fairy tales.

Ashe planted his feet wide and crossed his arms, ready to lecture. "Magic is dangerous. You know how the people over there got theirs." He nodded toward the mountains to the east. "They sell their souls, Ro, just like the Sorcerers in the old country. The Tyreans worship demons and a false goddess, not our God. We have to distance ourselves from that. I know Uncle Ches keeps the old story books in his library at Stone Ridge. I also know he and Aunt Victoria let you read them when you were little, and that was unfair to you. It warped your thinking. Magic isn't wise unicorns and pretty mermaids and benevolent magicians, understand?"

"I know the stories aren't true. I just wondered—"

"No. The real heroes are the magic hunters who keep us safe, and the soldiers who protect our borders against the Tyreans."

Ashe obviously considered the subject finished and turned to open the gate, but I held him back. I needed my mind to be still. "How do you know that our stories are true? I mean, there was a time when people told their children those stories. They must have thought magic was good, once."

Ashe folded his arms across his chest. "All right. Here's a story for you, little one, since you enjoy them so much. I said that there have been no large-scale attacks on us, and that's true. But I delivered a report this morning saying that a magic hunter was killed yesterday, his throat cut clean to the bone. There wasn't much left of the killer once the other soldiers caught him, but they're almost certain it was the hunter's own brother that did it."

My heart skipped at the news of the magic hunter's death. No one I knew, but still… "That's horrible." I pulled a lock of hair from its knot and twisted it between my fingers, a nervous habit I'd never outgrown. "But I don't see what their family problems have to do with magic or Tyrea."

Ashe sighed. "The ruling family over there, the Tiernals, they're really powerful. They say Severn, the one who's on the throne now, has even more magic in him than his old daddy did. His brothers are strong, too, and one of them, Aren, uses it to control people's minds." Ashe tapped a finger against his forehead, as if the point needed emphasizing. "There was a barmaid who said the killer was in her tavern the night before the murder and she thought he met with someone, but she couldn't remember what happened, or even what this guy looked like. She was terrified, thought she was going mad. Do you understand what I'm saying?"

It seemed impossible. An exaggeration, like I'd always assumed the old men's stories were. I shivered and pulled my jacket closer to my body.

Ashe glanced at the house and lowered his voice. "Rowan, these people aren't like us. Severn is ruthless. From what I've heard he could be insane, too. I have no doubt that the mountains are the only thing holding him back from taking our lands. We know less about this other one, but we know he's dangerous, and this isn't the first time he's been to Darmid. God willing, they'll catch him this time, but he's probably long gone."

"How do you know all of this?"

"I keep my ears open, and you should, too. The world's a dangerous place these days. The governor and councils don't want people to know about attacks like this because it would cause panic. I'm telling you because I've seen the kind of books you sneak out of the library, and I know you're curious about magic. It's all dangerous, and if you mess with it, you're jeopardizing everything good that's coming to you. Understand?"

My stomach clenched. I'd been trying to avoid thinking about those good things that I was supposed to be so excited about. Sympathy for magic held no place in my future. "Understood. You want to come in for lunch?"

"Nah, I've got work to do. You need anything else?"

"I think I can handle it. Thanks."

Ashe waved and jogged back toward town.

I stood for a few more minutes looking at the mountains and another shudder ran up my spine. *Magic,* I thought. I knew Ashe was right, but still. *What if?* I'd once spent my days acting out fairy tales in the woods. More recently, on days when the town and its rules frustrated me, I'd thought about taking our old horse and following the shore past the mountains, just to see what was really there before I had to settle down for good.

Dreams are for children, I reminded myself, *and you're not a child anymore. Good things are coming, remember?*

I sighed and rubbed my temples, where tendrils of pain once again crept forward. It was going to be one of those days when it came and went like the tide. The headaches were only becoming more frequent and severe as the years passed, but even town doctors were at a loss as to how to stop them.

At least there was one treatment that helped.

I opened the gate and followed the path through the yellowing grasses to my family's home. Out of habit,

I paused to rub my fingers over the rowanwood wreath beside the door. Nearly every home in town had one, thanks to an old superstition that said it would protect the people within from the dangers of magic. A tiny branch cracked off under my fingers, and I stuffed it back into the circle as another beat of pain thudded at my skull. No time to worry about a silly decoration. I had more pressing concerns to think about.

Chapter Three

Rowan

A note waited for me on the little table inside the front door. I unfolded it and read as I followed the long hallway to the kitchen.

Rowan,
I'll be at the workshop this afternoon. Please don't go out tonight. We need to talk.
-Mum

"Where would I go?" I muttered, fighting the urge to crumple the note into a ball and toss it on the floor. Whatever she wanted to talk about, it wasn't going to be pleasant for me. I left the paper on the kitchen table while I set the kettle to boil on Mother's new wood stove, then searched the cupboards for heartleaf bark.

The purple glass jar where I kept it was empty, though I was certain I'd just bought some. The emergency supply I'd tucked away under the sink was stale, but better than nothing. I poured a thin stream of boiling water over the strings of bark and let it steep for as long as I could, then gulped the hot, bitter tea down. A burned throat was a small price to pay for relief.

I carried a second cup of tea with me to my room and cleared a space for it on the little bedside table, sending several charcoal pencils clinking to the floor. I laid my bag on the bed and took out the book of fairy tales. The leather cover was cracked, and the gold leaf that had once highlighted the title worn. My Uncle Ches took far better care of his personal collection. Still, the book was over two hundred years old and still in one piece. I wasn't going to complain.

I turned to set the book down next to my tea. Something didn't look right. The book I kept drawings in sat on the far side of the table, under the oil lamp. Not where I'd left it. The papers that had been underneath it were stacked in a neat pile, not the disorganized mess I had left them in.

I grabbed the sheaf of papers and rifled through, but the letter was gone.

"No," I groaned. A black and white cat hiding in the pile of clothes at the end of my bed woke and yawned.

The letter had arrived a week before, and I'd panicked when I saw the return address and the neat handwriting on the envelope. I'd been expecting a proposal from Callum Langley, and should have been excited about it. After all, he was everything a Darmish girl could wish for—strong, handsome, son of one of the wealthiest and most powerful men in Ardare, and following in his father's footsteps as a magic hunter.

We'd met at a party the year before, when I visited

Ardare with my parents. I was trying to avoid another man who spouted poetry and insisted on comparing my eyes to storm clouds, dripping wine on my shoes all the while.

The hostess had been forcing her cousin on Callum. The woman was a simpering idiot who batted her eyelashes and laughed at inappropriate times when he was talking. He and I had started talking in order to avoid our pursuers and found that we got along very well. We always did, when he found time to visit. Still, I'd balked when he started talking about marriage. It felt wrong, too fast. And now, a letter. I'd meant to show it to my parents, but had hoped to work out my response first.

I pressed the heels of my hands to my eyes to push back the pain so I could think. My mother would never understand why I'd hidden the letter. At nearly twenty years old, I was practically a spinster by Darmish standards, and was well aware of how embarrassing it was for my parents. I should have been married and trying to have children by age seventeen. Darmish women had difficulty conceiving, and the magic that lingered in our land killed many babies when they were still too weak to fight it off. Some families never had a child survive its first year, and a family like mine with four grown to adulthood inspired both gratitude and envy in the community. Darmish girls grew up knowing that it was our duty to maintain the population.

I just couldn't help wishing it wasn't my personal duty. I liked children, but felt exhausted at the very thought of living like my older sisters, who spent their days chasing snot-nosed toddlers around.

If only I could be more like my beautiful, bubbly cousin

Felicia, who was constantly surrounded by suitors in the capital city and loved every minute of it. She was a few years younger than me and would be settling down soon, too. She'd find a perfect husband, have perfect children, and be happy making a perfect home.

I set the papers back on the table and wished I had someone to talk it over with. I couldn't tell my mother about my misgivings, but Felicia might at least try to understand. If only she lived closer. I had no friends in town I could talk to, and if my sisters ever found time to listen, they'd just call me a silly fool and tell me to grow up.

That didn't mean I had to sit around and listen to my mother's predictable rant and watch the accompanying hand-wringing, though. It suddenly seemed like an excellent time to visit the family I'd grown up with. I'd been meaning to go anyway, to help get my aunt and uncle's big, old house ready for winter. Going now would allow me a brief escape, and no one was likely to go that far to drag me home and face my mother. I'd think about sending Callum my acceptance when I returned. Refusing his proposal was out of the question, but...

"It just seems so final," I whispered. The cat ignored me.

The headache was fading, if only slightly. I took off my skirt and slipped into pants that would be more practical for travel, then tossed clothing into my old canvas bag, along with the book of fairy tales and the knife Ashe gave me as a sixteenth birthday present. There was no harm in reading the book, no matter what Ashe and the authorities might think. The old stories comforted me with their familiar adventures, the romance, and even the magic, and they took my mind off of my real-world problems in a way that nothing else could.

In just a few minutes I was finished packing, and I hurried to shove the rest of the bedroom's mess under the bed. "I'll miss you, Puzzle," I told the cat.

He twitched an ear and went back to sleep. *If only everyone else was so content to let me be,* I thought, and kissed his head.

My parents' house wasn't especially large compared to many in Lowdell, but Mother kept it meticulously clean and tastefully decorated. Today most of the windows were open, and the cream-colored, lace curtains lifted and swayed in the gentle breeze. I moved as quietly as I could through the kitchen, taking only a slice of buttered bread for my lunch and eating it as I piled meat and greens into a sandwich for the road. One of the beautiful glass flasks my mother made in her shop held enough water for the trip, and I threw in an apple for the horse. The back side of my mother's note was still blank, and I used it to scratch out the details of where I'd gone. At least she'd be pleased that I hadn't wasted paper.

The front door creaked open, and I froze.

"Rowan?" My mother's voice carried clearly down the hallway. "Are you home?"

Damn. She was early. I hesitated for a moment, then slipped out the back door. There was no point discussing the letter with her. It would just turn into a fight with her insisting that I accept the proposal before Callum gave up on me, and me pushing back, not knowing why I thought I needed to fight so hard. I understood that marrying

Callum would be the best thing for me. I would say yes, and make my parents proud. I would live the life I was meant to have, and I'd learn to be happy with it.

Everything would be just perfect.

The old wooden cart waited in our little stable, and I pulled a few things from the storage closet to take with me to Stone Ridge—a crate of preserves, sugar, sweets left over from the previous month's festival. It wasn't much, but taking supplies was a good excuse to make the journey.

I wondered what excuse I'd use to get away once I'd married and moved to Ardare. I'd have to find a way. They and their servants were more family to me than my mother, father, and siblings. But once children came along...

I gripped hard onto the side of the cart and took deep breaths to calm my aching stomach.

Jigger, our old chestnut gelding, watched from his stall. I slipped in beside him to crouch in the clean hay that covered the floor, and buried my face in my hands.

"It's going to be perfect," I told myself. "I'm going to have everything a girl should want."

I tried to imagine a big, beautiful wedding. Callum would look so handsome, and I would stand there in front of God and everyone and declare that I would love him forever.

My heart fluttered in my chest, like a bird frantic to escape a cage that was growing smaller every day. I took deep breaths and squeezed back the tears that stung my eyes.

"What is wrong with me?" I whispered.

Chapter Four

Rowan

The afternoon air was crisp, colder than it should have been before harvest's end, but the sun shone bright and the leaves on the trees were halfway to what would soon be a riot of colors. Jigger's hoofs crunched over those that had already fallen as we reached the shelter of the forest road. It was a perfect day for travel, and the weather did wonders for my mood. Soon I was able to leave my anxiety behind and let my thoughts drift to more pleasant things.

The sun had dropped behind the trees before we reached the rock formation that Stone Ridge was named for. The narrow granite and quartz ridge ran along the north side of the road, rising to twice my height in the middle and tapering toward both ends of its considerable length. It sat on the border of the property, and had marked the edge of my world when I was a young girl.

Back then I had pretended it was the back of a huge dragon sleeping in the earth, waiting to wake and snatch unwary travelers. It was a good game, but even then I'd known it couldn't have been true. My people drove the dragons out of Darmid long before I was born. Sometimes I still wished I could see one, just once. It was so easy to imagine a sleek, green form slithering between the trees in that forest, especially on foggy days.

You should ask Callum if he'll take you to Tyrea to see a dragon, I thought, and smiled. That might have been enough to get rid of him forever, if I'd wanted to. A respectable person would never be interested in such things.

I was lost in those thoughts when a crashing noise in the trees above us made me jump in my seat and let out a small scream. Jigger froze, ears forward and muscles quivering visibly under his shaggy coat. I understood perfectly how he felt—my own heart pounded, and I felt like I might throw up the sandwich I'd stopped to eat earlier. I scanned the trees overhead, and noticed a small patch of damaged branches over the long rock.

Maybe you called a dragon to yourself. The hairs on the backs of my arms prickled. I dug my knife out of my bag, then slipped down from the cart. It occurred to me that it would probably a better idea to just leave, as Jigger seemed eager to do. But these were my woods, and I'd always been insatiably curious about the things that lived in them. I didn't think I'd forgive myself if I didn't at least look.

It was probably nothing, anyway.

My knife looked laughably small, but it made me feel braver than I would have without it. I crept toward the ridge, and winced as the dry leaves crunched under my weight, the small sound amplified in the eerily silent forest. A moment later there came a shuffling noise from the other side of the ridge. It stopped, but something was waiting there, perhaps something more frightened than I was—or perhaps just waiting to attack. I leaned my chest against the cold, moss-spotted rock, breathed deeply, and peered over to the other side.

"SKREEEE!"

A high-pitched shriek pierced my brain in the spot beside my left eye that still ached. I glimpsed a large brown bird tucked beneath a fallen pine before I ducked back behind my own side of the ridge.

Not a dragon, then. I almost laughed at my wild imagination. Just an eagle, though not quite like the white-headed ones we usually saw near the water. I sheathed and pocketed my knife.

When I looked again, the eagle was waiting for me. It had backed as far as it could under the dead tree, but hanging branches blocked most of the space and prevented retreat. One wing lay outstretched at an awkward angle over the leaf-littered ground, displaying slick, wet feathers.

I'd never liked leaving an animal to suffer, but this one looked decidedly uninterested in any help from me. It held its yellow and black beak open, ready to strike, and glared at me from beneath the golden feathers that shadowed its eyes. I climbed over the rock, then crouched and made myself as small and non-threatening as possible.

The eagle wasn't fooled. It hissed and fluffed its feathers, apparently putting as much effort into looking intimidating as I was into doing the opposite.

"Shh, you don't have to do that," I said in my softest voice. I knew I sounded foolish, but kept talking. I glanced at the bird's long talons and hooked beak. "You're plenty intimidating as it is, my friend."

I had no idea what to do next. I wondered what Matthew, my uncle's hired man, would do. He'd let it die, I decided, and he would be right to do it. Having an eagle around wouldn't be good for the chickens and the sheep.

But I couldn't just leave.

"You're hurt," I told the eagle, and looked away from its fierce gaze. "It's going to get very cold tonight, and if I don't take you with me, you're going to die here. I don't want to hurt you." I shifted my weight closer to the bird. It pulled back a little, but didn't screech or hiss.

When I risked another look, it had laid its head in the dirt and closed its eyes—I suspected more from weakness than from my kind words. My jacket was off a few seconds later, covering the bird's eyes and body. It didn't object.

The eagle wasn't particularly heavy, but its massive wings made it awkward to carry. I was careful to keep a strong grip on its talons and to make sure all of the sharp bits pointed away from my body, but still spent the walk back to the cart half-expecting to get my innards clawed out. Jigger laid his ears back against his head and scraped a fore-hoof against the hard dirt. He only settled when he could no longer see me carrying that odd bundle.

I placed it in the back of the cart and took a closer look at the wing, careful to leave the eagle's eyes covered as I'd read about people doing with hunting falcons. Blood oozed from its wing and was already staining my jacket. I sighed and took two blankets—one to cover the back of the cart, and one to wrap around my shoulders. I left the jacket where it was.

Jigger had found his usual plodding rhythm again when the thud of faster hoof beats came from ahead of us, the horses and riders still invisible around a bend in the road.

I shivered, remembering what Ashe had said about the world being dangerous, and realized how foolish it had been to stop. *You could have been off the main road by now,* I told myself. *Idiot.* I reached for my knife, unsheathed it again, and tucked it between my thigh and the seat of the cart.

I didn't look up when the hoof beats grew louder, but watched from beneath the hanging curtain of my hair, hoping that if I didn't draw attention to myself the riders would pass without stopping. A pair of horses and riders approached, silhouetted by the lingering sunlight in the west, and they slowed as they came closer. Low voices spoke for a moment. Then one rider came closer.

Calm down, I told my pounding heart. *We're not doing anything wrong.* Still, I reached for my knife.

"Stop, please," he called. "Excuse me, Miss? I—Rowan?"

I looked up to see Callum's familiar face, and he grinned as I lifted my gaze to meet his blue eyes. I breathed a sigh of relief at finding a friend with me. He looked like he'd been on his horse all day and hadn't shaved for longer. His light brown hair was a mess and his clothing dirty, but he still looked good. Better than I remembered, actually.

"Hello, Callum. I wasn't expecting to see you out here." I signaled for Jigger to stop, and Callum brought his big black horse up next to the cart, leaving his companion to continue toward the stone ridge behind me.

"I wasn't expecting to be here, myself," Callum said.

"Are you all right? You seem flustered."

I slowed my breathing and reached up to smooth my hair. "I'm fine. Ashe had me concerned about the sort of people I might meet on the road, so when I heard you coming..." I shrugged, then forced a little laugh. "Silly, right?"

More hoof beats approached, this time from behind us, and four rough-looking riders came into view. They slowed to a walk as they passed, each of them giving us a careful look. They wore full beards and dressed in coarse, dark clothing. The one in the lead gave me a lewd wink and sneered at Callum, but none of them stopped or spoke.

Callum watched until they'd disappeared down the road. "He wasn't wrong," he said. "We need as many men as we can get out here, but I don't trust most of them." He grimaced and rubbed his forehead. "And they're not nearly the worst of it."

"Well, I'm very happy to see you, then. What brings you out this way?" I tried to sound pleasant in spite of the nervousness that gnawed at my stomach. Unless the eagle was dead, it would make noise soon. I didn't want to have to explain that one. Still, leaving would be rude. In spite of my reluctance to accept his proposal, I couldn't afford to push Callum away.

"Oh, sort of a hunting trip," he said. I raised an eyebrow, and he laughed. "Official business, though, I promise— nobody's taking time off these days. Actually, you might be able to help. Did you see anything unusual here when you were coming up the road?"

You might say that. The anxious fluttering moved up

into my chest. "What, right here? I don't think so. What are you looking for?" *Please don't say a bird.*

"Probably a large bird." *Damn it.* "Farmers in this area have been complaining that something is attacking their livestock, and we spotted an eagle a few minutes ago. My father shot it, but it flew on, and we can't find where it fell."

"Your father?" I twisted around in my seat. My day was going from bad to worse in a hurry. Sir Dorset Langley was renowned for his skill as a hunter and his cleverness as adviser to the king, but nothing I'd heard about the man had made me eager to meet him.

He rode back toward us, tall and straight-backed on a muscular gray horse that nipped at Callum's mount. "Father," Callum began, "This is Rowan, who I've been—"

Callum's father held up a hand to stop him. "I remember. What's in the cart?" Steel-gray eyebrows knit together over intelligent eyes that looked just like Callum's.

"I… nothing," I stammered. "I mean, I'm taking supplies to my aunt and uncle. Sir."

"Hmm." His gaze passed over the blanket-covered cart. "You didn't see anything?"

"Oh, no. Nothing like that, at least." I knew that I should hand the bird over to be killed. It was absolutely the right thing to do if it was causing problems. But I remembered the eagle laying its beautiful head in the leaves and dirt, and I couldn't let them hurt it. I didn't like the cold expression on Dorset Langley's face, and though his presence commanded respect, I didn't feel inclined to help him. I scrambled for words that sounded natural, and hoped he couldn't see the nervous sweat that I felt on my face. "I'm sorry I can't be more helpful."

"Open the cart."

"Excuse me?"

"Standard procedure."

I looked to Callum, who wore an expression of shock on his face. He leaned closer to his father and spoke quietly. "I hardly think this is the best way for you to introduce yourself to someone who might soon be family."

Dorset Langley looked me over from head to toe and back again, narrowing his eyes at my face.

I held his gaze as calmly and as openly as I could. *I have nothing to hide.*

"Perhaps a girl who wants to marry a magic hunter should be willing to aid us in any way we request."

"No." Callum nudged his horse to move between his father and the cart. "If it's gone, it's gone. We're wasting time questioning Rowan, and you're frightening her."

He arched an eyebrow. "Am I, now? My apologies, young lady. We've had a long week, and I'm not quite myself."

I thought this was probably exactly how he usually treated people he considered beneath him. His words sounded sincere, but that piercing gaze never left me. "That's fine," I told him. "Maybe we'll just start over next time?"

He just lowered his head in a sort of bow, then turned to ride back to the ridge. I looked at Callum, who was still frowning after his father. *Prince Charming himself,* I thought. *Chasing off the ogre to save his fair lady.*

"Well, I should get on," I said. "It was lovely to see you. I suppose we should talk more some time when you're not so busy." I urged Jigger on, down the road and away from Dorset Langley, but Callum kept pace beside us.

"Did you receive my letter?"

"I did. I passed it on to my mother to look at. I hope that's all right." At least it wasn't a complete lie.

"Oh, of course. I'm glad you're… yes, very good." He smiled, obviously pleased with the acceptance he antici-pated. "Would you like an escort?

I stretched my smile until I thought my cheeks would crack. "Oh, I'd like that, but I think your father is waiting for you. The turn-off is just ahead, I'll be fine." I wasn't sure what else to say. "Will you be in Lowdell any time soon? I should be home next week, if you'd like to come by."

"I don't know. Things are busy for us right now. But thank you. I'd like to talk to you about—"

"Callum!" his father called.

Callum sighed. "I should get back to it. Yell if you run into trouble. We won't be far."

I thanked him again, and my stomach clenched as I watched him ride away. Such a gentleman, so kind and so strong. But my chest still tightened when I thought of talking to him about his letter.

When I looked back one last time, Dorset Langley was pointing toward the broken branches overhead. I urged Jigger to move faster and get us away before Callum or his father could change their minds about letting me go.

Chapter Five

Rowan

The sun disappeared as we journeyed on, leaving the sky pink and purple overhead. The cart rocked and bumped over the uneven surface of the narrow road until the slate roof of Stone Ridge came into view over a low hill, followed by a crumbling rock wall and the heavy iron gates that had stood open for as long as I could remember. Jigger lifted his head. His ears pricked up and he threw his weight forward, perhaps recalling that the hospitality here was better than at home. I hoped that there would be supper waiting for me, too.

As we started down the other side of the slope, a slowly spreading warmth flowed through my muscles, erasing the tension that my meeting with Dorset Langley brought on. Though I'd been living with my parents for years, it was only when I returned to Stone Ridge that I felt like I was home. Stone Ridge meant love, family, and above all, freedom that I could never enjoy in the city.

I laughed when a scrawny, long-haired black mutt jumped into the road and gave a half-hearted snarl.

"Good evening, Micah," I said. The dog waved his curved tail and trotted alongside the cart as we passed between the gates and into the huge yard. Grass grew between the stones beneath us and weeds sprouted beside the roadway, but it was easy to imagine how beautiful the grounds must have been when the big house was new and filled with family and servants.

"Micah!" yelled a gruff voice from inside the carriage house. "Some guard dog you are!" My uncle's hired man Matthew came out and leaned against the doorway. The dog ran to him and lay on its belly, grinning. Matthew shook his head and ran his fingers through his thick, silver hair as he walked toward me, dog at his heel. He swung himself up into the still-moving cart and settled onto the seat beside me. The long hairs of his unkempt mustache twitched as he sighed. "I swear if anyone ever decided to rob the house, that mongrel would lead them straight to the good silver."

"At least he tried. You can't blame him, really. He knows he can count on me for a belly rub."

Matthew chuckled, then turned to me and scowled. "You should have told us you were coming. I'd have met you half way."

"I'm fine, Matthew. You worry too much."

"I don't worry. Just good to know what's what, that's all." He covered his smile with a work-roughened hand. He'd never admit to worrying, but Matthew had always cared for me like I was his own daughter. He and his wife Della had as much of a hand in raising me as my aunt and uncle did during my years at Stone Ridge. The hours he and I spent fishing at the river were among my most cherished memories, and he'd held me when I cried after I killed my first hen.

I may have had an unusual childhood, but it was a happy one.

"Is everyone else inside?" I asked.

"Your uncle is off to Ardare to advise on something at the university. He's been gone a lot these past few months. Della's inside seeing to Victoria. I don't say your aunt will be up for seeing you tonight. Hasn't been well." Exhaustion crept into his voice as he spoke. The house and grounds were too much for him and Della to care for on their own, but uncle Ches couldn't afford more help. "You want some help unloading, there?"

I almost said yes out of habit, but stopped myself. "Actually, would you mind taking Jigger after we get the cart to the house? He seemed to be favoring his right fore a ways back. Maybe you could give him his supper and take a look." I hated lying to Matthew, but I couldn't explain the eagle to him. Over the years he'd helped me bandage and care for injured rabbits, cats, and a saucy young crow, but I felt certain he'd draw the line at anything that might be a danger to the livestock or to me. Matthew was compassionate and talented with animals, but more than anything, he was a practical man.

He watched the horse, squinting in the fading light as we approached the stone walled house. "Seems fine, but if you can take care of the rest yourself, I'd be glad to." He jumped down as the cart rolled to a stop and removed the traces from Jigger. "I keep forgetting you're all grown up now."

Jigger seemed reluctant to leave, and kept looking at the cart, ears laid back. Matthew clucked his tongue and hummed a soft, lilting tune, and Jigger went with him. I waited until they were out of sight around the house before I pulled back the blanket that covered the cart.

Nothing had moved, not even the eagle. The bird lay still under my jacket. It didn't move even when I pulled the covering away and the cool evening air ruffled its feathers.

A lump formed in my throat. It shouldn't have mattered, but I had looked forward to caring for the beautiful creature. It would have been a far more interesting problem than the ones I'd tried to leave at home.

"I'm sorry," I whispered, and a dark eye opened. "Oh—I thought you'd gone."

The eye closed again. The golden feathers on the bird's neck seemed to glow in the light from the lamp outside the kitchen, and I reached out and gently ran my fingers over them. A shock pricked my fingers, and I pulled my hand back. The bird must have felt it, too. It opened its eyes again and tried to lift its head. I pulled the blanket back over the cart and hurried into the house. The heartleaf was wearing off, and I was anxious to get my work done.

There was no one in the big kitchen, but pots rested on the iron stove and the savory smell of supper set my stomach rumbling. "Hello?" I called, and set my bag down on the wooden table in the center of the room. "Della, are you here?"

Matthew's wife leaned her head out of the pantry door on the far wall. White streaks of flour marked her cheeks, and her brown hair was piled into a messy bun on top of her head.

"Hello, my girl!" she called in her musical voice. "I promised your aunt clean bedsheets tonight, and her supper's ready. Just give me a minute?" She went to the stove and piled food onto a plate, then disappeared into the hallway.

I turned on my heel and jogged back to the cart, lifted the eagle as gently as I could, and carried it up the narrow back staircase to my rooms, taking the stairs sideways so as not to nudge the dangling wing with my knees. I bumped the wall with my shoulder and a section of wood panels popped open, startling me. The building was full of those hidden closets. Useful for children's games and for storing spare bedding, but inconvenient now. Still, no one would miss those blankets if I made a mess of one. I shifted the eagle's weight to one arm and grabbed an old quilt, pushed the door shut with my elbow, and continued up the stairs. The eagle twitched, then relaxed.

The door to the old servants' quarters was unlocked, and I pushed it open with my shoulder. The sitting room of my private sanctuary smelled of fresh lilacs that stood in an old blue vase, mixed with the sharp cedar scent of the open wardrobe. I carried the eagle across the room and set it on the table I used for my drawings and collections, then lit the lamp, turning the flame low so as not to startle it.

Him, I thought, for no other reason than the fact that I hated calling an animal "it," even to myself.

The blood that streaked my jacket looked brown in the dim light. I left the bird on top of the old quilt and ran back downstairs to unload the cart, pain slamming in my forehead with every step.

I felt bad leaving him like that, but I had to take care of other things first if I didn't want anyone to follow me upstairs.

I put the kettle on to boil while I carried boxes into the kitchen. Della returned in time to take the last box of preserves from me, and I poured a cup of brewed mint leaves for each of us.

"How's Aunt Victoria now?" I asked.

Della blew into her mug and took a sip. "Probably as bad as you've seen her, but I suppose that's to be expected. It's been almost exactly a year since the accident, hasn't it? I've had a hard time just getting her out of bed these last few days. She was glad to hear you're visiting, but I'm afraid she won't see anyone but me right now. The memories are overwhelming her. She gets confused." Della rubbed her eyes with her free hand, and I regretted not coming sooner. I went to Della and wrapped my arms around her tiny waist, and she squeezed back.

"I'm sorry," I whispered.

Della released me and sat at the table. "Not your fault. Not hers, either. It's just one of those things." She looked thoughtful, then smiled and patted the seat next to her. I sat, though I wanted to get back to my rooms. "But enough about us. How are you? And your family? And… everything?"

I smiled into my cup. Della knew better than to ask directly about the marriage situation. "Fine, everyone's fine. There will be news on the other thing soon, I suppose."

I wondered how Della had felt when she decided to marry Matthew, who was nearly twenty years older than her. "If it's all right with you, I'm going to head up to bed. Do we have any heartleaf bark?"

Della nodded. "Of course. I don't suppose you can get it at home now."

"We're out of it. I was going to stop on the way out of town, and I forgot."

"Oh, my dear." Her frown deepened the lines on Della's forehead. "You didn't hear, then? They've just classified heartleaf as a highly suspicious species. Not to be collected or sold."

"What?" *Highly suspicious* was only a step below *confirmed magical*. Heartleaf trees would be extinct within a decade, at least in populated areas. "There's no magic in it," I groaned. "It's just the only thing that helps." I remembered the empty jar in the kitchen cupboard, and my jaw muscles tightened. "I can't believe Mother got rid of mine!" She knew how I needed it. But I supposed a magistrate's wife couldn't allow illegal substances in her house, no matter how badly her family needed them.

Della reached out and patted my arm. "Well, I suppose she felt it was the right thing. There was a letter about that a few days ago, but we ignored it. Even if they made us get rid of what we have, there'd still be three good trees on the property. Take some supper with you, dear, it'll help." She busied herself filling a plate with roasted meat, potatoes, boiled carrots, and a slice of buttered bread. My stomach groaned again.

Della poured boiling water into a heavy mug and set a

generous pinch of heartleaf bark strings next to it on the tray. "Sleep well, Rowan. I won't wake you, but there's plenty to be done tomorrow when you're ready." She kissed me on the cheek and hurried off to prepare plates for herself and Matthew, and I felt a pleasant ache in my chest. It was good to be home.

When I returned to my rooms, the lump on the table hadn't moved. I set the tray down next to my favorite old armchair and ate a few bites of everything while I tried to think what to do. I went to the bedroom and dug my sewing kit out from under the bed, and blew the dust off of it, then carried it and the mug of hot water over to the table. There were needles in the kit, strong thread, scissors, and a pair of pointed pincers buried beneath a tangle of string and fabric scraps. I dropped the pincers into the hot water, then pulled the ruined jacket off of the eagle and tossed it into the corner of the sitting room.

The bird watched with glazed eyes as I stripped off my heavy sweater and slipped into a long-sleeved button-up shirt. He didn't seem able to do anything else, except twitch for a few seconds when I lifted the injured wing to examine the wound. I hesitated for a moment, waiting for an attack, but he just lay there as I began my examination.

It was worse than I'd thought. A nasty rip through the skin and muscle of the wing left bone exposed, and I suspected a break farther down. I took the pincers and carefully removed a piece of wood that was embedded in the wound. It was splintered lengthwise, jagged at the ends. Part of the arrow's shaft, then, but it had a strange, sickly green color that shimmered in the flickering light. I dropped it onto the table and went back to work.

There wasn't much bleeding now, even with the wood removed, but I didn't know how I'd ever stitch the skin together. There were no clean edges to match up, and not enough flesh to cover the bone. I leaned back in the wooden kitchen chair and pressed the heels of my hands to my eyes.

"*Skrork?*" The bird was watching me again. For the first time I noticed the green flecks scattered through the deep brown irises of his eyes. They were beautiful. Cold, but expressive, almost human. Not like our chickens, which often seemed like alien creatures to me. I could almost believe that this bird understood what I was trying to do.

"I'm sorry," I whispered. "I'll do what I can, but I'm no doctor." The eagle closed his eyes and turned his head away from me. I pulled the lamp closer and cleaned the torn skin. If I could cover it and keep it clean, it might heal—but he would never fly again.

Sharp pain twisted through my head, and I picked up a few strings of bark to chew on. It didn't work as well as brewing them, but it was something. My eyes throbbed to the slow rhythm of my pulse.

I tried to stand to find something to cover the wound with, but felt light-headed and sat down again, suddenly feeling ill. The room wasn't spinning like it was supposed to if a person were fainting, but instead seemed to fade away. I could still see everything around me, but none of it seemed real. All of my focus was pulled to the eagle, its wing, the raw, bloody gash.

Nauseating pain washed over me and slashed at my

skull, but I couldn't pull back from the lamplight to find relief in the dark. White spots filled the edges of my vision. Something pulled at me, gentle but insistent.

The wing started to come back together. The veins knit themselves, and blood began pumping through them. My breath caught in my throat, my heart hammered. *Impossible.* I tried to look to the eagle's face, but couldn't shift my gaze away from what was happening in front of me.

I groaned as the pressure in my head increased to an unbearable level. My voice sounded far-off and weak.

Tears blurred my vision, but through them I watched as the healing continued. Muscles grew together over the bone, and the sharp bend in the wing straightened under the feathers with a soft cracking sound. Skin grew over the wound, dark pink and rippled, but nearly whole.

Grey patches bloomed out of the white lights and crowded everything else out. The world turned black, and I fell into darkness.

Chapter Six

Aren

Her magic disappeared from the room as she hit the floor, but it lingered in me, its glowing embers all that remained of the healing force that had taken me by surprise. I lifted my head and shifted my body to the edge of the table. There she lay, head cocked at an awkward angle and thick hair covering her face, chest rising and falling regularly. I closed my eyes, half-hypnotized by the strange feeling that flowed through me, pulsing outward from my injured wing. Hours before, I'd thought I was going to die, crippled, shot with an arrow that poisoned my blood and kept me from using my magic. Now I would live, if I could get away.

Perhaps a rest first, though.

I opened my eyes again, and blinked hard, fighting the influence of her magic, which felt so unlike my own in its warmth and gentle strength. It would have been easy to let myself drift off into it as it healed me, but I couldn't. I was still in danger, and needed to get home. It wouldn't be long before my body made the magic its own. I just needed to be patient.

I forced myself to my feet, bracing my talons against the flat surface of the table. I stretched my injured wing, resisting the contented laziness that infused my muscles. It wasn't fully healed, but that girl had done what I couldn't. She'd cleansed my blood of the poison, and healed my wounds far more efficiently than I'd have been able to under any circumstances.

There was no way I could open the window behind me without transforming back into my human body. I flapped to the floor and made my way through an open doorway into a tidy little bedroom, but the only window in there was closed, too.

There was nothing else to be done. I drew on that unfamiliar magic within me and transformed, sending the eagle's body away as I drew my own form back to myself until I crouched with my bare feet pressed against the smooth, wooden floorboards of the bedroom. The temperature in the room dropped as the process began. *Focus*, I told myself. Transformation was still a relatively new skill for me, and I had to be careful.

I wrapped myself in a quilt from the bed. Not for the first time, I decided that forming clothes after transformation was going to be the next skill I studied. At twenty-three I was far more powerful and skilled in magic than anyone had expected, but I couldn't let myself rest when there was still so much to learn.

The tiny sitting room where I'd left her was warmer and brighter than the bedroom. I sat in a worn-out armchair and examined my arm in the lamplight. The wound had transferred, as they always did, and it still throbbed with that unfamiliar magic. I found that I could think more clearly now that I had returned to my natural form, and several conclusions fell into place.

First, this young woman was no professional healer. The ability to heal another was among the rarest magical gifts. Besides that, anyone in my own country who regularly used magic to heal learned to strip their personal essence from the power before it left them, leaving it as blank as the ambient magic in the land around them. Their work felt nothing like this. Her magic was soft, yet powerful enough to make me feel light-headed. Her concern for me when the healing began was there, a feeling of peace and belonging that I hadn't felt in years.

The intimacy of it made me shudder. I didn't want this Darmish girl's magic and her essence to be a part of me. I hardened myself to its influence, and waited for the power to become my own. But as her influence began to fade, an ache spread through my chest, a feeling of regret which I refused to examine. The sooner I moved past it, the better.

I looked down at the still form on the floor. "Who are you?"

A Darmish woman with magic in her—just what I had been searching for. But the magic had hurt her. When I crouched beside her, I felt nothing. Had she not just healed me, I would have thought her just another useless, magicless body.

"Protected, then," I muttered.

It made sense. Anyone like her living in this country would have to keep that secret well-hidden from the magic hunters, their townsfolk and even their families. But from me? It should have been impossible.

In any case, she was exactly what I'd been searching for. If I took her back to Tyrea and handed her over to Severn, my work would be done. Delivering someone like this would win Severn's favor and once again prove my loyalty. If he trusted me enough to make me his Second, things would change for the better. My work might still occasionally involve manipulating Severn's enemies, but at least I'd be doing it in Luid instead of in the outer provinces or this gods-forsaken land. Taking this hidden Sorceress to Severn would buy me power and wealth—and anything or anyone those resources could buy.

And yet, this girl had saved my life at great risk to herself, and I needed to decide what that was worth.

I stood to open the window, and breathed in the cool night air. My brothers would call me a fool for even considering leaving her here. They'd have taken her in just to prove they didn't owe anything to anyone. Compassion was weakness, as was gratitude to those below our station, and my family had seen too much weakness in me when I was a child. I'd worked to harden myself to fear and love and everything else that makes one vulnerable, but suddenly found myself struggling again.

Wealth and power and freedom were within my grasp, and I was considering letting it go so a stranger could live. *Idiot.*

I flexed my arm again and felt its weakness. It would be too difficult to take her back in my current state, I decided. I would leave her, at least for now. If she was lucky, I'd find another.

The stairs creaked outside of the closed door.

Damn it. I'd forgotten to send my awareness out, lulled by that warm magic into a feeling of safety. I moved silently to the door and leaned against it. A single presence approached, female. Not threatening, but I doubted she'd be pleased to find a naked stranger in the house and the girl lying half-dead on the floor.

A knock. "Rowan? Are you awake? I'm off to bed, if you need anything." A soft voice, concerned but not overly so. When no answer came, she turned to leave. As soon as she left the stairwell, I locked the door.

"Rowan, is it?" I asked. The girl on the floor didn't answer.

The wagon ride had been torture. Every bump in the road sent fire burning through my veins, courtesy of the poison in my wounded wing. Still, I had listened, and heard much of her conversation with the hunters. Dorset Langley. I knew that name, though I'd never met the man. His reputation as a magic hunter reached far beyond his country's borders. And she was to marry his son.

"Why ever would you do a thing like that?" In their country those who fought against magic were heroes, and she would be marrying into a wealthy and powerful family. But as a magic-user, perhaps even a Sorceress, she was putting her life in danger to do it. So either she valued social status above her own life, or she felt confident enough in her ability to hide the magic that she thought it was worth the risk.

"Or she doesn't know what she is." An interesting idea.

I sat again and pulled my hands through my tangled hair, then tied the mess behind my neck with one of the strings from the sewing basket. As I ate what was left of the girl's supper, I glanced around the room to see what I could learn about her.

Illustrated books about nature lay stacked on one shelf, though I suspected they omitted many of the creatures we were familiar with on the other side of the mountains. There was fiction there, too, bound in leather and paper, probably nothing I would recognize. Scholars in Tyrea studied Darmish culture, such as it was, and I'd learned enough to know that their stories were like their land: scrubbed clean of magic.

And interest, I thought.

When I stood again, the heavy quilt I wore knocked the girl's travel bag onto its side, and another book slid out onto the floor.

As I flipped through the brittle old pages, I smiled. "That's more like it," I told her, and tried not to laugh. In my country, these were children's stories. There was a girl with a fairy godmother, as if the fairies would have any interest in the position. The prince turned into a monster and restored by love came next, followed by talking animals, burnt witches, and magic of the lightest and gentlest sort. But, I reminded myself, things were different here. The Darmish didn't allow their children to be exposed to these stories, which they considered heretical. Just possessing this book would get my unlikely rescuer into serious trouble if it were discovered.

She was a mystery, but one I couldn't dwell on for long.

When I extended my awareness again, the house was quiet. It would be safe to leave. But as I stepped past the body on the floor, she moved. Not much, just a slight arch of the back. Her head turned to one side, and the waves of tangled reddish hair fell back from her face.

She was lovely. I'd caught a glimpse of that when I was in eagle form, but had been unable to appreciate it fully. Now, in human form and with the pain receding, I could see it. The memory of her thick eyebrows knitting together over clear and intelligent eyes increased my pulse, as did the thought of her well-proportioned torso as she struggled out of her heavy sweater. No woman in my home city of Luid would have allowed herself to be seen in such an unkempt state, but there was something appealing about this girl's clean face and wild hair. Too appealing.

"Definitely time to go," I whispered.

I should have been able to leave her there. She'd served her purpose. If a night on the floor was the worst she suffered from meeting me, she would be better off than most. And yet, I couldn't do it.

I rubbed my hands over my face then wrapped the blanket around my waist. As I lifted her, her head rolled back, leaving her throat exposed as the collar of her shirt pulled open where she'd neglected to close the top few buttons. Such vulnerability should have seemed pathetic to me, but I found myself instead pulling her close to my chest and wanting to protect her.

It's her magic, I realized, and released the breath I'd been holding. Of course. It was still affecting me. Completely natural. Regrettable, but natural. *It will pass, and no one ever has to know.*

My left arm screamed with pain, and I hoisted the girl over my shoulder to carry her to her bed one-handed.

I gave into my weakness for another moment and made her as comfortable as I could, removing her boots, loosening the ties at the waist of her trousers, and pulling a blanket up to her shoulders. I reached out for her mind, but found that I couldn't see her thoughts. She was there, but blocked—another indication that her hidden magic was strong.

"Goodbye, Rowan," I whispered. "Best of luck to you with your magic hunter."

As I stepped out of the sitting room and onto the top stair, a certainty that she wasn't safe stopped me. She had used magic to help me. Would that change anything for her? Would her betrothed see what she was?

"Not my problem," I muttered, and forced my feet forward. Still, my mind wouldn't let go of her. *And how could she not know what she is? That was powerful magic that she used, that my body is still using.*

A memory from history lessons tickled the back of my thoughts, but wouldn't come forward. Something about a punishment that kings once used against rival Sorcerers.

This could be significant.

Pain twisted through the new scar on my arm. Perhaps it would be better to stay for just a few days, until my strength returned. I'd need it if I was going to risk returning to Luid empty-handed. Perhaps I would learn something useful.

Perhaps I'd change my mind about taking her when her

magic was no longer influencing me.

I returned to the sitting room and folded the quilt on the seat of the chair, then let magic flow through me and transform my body again. I found my eagle brain able to see the situation more objectively. *Only logical,* I thought as I settled in for the night. *Survival first. In a few days, she'll just be an unfortunate part of my past.*

Chapter Seven

Rowan

I've been having the same nightmare for as long as I can remember. In the dream I can't see or hear anything. All I'm aware of is something being wrapped tight around my body, squeezing. I try to inhale, but there's no room to breathe. That's where the dream ends, in suffocating darkness.

When I woke, it looked like I'd been having that dream again. The blankets were twisted around my legs, and at some point during the night I'd shoved my pillows onto the floor. I closed my eyes and tried to remember, but everything seemed jumbled in my mind, as though whatever happened the evening before had been mixed with surreal dreams. I remembered unbearable pain. I remembered trying to fix the eagle, and I remembered fainting. Nothing more.

I kicked the blankets away and rolled gingerly onto my side, careful to not waken the pain that had faded to a bearable ache as I slept. I was still dressed, but my boots stood neatly paired beside the bed, and the laces on my pants were undone. I didn't remember going to bed. Had Della come up and found me on the floor? If so, had she seen the eagle?

The eagle. I closed my eyes again and sighed. *The poor thing probably died while you were passed out on the floor, you silly thing. So much for your life-saving skills.*

I changed into fresh clothes and hurried through the sitting area to the washroom, not daring to look around yet, and took my time getting ready for the day. Only when I couldn't stand it any longer did I go back to the sitting room.

Nothing. No body on the table, no bloodstained jacket in the corner, not even the strange, green piece of wood I vaguely remembered pulling from the bird's wing.

"*Skraaw?*"

I spun around to look for the source of the soft croaking noise. A brown and gold eagle perched with its talons sunk deep into the upholstery of my armchair, but it couldn't have been the same one. Far from looking like the bedraggled, nearly dead thing I remembered, this bird was alert and healthy, though one wing drooped slightly. I took a step forward, then hesitated. That beak looked even more intimidating than it had the evening before. The eagle didn't move, but watched calmly as I edged closer, as though he was accustomed to human company. A hunting bird, maybe.

As if to demonstrate his good health the eagle stretched, wingtips reaching out as wide as I was tall. He pulled them back in, right wing still held slightly askew, and began preening his glossy feathers.

I'm losing my mind, I thought, and looked again. The wound, while still visible, had done an impossible amount of healing for one night. This was a strange animal, or I'd been asleep for a lot longer than I thought.

I backed slowly toward the bookshelf and grabbed "The Illustrated Field Guide to Birds Vol. II." I'd borrowed it from my uncle's library thinking I could use it to practice drawing, but had never found time.

I had no idea what might have become of volumes I or III, but this book had exactly what I was looking for. On page twenty-six, perched between the White-Headed Eagle and the Fish Hawk, was my house-guest, the Golden Eagle. There was no other useful information, but it was good to have a name to put to the bird.

A name... When I glanced up the eagle was still watching me with his head cocked to one side. The feathers over his eyes gave him a stern and serious look.

"I don't know how long you're going to be staying, but I can't be calling you 'hey you' or 'fella' while you're here," I told him. "We even name the chickens, and we *eat* them." I tapped a fingernail against my teeth as I considered the problem. "I once read an old story with an eagle called Aquila in it. Suits you well enough. What do you think?"

I didn't expect a reaction, and I didn't get one. The eagle just stared at me, somehow appearing relaxed and vigilant at the same time.

He stretched again, hopped down to the floor and flapped up to the table, scattering my drawings and a few books. The window was open, and he shuffled over to the sill and onto a cherry tree branch that grazed the side of the house. He seemed perfectly content to sit there, ignoring me. I stooped to pick the books up. One was the old fairy tale book from the library, though I didn't remember taking it out of my bag.

"It's magic, isn't it?" I asked as I leaned out the window. "That's how you healed so quickly. Did you come from over the mountains?"

The eagle didn't respond, but a thrill rushed through me. There was simply no other explanation. Then, just as quickly as it had come, the excitement dulled. I remembered what Ashe had said about magic, and everything we'd been taught about the need to protect ourselves from it. This was real life, now, not a fairy tale.

But still, he was just an animal. There couldn't be any harm in helping him, could there? He seemed normal, aside from the overnight healing.

"You're not dangerous, are you?" I asked. Aquila stared at me for a moment, then slowly clacked his beak. Not threatening me, but I didn't know what it meant. Maybe nothing.

"So what am I supposed to do with you now?" I paced between the chair and the bookcase, and Aquila watched from the window. "If I tell someone, I don't know what they'll do to you. I doubt it'll be pleasant, if Dorset Langley was after you. But if I take you back to the forest before you're ready, you won't survive." I tugged at my hair as I thought. "Tell you what. You can stay just a little longer, but I'm watching you." I hardly wanted to admit to myself that I was feeling the excitement again. "You hurry up and finish healing, and then you'd better get out of here if you know what's good for you."

Aquila fluffed his feathers and settled his head on his breast. At least someone was comfortable with the arrangement.

"That's settled, then. You do what you want, just stay out of trouble. If you fall out of the tree I can't risk smuggling you in again, and if Matthew sees you, I have no idea how you got here. I'll try to bring you something to eat later."

I spun around and raced downstairs, excited about something for the first time in as long as I could remember.

#

I fell easily back into the routines of life at Stone Ridge, helping Matthew prepare the gardens for winter, putting up storm windows, feeding the animals and cleaning the barn. Aquila watched us from the tree, huddled close to the trunk where he was nearly indistinguishable from the bark.

I tried to visit Aunt Victoria that afternoon, but her bedroom door was locked, and she refused to answer when I knocked. She rarely left that room anymore, but I'd hoped she would at least let me in.

After Della and Matthew went to bed that evening I sneaked some raw meat from the cold storage to my room, and Aquila ate while I went to the bedroom and changed into my sleep clothes. When I returned, he seemed to be waiting for me. I took out my charcoals and sketched him for a while, but it didn't relax me the way it usually did.

After a few hours of lying in bed with thoughts churning through my mind, I got up to find a book to read.

Aquila was dozing on a chair, and woke when I passed. He hadn't done anything unusual all day. Maybe I'd been wrong about the magic.

He stretched his neck out toward me, and I reached out tentatively to stroke the feathers on his head. He *squorked* softly as he side-stepped his way toward the table and the window. I decided to leave the books alone for a while and followed him instead.

The moon was full and hazy behind the thin clouds that stretched across the sky, bathing the flower garden beneath my window in cool light. Most of the flowers had died off or gone to sleep for the winter, but the cherry tree still held its strange mix of flowers and fruits, and the rose and lilac bushes were covered in blooms. I opened the window, and Aquila stepped out.

"It's funny, isn't it?" I asked, and he glanced back from his perch in the tree. "I was six years old when my parents sent me to live here. I hated it here at first, but I remember how pleased I was when I learned that the flowers didn't wilt or fade until well into the winter. Everything in the garden bloomed longer back then, the flowers and the trees. When I was little, I used to think it was because the garden was in love with my aunt. She cared so much for it, like it was a child or a friend, and I thought that the flowers were the garden's way of loving her back. Now that she doesn't go out there anymore, the flowers only bloom when they're supposed to. The trees have longer memories, though."

Aquila fluffed his feathers.

"I know, it's stupid." I leaned farther out the window.

"Matthew told me it's just because the trees were cultivated over generations to bloom long and bear extra fruit. He doesn't have as much time to tend the flowers as Victoria did, so they die off more quickly. I still sometimes like to think it was magic, though. It was the only bit of it I ever really had, until you came along."

I was about to duck back into the warm room when a frail shadow passed through a patch of moonlight below us. Aunt Victoria's thinning blond hair was twisted into a bun that left strands floating loose around her face. She wore only her nightgown, but carried a winter scarf in each hand, trailing on the ground. She paused for a moment, then hurried down a side path before I could call out to her. I ran to the bedroom, pulled on a sweater and grabbed a second one for her, and raced down the stairs and out the kitchen door.

There was no sign of her when I reached the garden. I searched down the path, circled around past the peonies and looked in the dark stone garden shed, then took my time searching the area again. She was gone.

I turned back to the house, where a thin silhouette paced by the windows in my aunt's room. *At least she's warm now,* I thought, but it didn't ease my nerves. She never went near the gardens anymore. I pulled my sweater tighter to my body and walked back to the corner where the old well lay buried in rocks. The breeze shifted the branches above me, and a patch of moonlight revealed the dull nighttime colors of the hand-knitted, wool scarves she'd left on the ground.

Something crashed into the bushes. An airy shriek

escaped me before Aquila climbed out of the tangled mess of ivy vines that covered the ground beneath the rose bush. He managed to flap onto the bench behind me, and I laughed a little at the sight of him standing there with his long toes splayed out on the cold stone, acting like nothing unusual had just happened. He glared at me, and it was hard not to laugh harder at how insulted he looked.

I sat beside him, pulling my feet close under my body to warm them. "It feels strange to be laughing out here again." Aquila wouldn't understand, but I wanted to talk and he seemed like a good listener. A tolerant one, anyway.

"They died right over there. The twins." My voice caught in my throat, all traces of laughter gone. "I didn't know them well. My mother had me move back to town when Aunt Victoria was pregnant. I wanted to stay and help, but Mother said that finding a husband had to be my priority. Aunt Vic and Uncle Ches were so excited to have a baby. They'd given up hope." I smiled a little at the memory, bittersweet as it was. "When we found out it was twins, my mother practically had to chain me to the floor to keep me from coming back. I met them a few times. They were sweet little boys. Uncle Ches always said they'd be a boatload of trouble later, but he laughed whenever he said it.

"I wasn't here when they disappeared, a while after they started walking. They were gone for three days and every person in the area was looking for them when—" I had to take a few deep breaths before I could finish. "When Uncle Ches found them in that old, dried-up well. I don't think anyone even remembered it was there. We don't know what happened, how they got out of the house, whether one followed the other or they went in together, whether they died right away or…" I couldn't finish that thought. "Anyway, Ches and Victoria have gone through hell this past year. He's tried to move on, but she can't. She spends most of her time in her rooms thinking the boys are playing somewhere else in the house. When she remembers that they're not, she won't get out of bed. Won't see anyone.

"This garden was one of the best parts of my childhood, and it should have been for Jacob and Leram, too. None of it makes any sense."

I squeezed my eyes shut, and tears started rolling out. By the time most of them had soaked into the sleeves of my sweater, the cold had caught up with me and I was shivering hard.

"I guess me freezing to death out here's not going to change the past." I wiped a sleeve across my face and stood. "Thanks for listening." Aquila looked up at me, then out over the garden. I went to the pile of stones that covered the well and placed a rock on top of the scarves to hold them in place. "I'm going in," I told him. "You'd better decide whether you're in or out tonight, because I'm shutting the window."

He chose in. I collapsed into bed and felt the approach of the deep sleep that had eluded me earlier. The last thing I heard was the rustle of feathers in the next room.

Chapter Eight

Rowan

Three days passed in relative peace. My aunt didn't return to the garden, but she did allow me to have tea with her one afternoon. Aquila showed no further signs of being unusual, except that he was the quietest and cleanest animal I'd ever met and managed to stay hidden from everyone else in the house. When the rain forced me indoors, I kept myself busy organizing my uncle's library.

It was a fine respite from my regular life, but I knew it couldn't last.

On the morning of my fifth full day at Stone Ridge the door to my room slammed open, jolting me awake. Foot-steps thundered across the wood floor of the sitting area and into my bedroom. Someone landed on top of me with a loud cry of, "Get up, get up, get *up!*"

I grabbed the heavy feather pillow from under my head and used it to whack the intruder, who shrieked and bounced back onto the floor. I groaned as my cousin ripped the blankets off of the bed and flopped down beside me, out of breath and laughing. "Come on, sleepyface," she said, grinning. "Aren't you glad to see me?"

I squinted at her and tried to look angry. "Felicia, I wouldn't be happy to see Prince Charming himself if he woke me up by jumping on me."

She giggled and brushed her golden curls back from her face. "That might not be so bad, you know."

"Filth," I muttered, and grinned back at her. That was the problem with Felicia. She was always so damned happy that I couldn't stay mad at her, even when I wanted to. When I was a child at Stone Ridge, I looked forward to visits from Felicia more than I did trips to see my parents.

She rolled over and stared at me with a mock-serious expression. "We have much to discuss. But first, get thine self to a washing chamber and clean thy teeth. Thou art offending my delicate sensibilities."

"Says the girl who smells like the horse that brought her here." I rolled out of bed and raced through the doorway before she could smack me. Felicia always got me into trouble when we were kids, getting me to join in on whatever trouble she was causing. Now that we were grown, she still brought out the wildest and most childish part of me. I'd missed that.

There was no sign of Aquila in the sitting room. I couldn't blame him for disappearing when that strange, noisy person burst in. I leaned out the window and came face-to-beak with him sitting in the cherry tree. "Sorry," I whispered. He didn't look impressed.

When I returned, Felicia was looking at the books on my shelf. She took a seat in an armchair with her legs crossed under her, and I sat in front of her on the floor.

She pulled a brush out of her bag and went to work on my hair. She'd treated me like a doll since the first time she came to visit me at Stone Ridge. I never complained. It was relaxing.

"You know why I'm here?" she asked at last.

"You missed me?" I winced as she tugged at a knot in my hair. I'd known as soon as I saw her why she'd come. I might have temporarily forgotten about Callum's letter, but my mother hadn't, and she'd sent someone to remind me. I gritted my teeth, and reminded myself that it wasn't Felicia I was angry with.

"Ro, you have a proposal. A good one, from a great guy. I'm here to make sure you don't make a mess of it."

"You don't seem to have much faith in me."

Felicia sighed and set the brush in her lap. "You know I love you like a sister, right?"

"Yes."

"So it's with love that I say no, I don't. Remember when you had a proposal from that mayor's son, and you turned that down? I supported you. He was dreadfully dull, and obviously wanted you for your family history."

Harsh, but true. My mother and my sisters' success in having healthy children, plus the fact that my family had no history of adults using magic, made me more desirable than I'd have otherwise been. Felicia would have managed to use that to her advantage. I hadn't.

"But Callum," she continued. "He's perfect. He's rich, he's sweet, he's gorgeous. He's going to do great things. I can't tell you how many girls in Ardare would love to get their claws into him. But he's ignored them and courted you. He sent you a proposal, and you didn't even tell your mother, or send me a letter to let me know." She sounded hurt. "It seems like you're still undecided, and I'm sorry, but you really can't afford to be. What's going on?"

"I don't know what my problem is." I tried to keep my voice steady. It always betrayed me when I was upset. "I know what's expected of me. Even if Aunt Vic and Uncle Ches didn't make a big deal out of it, I've always known. And I know that it's inevitable. I'm not going to disappoint my family and hurt Callum, and if I did I'd regret it, soon. I care about him, I really do." I reached up to play with my hair, and Felicia leaned forward to gently move my hand away.

"But you're not happy about it."

The concern in her voice undid me in a way my mother's nagging never could. My throat tightened. "I want to be happy. There's something wrong with me, Lecia. I don't think I love him."

"Oh, honey, you will!" She leaned forward and wrapped her arms around me. "You just don't know him well enough yet. I wish your parents had let you move in with me. You would feel so much better about this if you lived in Ardare and saw Callum more often."

"Maybe." I scooted around to face her. "It just seems like I should feel more for him. He's amazing. I just don't feel any passion when he kisses me." My cheeks grew warm. I was used to reading about this, not discussing it. "I don't burst into flames when he says my name. I don't pine for him when we're apart. I don't feel… *that*. And I don't know that he does, either."

She tilted her head to the side. "So you haven't slept with him yet?"

"No." My face grew warm. "It's not that I'm opposed to the idea, but it's never seemed right. And when I think about it, I just hear Miss Persimmon's lectures from that marriage preparation class Mother made me take last year."

Felicia laughed. "I promise, it's far more enjoyable than the old ladies make it sound. They just want to make sure you know how to make babies, but you only need to worry about that in the weeks before your annual cycle. The rest of the time it's fun and practice. And more fun. Maybe even a happy accident. When's yours due this year?"

"Just finished," I admitted.

"Ugh. Don't tell anyone. Let them think you can make a baby sooner. Like, right after the wedding. Or before, even."

"Callum didn't drop me when I told him about my headaches. I doubt a year of practice before my next chance to get pregnant is going to end things." I thought back to the last time Callum had kissed me. It was sweet. Safe. Warm. *Maybe that's just how it starts.*

Felicia reached out to squeeze my hand and got up from the chair. Cold panic washed over me as she went to the window and leaned out for a breath of fresh air, but it seemed Aquila had moved. Something on the table caught her eye, though. The fairy tale book. Felicia held it up and raised her eyebrows. "Are you supposed to have this?"

I pushed up from the floor. "No. But the books aren't the problem." She'd heard a few of the stories when we were children, but had lost interest when she discovered the delights of real life in the city.

She flipped through the brittle pages, pausing now and then to read or to look at a picture. "Don't you want your happily ever after?"

"Sorry?"

She held the book out to me. "This."

The drawing was simple, but the lines on the yellow page captured every important detail—the benevolent smile on the prince's face, the admiration on his bride's as she looked up at him. The long gown, the doves perched in the rafters of the church, the flower petals scattered on the floor. Everyone looked so happy, from the prince to his proud mother and father, and especially the girl. So why couldn't I picture myself there?

I flipped a few more pages back and found an illustration of a turreted, stone castle surrounded by a moat, and a dragon attacking it. That same prince stood with his feet planted firmly on the drawbridge, ready for battle. "I feel like I've skipped a few steps on my way to happily ever after," I said. "Isn't there supposed to be more?"

Felicia stepped around to look over my shoulder at the picture. "Rowan my dear, your prince *does* slay dragons. Literally. You know that, right?"

I sighed. "The dragon's not the point. It's the adventure, the passion, the excitement. So these stories are made-up and completely wrong about magic, I understand that. But surely there's more out there than we've been told?"

"Not much that's good. The feelings will come, believe me. You'll find what you need with Callum. Everything else is better left in stories." She took the book and stretched to place it on the highest shelf in the room, out of sight.

"You don't seem too eager to jump into your own happily ever after," I said.

She smiled. "You didn't even notice." She held out her left hand, where a gold and amethyst ring sparkled on her slender finger. "Robert asked me a few days ago."

"Oh, Lecia!" I hugged her, and she laughed. "I'm so sorry I didn't see it. That's wonderful news!"

She took my hands in hers. "And it's perfect! Robert and Callum are best friends, they're both magic hunters… this is it, kid. All you have to do is say yes, okay? Stop dreaming about lives you can't have, things that aren't even real. Focus on what you *can* have before it's out of your reach."

"I want to want that," I told her, and it was true. I wanted to stop fighting, to let go of the silly doubts that were holding me back from the happiness that waited for me. "Will you help me write the acceptance letter?"

"Of course! And you can stay with me in Ardare until the wedding. Spend more time with Callum. See what happens." She winked and wrapped her arms around me again. "It's going to be great, you know. The two of us in the city together?"

She went on about the stores we'd visit and the important people she knew as she let go of me and wandered into the second bedroom, and I thought of Aquila again.

"Hey Lecia, are you staying up here?" I called. "I don't see your things."

She laughed as she came back toward me. "Nope. Robert accompanied me here, and we're staying downstairs overnight. Wouldn't want to keep you awake." She winked.

Right. At least I didn't have to worry about more than one guest sharing my space.

She left to take a bath before lunch, leaving me alone again. Aquila appeared in the window and side-stepped cautiously over the sill to stand on the desk. He tilted his head, questioning.

"You'd better go," I told him. "Matthew's been too busy to notice you, but Robert won't be. It's not safe for you here with a magic hunter around." He shuffled closer and arched his neck, and I ran my fingers over the soft, dusty feathers. "I'm going to miss you. I'm glad I helped you, but you need to go back to wherever you came from, and I need to get past this curiosity about magic."

No magical speech poured from his beak as it would have in a story book. He didn't thank me for my help by offering to grant wishes, and he didn't leave a magic feather I could use to call him if ever I was in trouble. Those odd, beautiful eyes just stared at me for another moment, and then he was gone, soaring toward the forest.

Chapter Nine

Aren

I flew from that country as quickly as my wings would carry me, soaring over the mountains and relishing the feel of the magic that surrounded and restored me in my own country. It wasn't a gift I was likely to take for granted any time soon.

After several days' hard travel I reached the outer wall of Luid. Pale gray stone snaked around the outside of the city from port to forest and back, protecting it from attack on all sides. Light and noise flooded through the main city gates. I had forgotten about Severn's birthday, which when combined with the harvest festival had become the single most lavish and wanton party of the year.

A string of three horse-drawn carts passed below me as I landed in a tree, nearly missing the branch. Even after three years of irregular practice at flying, I still had trouble with landings. The occupants of the carts didn't notice me, but shouted and laughed amongst themselves. A woman shrieked and threw her head back, sending out a dazzling display as her dress reflected the moonlight in bright flashes. The others riding with her were no less elaborately costumed. Wealthy folk, perhaps people I would recognize, perhaps not. It was difficult to remember all of the names and faces that passed through.

Someone tossed a wine bottle up in the air. It flashed for a moment in the moonlight, then shattered on the road. Everyone laughed as they went on. I studied the glinting glass shards as I considered my position.

The question of whether to take Rowan back to Severn had gnawed at me every moment I spent in her home. The sensible option would have been to recover my strength and then make her go with me. She was as defenseless as she was ignorant of magic. Though her magic would protect her mind, I had other ways of making her co-operate.

And the rewards would have been sweet. The arrival of summer would mark three years since our father's disappearance. He would be declared dead, and Severn would become a king in need of an adviser. Acting as his Second wouldn't be an easy job, but I was well-prepared, and more than ready for the power and wealth that would come with it. I'd worked hard to escape the shadow of my mother's dishonorable death, fought to win Severn's respect and trust even as I hated him for his cruelty. I'd come so far, and my reward was so close.

And yet I had chosen to return to my brother empty-handed. I couldn't repay my rescuer's kindness with betrayal, especially when I didn't know what Severn planned to do with her. She had impressed me with her courage in standing up to the magic hunters, and she had healed me, fed me and sheltered me. Even after the influence of her magic faded, I had no desire to let Severn harm her.

And that's all it is. I fluffed my feathers against the wind and hardened myself to the memory of her. *I don't care for her,* I told myself. *It's only a debt that I'm repaying. Her kindness, her laughter, and her interest in the world beyond her people's stifling beliefs mean nothing. It's over.* I'd indulged that weakness enough already.

I preened my feathers, taking my time, not ready to return home. I would have to transform again before I got there, find clothing before I entered the palace. Severn didn't know about my eagle form, a skill I'd developed in secret. He had directed much of my schooling, had suggested that I develop a small talent for reading people's thoughts into the ability to control them. Hard and cruel as his tutelage had been at times, he'd shaped me into the man I was. Still, it wouldn't have been wise to let him know everything I was capable of. I walked a narrow line between his approval and his potential jealousy, and keeping my balance grew more difficult every year.

I pushed off from the tree and soared over the city wall. The sounds of laughter and music became louder, and the smells of street festival foods wafted up to greet me—candied flowers guaranteed by Potioners to delight and captivate the mind, hot sweet drinks in a hundred flavors, frying slabs of moist dragon meat that most people would have few opportunities to taste in their lifetimes. The scents and sights reminded me of how badly I needed a good meal and some excitement that wasn't life-threatening, but I doubted I'd find time to join in the people's revels.

I dropped directly to the ground in a dark alley behind a small mercantile, not risking a loud landing on top of anything that would have kept me out of the mud. The shadows protected me from curious glances as I transformed and broke a window so that I could unlatch it and climb in. No one would take particular notice if a few items of clothing went missing during the festival. It was a celebration, but also an opportunity for crimes such as this. I left the doors locked and exited the same way I went in.

A young woman collided with me as I left the alley. Her mind was open, her thoughts as overpowering as the smell of strong wine on her breath. Interest, at first, until her drunken thoughts coalesced enough to recognize me. Fear took over then as she considered what might happen with a man who could make her do anything—or so said the rumors she'd heard. I turned away before I could see more.

Everyone else avoided me. Perhaps the expression on my face told them I was in no mood for whatever food, drink, or flesh they were peddling that night.

The turreted palace came into view as I entered the square, its imposing stone façade only slightly softened by the colored glass windows my grandmother had commissioned when she ruled. I slowed as I passed the public fountain, wishing I had more time to prepare.

Any hope I had of my presence going unnoticed was dashed when a pair of burly palace guards met me at the kitchen entrance. Without a word, they escorted me toward Severn's quarters. Neither laid a hand on me, perhaps because they were only a little less afraid of me than they were of Severn, but their presence was a threat in itself.

The stone walls and rich furnishings we passed were as familiar to me as my own reflection, but returning home offered little comfort. So much depended on my brother's mood and whatever had happened in my absence.

Severn himself met us at the door. His white hair, an effect of advanced magic he once tried to work before he was ready, hung loose over his shoulders. Nearly as tall as me, with a regal bearing and piercing blue eyes that missed nothing, he looked every inch the king he would soon be. Even in casual surroundings, clothed in nothing more than simple cotton pants and his silk dressing gown worn open, he commanded the room.

I couldn't let my nervousness show. Severn was like a dog, and would attack at the first sign of weakness.

He dismissed the guards with a wave of his hand. They bowed and retreated, closing the door tight behind them. Severn turned and led the way through the lavishly decorated receiving room and between the heavy wooden doors that led to his personal living space. Empty bottles and half-filled wine glasses littered every flat surface, and piles of discarded clothing covered the floor in patches. The scent of sour grapes and sweat hung thick in the air.

Severn leaned against a marble-topped table and picked up a glass of pale wine. Hard blue eyes regarded me as he sipped, taking in every clue I might reveal about my absence.

"How wonderful," he drawled. "Just what I wanted for my birthday. A ghost."

I didn't speak. I'd learned over the years that if I didn't have an answer that would satisfy Severn, it was best to say nothing at all.

"We thought you were dead," he continued, his voice as cold as I'd ever heard it. "It's not like you to disappear. You know how I worry."

"I was injured escaping from the mountains. I needed time to recover, and had no way to contact you without being seen."

Severn poured a glass of wine and offered it to me. I drank it, not because I wanted it, but to show that I trusted him not to poison me. That, or I feared him enough to do as he wished with no thought for the consequences. It didn't matter to Severn. Respect and fear were nearly the same thing to him, and he would accept either from me.

"And why was escape necessary?" He took my glass to refill it. "Surely you didn't make such a mess of that simple mission that you brought the magic hunters down on you." He arched one thick, dark eyebrow. "When I heard that one of Dorset Langley's top magic hunters had been murdered, I assumed it was your doing. Got in your way, did he?"

"In a sense."

"You need to control that temper, brother. I have other people I can use if I want to stir up trouble. From you, I require control and forethought."

"It won't happen again." I didn't ask how he knew. Though he couldn't see into people's minds like I could, he had some skill that seemed to bring him information on occasion. It wasn't anything he'd ever explained to me, which made it all the more unnerving. Every secret I kept from him was a gamble. They had paid off so far, but there were never any guarantees where Severn was concerned.

He handed my glass back. It was several uncomfortable moments before he looked away and sipped again from his own. "You're ruining my party. Tell me what happened, and go."

"I learned that the hunter had executed every magic-user in the area, and I became angry. I manipulated his brother's mind and sent him to kill the hunter."

Severn sneered. "I'm not sure whether I'm impressed by your skill or disgusted with your unwillingness to dirty your own hands. Either way, what's done is done. I can't say I'm sorry." I was certain he was pleased that the man was dead, but this was the most praise I could expect for it. "I assume you were unsuccessful in procuring a Sorcerer for me, if things ended so badly for you."

"I was busy trying to escape. The magic hunters were after me before I left the mountains, before I could search further."

Severn stepped closer, less than an arm's length away. A smile twitched at his lips, but came nowhere near his eyes. "You're a good liar, Aren, but I know you too well. There's something you're not telling me."

I was nearly as familiar with Severn's magic as I was with my own, and felt it immediately when that power pulsed around him, ready to be used against me. Pain erupted deep in my right shoulder, in the spot where he'd once injured me with a blast of pure magic. What he was giving me was only a reminder of what he could do, but it was enough.

"I may have found another." I fought to draw in a breath. "The hunters attacked before I could bring her in."

The pain diminished slightly, and I breathed normally. Severn leaned back against the table again. "Her? Interesting. Where?"

I fought back the tension that cramped my shoulders. "Near the border." Truth, but not the whole truth. I cursed the weakness in me that insisted on protecting her. "What do you want her for?"

He frowned and set his empty glass down. "I wonder why you can be bothered to ask now."

"I'm only curious. It's not important."

"It is, though." The mask of confidence and certainty slipped from his expression. "It's our magic, you see. In the centuries since the Darmish settlers arrived over the mountains and began destroying the magic in their lands, ours has suffered. Their position on the isthmus is keeping magic from the lands beyond them from moving through ours. Our power is growing stagnant."

"I don't understand. Magic is everywhere. It doesn't require a trade route."

Severn cleared his throat and took another sip of wine. "I would prefer to speak of this another day, but you should understand." He dropped the glass and reached out to grab my left wrist. "Imagine that the blood is cut off from some part of your body. What happens?"

I fought the urge to pull away as his grip tightened. "Exactly as you've said. The blood that's trapped there becomes stagnant."

He nodded and released me. "Precisely. And eventually that hand or finger or foot dies. I believe it's the same with magic, and we are suffering for their foolishness."

"Not you, personally."

"Perhaps not. Or perhaps we would all be more powerful without the Darmish destroying their land. It's not something that's noticeable to most, but the magic in Tyrea is less vital than it once was. I wish to know why."

"Your scholars believe that the appearance of Sorcerers in Darmid somehow proves this?"

"It speaks to the magic still trying to manifest in their land, doesn't it? But that's not why we need them. There are experiments to be done, tests to learn about the quality of magic in their land. Perhaps whether it can be recovered. Much like yourself, I'm only curious. For now."

"Why didn't you tell me? I'd have been more careful if I had known how important it—"

"It shouldn't have mattered." He glared at me, then turned to look out the window. "It's imperative that we keep this secret until we have proof. I'm sure you can imagine the legal difficulties I'd face if anyone found out what I was doing to a Sorcerer. Or Sorceress, if we find this woman you mentioned."

"I can. Though I suppose there would be less fuss over one from Darmid."

"Perhaps not. Our laws leave no room for interpretation in that regard. I've looked." He rested his hands on the window ledge and pressed his forehead against the glass. "I've wanted to rule for as long as I can remember. It's what I was born to do, but it's not easy. I have to do what's best for this land and its people. This means making sacrifices, bending the laws."

Memories of the sacrifices he'd forced me to make years ago flashed through my mind before I could block them off. But that was all in the past. There were more important things to focus on now.

"I regret that my actions in Darmid caused trouble for you."

Severn turned back to me. Though he was still careful to guard his thoughts, his expression was more troubled than I'd ever seen it. "They haven't yet. Your apparent desire to withhold information and distract me from speaking about this Sorceress does concern me, though."

I gritted my teeth as the pain traced deep lines over the skin of my back, spreading outward from its source in a familiar pattern. "I want to help."

"I hope so. Otherwise, I might regret my choice of Second. I selected you for many reasons, Aren, in spite of the many failings of your breeding and your character. Your power is impressive. Your dedication to your studies has brought you knowledge and skill. If I've been hard on you in the past and forced you to do things you disliked, it's only because I saw your potential. I had to force you to achieve more than you understood you were capable of. And in recent years, you've done well."

This was the closest Severn had ever come to appreciation or apology, and I wasn't sure how to respond. I hadn't realized until that moment how badly I needed his approval, in spite of everything. I understood manipulation better than most, and recognized how he was using his words to win me over.

But damned if it wasn't working.

"We could do great things for our people, Aren. I have far grander ambitions than our father ever had." He breathed heavily, and the usual hard look returned to his face. "Now, tell me more about this woman."

I drank my second glass of wine down. "I don't know that she'd be any use to you. She seemed to be unable to use her magic. Unaware that she even has it. I suspect that it's been bound, but I couldn't say how."

"You're saying that someone—someone in Darmid, no less—used magic against this woman so that her magic would be permanently trapped within her?" Severn's grin sent shivers up my spine. "Fascinating! I haven't heard of that being done since well before Father's time. I'll have to look into it before we bring her in." He tapped a foot on the floor as he thought. "What makes you think—" he began, and then shook his head. "We'll discuss that tomorrow."

Uneasiness crept over me, and I pushed it aside. My loyalty was to my family and my country, and telling Severn about her was in my best interests and his. Still, if I could keep my rescuer out of it, I would. "I don't recall ever hearing about it being undone. It might be easier to keep looking for another."

Severn narrowed his eyes. "Hmm. And yet, bound magic would make it much simpler to bring her in, wouldn't it? No question of anyone objecting to holding a simple Darmish prisoner if she couldn't prove she was a Sorceress. It might be interesting to experiment with her condition. Push her. See what happens under stress and pain." He watched me carefully.

"That's true. I only wonder whether it's worth the effort."

Severn let out a bark of laughter. "By all of the gods, Aren. Are you going soft? Do tell me more about this woman who has so bewitched you. How exactly did she convince you to protect her? As if I couldn't imagine."

"I'm not—" The pain whipped across my skin, harder and deeper than before. I fell to the floor and Severn dropped to his knees beside me, pushing on my shoulder so that I rolled on to my back.

"Don't lie to me." He pressed down on my chest. "I need to be able to trust your loyalty, Aren. A Sorcerer I couldn't trust might find himself in prison instead of holding the second-highest position in the land. He might find himself in constant agony." The pain drove deeper until it wrapped around my heart. He released me and I curled up on my side, breathless, every muscle in my body tight.

"Choose, Aren. Where does your loyalty lie? With your family, your country, your magic and your future king, or with a worthless, Darmish tramp?"

"I'll find her," I gasped.

"Good." He moved a few paces away. I remained on the floor, unable to stop the shaking that gripped my muscles even as the pain disappeared. "I'll come with you."

I pushed myself up onto my hands and knees, and waited for the white lights to stop flashing before my eyes. "That won't be necessary. You have enough to deal with here. I'll bring her in."

"I don't think you will. Besides, I need a little fun." His smile reflected cruel amusement. "I think this will be interesting. Now get out, I have business to attend to."

He pulled a heavy silk cord than hung next to his bed and an attendant rushed in, eyes lowered. Severn spoke quietly to him as I struggled to my feet. The man disappeared, trailing behind him nervousness so strong that I barely had to reach out to feel it. It was a wonder he didn't leave a trail of piss behind him.

I retreated to my own rooms and went straight to bed. The open window let in cold air and the sounds of the streets, but the idea of an escape route helped me relax.

How long had it been since I'd contemplated leaving? Years. I was seventeen the last time I ran away, and when my father brought me back he decided to let Severn handle my training. How I hated them both, then. Over time I'd become accustomed to my brother's demands and his volatile temper, and had accepted that it was my duty to support the king, whether that meant my father or Severn. I was grateful for the things I'd learned from him, if not for his methods. And in the end, he was all I had.

I turned away from the window and pulled the feather pillow over my head to block out the noise, but I couldn't escape my doubts.

I wasn't born to be a hero.

No, I was born to be Severn's puppet, wasn't I? I gritted my teeth and forced the resentment away. Perhaps he had manipulated me, but I sensed that he did have our people's interests in mind when he spoke why he needed a Darmish magic-user. Maybe he was right, and I needed to get past this weakness before I could reach my full potential.

The question wasn't whether finding Rowan again

would be right or wrong. It was whether I was willing to do what was necessary for the greater good of my country and my family. For magic itself.

I would take Severn to Darmid, but I would wait as long as possible. With any luck she'd be safe in their capital city before we raided her home, and I would find another Sorcerer for Severn. If not, Rowan would learn exactly how cruel the world can be to a compassionate soul.

With that thought, I closed my eyes and tried not to think about the peace and kindness that had overwhelmed me after she healed me, or the light dusting of freckles on her nose.

Chapter Ten

Rowan

A week after my conversation with Felicia, I was ready to leave.

With all of my things boxed up, the rooms didn't feel like mine anymore. They seemed larger, less friendly, as though the house had already forgotten me.

I spun in a circle, but my skirt didn't flare out the way I'd have liked. Felicia had insisted on leaving one of her own outfits for me to travel in, something fashionable for my arrival in Ardare and the start to my new life. The knee-length brown skirt was pretty and dignified, but closer-fitting than I found comfortable. The blouse and jacket weren't so bad, though the jacket was too structured, and made it difficult to lift my arms. It was a grown-up outfit. No running and playing in this one.

Better get used to it now, I supposed. I hoped Felicia's enthusiasm for fashion would prove contagious. I certainly wasn't feeling it.

The dainty heels on my boots clicked as I crossed the floor, and I checked one last time to make sure the rain-streaked window was locked. As I turned, something on the bookshelf caught my eye, high up where I didn't usually store things. I leaned forward onto my toes as much as the stiff leather boots would allow and grasped the fairy tale book with my fingertips, pulling it forward until it dropped into my hand.

So many memories.

"You ready?" Matthew stood at the top of the stairs, dressed in his striped shirt, his newest black pants and matching suspenders, holding his hat in his hand.

"Matthew, you didn't have to dress up."

"It's a big day for us, isn't it? I know it's been years since you lived here, but you're still part of Stone Ridge. Today our only chick is leaving the nest." He stepped into the room and made a slow, thoughtful turn. "Looks different. They'll send someone for all of this later?"

"I think so." I laid the book on a lower shelf.

"I still say I should've been the one to take you."

I laughed. "You hate the city. Besides, what would they do without you here, even for a few days? Callum is going to meet us in Lowdell, and he promised that he'd send the family's—"

"Most trusted servant, I know," Matthew muttered. "But if your uncle was home to help out, I'd brave the city for you."

It might have been the oddest declaration of love I'd ever heard. I didn't want to laugh at him, and I wasn't supposed to cry. Instead, I hugged him. "I know." He kissed the top of my head, and seemed to have trouble letting go.

Matthew cleared his throat. "Well, the carriage is here,

and loaded with the boxes you had downstairs. Just the one, though. I thought you were going with a group of merchants or something."

"We are, we'll meet them at the main road. No need to clog ours. Callum said there would be a large enough group that we wouldn't have to worry about anyone bothering us out there. I'll write as soon as we reach Ardare, I promise."

In truth, I would have been far more comfortable traveling with Matthew, but I couldn't let him worry about me.

He nodded and picked up my travel bag. "I can take that," I said.

He raised a shaggy gray eyebrow as he looked at my skirt and boots, but handed it over with a grin and a low bow. "Whatever you like, ma'am. Anything else?"

"I think anything else I need to take today is down there already. I'll be along in a minute."

When I was alone again, I picked up the book and paged through it. Monsters. Dragons. Witches and fairies, stepmothers and godmothers, all outlined in black and white on the illustrated pages. And happily ever afters, plenty of those. I hesitated for a moment, then slipped the book into my bag and hurried from the room before anything else could hold me back.

#

The coach waited outside, a black-stained wooden contraption like I'd seen on my few visits to Ardare, with an enclosed passenger compartment and a driver's seat outside, drawn by a pair of black horses. I wiped my boots carefully on the bristle-brush mounted outside so as not to stain the cream-colored carpet. The interior was more luxurious than I'd expected, with painted walls and cushioned leather seats for a long trip. Curtains kept the space private for the wealthy folks who were accustomed to such means of travel. The whole thing creaked and rocked as we got going, but settled into a smooth rhythm when we reached the main road.

Daryll, a quiet, unobtrusive fellow, filled his half of the coach with his broad shoulders and long, black raincoat. He seemed out of place in the small space, like a guard dog forced to sit quietly in a parlor, but if he was uncomfortable he didn't show it. We sat in silence for a while, until I asked, "How long have you been with the Langleys?"

"Twenty years." His voice was soft and smooth, an odd complement to his imposing physique. "Callum was just a little fellow when I joined the household. I've been with them for longer than anyone else. They trust me." He gave me a kind smile. "Callum insisted that I be the one to escort you to the city."

"He told me he'd send someone he would trust with his own life," I said, and Daryll seemed pleased. I tried to stifle a yawn behind my hand, but he noticed and checked his watch.

"Forgive me if I'm keeping you awake," he said. "You're probably tired from your recent excitement." In truth, I was exhausted. I hadn't been sleeping well, spending my nights fighting strange dreams, and the previous evening had been a late one, filled with goodbyes and last-minute plans. Daryll pulled back the curtain and leaned forward to watch the forest go by. It had stopped raining, though water still dripped from the leaves overhead.

"I'm going to ride with the driver for a while," he told me. "We have a few things to discuss. If you'd like to close your eyes and rest in private while I'm gone, it might make the time pass more quickly. We have a long journey ahead of us."

I decided that I liked Daryll very much. "Thank you. And thank you for traveling with me. It makes me feel better knowing you'll be up there."

Daryll nodded and gave a little smile. "We're not expecting any trouble, Miss Greenwood, please don't worry about that. You're safe with us." He opened the door and climbed toward the driver's seat without signaling for the carriage to slow. His coat fell open, revealing a quick flash of dagger hilts that identified him as a Makai, one of the trained protectors employed by the wealthiest citizens of Darmid. I should have known Callum wouldn't send just any servant.

The door clicked shut, and I stretched out on the seat and rested my head on a soft cushion. The smooth side-to-side rocking soon relaxed me, but my mind was racing too fast for sleep to catch it. I pulled the story book out and passed the time reading.

I'd almost reached the end when the carriage lurched to a sudden stop, sending me tumbling to the floor and the book skidding into the darkness beneath the other seat. Voices yelled outside, angry and frightened. The hairs on my arms prickled, and I shivered.

This is wrong. I reached into my bag for my knife, but

didn't know what to do next. I sat there turning the blade over in my hands, fighting to keep calm. *It'll be fine, Darryl is right there.*

Someone yelled, but the words were muffled. The door popped open and Darryl appeared, leaning from the driver's seat in front. "Stay here," he ordered. "Leave the curtains closed, lock the doors, and don't open them for anyone!" Then he was gone, and the door slammed behind him.

I reached over and twisted the silver locks on both doors, then slid back to the center of the seat and waited, trembling. There was more yelling and a sound like a tree snapping in half. A horse screamed. I stayed where I was, surrounded by chaos, but insulated and separate from it. I knew it was only an illusion of safety, that the thin wooden walls offered no real protection, but I couldn't think of what to do except stay where I was and trust that the others would protect me. Never in my life had I felt so helpless.

Unfamiliar voices approached, growing louder until they stopped just outside. Someone tried the door on my left, but the lock held. A low, rough voice cursed, then called out. I held my breath. A wide shadow fell over the curtain, and the hinges creaked as someone hauled back on the door handle.

Every muscle in my body tensed until they felt ready to snap. I pulled my feet up onto the seat, making myself as small as I could. *This is not happening.* I mentally cursed Felicia's choice of clothes, and wished I had my pants and flat boots on.

The door came off of the carriage with a loud crack, and

a bald man leaned in, his shoulders filling the wide opening. He grinned, revealing several broken teeth. Blood dripped into one of his eyes from a gash in his deeply lined forehead.

He chuckled, and my own blood froze in my veins. "My, my. Not what we was expecting!"

Someone shouted outside, and he turned to look.

I kicked my left leg out, and the dainty heel of my boot struck him in the eye. He roared and pulled back from the doorway, and I launched myself out onto the road.

Everything was confusion. I caught a glimpse of huge hands shooting toward me, but the big man's aim was off, and he only managed to tangle his fingers in the ends of my hair. I shrieked as he ripped several strands out, but I hit the ground running, straining the seams in my skirt with every step.

I stumbled into the unfamiliar forest and toward a nearby river that sparkled in the thin sunlight breaking through the clouds. Faint hope swelled in me as I drew closer to the water, and a chance at escape.

I wasn't fast enough. Over the sound of my rasping breath I heard someone thudding along behind me, getting closer with every step. I adjusted my grip on the knife's handle and prepared to turn and fight, but my feet went out from under me as I slipped on one of the loose, flat stones that littered the ground near the river. A sharp pain pierced my ankle as it twisted under me, and I fell.

I hadn't even got one leg back under me when a crushing weight landed on my back, pinning my left arm beneath me. A meaty hand grabbed my wrist and squeezed. I dropped the knife and screamed as he wrenched my arm behind my back, straining my shoulder until I thought he was going to rip my arm off.

"Don't think so, sweetheart," the bald man snarled into my ear, his breath sickeningly wet and warm on my face. He sat up a little and I pulled in a deep breath, but I couldn't move. Tears of pain, frustration, and fear burned my eyes, and I screamed again.

I was aware of the sound of another set of feet clattering toward us over the broken rocks, but couldn't turn to see who it was. I had little hope at that point that it was Darryl coming to save me. The footsteps didn't slow as they came closer. The weight on top of me shifted. "Hey, lookit what we found in the—" My attacker's words cut off as something hit him. He collapsed back onto me, and the air rushed out of his lungs in a quick, foul breath. He rolled off, gasping.

As soon as that weight was gone I pushed with my feet, crawling toward the water and fighting to catch my breath.

Above the buzzing in my ears I heard the thug talking. "What're you on about, she's just a—"

He was interrupted by a cracking noise and a scream that I sincerely hoped was his. I tried to stand, but my ankle buckled, and I bit back a cry of dismay as I hit the stones. I'd reached the edge of the wide, shallow river. I was a good swimmer, but the current was moving fast and rough over mostly-submerged rocks. In my condition, I'd be dashed to pieces before I made it half-way across.

The scream stopped, and footsteps followed me, more slowly now. I'd lost my knife, but I picked up a sharp rock, flipped myself around, and pushed my back up against a boulder.

A shadow fell over me, and I looked up to see another stranger. He was far leaner than the bald one, younger and taller. The way he stood gave an impression of graceful strength that made me more afraid of him than I'd been of the mass of muscle that attacked me. The sun behind him left his face in silhouette. His hair was dark, just long enough for most of it to be pulled back and tied behind his neck.

Darmish men don't wear their hair long like that.

He watched me, catching his breath and apparently considering my situation. I glanced back at my previous attacker, who lay flat on his stomach with his face pressed into the rocks, not moving. Nausea washed through me, and I grasped my chunk of rock so tightly that it cut into my fingers. I wasn't about to go quietly.

The stranger stepped back, allowing sunlight to fall on his face as he watched me. I had expected a scarred warrior, but found quite the opposite. His unblemished skin and high cheekbones would have seemed more at home on a pampered aristocrat or a prince. His brows shadowed dark eyes in a stern expression that seemed familiar, though I was certain I'd never met anyone like this before. He reached up to rub a hand over the dark stubble on his jaw.

"It's all right," he said, his voice calm and heavily accented. He stepped around so that he was standing beside me, then crouched. In a movement that was too quick for me to follow he caught my left hand in his own. I tried to pull back, but the strength drained from my arm, and the rock clattered to the ground. I was completely at his mercy, and though he'd saved me from my attacker, something about him filled me with terror. I met his gaze, and my mouth went dry at the sight of his cold, green-flecked, brown eyes.

I'd been wrong when I thought this man was completely unfamiliar.

He let me look for a few seconds, then said, "I'm not going to hurt you. Will you listen while I explain?" His speech was clear, but his accent made everything sound strange.

I was afraid to answer. Someone yelled from near the road, and the stranger frowned.

"I'm sorry." He reached his free hand toward my face. Blood streaked his knuckles. I flinched, expecting him to hurt me, but he only laid his hand on my forehead. The world grayed out, and I fell away as I had the first time I looked into those strange, beautiful eyes.

Chapter Eleven

Rowan

Everything hurt.

I lay with the left side of my body pressed into a soft surface, with something wedged behind me that kept me from rolling backward. It felt like the room was rocking. Without moving my head, I opened one eye just enough to get a blurry look at my surroundings. The bed I lay in took up one end of a narrow room with boxes lining one wall, a writing desk and built-in wardrobe the other. A heavy curtain was pulled across a small window, and the only light in the room came from a pair of oil lamps. The air smelled of something sweet and herbal that I couldn't identify.

There didn't seem to be anyone else in the room. I opened my other eye and lifted my head to look around a bit more.

"Welcome back," said a smooth voice from somewhere near my feet. I froze, my flesh crawling. "Sorry I had to do that. I don't imagine falling unconscious is fun, but I'd say you're becoming accustomed to it by now."

I looked toward the end of the bed and there he was—the young man with Aquila's eyes. The rest of his face would have been attractive if those eyes weren't so cold, or if he would smile. As it was, just looking at him frightened me in a way that seemed to come from instinct as much as it did from the situation. He leaned back in an armchair next to the end of the bed, long legs stretched out in front of him, apparently waiting for me to say something. I got the feeling he could wait all day if he had to.

"Who are you?" I asked, my voice rasping. "What's happening?"

"My name is Aren. You're on a trading ship bound for Tyrea. My brother Severn needs you."

"The…" I tried to moisten my lips with my tongue. "Severn is the king, isn't he?"

"Close enough."

I struggled to remember what I'd heard about Ulric's sons. I couldn't make my thoughts line up properly. Was Aren the one who read minds? No, controlled them. Unless I was missing something, he could certainly turn into an eagle. Those eyes were unmistakable.

Aren leaned toward me. "You should know that you're in more trouble right now than you can imagine."

I could have guessed that, I thought.

"I'm telling you this because you don't have much time to decide what you're going to do about it. Severn will—" He paused. Distant shouting echoed outside the room, and my heart beat harder, pumping fresh fear through me.

"Speaking of whom…" Aren stood and stalked to the door, then stopped and turned back to me. "I suggest you close your eyes again and that you not move until he leaves. Things will get worse for you in a hurry if he knows you're conscious." He came back and untied a set of white curtains that closed between the bed and the rest of the room, sheer enough that I could see out if I squinted.

There was a single hard knock at the door. Brighter lamplight flooded in from outside as Aren opened it and and a white-haired person stepped in, looked around, then closed the door.

"Where is she?" he asked. Aren gestured toward the bed, and the man who I assumed was Severn strode toward it. My eyes snapped shut just before he pulled back the curtain. His clothing rustled as he leaned over me, and I fought to keep my breathing slow and even. He smelled smoky, like my hair after I fell asleep beside an outdoor fire. I struggled to remain still, and to keep by breathing slow and even.

"This is her?" There was a sneer in his voice. "Not much to look at, is she?"

"She doesn't usually have those bruises." Aren sounded like he was trying not to laugh.

You bastard.

"Has she wakened yet?"

"Not since I've been here. Sara was in to tend to her wounds earlier, and gave her something to keep her quiet. She'll be fine."

"Hmm." Severn leaned closer for a moment, his breath tickling my skin, then stood and turned away from the bed, letting the curtains fall closed.

I took a deep, trembling breath and let my eyes open

again, just enough so that I could watch.

"About that temper of yours," Severn said.

"This was completely different. You saw what happened. Morten got carried away, and I did what was necessary to protect your interests."

Severn's chuckled. "I wonder whether killing him was completely necessary. Still, it's a small loss." He gestured toward me. "You're certain about her? I don't feel anything."

"No. Whatever they've done to her has been effective enough to keep her magic hidden from her people for all these years."

The skin on my arms prickled. *Who do they think I am?*

Severn sat in the chair and removed his gloves, then leaned back far enough that I couldn't see him. "Perfect. We'll still try to keep this quiet, but getting her into the city will be easy enough, even if someone stops you."

"Are you leaving?"

"Is that a problem?"

Aren shrugged. "She won't be a problem. I thought you'd be sailing with us."

"Hmm. No, I have the horse. I'll fly back. I don't like to leave the city in anyone else's hands for too long. I suppose I could try to take her with me, if you don't want the responsibility."

"It will be fine. Sara will put her under again if she wakes." Aren didn't sound any more pleased to be stuck with me than I was to be trapped with him.

"Very well. No sign of anyone following us yet? Her husband-to-be, his father? Anyone?"

"Nothing."

I thought back to the day I'd rescued the eagle with Aren's eyes, the conversations I'd had with Callum and Felicia when he was within hearing distance, and fought back a wave of nausea. It had been this man, this Sorcerer, listening to my stories and sleeping in my rooms that whole time. *I should have turned him over to Dorset Langley when I had the chance.*

"Let's hope it stays that way. Much as I'd love to see what you'd do if Dorset Langley himself angered you, I'd rather keep this quiet." Severn stood and looked at me through the curtains again. "I'd almost say we were doing her a favor by getting her away from them."

Aren rocked back on his heels. I couldn't see his face clearly, but when he spoke there was a hint of a smile in his voice. "I doubt she'll agree once she gets to Luid and finds out what's waiting there."

Severn chuckled. "No, certainly not." He reached out to clasp Aren's arm with his hand. "I'm pleased to see that your view on these matters has improved. This is for the best."

Aren cleared his throat. "Indeed."

Severn took a sudden step closer to Aren. It startled me, and had Severn not been nose to nose with his brother, he'd certainly have seen me twitch. "Don't disappoint me."

"Never again."

Severn held his position for a moment, then stepped back and left without another word.

Aren stood frozen in the center of the room, fists clenched. He breathed in, sighed, and collapsed into the chair, resting his face in his hands. I propped myself up on one elbow and winced at the pain that twisted through my arms and my torso as I moved.

I wanted to speak, but couldn't find words. Though I waited, Aren said nothing.

"I think there's been a mistake," I whispered at last, and pushed the curtain aside so I could see him better. "I'm not whoever you think I am. I understand you not wanting to keep me here…" I trailed off and tried to wet my parched lips with my tongue. "I'd be happy to go."

Aren raised his head just enough to look up at me, and a look of slight amusement touched his eyes. "No, there's been no mistake. I wish there had."

"I'm not—I mean, I don't use magic. Please, just let me go home."

Aren leaned back and stretched his legs out in front of him. "Let me think." He closed his eyes, and I waited. I thought he'd fallen asleep when he said, "Gods damn the whole business." He opened his eyes to glare at me. "If I turn you loose, he'll find you again."

"But—"

"Not to mention the fact that my life will be worth less than nothing when he realizes what I did. I can't let you go." He stood and tied the bed curtains back.

"Please," I whispered again when his gaze met mine. I fought back the tears that filled my eyes, not wishing to appear weak. I doubted crying would buy me any sympathy from a person like him. "I'm not what you think I am."

His jaw muscles tightened and his eyebrows pulled together in a deep frown. He turned away and took a heavy-looking brown coat from a hook by the door. "I have to leave for a while. Sara will be in soon to change your bandages. I'd suggest not talking at all, especially about what you think you know about me, even to someone who seems trustworthy. Everything gets back to Severn. I'll answer your questions when I return, if I'm able to."

Before I could ask whether it was his return or my answers that were in question, he had left. The lock clicked into place. I was alone, a prisoner.

It felt like I was watching all of this happen to someone else. *This is a dream, this is a story book. This is not my life.*

But I couldn't wallow in my disbelief and panic. I'd have to figure out how to escape, to get home or to a place where I could send a message to Callum. I suddenly found myself longing for that safe feeling I had when he was around, and wondered why I'd ever desired anything more. All I wanted now was to see him again.

Hot tears slipped down my cheeks. They had to come out some time. I allowed myself a few minutes of sobbing quietly into the pillow, and when I'd finished, my mind felt clearer.

Take stock. What do you know?

I knew that my body hurt. I tried to sit up, but the muscles in my stomach wouldn't support me, and when I moved my legs my ankle burst into pain. I knew that I was afraid, and that I was in trouble.

What else?

Aren was a Sorcerer. I saved his life, and now for some reason he wanted to take me to Tyrea. I'd seen him kill a man.

I didn't much care what had happened to the one they

called Morten, but I wondered about the others. Darryl was certainly dead. If Aren was leading that group that attacked us, he was responsible for that.

A chill washed over me. *What if Matthew had come along like he'd wanted to?*

There was no time to think about it more. The door creaked open and a pretty young woman with long, honey-colored hair slipped into the room. She moved slowly and purposefully as she pulled a variety of items out of her basket, but she kept looking over her shoulder, and twitched when footsteps passed outside the door. I didn't answer when she asked how I was feeling.

"I'm going to check your wounds and change the bandages," she murmured in a warm Tyrean accent, and I closed my eyes. If she wanted to fix me, it would only help me when it came time to escape. The air felt cold on my arm when she uncovered it, and my skin tingled as she rubbed a thick ointment into it. That explained the strange smell in the room—some kind of herbal remedy for injuries. She worked it into my shoulder, and tendrils of warmth swirled deep into the muscles.

"The arm wasn't out," Sara told me, "but it's been pulled too far. You shouldn't use it for a while, and rest that ankle while you can. The other cuts and bruises will heal soon enough."

I flinched when she rubbed the stuff into my cheek. When I tried to touch it, she pushed my hand away. "Look at me, please."

After a few moments I turned my eyes to her, but kept them unfocused. Sara leaned in close and pressed her lips into a thin line. "We'll see how things look in the morning." She held a cup of water for me to sip from, then stood and gathered her supplies back into the basket, which she left on the desk.

"You'll be fine," she said softly, and laid a cool hand on my brow. "Just don't cause trouble. It's better that way." And then she left. I didn't hear the lock click into place.

I waited until I was sure she was gone, then tried to sit up. The room spun and heaved, and my thoughts became disordered. I grabbed on to the pillows to keep from falling to the floor. My thoughts of escape faded as I fought a losing battle to stay above the waves of unconsciousness that pulled me under.

The hours that followed were a blur of nightmares and surreal visions, most of them set in a strange labyrinth. Light from invisible fires flickered against stone walls, and tentacle-vines reached up from the ground to wrap around my ankles and trip me. I thought I woke and saw Sara a few times, but I couldn't be sure whether I was really awake. At one point she had snakes instead of hair, and dripping fangs sprouted from a grin that was somehow wider than her head.

I woke completely exhausted. I knew I'd had no reason to trust Sara, but still felt betrayed that she would drug me after she'd tried to heal me. Aren had been right about that one thing, at least. I was glad I hadn't spoken to her.

Though the room was dark and the bed comfortable, I fought off my need for sleep and pushed myself up to sit. My ankle screamed with fresh pain when I put weight on it, and I leaned on the walls and furniture as I made my way to the door, dressed only in my underthings. Perhaps there was nowhere for me to go, but I had to try.

The room tilted slightly and I tumbled, slamming hands-first into the door. I breathed deeply through gritted teeth until my shoulder quieted, and I reached for the door handle. My heart leapt when it turned under my touch, then sank as I realized that the deadbolt above was locked again.

A lump formed in my throat, but I was done feeling sorry for myself. I would take Aren's advice and trust no one, especially him. I'd just have to wait until someone came back, and see what was to become of me.

Chapter Twelve

Aren

What the hell am I doing?

I shrugged into the brown coat and leaned against the door that held her captive. I'd had to leave, but probably not for any reason she might suspect. I couldn't trust my own thoughts in there, and I needed a clear head.

This wasn't how Severn and I had planned it. He'd chosen his men, all of them strong and trustworthy, but accustomed to action. They grew restless on the road, and when we ran into the traveling merchants, Severn told our men to kill the men and take whatever they wanted from what was left. I'd kept my distance until Rowan came bursting out of that coach and took off into the woods with Morten in pursuit. Whether he counted Rowan amongst the "men" or the other items, I didn't like her chances. I went after them, but wasn't fast enough to keep him from harming her.

I tried to tell myself that it was a stroke of luck that we'd found her so easily, and sooner than we'd expected. We were far from any town, and the only witnesses were dead or dying. I was only a few steps away from securing my future. But when I saw how frightened she was of me, I wanted nothing more than to tell her that I would never hurt her. It would have been a lie, but I wanted to say it just to make her stop looking at me like that.

As if it mattered what she thought of me.

I considered letting her escape into the woods, but Severn had already seen us. I thought about lying and saying I didn't know who she was, but he'd have had her killed if she hadn't been the Sorceress we wanted. She was so terrified and so overwhelmed that I'd been able to use my magic to push her over the edge into unconsciousness, and I told Severn that was how I'd found her.

I brought her back and got Sara to fix her up while Severn covered our tracks. I stayed and watched over her, and kept telling myself I was doing the right thing in letting him have her. I was acting in my country's best interest, helping to preserve or restore the balance of magic. Advancing scientific interests. Keeping Severn happy.

All of that paled, though, when I really looked at her. A Sorceress deserved better than to be beaten, chained, hurt, and humiliated. Even a Darmish one. Even for the good of magic.

Severn's glee over the prospect of torturing her had finished it for me. That, and his satisfaction in bending my will to his. In that moment every reason I'd ever had for wanting to escape had come flooding back, filling me with the hatred I'd fought so long to suppress. It took all of my strength and self-control to continue the ruse, to make him believe I was still with him. Even as he was walking out the door, I was beginning to make my plans. Get her away, leave her somewhere relatively safe, and find a new life for myself somewhere far from my brother.

I still had no desire to be a hero or to sacrifice everything I'd worked so hard to gain, but here I stood preparing to do just that.

I sent my awareness out to search for him, but Severn was gone. "I'm not yours to control anymore," I whispered. "Damn you. Damn the consequences." I'd lost my balance at last, and fallen from the wrong side of Severn's favor. It felt surprisingly satisfying.

Sara approached with her basket of supplies in one hand. She didn't look up or speak, only stood waiting for me to move so she could enter the room. "You might as well leave the basket there," I told her, and she nodded.

I made contact with as many people on the ship as I could, suggesting that they wouldn't think anything of it if they saw me leaving with the prisoner, helping Severn's guards realize they had somewhere else they needed to be, and arranging for our departure. The ship was still moored in the choppy waters of the little harbor, and I made my rounds in the shipyard as well. It was a far larger group than I'd ever attempted to manipulate at one time. It took the entire night for me to do my work, and with every person I affected I felt the magic draining from me.

At least most of them were too afraid to put up a fight when they felt me enter their minds.

Sara was leaving when I returned to the room at dawn. Rowan still lay in the bed with the blanket pulled up over her, a small breakfast of toast and stewed berries untouched on a tray beside her. She looked better, but her cheek was still marked by scrapes and bruises, and fresh bandages covered her shoulder. She watched warily as I paced, as though someone had released a wolf into the room with her.

"The ship leaves in less than an hour. We need to be off by then."

Her eyes widened, and she twisted her body to try to look out the window. "We haven't left yet?"

"No. The sailors decided to wait for the tide, and Severn ordered them to keep distance between ourselves and the decoy ship he sent out."

She frowned. "Wait—*we* have to be off? And where are we going? I thought you said you couldn't let me go. I mean…"

I sank into the chair at the end of the bed. It occurred to me that it wasn't too late to change my mind. Severn would never know.

Instead, I said, "You want to get out of here, right?" She nodded vigorously. "Well, I'm going with you. You need someone to help you get to a safe place, and I'd just as soon not be here when Severn returns." I leaned back and closed my eyes to rest while I could.

"But your men attacked me," she said. "You brought me here. Why would you help me now?"

I forced one eye open. She sat up in the bed and clutched the blanket to her chest. Her eyes searched mine, perhaps wanting to believe me. I had no way of knowing what she was thinking, or what I could say to make her trust me. It might have been easier to explain my actions to her if I'd understood them, myself.

"It's your decision," I told her. "You're free to do as you please. If you insist on staying here and waiting to see what happens to you in Luid, I'll stay, too."

"But I—"

"You should know that this is the last time I'm going to offer to help," I added. "It will be too dangerous later."

Her mouth dropped open, and she winced as the raw skin on her cheek stretched. "How can I believe anything you're saying?"

I didn't let my irritation show. Heavy footsteps passed by the door. Someone hollered far down the corridor. The ship would be leaving soon.

"Maybe you can't. But you saved my life, even if you didn't mean to. I don't have time to explain more right now." It was the reason I thought she'd be most likely to give if she were in my position. My family may have considered compassion and kindness the flaws of weaker people, but they ran deep in her.

I glanced at her breakfast. "The bread should be fine, if you're hungry. I wouldn't try the berries or the water." Sara had no more interest in angering Severn than I usually had, and she'd be doing everything in her power to keep Rowan incapacitated. I poured a cup of fresh water from the pitcher on the desk and offered it to her.

She drank it all, and ate the toast. I turned away to retrieve my travel cloak from the wardrobe and pulled it on over my coat. When I turned back she was watching me. Making her decision.

"When do we leave?" She pulled the blanket tighter

around her body, and I helped her sit up on the edge of the bed. She flinched when I touched her, but almost toppled over when I let go.

I nudged an old knapsack that waited on the floor. "Those are your things in the boxes. Get dressed quickly. Pack what you need. I suggest warm clothes, whatever you can manage. I have food and bedding. Stay here, don't open the door until I return."

"We're just going to walk out of here?"

"I think riding would be faster."

I collected supplies and food as quickly as I could and carried the bags one by one up to the deck, where I left them piled in a dark corner. When I returned to the room Rowan was dressed in trousers, brown leather boots that laced up to her knees, a heavy sweater and a jacket. Her pack was stuffed full, and Sara's basket of ointments and potions sat empty on the bed. I handed her a charcoal cloak with a deep hood. It was Sara's, the only one I could find that was small enough that Rowan wouldn't trip over it. She ran her hands over the rough wool and the smooth, pink lining before she pulled it around her shoulders.

"Keep your face hidden until we're clear of town, and don't say a word until I tell you it's safe," I said. "When Severn comes looking for us, I don't want anyone to have seen you."

She looked like she was going to say something, but instead reached for her hood and pulled it over her head.

"We only have one chance to get away from here unnoticed. Keep your eyes down, and we'll be fine."

She limped toward the door, and reluctantly accepted

my arm when I offered it.

Wooden boards creaked under our feet as we stepped into the passageway, and Rowan hesitated. "It's fine," I whispered. "Just keep moving."

A door ahead and to our left creaked open. One of Severn's uniformed guards stepped out, yawning, and turned toward us. I released Rowan's arm and readied myself for a fight. He squinted, nodded, and turned to lock the door behind him. He saw us, but took no notice of us, which was as much as I'd hoped for. I released the breath I'd been holding as he passed us and continued down the passageway.

I took Rowan's arm again and urged her to move more quickly. The sooner we got off of the ship, the better.

I took Rowan's knapsack and went ahead when we reached the ladder that took us up to the deck. A cold wind blew in off of the ocean, and I pulled my cloak tighter as I offered a hand to help Rowan up. She looked around and blinked in the cloud-diffused sunlight, took in the sight of the men working to prepare the ship to sail, then looked down at her feet and waited for me to retrieve our supplies. If she was going to run, she was smart enough not to risk it yet.

A pair of gray horses waited for us at the bottom of the gangplank, as I'd arranged. I tied the bags to the saddles, then offered a hand to help Rowan up. She hesitated, but accepted. She took a few deep, shaky breaths as I mounted my own horse, but still said nothing.

We passed a few workers in the shipyard, all of whom ignored or seemed to look right through us as though we were ghosts. As we passed the fence a sailor staggered out of a dingy bar and looked at us with bleary eyes. When I reached out to take in his thoughts I found him struggling to remember some instruction. Something he was supposed to watch out for, to alert someone if he saw someone… something. He squinted at us.

"Say, you're not… um," he mumbled.

Shit.

I'd hoped that manipulating so many people would create a group effect that would draw in anyone I'd missed, but this one seemed unaffected.

"No," I said. Had I been alone I might have taken care of things differently, but I glanced at Rowan and saw her watching from under her hood. Her hands gripped the reins tight, ready to take off at the first sign of trouble.

I reached out to change the sailor's mind, to make him forget his instructions. I felt the magic go, leaving me weaker. The magic here near the border was stronger than it had been elsewhere, but I needed to get back to Tyrea soon to replenish.

The sailor's drunkenness worked in my favor. He took a step away, stumbled, and went back toward the ship without further comment.

We went on, Rowan riding beside me down the hard-packed dirt road that led through town and toward the nearby mountains. We wouldn't be safe until we'd left the obvious path and put distance between ourselves and the ship. Even then, Severn would be after us long before I was ready for him.

I gritted my teeth and urged the horse to move faster.

Chapter Thirteen

Aren

Rowan stayed close behind me as we climbed steep, winding roads, crossed the square and continued up a side street. The little town was packed into the foothills of tree-covered mountains, and the streets twisted back on themselves and met at strange angles with whitewashed buildings packed into every spare bit of space.

Few people were out so early, and those that were gave us no more than a look. They knew to mind their business and no one else's. Not all of the Darmish were loyal to their own country, and my people used this particular harbor frequently. We were generous with the people, and they repaid us with safe passage and with information when it was available.

They were Severn's allies, though, not mine. If he came asking questions later, they wouldn't hesitate to answer.

A curtain twitched in a kitchen window, and an elderly woman squinted down at us. I looked away. As long as we got out of town, it didn't matter what she saw. Severn would find out soon enough that we were missing, and one old hag noting which direction we'd headed would make little difference.

I closed my eyes to sharpen my focus and sent my awareness back in the direction of the ship, searching for chaos, confusion, or any sense of someone following us. There was nothing yet.

We rode without speaking, accompanied only by the sounds of a far-off pair of crows, the twittering of a few birds, and the sound of our horses' hoofs as they scuffed through the drifts of pine needles that covered the long-un-used logging road we followed toward the mountain. Late in the morning Rowan rode up beside me, looking like she wanted to ask a question, but I shook my head and she dropped back without a word.

Perhaps it would have been polite to ask how she was feeling, but it didn't matter. We weren't stopping, no matter how uncomfortable or frightened she was, or how badly a part of me wanted to haul her hack to the boat and insist that I'd caught her trying to escape.

I glanced over my shoulder. Rowan had let her hood fall, and she was watching a raven that flew overhead. My stomach turned every time I saw the bruise on her face, a reminder of how ill prepared I was to protect anyone. She looked calmer now than she had when she was trapped on the boat, though, and for a moment I felt as though I'd made the right choice in helping her.

Hours passed and the sun broke through the clouds. As we moved away from the immediate danger of the ship, doubts crowded my mind. In a moment of irrational anger I had thrown everything away—my family, my future, my identity. If I'd wanted to leave on my own, I could have planned a better escape. What I'd done was stupid and impulsive. But there was no changing the past. I locked those thoughts away and focused on keeping Severn from finding us. Worrying about what I'd done would only distract me from that.

After several turn-offs the road became little more than a path. We crossed a slow-running river shortly before noon and I turned my horse off of the road, letting him pick his way through the sparsely wooded forest for a few minutes before we stopped. "Do you want something to eat?" I asked Rowan, and swung down to the ground.

She opened her mouth, but didn't say anything for a moment. Perhaps she was becoming as accustomed to the silence as I was. "We can talk now?"

"We could have hours ago. I just didn't want to." She shot me a look that would have frozen a dragon's insides, but it disappeared almost instantly. I wondered whether she expected an apology. She'd have to get used to going without.

When I offered my hand, she refused to take it. "I'll manage on my own, thank you."

It took her longer than it should have, but she made it safely to the ground. She limped past me into the woods as I tethered the horses and pulled fresh fruit and dried meats from the bags, eating as I offered the horses a little grain. When Rowan returned, she sat in a sun-lit clearing and devoured her meal. I'd have offered more, but we'd have to make our supplies last. We wouldn't be going anywhere near a town as long as I could avoid it.

She sat with her knees tucked up against her chest and winced as she bit into an apple. The bruises had faded over the past few hours, thanks to Sarah's impressive gifts as a Potioner. Still, there was only so much her ointments could do. Morten certainly hadn't showed Rowan any mercy. I had occasionally regretted killing people in the past, but I certainly didn't this time.

Her gaze darted away from my face every time I caught her looking at me.

"I'm not going to hurt you."

"No? Where I come from abductions don't usually end well." She winced at her own words. "Sorry, I'm just…" She pressed her lips together and closed her eyes.

"Nervous?"

She swallowed hard. "Terrified, actually."

Her openness surprised me. I tried to reach into her thoughts, but didn't have any more success than I had before.

"You're safer with me at the moment than you are anywhere else," I said. "Severn will be searching for us in this area, but we'll get away from here as soon as we can."

"Good." She shivered and wrapped her arms around her knees.

"If I was going to hurt you, I wouldn't be helping you, would I?"

"I suppose." She still wouldn't meet my gaze. Perhaps now that Severn was gone, she considered me the most immediate threat.

I wouldn't be hurt by that. It didn't matter whether she liked me. I was already toying with the idea that I could use her somehow, now that Severn was my enemy. That would mean keeping her around, trying to break the binding that had her magic trapped. It hadn't been my original plan, but perhaps we'd both benefit, if only she would trust me.

"If you're finished eating, we should keep moving."

She struggled to stand as I went to untie the horses. I soon realized she hadn't followed me out of the clearing. My anger caught me by surprise, and I tried not to let it creep into my voice. "I'm not going to rape you, either, if that's what you're worried about." Her eyes grew wide. "Where I come from we believe that's the territory of weak men and cowards. I am neither."

"I didn't mean any disrespect, mister—"

"Aren, please."

"Aren." She pushed past a low branch to follow me into the shadows beneath the trees, and reached out to stroke her horse's nose. "I'm sorry. I've never been in a situation like this. I don't know what to think or expect. Can I ask where we're going? And if we can talk now, I'd like to ask about why your brother wanted me."

Before I could answer, a shadow passed over the place we'd just been sitting. Rowan hobbled out from the shelter of the oak trees, shading her eyes against the sun. "What is that?"

"Rowan!" I whispered as loudly as I dared, but she kept going. The shadow passed again. I grabbed her arm to pull her out of the clearing.

"Hey!" she yelled, and I clapped a hand over her mouth. She struggled against me, but stopped when a dark silhouette passed above the trees, feathered wings spread out to soar toward the mountain. For a moment I thought it was Severn's horse, a winged beast he'd captured years ago. It wasn't, but it could have been just as problematic. Four legs were tucked up close to its body, and a sharp-beaked head moved side to side, watching the ground. I let go, and Rowan staggered back to lean against a tree.

"What—"

"Gryphon."

"But we don't have those in Darmid."

"Welcome to the borderlands. At least it didn't see us or the horses. We should move on."

I tried not to let her see how shaken I was. The gryphon wouldn't be a problem, but there were worse things hunting us.

I closed my eyes, focusing inward, and sent my awareness out again, more focused than it had been before, searching for Severn and then for any human presence. There was nothing.

When I opened my eyes Rowan whispered, "What did you just do?"

"I'm keeping us safe."

"Was that magic?"

"Yes. Does that bother you?"

"No." She hobbled back toward her horse and allowed me to help her into the saddle, and we moved on.

I waited for more questions, but Rowan seemed to be lost in her own thoughts. The quiet forest reflected a calm I wished I felt. Conflicting plans and desires battled within me, but no obvious course of action revealed itself. My thoughts spoke over each other in an argument with myself that I couldn't win. *Take her home.*

Dump her in the woods.

Help her.

Send her away and board the next ship away from Darmid and Tyrea, alone.

No, free her magic and see how powerful she really is, first—she could be a strong ally.

I've done enough. If she wants to go home, let her deal with the consequences.

I rolled my shoulder muscles to ease the tension that weighed them down. I would try to make her understand the danger she was in, offer to help, and let her decide. If she chose to leave, I wouldn't feel any guilt over her fate. And yet, I wanted her to stay. Perhaps it was some lingering effect of her magic, affecting me again now that she was close by. Nothing to be concerned about. It would fade again.

"Are you going to take me home?" she asked a while later.

"Not yet. Right now we need to focus on getting as far from the ship and Severn as we can. He'll look for us going that way first."

"He knows where I live?"

"Yes."

Her face paled. "But my family—"

"They'll be fine. He won't attack unless he's sure you're there, and he'll try to cut us off before then. Let's find a safe place to spend the night, and I'll try to explain everything."

She frowned. "Sure."

We'd want a fire, but we needed more cover than the

trees would provide.

"What's that? It's beautiful." Rowan pointed toward the nearby mountain face. Erosion had exposed diagonal layers of rock, variegated shades of gray with lighter brown streaks.

"Lovely." Useless, but very nice to look at. I knew people like that.

Or was it useless? I rode closer to an outcropping in the rock and ran my fingers over the brown stone. My fingers came away dusty, but left no mark on the rock. "We might be able to find shelter here and build a fire," I called, and Rowan came up beside me. "There may be caves."

I dismounted and led my horse over the rocky ground as Rowan rode along the edge of the forest below, stopping to dismount and look at something in the woods. The first shadow in the rock I explored was only a hollow that wasn't nearly deep enough to offer protection. A dark space up ahead looked more promising. I left the horse and stepped into a cleft in the rock that continued deeper into the mountain on a shallow upward slope, turning into a tall, narrow cave farther in. I wanted to explore further, but I hesitated as an uneasy feeling crept over me. I sent my awareness out.

Severn. He wasn't on top of us yet, but he wasn't far. My skin prickled with cold fear as I darted back into the sunlight.

Rowan was busy picking up an armload of firewood. "Rowan," I called, and she looked up. I didn't want her to panic, but he was getting closer. Too close. "Severn is coming."

She stumbled forward, clutching the bundle of dry branches to her chest while she held her horse's reins with the other hand.

The crack in the stone was barely wide enough for the horses to enter, but we had no other options. Mine pulled back and shuffled her feet against the dusty stone floor as the space narrowed and the walls came together overhead, but I urged her on, hoping we wouldn't become trapped if there was nowhere to turn around.

The passage opened in a wide, enclosed space with an uneven floor and a ceiling that was just tall enough for Rowan to stand comfortably, but the horses and I had to keep our heads down. Rowan's horse let out a nervous snort. I stepped aside and let Rowan and her horse pass, and handed her the reins for mine. She led them to the rear of the cave and stroked their faces, quieting them.

Severn was still coming closer. I felt his wrath in my bones, and his voice echoed in my mind as he cursed my name. My heartbeat sped up and sweat broke out over my body as I remembered other times when I'd hidden from him, when I was much younger. I'd succeeded a few times, before he forced me to stop. But it had been too long since I'd tried it. I wasn't prepared.

Severn's approach slowed. He'd sensed my magic and was trying to locate me. If I didn't act, we were finished. I closed my eyes.

My thoughts turned away from Severn and back to the cave, making it an impenetrable fortress in my mind. Nothing happened. Then the temperature in the cave plummeted, raising goosebumps on my skin. I backed away from the entrance and hoped the change wouldn't extend to outside, alerting Severn. A horse squealed, and Rowan began speaking to it softly. In my mind the cave sealed itself, rock closing out the light and any sign of our presence.

Still he came closer, his mind open to me for the first time. *He's baiting me.* If I took the opportunity to look into his thoughts, he would feel me. I shut him out and quieted my own mind as well as I could.

Minutes passed, and no one entered the cave. I risked reaching out, and found Severn's presence fading. I stayed where I was, waiting until I lost all sense of him. When I opened my eyes, I was surprised to see that nothing had changed. Sunlight still filtered in from the open entrance. It had all seemed so real in my mind.

When I turned back Rowan was staring with wide eyes, holding both horses' reins in one hand and pulling her jacket and cloak tight to her body with the other. Her breath came out in smoky white plumes that faded as the cave warmed.

"Is he gone?" she whispered. I nodded, and she relaxed slightly. "What was that? Why did it get so cold?"

"Do you know anything about magic?"

"Um… no. Well, I've heard that you—I mean people sell their souls to get it." She offered a nervous half-smile. "I sort of hoped that wasn't true, though."

"No. If I'm damned, it's not for that." I meant it as a joke to put her at ease, but she didn't seem to think it was humorous.

"So what is it? How does it work?"

How to explain magic to someone as ignorant as her? I'd studied it all my life and still didn't understand it.

"Magic is energy, like sunlight or a thunderstorm or the life in your body. It's everywhere, or it should be. Some creatures wouldn't exist without it, like flying horses, gryphons or the Aeyer—"

"Aeyer?"

"Winged people. Mountain folk. Other creatures and people are able to use it to do various things. We don't all have the same abilities, and it takes a lot of training to learn how to use them properly."

"For example?"

I wasn't eager to talk about my natural abilities concerning mind-control. "For example, Severn has natural skill with fire. That talent showed itself long before he learned to control it. What I did a few minutes ago was an attempt to keep him from locating me, creating a magical shield of sorts. It's not something I've practiced, or even planned. It worked, but the process also took a different kind of energy from the air in here, making it cold. We're lucky that's all that happened." People had died attempting less, but that information didn't seem like it would make her any more comfortable with the concept.

I stepped toward my horse, and she shied away. Rowan took the bags off of both horses as I turned to set up the firewood in a depression in the floor, stripping bark and piling it beneath the branches. Rowan carried the saddles to an out of the way spot in the cave and brought our bags to the fire pit, limping on her injured ankle.

"So does everyone in Tyrea use magic?"

"No. Most can't at all. Some have very low-level magic, and use it as they can. Their skill sets tend to be very narrow. Sorcerers have more magic in us, and it replenishes faster after we use it. We have a wider range of natural gifts, and if we're willing to risk those unpredictable outcomes, we can expand beyond that. Like me changing into an eagle. It was a risk the first time I tried it. Very dangerous, even after study. But it worked." I took a fire striker from my bag and lit the kindling. "Sadly, some skills seem destined to remain forever out of my reach."

She smiled at that. "Being able to make fires would be convenient." She sat across from me with her legs stretched out in front, head tilted to one side. "There's so much I want to ask about magic."

"But?"

"But I think the more important question is why I'm here. Why did Severn want me? You said I have magic, but I don't. I'm not like you. I don't start fires, or make strange things happen."

"You healed me."

"I didn't. I believe that magic healed you. There's no other explanation. But it wasn't mine." She took off her boot and pulled Sara's ointment from her bag to rub onto her injuries. "Is this magic? Is Sara like you?"

"No, she's a Potioner. It's different, and not important right now. She's not a Sorceress. Not like you."

Rowan set the jar aside and leaned forward. "Please stop saying that."

"My body heals far more quickly than the average person's. Any Sorcerer's does, but it's nothing on that scale.

And what happened that night goes beyond simple healing. The magic hunters treated their arrows with a substance that kept me from using my magic. You destroyed that poison. Your magic flowed through me, repairing the damage until you fainted, and then it ended." I couldn't sit still anymore. I stood and paced the cave, though there was little space. "Do you remember any of it?"

"No. I remember a crazy dream, and darkness. Pain. Everything was so confused. But as far as what actually happened, I remember wanting something to cover Aquila's—I mean, your wounds, and getting dizzy. So maybe you used unfamiliar magic when you healed yourself, and causing me pain was the unexpected effect?"

I stopped and stood opposite her, with the fire between us. "Why are you fighting this?"

She pulled her boot back on and laced it tight. "I'm not fighting, I'm being rational. I'm not like that." She said it as though magic were a curse or an illness. But then, according to what she'd grown up hearing, it was.

"There's powerful magic in you, Rowan."

"But I-"

"Please, let me explain. You once told me you wanted magic in your life. At least give it a chance."

She clamped her mouth shut and motioned for me to continue.

"Your magic healed me, but it hurt you. I believe that's because when you were young, someone found out about your power and decided it needed to be locked away inside of you. It's a process called binding, and it hasn't been done for centuries, at least not according to any records I could find."

She looked like the objections or questions were going to come exploding out of her at any moment, but she held back.

"Go ahead."

"How? And who would do that? And if I believed you, what would you propose I do about this binding thing?"

"I don't know, and I don't know, and I'm thinking about it." I untied a blanket from my pack, laid it out on the floor, and sat. "I suppose might have some luck finding help or answers in Tyrea, though the libraries in Luid are out of the question now. There might be others who could help."

She raised an eyebrow. "Forgive me, but going toward your brother doesn't sound like the best plan to me."

"When we're in Tyrea my magic will be stronger than it is here. I can protect us. And magic has to be the answer to this. There must be someone in Tyrea who knows what kind of magic can break a binding, and once we do that, you'll be able to use your magic to defend yourself." I heard the excitement in my voice, and took a breath to calm myself. It would take time for her to learn, but I was sure she could do it. "You'll find protection in Tyrea, especially with other magic-users, if people know what you are. If you go home now and your magic remains hidden, you'll never be safe from Severn, or your own people if it gets out."

She glanced at the flames dancing in the fire pit and chewed on her lower lip. "When I woke up on the ship and you said I was in more trouble than I knew, you weren't just referring to Severn, were you?"

"No. He was and is the most immediate danger, but there's more. There's the binding, which I think is only going to cause you more pain as time goes on and your magic grows stronger." The idea that it might kill her had occurred to me, but the look of horror on her face at the mention of more pain made me keep it to myself. "There's also the fact that you're a Sorceress who's a Darmish citizen and planning to marry a magic hunter."

She shivered in spite of the heat from the fire. "I have to go." She used the rough stone wall to pull herself up, then limped toward the cave entrance.

"You can't just leave."

She stopped, but didn't look at me. When she spoke again, her voice was weary. "I just have to pee. I'll come back. Give me a few minutes alone. Please."

I allowed some time to get away from the cave, then tethered the horses outside with water and grain rations. I watched from a distance as Rowan returned to the cave, and decided she could use more time alone with her thoughts. Perhaps she'd realize I was right.

We needed to add to our food supplies, anyway. I walked farther into the woods, undressed, and transformed into my eagle's body.

#

Prey was scarce on the side of the mountain, but I spotted and killed a fat rabbit. I changed back into my own body and returned to the tree where I'd left my clothes and hunting knife, and cleaned the carcass. It wasn't much, but it would be better than nothing.

I hesitated before I entered the cave. If only I could sense Rowan's mood and her thoughts. Had she been a normal citizen of her country, I could have forced her to understand. But then, if she'd been normal, she would have been safe from all of this.

She was lying on her bedroll with a sweater folded under her head, her bandaged leg elevated on rock that hunched up from the cave's floor. The smell of Sara's healing mixture touched the air, mixed with a hint of burning pine. Rowan didn't look at me or say anything while I set up a makeshift spit over the fire. Just before the meat was cooked, she asked, "Where's the smoke going?"

"Pardon?"

"The smoke. We should be choking on it by now. Did you do something to the wood?"

"No, it's the smokestone. This part of the mountain is full of it. Absorbs smoke, and some of the smells from cooking. Usually forms around air pockets, which is why I thought we should look here for shelter. Not strong for building, but it can be useful."

"Huh." Her voice was flat, exhausted.

For a while the crackling of the fire was the only sound. When the food was gone and the remains taken far from the cave, she sat cross-legged on her blankets and spoke. "You remember what you said before?"

"Vaguely."

The arch of her eyebrow could have been mild amusement or well-contained annoyance. "I've been thinking about it. There was a time when I'd have been excited to hear that I was a Sorceress, but that was before I understood the truth about it. About what magic means to someone in my country, how it's feared and hated. If what you said were true, I would lose everything. My family, my home, Callum, my future, any hope of a normal life. Do you understand that?"

"I do. But none of that changes what happened that night. You healed me. The magic is there, whether you want it or not."

The corners of her lips twitched upward. "Is this the part where you tell me there's a prophecy about someone like me? No, wait. I'm a long-lost princess, right? Hidden from the evil fairy for my own good? And I need to seek out the magical amulet, or be saved by prince charming."

I was confused for a moment, until I remembered the story book I'd leafed through in her room. "Funny, but no."

She rubbed a hand across her eyes, and winced as it brushed the bruise on her cheek. "So you think this binding thing can be undone? Assuming I wanted that. I mean, I want the headaches to stop, but having magic would finish me in Darmid. They'd kill me as soon as look at me."

"Even your family?"

"My father's a magistrate. I don't think that would make things easier on me." She lifted her gaze to meet mine. "I'm going to need to think about this. I understand what you're saying about the healing and all of that, but it just doesn't make sense to me. And going to your country is just…" The end of her sentence disappeared in a yawn.

There was no point arguing when we were both tired. "Here," I said, and handed her my bedding. "I'm going to change and sleep outside so I can keep an eye on things."

I thought she'd also sleep better without me in the cave, but would be either too polite or too frightened to say so. I'd also have an easier time staying alert if I wasn't in my human body. Now that we were away from the destruction of Rowan's people, my magic was replenishing itself. I could afford to use some for her comfort and mine.

I stepped out into the forest and searched for Severn, but felt nothing. I let my clothes fall into a heap as I transformed and took off to find a place in the treetops where I could watch the horses and the cave.

I doubted I'd be getting much rest.

Chapter Fourteen

Aren

I never slept as deeply in my eagle's body as I did when I was a human. I passed the night without dreaming, and managed to keep a faint awareness of any human presences that might be approaching. There was no one, save for the woman sleeping in the cave.

I woke before sunrise. While I changed, dressed and collected the horses, I considered the problems Rowan brought with her.

She understood what I'd told her, but didn't want to believe it. If she didn't believe, she wouldn't go to Tyrea to look for help. I doubted she'd stay with me simply for the pleasure of my company. All I needed was for her to see the wrongness of what had been done to her, to get angry about it, and to fight against everything she'd been brought up believing about herself, magic, and my people.

"That's not so much to ask, is it?" I asked my horse as I offered her a morning grain ration. She rolled an eye at me and flicked an ear. "No, should be easy enough. Maybe she had a miraculous vision overnight that convinced her."

I led both horses back to the cave and heard Rowan moving about, packing her things. She nodded to me when I entered, but didn't speak.

"What, not even a 'thank you for not murdering me in my sleep?'" I asked as I laid the saddle pad on her horse.

She smiled and came to help me. "I'm very grateful. Did you sleep well?"

"Well as I ever do." I didn't ask her the same. The shadows beneath her eyes spoke of a restless night. She was moving more easily, though she still limped when she walked, and her face looked better than it had the day before. She'd brushed her hair out and braided it, and changed her clothes. I had hoped that I'd only found her attractive when I first saw her because of her magic's influence. It seemed that was wrong. Injured and unwashed as she was, she still looked good.

I turned away before my body could make me understand just how good.

We left the cave, and Rowan winced as she settled herself in the saddle. "Too much riding yesterday."

"There's still a long way to go," I told her. "We should make it to Tyrea tonight if we keep a good pace."

"We? Does that mean you still want to help me?" She seemed genuinely surprised.

"I do. I'm absolutely certain of what I told you last night."

"But—"

"I wouldn't have stayed at your house if I wasn't. I wouldn't have even bothered to pick you up off the floor."

She winced. "You put me to bed when I was passed

out?" I nodded, and she looked thoughtful. "You know, that kind of thing always works out well in fairy stories. In real life it seems a little awkward."

You have no idea. I tried not to think about what I'd felt that night, with her magic in me. How she'd looked, how I'd wanted to keep her safe. "I think the princes in those stories usually have better reputations than I have."

"True. I just never thought about how creepy it all was, them kissing sleeping girls and all of that."

"I promise that was the only time I wasn't an eagle when you were in the room."

"I appreciate that." She seemed to be mulling things over as we rode away from the cave, still moving east, picking our way through the sparse forest. "So," she said at last. "I was thinking about whether I'm going home, or going to Tyrea."

I tried not to look like I cared, and reminded myself that escape would be easier without her. "Yes?"

"I should want to go home. The thing is, I was just saying to Felicia that I wanted adventure in my life."

"I remember."

"The point is, I used to want this. I've heard stories about Tyrea and wanted to see it for myself. I once met people from there. Wanderers. Do you see them where you live?"

I nodded. Wanderers were hardly what I'd call Tyreans—they didn't claim any nationality, refused to pay taxes, and went where they pleased. They were an irritation at best, and a security risk at worst. But if she thought highly of them and it made her think well of my people, so be it.

"There was a little boy who told me a few things, but his mother shushed him. Probably didn't want to get them in trouble. I tried to forget like Matthew told me to, but I don't think I ever got over the curiosity. Maybe that's why I loved those stories so much." She smiled and shook her head. "But I made a promise to Callum, and I'm happy with that." She hesitated slightly before the word *happy*. "I can't leave him because of a childhood dream that was foolish and dangerous to begin with. And I especially can't go with you."

"Of course you can't. I'm everything you've been taught to fear. You believe what you've been taught about magic and about my people, so obviously you wouldn't want to give me a chance to prove that wrong."

She frowned. "I'm not like that. And don't do that, it's not going to work."

"Do what?"

"Telling me I'm something that I'm not just so I'll have to prove you wrong. It's tricky. I don't like it."

Perhaps she was smarter than I'd thought.

"So what I'm thinking is that maybe I'll stay with you until we get to the border. You can tell me more about magic, and about your country. If by then I think you're right about me, I'll keep going. If you want me to."

"I do."

She turned to me with narrowed eyes. "Why? Why are you helping me?"

"I already told you. I'm repaying you for saving my life."

Her frown wrinkled her nose. It would have been oddly attractive if I'd let myself think of her in those terms. *Which*

I don't.

She studied me for a moment longer, then looked forward and straightened her shoulders. "You really think there's a way to get rid of the headaches?"

"I'm sure there's a cure for you." I hadn't found any information in Luid of how bindings were performed. Severn hadn't given me many chances to look through the old court Sorcerers' records. Still, there had to be some way. "And maybe you'll enjoy life in Tyrea. If you go that far, of course."

She was silent for a while longer, save for asking whether we could ride and eat at the same time. We could, and did. Her ruminating suited me. I was accustomed to being alone, and much preferred traveling in silence.

"This is probably the stupidest thing I've ever done," she said at last. "I should go straight home and forget all about this, but I've spent my entire life wanting to know more about magic, dreaming about an adventure like this." She tilted her head to one side. "Though I might have preferred that the magical, mysterious stranger who saved me from the bad guys wasn't terrifying and possibly evil."

"Well, no one is perfect."

She grinned, looking truly amused for the first time since I found her by the river. "I know I'll regret it if I don't take this opportunity. This might be my only chance to fix whatever's wrong with me, and I believe you want to help. But you should know I'm going to have a lot of questions, and I need you to answer truthfully. Can you do that?"

"I'll do my best." Not an appealing prospect, if it meant endless conversation like she seemed fond of when she was with her family. Still, it would keep her around until I could convince her of her magic, and there would be dangers ahead far worse than a lone gryphon that she'd need to learn about.

She still looked troubled. "This is a bad idea, I know it is."

I couldn't disagree.

#

It took her far too long to understand that I wasn't willing to talk about myself. I tried to be patient, politely deflecting her inquiries when she asked about what I'd been doing when she found me half-dead by the road, how exactly I "did magic," my family, where I'd grown up, whether I had any pets or friends, what I did when I wasn't out abducting people. I had agreed to tell her about magic, nothing more.

She became increasingly frustrated with each refusal, and with each question she pestered me with I came closer to abandoning her in the woods. In theory, I admired her curiosity. In practical terms, it was going to drive me mad.

"I would feel better about all of this if you would tell me just one thing that makes me think you're anything other than a creepy bad guy luring me off into the woods to feed me to a dragon," she said.

"The fact that you're still here leads me to believe that you don't think that at all."

She flipped her braid back over her shoulder. "I'm still just a little uncomfortable. You seem to know so much about me. Tell me something. Anything. Tell me your brothers' names."

I gripped the reins tighter and took a deep breath. "What difference does it make?"

"None, I suppose," she said. "But I'm putting a lot of trust in you, and you haven't given me anything in return."

"Besides not killing you?"

She sighed. "You're right, I know. Coming along was my decision, and I appreciate what you're doing for me. I'm just—"

"Severn, Wardrel, Dan. Those are my brothers' names. They're not as friendly as I am."

She snickered. "I picked up on that from Severn." She looked over at me and seemed to be considering something. "Thank you."

I reminded myself that she probably still saw me as something of a monster. Not being able to read her was throwing me off, and if I wanted to help her—and it was too late to change my mind on that—I'd have to try to make her comfortable without letting her get too close.

"You didn't know there were gryphons in the mountains?" I asked.

"No. I've read about them before, but I didn't ever expect to see them in Darmid."

"Normally you wouldn't. Your people have done a surprisingly good job killing off every bit of magic in the populated areas of your country, but the mountains are still wild. Out here you'll want to watch the skies for gryphons, be wary of the paths that a dragon might use for hunting, watch for burned trees. This is probably where they've fled to, if your hunters have left any alive." I tried to keep the bitterness out of my voice.

I must not have succeeded. Rowan grimaced and looked away. "I guess that's a sore spot for you," she said. "For what it's worth, I'm sorry. But you can't be upset with us for protecting ourselves against gryphons or dragons, can you? They're dangerous."

"Dangerous, but necessary for most of us. Everything is connected. Without dragons and every other magical creature, there's nothing to keep magic in the land. Your people understand that, and push all the harder to be rid of it completely. It's causing problems in Tyrea. That's actually why Severn wanted you."

"For information?"

"Experimentation."

"Oh." It seemed enough to buy me a few minutes of silence as she mulled it over. Perfect. If I could interest her with those things, she'd have a reason to stay with me, and I would avoid talking about myself.

We rode farther from the mountain's slope as the day passed, under cover of the forest. Rowan looked around, taking in the trees and the rocks, and the occasional animal that darted across the path. I was doing the same, but I soon realized she wasn't seeing the same things I was. To me, every noise was a reason for caution. I looked at the trees for signs of damage, anything that might indicate what sorts of creatures lived in the area. I watched the sky for potential attackers.

Rowan seemed to be simply enjoying the colors of the leaves. She took deep breaths of the earth-scented air, and smiled when a doe paused in the path ahead of us before leaping away into the underbrush.

I only wondered what the deer might be running from. *You have a lot to learn about the world, Rowan.*

"So tell me about dragons," she said after the deer fled. "I don't know much about them, except that there's a skeleton at the university, and Dorset Langley has a bow made from a rib he took from the first one he killed."

"How very impressive. What do you want to know?"

"Everything."

Of course you do. "Your people's perceptions of dragons seem to be based on younger dragons. They're nasty beasts, violent and thoughtless. If we have to kill a dragon, it's usually not more than a few hundred years old."

"So you do kill them? I thought you needed them."

"We do. And they don't often bother us enough that we'll hunt them. Farmers in dragon lands accept the loss of a few animals every season as the price they pay for living there, and they take precautions against it. Once in a while a young dragon will develop a taste for human flesh, though, and discover that we're easy prey. Then we have no choice. When they're older, they know better."

"How old is old?"

"A dragon could in theory live for thousands of years. They don't let it go that long, though. As they get older, they become more like us. Their minds change, they think and speak like we do. And they hate it."

She seemed surprised. "Are we so terrible that an animal would rather die than be like us?"

"They spend hundreds of years living without greed, envy, betrayal, sadness, anger. Even the things we might consider good are confusing to them. It becomes much harder to kill or steal when you start to think about what it does to someone else."

She gave me a look that said she was reading too much into that statement, then asked, "Do they love?"

"I think any respectable dragon would kill itself before it let things get that bad."

My answer seemed to please her far more than I'd expected. Strange woman. I'd thought I had her figured out. Easily distracted by daydreams, rebellious only when it was safe and suited her whims, kind but somewhat self-ish, probably a horrible romantic. Smart, but dangerously unobservant. Perhaps I was only mostly right.

I realized that I'd let my awareness slip for far too long, and took a moment to check the forest around us. No humans. I'd have to watch that, though. Having company made for too many distractions.

Rowan appeared to be enjoying the conversation, and seemed to be growing less wary of me as the day wore on. "Is it true that they steal treasure? Is that a part of them becoming like us?"

"Partly. Dragonlings are quite fragile. They consume hard gemstones and minerals, and those substances are incorporated into their scales. It's entirely natural that they'd seek them out for that purpose." I'd learned all of this when I was a child, and it amazed me that the Darmish could be so ignorant. "But yes, when they get older they begin to hoard things they think are beautiful, and later the things that are valuable to other creatures. Gold isn't good for a dragon to eat, it's much too soft. But an old dragon might have more of it than most city treasuries, simply because someone else wants it. Of course, it benefits the dragon when people hear about their treasure and try to steal it. An old dragon doesn't need to eat much, but they always appreciate fresh meat."

"Is that treasure cursed?" she asked, whispering the last word. She was watching me so intently as she waited for an answer that a low-hanging branch nearly knocked her off of her horse. She ducked at the last moment, and turned to face forward again. I hoped she hadn't seen me trying not to laugh at her.

I cleared my throat. "You know, I think that's enough questions for now."

"You promised me answers!"

"I didn't promise all of them at once. I'm trying to focus on keeping us safe. Curses and everything else will have to wait until we stop for the night."

Of course the treasure was cursed. Possessing it invariably turned people into the very worst parts of themselves, cruel and selfish and murderous, caring nothing for anything but their own pleasure. It would have been exhausting to try to explain it all to her, though, and I was tired of talking.

"But what if—"

"Shh." I held up a hand to silence her. "There's someone here." I relaxed when I realized that it wasn't Severn I'd sensed, but that didn't mean we were safe. It felt like two men behind us, still far enough off that they wouldn't know exactly where we were, but close enough that I wasn't just going to wait and hope that they'd go away. They didn't feel familiar. Darmish, perhaps, though I couldn't tell whether they were magic hunters.

Either way, I would deal with them. I just hoped it wasn't the Langleys. That would be particularly messy.

A strip of grassy, treeless land stretched out to either side of us like a deserted road. I urged my horse forward, into the shelter of the trees on the opposite side, and Rowan followed.

"What's going on?"

"Wait here," I said, and handed her the reins while I dismounted. "We can't have people following us. I'll take care of it."

"How?"

I looked down the broad path in both directions. The trees on either side reached branches across, and the ground was overgrown with grass and saplings. Definitely unused, but still… "Don't go anywhere, and try to be quiet. I don't think there's anything here, but it's best not to take chances. Just stay well off the path. If anything threatens you, leave the horses and run. I'll be back."

"What is it?"

"Dragon path."

"Really?" She leaned forward and squinted as she looked toward the place where the wide path curved back into the trees.

I tried to forget about her as I crept back through the forest toward whomever was unlucky enough to be on our trail.

Chapter Fifteen

Aren

The men were easy to locate. They were locals sent to search the woods for us, careless and unaware of how close they were to success. I heard and saw them long before they knew I was there.

"Do you see anything?" His Darmish accent made it come out, "D'you see hennyting?" His thoughts were easier to follow than his words.

"Same as. Are we going to turn back? I'm about ready to get back to my Mary and a home-cooked meal."

"Nuts to your Mary. Give it another few. We'll never hear the end of it if we're first back."

"Imagine if we did find them?"

The first speaker snorted, then wiped his nose on his sleeve. "Gawd, I hope not! Magic stuff gives me the creeps."

They certainly hadn't located us through any skill of their own. More likely they'd been sent off in our direction, picked up a few signs of someone passing, and followed because they'd been instructed to follow every clue. What a shame for them that they were so keen on doing their duty.

They were alone, and hadn't thought to send word back to the magic hunters. The second one told me so before I broke his neck.

I dragged the bodies to a shallow ravine, then hurried back to where I'd left Rowan.

That could have been worse, I thought. I didn't enjoy dealing with situations like that, but if those two incompetents were the worst thing we had to deal with before we got to some kind of safety, I wouldn't complain.

The horses were still there, tearing away at the leaves of some low redberry bushes. Rowan had left our bags piled under the boughs of a thick pine, but she was gone. I hoped she'd only gone to look for food, but I knew better. I left the horses where they were, took the bags with me, and set out down the dragon path, heading toward the rocky hill to the North.

She'll be fine, I told myself. *Just a young dragon, long dead. Dorset Langley probably killed it and made a piano bench out of its bones.* Even if it had been an older dragon that left its treasure behind, Rowan would know not to touch anything in its cave, wouldn't she? Perhaps not.

I pushed my feet harder into the grassy earth and ran.

The cave entrance was wide and low, opening beneath an overhang of dark rock. The leaves littering the ground were another reassuring sign. If a large dragon had been going in and out, its belly would have cleared the debris. I left the bags outside and ducked my head to creep into the cave.

The cave Rowan had slept in the previous night had been damp and cool. This one was warm and dry enough that I had to breathe slowly so as not to cough. My stomach tightened with apprehension, but I forced myself to go on. Something rumbled in the cave ahead, but the echoes and the curves of the tunnel distorted the sound. The passage grew lighter, not with daylight, but with a red-gold glow.

Had that not told me what lay ahead, the strong magic in the air would have. Had Rowan felt it? Could she? Perhaps that had been enough to warn her off. But I had to know.

I stayed close to the smooth wall, creeping forward until the tunnel opened onto a larger cavern which was almost entirely filled with a massive dragon.

The light in the cave came from the dull glow of the creature's red scales. Its thick body rested on the floor, and great clawed feet curled at the ends of four muscular legs. Relaxed, not aggressive or defensive. The tail curved around the wall of the cavern toward me, and the head, which was half again as large as one of the horses I'd left outside, was raised at the end of a sinuous neck, gaze directed at a spot just to the side of where I stood in the shadows. I leaned forward. Rowan crouched on a stone outcropping with her back pressed to the wall, her attention fixed on the massive face in front of her. She appeared unharmed, but frightened.

"I think we have company," the dragon said, and a chill spread from the base of my spine through my body. The rasping voice spoke with our words, but sounded nothing like a human. The dragon and Rowan both turned to look at me.

"Aren, run," Rowan ordered.

"Don't be rude, girl," the dragon replied. Its green eyes were surrounded by scales that were the same deep gray as its neatly folded wings and the narrow spines crowning its head and tracing the length of its back. "Come in, please."

I stepped into the cavern, but stayed near the entrance. There was no point trying to reach Rowan. We'd both be dead before we took one step toward freedom. The dragon shrugged, a gesture that rippled down the length of its body and ended with a flick of its tail. "Good enough. This young lady was just telling me about this journey that the two of you are on. Seems strange to me that you'd help her. Out of what? The goodness of your heart?" The beast lifted its lip in a sneer. "I hardly think there's much of that in you."

"You know who I am, then?"

"I do. I rarely care for the short-lived concerns of humans, but your family is familiar to me."

"I'm sorry," Rowan said. "I just wanted to look, and then Ruby invited me in, and I didn't think I should say no."

"Ruby?"

Another flick of the tail. "The girl wanted to know my name, and I told her dragons don't have them. She asked me what I ate to become such a lovely color, and I told her." The dragon blinked slowly and fixed its gaze on my hands. "Very nice gloves you have there. Dragon skin?"

"Yes." There was no point lying. "He killed a dozen people before we killed him. Fourteen if you count unborn children."

"I don't, but I suppose you are correct. He earned his death." It stretched its forelegs and flexed its claws, clearly not intimidated by my presence. "If I kill her, will you do the same to me?" There was a mocking tone to its voice.

"I'll try."

Rowan sighed. "I told you not to come in. *Are* you going to kill me?" she asked the dragon.

"Of course. You're not much, but my young are hungry."

I hadn't noticed the pool of still water between the dragon's forelegs. Beneath the surface I could just make out the pale shapes of a trio of dragonlings, still too young and soft to survive the air their mother's heat made so dry. That was why the path appeared unused. Mother dragons guard their eggs and their young more carefully than any other creature, forgoing food and exercise in order to protect them.

"Your story has entertained me," the dragon continued, "and I thank you. But if you're finished, I have no reason to spare you. Or him." She leaned her head closer to Rowan. "But I'll let you choose flames or claws, by way of thanks."

I scrambled to think of a way to get us out of there, but couldn't come up with anything that would work fast enough. All I had was my hunting knife and magic, neither of which would work fast enough to save us.

Rowan stood, slowly and unsteadily. She reached out a trembling hand and laid it on the glowing red snout. "I think you should let us go."

It was a lucky thing the creature didn't snort in surprise. It might have cooked Rowan where she stood. "Why ever would I do that?"

Rowan closed her eyes and took a deep breath.

Come on, I thought. She'd have to find a way to use

magic again. I didn't know what she'd be able to do with it, but we were both going to be eaten if she didn't think of something.

"Because," she said, and looked up. "You want to know how the story ends."

The dragon opened her mouth, then paused. She pulled back, neck curving into an S-shape. "*This* is how it ends."

"It could be. But if you let us go, there will be more for you to hear. I don't know what's going to happen. Neither do you. I think you're curious, that you'd like to find out. Isn't that better than a tiny little meal?" Her voice shook, but she stared steadily at the dragon's horrible face.

A few seconds passed, and then a rumbling noise began deep in the dragon's massive chest. It took me a moment to realize that she wasn't growling, but laughing—or as close as a dragon could come to it. Her tail thumped twice on the floor.

"I almost wish I could like you," she said, and bared her teeth in a grotesque parody of a grin. "You're amusing. I think your story would be worth hearing, but what's a little human's word worth, eh? Now, a sorcerer's, perhaps..." Her head swiveled toward me. "What do you say, king's son? Will you give me your promise that neither of you will tell anyone what you've seen here, and that you will come back to tell me how the story ends? Soon, I mean. If you don't, I will find you, and I promise that the ending of this little story will not be pleasant."

I tried to erase the look of shock I felt on my face. Was this dragon actually offering to let us go? True, an agreement with a dragon was never to be entered into lightly, and the consequences could be unpredictable. But if the alternative was death…

I nodded. "I promise, you'll have your story."

Ruby drummed her clawed fingers on the floor, then stood and stretched, arching her back so that the gray spines scraped the ceiling. Her mouth twisted into a sly smile as she reached into an alcove and pulled out a mass of gold coins, jewelery, ornaments, and unrefined ore, all of it littered through with precious gemstones that would have made any jeweler in Luid weep to see them.

"Very well, with two further conditions. First, you leave the horses. I can smell them on you, and it reminds me that my young are old enough to taste meat. Second, as a symbol of our agreement, I insist that you choose a bit of my treasure to take with you." It seemed she was going to make sure the story that came back to her was worth the price she was paying for it.

"Oh, I couldn't," Rowan stammered. "You're very kind, but—"

"I insist. Come, child. You must like pretty things. Choose, or stay for supper." Rowan turned to me, eyes wide and frightened. "No," Ruby said. "Not him. He's got his gloves, he needs nothing more from us, and you need no help from him. Choose your prize, and I'll let you go. Both of you. This is my offer."

Rowan's shoulders sank, and she lowered her gaze. *Don't*, I mouthed, but she didn't see. I was sweating in the warm air, but my skin felt chilled. *Please.*

She clenched her hands into fists, then forced them to relax. "Any treasure of yours, and we can go? I have your word on that?"

Something like a smirk crossed the dragon's face. "Any that's in this cave. Let it not be said that I'm not generous."

"Then I suppose I'd be a fool not to take your greatest treasure."

"You would."

Rowan looked up, straight into the beast's eyes. "Then kindly bring your children out of the water so I can choose which I like best."

Ruby's gasp was nearly drowned out by the sound of my heart pounding in my ears. I didn't know whether what Rowan had just done was brilliant or insane. Maybe both.

Ruby lay down on top of the pool. "You wouldn't."

"I could, according to the terms of our agreement. Perhaps I won't. And perhaps you'll remember that before you try to trick us again. No more games. We go, you get your story. That's all."

The air warmed as the dragon let out a deep, shuddering breath that made my mind hazy when I breathed it in. "Agreed. But name your prize. You already said you'd take one. What do you want the most?"

Rowan's gaze passed over the heap of gold, along the great crimson body, toward the far end of the cavern. "There," she said, and jumped down from her perch. She walked closer to the dragon's rear claws than I would have dared, and stooped to pick something up off of the floor. *Don't take anything, please*, I thought.

"This," Rowan said, and held up what looked like a shallow bowl. "I told you I've waited my whole life to meet a dragon. I can't think of a better prize than one of your scales."

Ruby's jaw opened, and she cocked her head slightly to one side. She turned to me. "She's not even lying, is she?"

"I don't think so."

The dragon tapped a foreclaw on the ground and sighed. "Go, then. Take your prize, and let it be a reminder of your promise to return." Rowan clutched the scale to her chest and ran toward me. Ruby watched her go by, then studied the two of us for a moment. "Well. I think this could be interesting, indeed. Go on."

"Thank you," Rowan said, and the dragon nodded.

I pulled Rowan up to the tunnel entrance, holding onto her arm to support her. Her whole body was trembling.

Ruby's head turned to follow us. "Don't forget to leave the horses."

Rowan looked down at her injured ankle, then back at the dragon. She looked like she was going to object.

"Don't," I whispered. "It's a small price, believe me."

She nodded, and led the way through the tunnel. My gloves fell to the ground as we ran. I didn't stop to retrieve them.

It seemed strange that the sun still shone through the colored leaves when we emerged, as though nothing in the world had changed.

We left the cave, turning away from the path. Ruby would find the horses soon enough, and we didn't need to be there when she did. I hoped she'd find the bodies I'd left. It would be better if they disappeared completely.

I handed Rowan her bag and bedroll, and we ran as far as we could before her ankle gave out and she had to stop to treat and re-wrap it.

After she finished tying her boot, she covered her face with her hands. "That was horrible!" she cried.

"Well, what did you think was going to happen?" I tried not to yell, but I spoke more loudly than I'd intended. I was impressed with her quick thinking, but that didn't do anything to cancel my anger at her. "At what point did you realize it was a bad idea? Obviously not when I said 'dragon path'. Was it when you discovered that there was a live dragon in there, or only after you started having a friendly conversation with it?" She didn't look up. I took a few deep breaths, then knelt in the dirt beside her. "Rowan, you could have died in there. You're lucky that's not the first thing that happened. If that had been a younger dragon..."

"I know." Her voice cracked.

"How did you know not to take the treasure?"

"Stories. I didn't want to risk it."

"Well, good. But that doesn't change the fact that under any other circumstances, we both would have been roasted."

"I'm sorry." We stood and she wiped her eyes on her sleeve, then slipped the gray traveling cloak around her shoulders and pulled up the hood. "I need to go home."

"You can't, we haven't found help for you yet. Even if you don't believe me about the magic, we can get help for your pain."

When she looked up at me, any trace of happiness or excitement that might have been there before was gone. "I thought I wanted an adventure," she said, "but this isn't at all what I expected. I don't have magic, and you can't fix me. It was stupid of me to let you try. I'm going home, and I'm going to put all of this behind me. Maybe it's not too late for that." She picked up her knapsack and bedroll and started down the hill, deeper into the dimly lit woods.

"But you just got us out of a dragon cave," I called.

She turned back. "Yes. Right after I got us *into* a dragon cave. I'm obviously not ready for any of this. Which way is the border?"

I picked up my own things and followed her. I couldn't let her go home to be captured by Severn, or to marry a magic hunter who would probably turn her in or kill her when he realized what she was. I still wasn't entirely sure why it was so important to me, but it was.

If I could arrange it, I might get one more chance to convince her of her gifts, to make her stay and fight to save herself. I didn't like to think about what I'd have to do, but I had no choice. It was time to try something drastic.

Chapter Sixteen

Rowan

Painful as riding had been, walking was worse. Aren took the lead and I limped behind, trying to keep up with his long strides, occasionally catching up when he stopped to look back. My stomach grumbled as supper hour passed, but we'd lost too much time. I doubted there would be any stops before nightfall.

He wasn't speaking to me now, and that was fine. I didn't blame him for being angry. I'd been too impulsive, forgetting that the dangers out here were far different from any I'd known at home. Aren wasn't always nice about giving orders, but he'd been right, and like an idiot I hadn't listened. I wanted to talk about it, but decided to wait until he was ready. I needed some space to think, anyway.

Staying with Aren had been a terrible idea. I'd been curious about magic and thought, for just a moment, that he might even be right about me. I had acted without thinking of the consequences, and what had my stupid curiosity brought me? I'd almost gotten us eaten.

And those poor horses. Aren had called them a small

price to pay, but I kept thinking about them. They should have been back at the docks, getting their supper. They'd done nothing but carry us without complaint for two days, and now they were as good as dead.

I had made a terrible mistake. It was time to go home. Even if Aren couldn't straighten Severn out on what I really was, Callum would protect me. Not only that, but I'd be able to tell him what I'd learned about Tyrean magic, and how wrong we were about it. They didn't sell their souls, and those people who used magic in Darmid really were born with it. It would change everything. Maybe useful information like that would make up for not telling him about the eagle.

My head was throbbing with heavy pain again, but I kept putting one foot in front of the other, crunching over dead leaves in a faltering rhythm as the afternoon passed. Aren walked with his head down, jaw clenched, frowning. I felt badly for him. It was clear that he couldn't go home after what he'd done. Would that have worked out differently if he'd been right about me?

Not your problem, I told myself. *You never asked him for this.* He took a gamble, and it wasn't paying off. I tried to tell myself I had bigger problems to think about, but couldn't help worrying about his. He wasn't a friend, but we were in this together.

Late in the afternoon we reached a place where the forest ended, cut back in a straight line. Harvested fields sprawled in front of us, and in the distance dark trees crowded up against a cluster of whitewashed farm buildings. In between, placid-looking horses grazed in a large paddock.

Aren stopped and leaned on the fence. "Are you tired of walking yet?"

"Yes." Most of my injuries were nearly healed, but my ankle and shoulder still ached. "Why? Are we going to try to buy horses?"

"What? No." I thought the expression on his face was probably the same one I'd worn when he tried to tell me I was a Sorceress. "Can you ride without a saddle?"

"It's how I learned. But we can't just take someone's horses. That's stealing."

He gave me that *Are you serious?* look again. I thought I'd see a lot of that one if we spent much more time together. He dropped his backpack and bedroll, and boosted himself over the fence.

"Rowan, we have people hunting us who aren't going to treat us very nicely if they catch us, so I think moving more quickly might be a really good idea." He was talking like I was an idiot, and I wanted to slap him for it. "I was lucky earlier today," he continued in a more normal tone. "The two men who were following us weren't being careful, and it was easy for me to surprise them. We might not be so fortunate next time. Come on, there's no one home here. It will be easy."

I had forgotten about the men who were following us. "Did you kill them?"

"I did what I had to do."

How many people did you have to kill before you could just say it like that, without showing any more remorse than you would for killing a rat?

"If it makes you feel any better," he added with a sardonic smile, "I didn't pay for the other horses, either. You're already a thief and on the run from parties in two countries. A few more horses won't hurt."

"Fine. It's still not right," I said, and dropped my own things onto the pile. "Let's just hurry."

He held out a hand to help me over the fence. "Sometimes necessary has to come before right," he said. "And look at it this way. Your new friend Ruby seems to be ready to get out hunting again. We're saving a few of these horses from her." He took a few steps, then turned back. "And no, we can't take all of them."

"I wasn't even going to suggest that."

We didn't speak as we crossed the back fields. We entered the paddock, which sloped downward at the far side into a wooded area contained within the fence.

From a distance, the herd seemed to be a common enough mix of work and riding horses. As we approached, though, I saw that these horses all had heavy jaws, and thicker legs than the horses I was accustomed to. Their hooves were massive, and their lower legs all covered in long hair that matched their shaggy manes and tails.

"Wait for them to come to us," Aren said.

"What are these?" I whispered.

Aren reached out to stroke a black mare's white-blazed face as she approached. She shied at first, but seemed to warm to him quickly. He smiled. "Proper Tyrean horses. This will make things easier."

Another of the mares approached me, a stocky piebald-coated creature with the largest brown eyes I'd ever seen on a horse. She sniffed at my cloak and snorted. "You don't like dragons?" I asked her. I reached out, and she allowed me to touch her face. "Aren, we're still in Darmid, right?"

"We are," Aren said. "I'd say these are quite illegal because of their magical ancestry, but people are smart to keep them. They're tougher than the horses you're accustomed to. If they learn to trust us they'll forage without wandering off or getting lost, and they can eat almost anything, plant or animal. They're stronger, faster and more sure-footed than your horses, too. Gods, I miss Tyrea." He left to search a nearby shed, and came back with a pair of simple leather bridles. "Your people's stubbornness about this land makes your lives far more difficult than they need to be."

A pale gray mare trotted over and bared her teeth at my new friend, revealing long, sharp canines. She gave a friendly nip, then returned to the herd.

We were adjusting the bridles when a brain-piercing scream ripped through the cold air from behind us. Somewhere near the house a dog added its howls to the racket.

Aren cursed. "Hurry. We need to go."

What seemed to be a white stallion emerged from the trees below us and stopped at the top of the hill. It didn't sound like any horse I'd ever heard, though, and when I risked another look back I saw the long teeth that curved up from either side of its mouth. Its eyes burned like hot coals, and the ground shuddered when it stamped a hoof.

"Rowan, go."

There was nowhere to mount, and the horse was too tall for me to climb. I settled for taking the reins in hand and running. The mare seemed eager to escape, too, and tried to pull ahead. Aren and his mount kept pace beside us.

"What *is* that?" I yelled.

"Tusker," he called back. "Nasty beasts, used for breeding these horses every ten generations or so. Didn't think anyone was crazy enough to keep one loose with their mares."

We kept running, but the tusker was too close. He'd catch up when we stopped to open the gate, and I doubted he'd be content to just take back his mares.

I caught a flash of movement from the corner of my eye as Aren leaped and pulled himself up by his horse's mane. They sped ahead. *You bastard*, I thought, and in a moment of panic I almost let go of my own horse and ran for the closest fence in hopes of diving under it. When I looked ahead again, Aren had reached the gate. I expected him to try to jump it, but he swung down to the ground and started working at the lock, giving it a hard smack and hauling back on it until it popped open, sending sparks flying into the air. He hurried his horse through, and waited.

The tusker's hoofs pounded the grassy earth behind me, gaining with every step. I pushed my legs to move faster than they'd ever had to before, ignoring the pain that burned in every muscle and shot up from my ankle.

We made it through the gate and Aren slammed it closed behind my horse's tail, then reached through to snap the lock shut moments before the tusker slammed into the fence, bucking and shrieking. Aren yelled, and the tusker's head snapped back as though it had been slapped, long white mane flying. It pawed at the ground and screamed, but didn't hit the gate again.

Aren stepped back and examined his hand. The skin on his palm was red, burned and blistering.

"What happened?"

He grimaced. "I couldn't get the lock open. I tried to use magic. At least it worked, right?"

We mounted our horses and raced back to pick up our things. The tusker continued his tantrum behind us as we rode off into the woods. My mare kept looking back, but settled when we were far enough away that she couldn't hear him anymore.

We stopped beside a wide stream to catch our breaths and let the horses drink.

"There," Aren said. "Wasn't that easier than walking?" He was almost laughing. Unbelievable.

I took a few more gasping breaths. "You knew there were people following us back at the dragon path, you felt Severn coming after we left the boat, but you didn't know about *that*?" I crouched by the water and splashed some on my head and face, letting it run down the back of my neck. If it had been summer, I might have jumped into the river clothes and all to wash the sweat and dirt away. I still felt guilty for stealing the horses, but at that moment I would happily have broken into someone's house for a bar of soap.

Aren followed my example, and raked his wet hands through his hair. His expression and voice turned serious. "It's not easy, you know. Just trying to be aware of human enemies takes concentration and energy. Focusing on everything else that might be out there is impossible. For me, anyway." He shook his hands, sending droplets of water back into the river.

"I'm sorry, I didn't mean it like that. You're doing a great—"

"We should keep moving." His words were clipped, his voice tense. "There was no one home at that farm, but they'll be out looking for us when they get back and find their monster upset."

We rode upstream in the shallow water until a short run of rapids blocked our path, then finished our crossing. The sun had set, and we had to move slowly through the woods. Still, Aren was right. It was better than walking.

"Are we almost to the border?" I asked. "I think I've had enough adventure to last me the rest of my life."

He didn't answer.

#

Aren was quiet while he built the fire in a sheltered place beside a cliff in the forest. I was starting to feel lonely having no one to talk to, but what was there to say? At least he seemed to have let go of the idea that I'd healed him that night at Stone Ridge.

He'll probably be glad to get rid of me.

There wasn't much food left, but it was probably too dark for Aren to change and go hunting. I hoped he'd do it again, though, that I'd see the eagle I knew as Aquila one more time before I left him. The whole situation was beyond strange, but fascinating when I thought about the magic instead of how he'd deceived me. In a way, I missed Aquila. He'd been good company.

Aren hardly ate anything, just sat watching the fire

burn. I tried to leave some food for him to have later, but it was difficult. Excitement, exercise, and missing meals had made me ravenous.

"If I'd been human that day you found me, would you still have helped me?"

His voice startled me. "Yes."

He rolled his dirty white shirt sleeves up to his elbows and leaned forward. "If you'd known who I was?"

"I don't know. I would have been frightened of you."

He didn't speak as I put the rest of the food away, then asked, "Would you let me die now?"

"What do you mean?"

"If you saw me injured and dying again, knowing what you do now, what would you do?"

I didn't understand what he was getting at. "If I saw you hurt like that again, I couldn't leave you. I don't know how I would help."

"You still think I'm wrong about your magic, but you'd want to help me?" I didn't like the way he was looking at me. Not threatening, exactly, but he looked half-insane in the flickering firelight.

"Yes."

"I believe you." In one smooth motion he reached into his knapsack, produced a long, dark-bladed hunting knife, and plunged it into his left wrist. I screamed. He gasped, then pulled the knife through the flesh of his arm, twisting it near his elbow. The blade must have been sharper than any I'd ever come across before. It cut through muscle and tendons like they were liquid. Blood gushed from the wound.

"What the hell are you doing?" I shouted. Aren held his arm away from the blankets so that his blood poured onto the ground, burning on the fire-baked rocks.

"This is up to you," he said, speaking calmly. "You probably have a few minutes, but I'd appreciate it if you didn't leave it for too long."

"No." My legs went weak, and I had to sit down and push with my feet to back away. "You're crazy."

"And I'm dead if you can't manage a repeat performance. I…" He grimaced. "Gods, that hurts."

I told myself that he was tricking me, that this was some kind of illusion, but as his eyes grew glassy and his breathing shallower it became harder to believe that. "You ass," I whispered, and he tried to laugh.

"Rowan, I can't—"

"Shut up." I picked up the knife and used it to cut into a blanket so I could tear off a ragged strip. I dropped the knife and kicked the handle as I stepped back toward him, sending it spinning into the trees.

He looked at the fabric in my hands. "You don't need to do that."

"I said shut up!" The sight and smell of blood sickened me. Panicked tears made the world tremble, but I managed to start wrapping the cloth tight around the butchered arm to try to slow the bleeding.

Aren placed his other hand over mine, then unwrapped the bandage when I pulled away from his touch. "Don't. You can do better than that."

I pressed the heels of my hands to my eyes to stop the tears, then grabbed Aren's injured arm in both hands and squeezed. He yelled.

"You deserved that," I whispered, and forced myself to look at the gaping wound. It was a cleaner cut than the one the arrow had given him, but longer and deeper, and there was more blood. The flesh twitched at the edges, trying to come together, but it seemed that his magic wasn't able to take care of such a severe wound.

My focus was drawn toward it, slowly. Suddenly I remembered every detail of the night I'd found Aquila in the woods.

The back of my head began to pound with a heavy and increasing pain. The flesh twitched again, but this time the muscle pressed together, starting near Aren's elbow and closing down to his wrist. I wanted to close my eyes or to run away, but I didn't.

I'm doing this. A wave of joy washed over me at the real-ization, but pain burst from the back of my head, drowning it completely. I fought to stay conscious when white spots appeared in my vision. I needed to see what was going to happen.

The bleeding slowed, then stopped. I felt his magic responding, drawing mine deeper, accelerating the healing process. Seconds later, all that was left was a long, red scar twisting its way up his forearm.

Aren's blood was everywhere, on the blankets and my hands and our clothes, but when I looked back at his face, he seemed relaxed. Almost happy.

"Thank you," he whispered.

I turned and crawled away from the fire and threw up my supper under a tree. Sharp pain hit between my eyes and my arms gave out, sending me crashing into the musty leaves.

I wanted nothing more than to faint as I had before, but it didn't happen. I had to let Aren help me back to my bed. The light made everything hurt more. I turned away from the fire and pulled my knees toward my chest.

Aren pulled a blanket over me, and I pushed his hand away. "Leave me alone," I whispered. He'd been right about the magic in me, but I wasn't prepared to thank him for what he'd done.

"I'm sorry I had to do that. I didn't think—"

"Just go." His shadow moved away, and I was left shaking and trying to hold back tears that would only make the pain worse if I let them come.

Chapter Seventeen

Rowan

Aren was nowhere to be seen when I woke the next morning—not that I spent much time looking. The previous night's pain lingered, and the rust-colored stains on the rocks beside the burned-out fire were vivid reminders of what had caused it.

It seemed I had what I'd always dreamed of, but it was nothing like I'd expected. The healing had been beautiful, but the memory of the pain tarnished any sense of wonder I felt at it. I didn't want to think about what any of this meant for my life back home. I just wanted to get away, and think about it all when my head was clearer.

I found Aren with the horses. He didn't say anything, but at least had the decency to look concerned. I ignored him, still not ready to forgive. He packed up the campsite while I went out into the woods to strip a bit of sweet-smelling bark from a heartleaf tree. Taking too much would have caused permanent damage to the tree, but I thought about doing it. I'd need it later.

Your species is in trouble, my friend, I thought as I tucked some bark into my pack, and reached up to rub my fingers over a sweet-smelling pink leaf. *You and me, both.*

Neither Aren nor I spoke as we rode away. That suited me at first, but after a while I began to wonder if he wasn't speaking because he was angry with me for almost letting him die. Not that it would have been my fault, but he seemed to have strange ideas about these things. Finally I asked, "Are you mad?"

He snorted. "Angry, or crazy?"

Good question. "I meant angry."

"Then no, not at all. I have no reason to be. I just didn't want to say anything until you were ready to talk."

"I'm not."

"All right, then."

I knew he'd been trying to help, and he had. He'd showed me my magic. But the way he'd done it was horrible. What if he had been wrong about me, and he'd died? I leaned forward to rest my forehead against my mare's strong neck. Her mane smelled like clovers.

That would be a good name, I thought. *Clover.* Getting attached to animals seemed like a bad idea, but I couldn't help it. She was the closest thing I had to a potential friend at that moment.

What followed might have been the most awkward hours of my life. At least, they were uncomfortable for me. The silence didn't seem to bother Aren. He was either used to traveling alone, or to having people angry with him. He didn't even speak when we stopped around midday and he wandered off behind a cluster of boulders, leaving me holding his horse's reins with no explanation of what he was doing. I didn't have to wait long to find out. A familiar avian shape appeared at the top of the tallest rock, feet scrambling to hold onto the steep surface. He gave up and glided toward me, then past me, and crashed into a patch of low scrub bushes. I laughed.

"Nice. Very graceful."

He backed out on foot and shook his feathers out, and I dismounted. He looked toward the sky.

"You're leaving?"

He shook his head.

"Hunting?"

His head bobbed up and down, and he shuffled closer, until he was almost standing on my boot. I sighed and sat on a rock. "Just because you look different, that doesn't make it easier to forgive you." Still, I couldn't help reaching out to touch the soft, golden feathers on his head. He arched his neck under my hand.

I pulled back, and he shuffled away. "Nice try, though."

He dipped his head toward the ground, then pushed off and climbed into the air until he was only a black dot against the blue sky.

I didn't know what the plan was, but it seemed like there was enough time to let the horses rest. I gathered wood for a fire in case we were stopping, then watched the horses graze while I waited for Aren to come back. We'd have to talk when he changed back. I needed to make a decision.

As I saw it, I didn't have a single appealing option. Go home, knowing what I was… and what? Marry Callum and hope he never found out, and risk ruining him if my secret came out? Not likely. Go home, quietly break off the engagement, adopt some cats and move to a small town where no one knew me, shut people out forever? Also not appealing, but the other option was staying with Aren and trying to fix whatever was wrong with me.

I rubbed the back of my neck, trying to ease the tension and the pain. Maybe I hadn't given him any choice. I hadn't exactly been open to listening to him.

He never said he was a nice person, did he?

A snapping noise startled me, and I turned to see Aren approaching, dressed and carrying a pair of skinned and cleaned partridges. He lit the fire, and warmed himself by the flames. He looked up at me and raised his eyebrows.

"Yes, we can talk," I muttered, and moved closer to warm fingers that were going numb in the cold air.

"How's your head?"

"Better than last night. How's your arm? And your hand?"

He held up the hand he'd burned on the lock. Had I not seen the injury, I wouldn't have believed it had happened. He rolled up his shirt sleeve, revealing a thick scar twisting up his arm. I grimaced. "That'll fade," he said. He spitted the birds and set them over the fire. "I'm glad your head's not too bad."

"Does any of this affect your theory about my magic being bound? I thought I wasn't supposed to be able to use it."

He shrugged. "This is why we need to look for answers. Maybe I'm wrong. Maybe you're too strong for whatever they did to you. But there's magic, you didn't know about it before, and it's hurting you. And we're going to find help."

My anger melted. "Aren, why was all of this so important to you? You didn't give me a good answer before."

"No, I couldn't." He looked down and studied his hands, turning them over, brushing invisible dirt from his palms. "Taking you off of that ship was the most foolish thing I've ever done, but once we were off, there was no turning back."

"You could have left me on the boat, though. Let Severn have me."

"Could have." He shrugged. "I don't understand it, myself."

"Do you regret it?"

He sighed. "Regret is pointless. I don't know why I thought I had to help you. Maybe I just thought that a Sorceress deserved better." He shifted uncomfortably and squeezed his eyes shut. "No, that's not all of it. I don't know. You showed me kindness, and you helped me because you cared, not because you wanted something from me. I hadn't experienced that in a long time. Maybe I just couldn't let him destroy that." For a moment he seemed vulnerable, open. It disappeared quickly, replaced with the stern, closed-off expression that seemed to be his default.

"Oh. Well, thank you." I wanted to reach out to touch him, but didn't know how he would react to that. I let it go.

He took the birds off the fire. It seemed too soon, but the meat was cooked and falling off the bones.

"What will you do now?" I asked.

"Why, are you leaving?"

"I don't see what other choice I have. I appreciate everything you've done. Well, almost everything." He winced, and I smiled in spite of myself. "But I have to go home. Try to get by." I broke a leg off of my bird and bit into it. The meat was dry and unspiced, and perhaps the best thing I'd ever tasted.

Aren finished his food first, then watched as I picked the last of the meat off of the bones and licked the grease from my fingers. "We should keep moving," he said. "We're not far from the border."

We led the horses to a cool stream that flowed through the field and let them drink, then filled our water bags and rode on.

"You could keep going," Aren said. "I meant it when I said I'd help you find answers. If there's a way to undo this binding, you could do great things. You deserve better than your people can offer you. I mean, you're not perfect. You talk too much, you're ridiculously uncooperative, and I don't know if you ever think before you act. You're completely blind to your people's cruelty—"

"Says the man who comes from a family that's too horrible to talk about. What's so bad about mine compared to yours?"

He looked steadily at me. "I didn't say anything about your family. But as a people, the Darmish are ignorant and cruel. Even that dragon you met would die defending her young, but your people let their babies be killed if they're born like us."

"That's not true! We value every child that's born. We have so few of them."

"And fewer that survive the first year, if I recall correctly." He frowned. "You really think they're taken by disease, or by magic?"

"No, it's—"

"I know what they've told you. Think for yourself, Rowan." Not an order or an insult, but a plea. "Does it seem likely that you're that unusual?"

I thought back to the wanted posters I'd seen, and the few magic-related trials I'd sat through when my father needed an extra clerk. Were they all like me before they died? Were we all born that way? A lump formed in my throat. *It can't be.*

Aren shook his head. "I don't think the mothers usually know what happens, but it gets taken care of one way or another."

"You're wrong."

"Am I?" He reined his horse in, and I turned mine to face him from the opposite side of the path. "You really think your little cousins' deaths were accidental?"

His words were like cold water thrown in my face. "That's not true. It's the magic still in the land that makes babies fragile. My mother had a baby before me who died from it when she was a few weeks old, and…" I trailed off as a lump formed in my throat. "No one's killing them. It's just a sad fact of life."

"Really?"

"Really. People who need more children so badly that they'd practically force us into marriage to make sure we have them would never throw away a human life."

"And what about a monster's life?"

I shuddered. The idea that someone would have hurt Ches and Victoria's children because they were like me was unthinkable. My aunt and uncle's grief-stricken faces flashed before me.

No, it's impossible. No one could be that cruel. And if someone was killing those babies, they knew the truth about magic. At the very least, the king and his magic hunters were lying to the rest of us. No wonder they thought fairy stories were dangerous. But not Callum. He had just started. He couldn't possibly know.

My stomach roiled, but I forced my food to stay down.

Aren watched, his expression more compassionate than I'd ever seen it. "I know this is hard," he said, and smiled sadly. "I understand what it means to throw your life away and start over. It's not pleasant, but there is a certain freedom in it."

He turned his horse and started down the road again, and we stopped at the top of a small rise. In the distance, smoke rose from a group of buildings.

"Is this the border?" I asked.

He nodded. "This is as close as I'll be getting to those people. If you want to go to them, you're free to do so. I'm sure your future husband's name will be enough to ensure your safety until he comes to get you."

"What?" I couldn't follow his thoughts while mine were still reeling from what he'd just told me. "You say you've thrown everything away to help me, you almost kill yourself to make sure I understand what I am, and now you're telling me to forget it and leave?"

"I don't want you to leave," he said quietly, "but I didn't think all of this through before. I wanted to help, but all I've done so far is put you in danger and cause you pain.

I've done everything I'm willing to to convince you to see this through. You're not a prisoner.

"Maybe you're right," he continued. "Maybe you can hide what you are and have the life you were expecting, marrying a wealthy magic hunter and having lots of babies to support the pure and normal population of Darmid. Maybe you'll be really lucky and none of them will be freaks like you. But you should have so much more than that."

I hated him a little when he called me that, using my people's words against me, reminding me again of how they hated what I was. It seemed impossible that anyone would murder infants, but when I thought about how passionately the people I'd met in the city spoke against magic and how they pushed for its complete extermination, I could see it.

I might manage to never use magic again, and perhaps Aren was wrong about the pain getting worse. I could manage. But what if someone I loved got hurt? I would never let someone die to protect my secret. I would try to heal them, and then I'd find myself arrested. In court. Convicted. Dead. And my family shamed forever.

I glanced at Aren. He was looking down the path, which curved away from the border-guard station. Toward Tyrea.

There were no guarantees of what would happen if I went that way with him, either. Even if we found someone who could help me, what then? There would be no returning to Darmid. Physical pain gripped my chest at the thought of never seeing my aunt and uncle again, or Felicia. My parents and Ashe. Tyrea would be dangerous for me on my own, and worse if I was with Aren, with Severn hunting him. He'd helped me, but he'd hurt me. And I didn't want to let him leave.

Aren urged his horse forward at a slow walk. "What will you do if I go?" I asked.

He stopped. "I'll take my chances in Tyrea. I don't want to rush you, but Severn or his people will likely be here soon. You'll be safer with those guards."

"They won't find you? Severn, I mean."

"He will, eventually. But I still don't regret any of this." He nudged the horse, and they continued down the path. He didn't look back before they disappeared into a patch of trees.

If I listened carefully, I could make out the sounds of laughter coming from the border-guard station. Aren had brought me far closer than was safe for him. He was right. I'd be much better off with the guards than I'd be on the road with him, with his horrible brother trying to capture us. Perhaps there would be a cure for me among the doctors in Ardare. Or I could just break off my engagement quietly and live far from magic hunters and cities. I could find a life somewhere that didn't involve magic, or running from a Sorcerer who wanted me dead. I could forget about all of this, forget about Aren and what I might find over the border.

I took a deep breath, and decided.

"Wait!" I called, nudging Clover into a swift trot that was far from comfortable for me.

He'd moved to the side of the path and stopped. Clover leaned her head toward Aren's horse and snorted.

"I hope I don't regret this," I said as we started forward again.

"Me, too." Aren didn't look at me, but he smiled, and something in my chest slipped a little.

Don't be stupid, I thought. *He's not your friend. He's barely even not your enemy.* But that relaxed grin suited him, and made me feel far better than it should have.

We came to a place where the trees thinned, then disappeared, leaving us at the top of a hill that rolled down toward an uneven landscape littered with boulders, long grass, and stunted trees. Far to our left, the main road flowed down the hill toward a few small farms surrounded by a patchwork of gold and brown fields, and beyond them a tidy-looking town. The buildings looked like dollhouses from where we sat.

"Welcome to Tyrea," Aren said.

A shiver flowed through me that was part apprehension and part excitement, and I followed him toward the road.

Chapter Eighteen

Rowan

The other side of the mountains. How many times had I wished for exactly this? It didn't seem so different from the land I was familiar with, really. The same rugged beauty, the grasses turning brown as winter approached, the rocks beneath pushing through at the high points.

Well, what did you expect? A flock of fairies handing out magical guidebooks? I smiled and breathed in not the ocean-and-seaweed smell of Lowdell or the pine forest air of Stone Ridge, but air that was fresh and cool and pleasant, nonetheless.

Aren smiled. "You like it?"

"So far, so good." Now that we were past the border and my decision made, I was beginning to enjoy the journey.

You'll have to watch that, I reminded myself. *You're still in more danger than you've ever been before.* The headache was growing stronger, and I took a few strands of heartleaf bark from my pack. "Just out of curiosity," I asked, "is this stuff magic? They've banned it back home."

"In a way. Plants like that certainly have properties they

wouldn't have without ambient magic." He took a strand of the dry bark. He rubbed it between his fingers. "This is weak," he said. "You're probably used to that. I assume the magical plants in your land are less potent than the ones in most of Tyrea. Sara would have been able to tell you more about that than I can."

"Sara works for you?" I remembered her wariness and her warning that it was better not to cause trouble.

"No, for Severn. Why?"

"No reason." A pair of hawks wheeled slowly through the air above us. One dropped, then plunged to the ground not far from us. "Can I ask you something else?"

"I can't stop you." He didn't sound keen on talking, but I still needed answers.

"Why an eagle? I don't suppose it's easy to learn to do something like that. Is that the only thing you change into? Did you have a choice about your form?"

"It is, and I did. Why not an eagle? I grew up with hunting birds, and was able to study their physiology. I can get myself where I need to go more quickly flying than I can on foot, and usually without being noticed. I can fight if I need to. It's been useful for hunting, hasn't it?" I nodded.

I remembered the beak and talons that I'd been so cautious of, but also thought of how little that body weighed when I picked it up, how fragile the bones seemed, and how impossible it was for him to get away when he couldn't fly. A wolf might have been a stronger choice for survival and fighting, or maybe a dragon if he needed to fly. I wondered what form I would choose if I had the chance—but that could never happen.

Or could it?

With that thought I suddenly understood the full meaning of what had happened the night before. I had magic in me. Yes, it had hurt me. But if Aren was right about finding a way to break the binding, I might be able to do anything. It was too much to think about, like trying to look directly at the sun. Excitement and happiness lifted me, warming me to my toes.

The town was farther away than I'd thought, and it was late afternoon before we arrived. A boy stopped his game of marbles for long enough to direct us to an inn down a side street, a wide, white building with a handsome stable around back. A groom took the horses and promised to treat them to the best night of their lives. Aren started toward the inn, then stopped and held out his hand.

"What?"

When he spoke, he sounded apologetic. "They should probably think we're together. It makes more sense than an unrelated man and woman traveling together for no obvious reason, and we don't want to be memorable if we can help it. Two rooms would cost more than we have available, so we just got married."

"Oh. Well, congratulations to us," I said. "They're going to remember us anyway, if someone asks. We're not exactly disguised."

Aren stepped in front of me and pulled the hood of my cloak up so that my face wasn't hidden, but shadowed. He held it and looked into my eyes for just a moment longer than he needed to. My mouth went dry.

"Don't worry about that," he said. "Just act like everything is normal. Happy, even. And try to stay quiet."

I took his hand and walked beside him through the front door of the inn. His long fingers were cold, either from the weather or the blood loss. I sat in a plush armchair while he paid for a room.

It was a beautiful place, nicer than any inn I'd seen back home, small but richly decorated in polished wood and luxurious fabrics. Several people ate their suppers in a brightly-lit dining room, and the smell of roasted chicken and rosemary wafted out into the lobby. I should have been interested in all of it, but I found myself watching Aren instead of enjoying my surroundings.

His hands rested on the dark-hardwood desk, and he smiled and laughed quietly with the clerk. She blushed. He looked exhausted and pale, and like he'd been on the road for far too long. In spite of that, I understood why the woman behind the counter found him so interesting. It wasn't just the way he looked. There was also the way he carried himself, his quiet confidence, the way the corners of his eyes crinkled on the rare occasions when he really smiled. I shifted in my seat, which had suddenly grown uncomfortable.

The woman behind the desk giggled quite unprofessionally and handed a key to Aren. She leaned over and whispered something as he was turning away, to which he replied "No, but thank you," and came back toward me.

I stood too quickly, and faint gray spots appeared in front of my eyes. Aren rested his hand on my waist and guided me toward the stairs. I suddenly felt warmer than I had by the door, and my heartbeat quickened.

After a few nights on the road, the room looked like heaven. The head of the bed was piled with big, fluffy pillows, and thick quilts were folded at the foot. A chair and small, formal-looking sofa faced a stone fireplace, and when I took off my boots, the carpet was soft and deep under my feet.

"Oh," I groaned, and flopped face-first onto the bed. Sleep began to crowd my mind as soon as my face sank into the feather mattress.

"You go ahead," Aren said from somewhere very far away. "I'll sleep on the chair."

"Hrmflphmrm."

"Pardon?"

My head weighed a thousand pounds, but I lifted it to tell him, "I said, 'that's not fair, you take the bed.'" I mashed my face back into the sheets, then lifted my head again to add, "It smells so clean!"

I heard him moving around the room, but couldn't open my eyes. "If I change, I'll be more comfortable perched on the chair than either of us would be on the sofa," he said. "Go ahead and sleep for a while, I'll see what they have to eat around here." I barely heard him, and was only vaguely aware of him pulling a blanket up to cover me.

#

The most beautiful scent greeted me when I woke form my nap, clean and floral. I opened my eyes to the last of sunset's light filtering in through the window. As much as I wanted to stay curled up in that beautiful bed, I had to see where the smell was coming from. After three days on the road, I knew it wasn't from me. My hair was greasy, and my skin felt like it had a layer of dirt and smoke ground into it. If only it was—

"A bath!" A door I hadn't noticed before stood open, revealing the edge of a tub in a small room, steam rising from its bubbly surface. I nearly cried, it looked so good.

"Excellent timing." Aren sat in the chair next to the fireplace, reading a leather-bound book. His damp hair left wet patches on his clean shirt. "I asked them to prepare a bath for you. Nothing personal. I just thought you might like one."

"That's all right," I said as I climbed off the bed. "I know I stink." He grinned as I walked past him and into the bath room. A washbasin stood in the corner with a round mirror hung over it, and a wooden bench next to the tub was stacked with soaps and fluffy towels. There were no windows, but oil lamps burned bright on the walls, creating an inviting atmosphere. I cleaned my teeth with one of the mint-flavored cloths on the edge of the wash-basin, made sure the door was closed tight, then stripped off my dirty clothes and stepped into the tub.

The water was hot enough to turn my skin a deep pink as soon as I slipped in, but I didn't care. I was happy to let it burn the grime of the previous days out of my skin and hair. I soaked until my skin wrinkled and used a heavy bar of soap to scrub every inch of myself twice over.

The door to the bedroom opened slightly. I scrambled to grab something to cover myself, but it was only the maid. "May I take your clothes for cleaning, ma'am?"

I willed my heart to slow. "In a minute, thank you." The

door closed again, and I slipped my head under the water again. *Silly thing. Who else would it have been?*

The towels were like nothing I'd ever used before. Thick and fluffy, they seemed to drink the water off of my skin. A clean nightgown and robe hung on the back of the door, and I slipped into them. It almost made me feel like myself again.

The maid was bringing in supper when I left the bathing room. "Your husband said he'd be back soon, ma'am," she said in a lilting Tyrean accent thicker than Aren's. She placed a plate of chicken, roasted potatoes, and unfamiliar greens on the small table, then went to the other room to collect my dirty things.

"If I may say," she added as she collected my boots and my extra clothes for cleaning, "he seems like a real gentleman, and I hope you'll be very happy together."

I bit the inside of my cheek to keep from laughing and nodded. She smiled and backed out the door.

"Thanks," I said, but she was gone. *If only you knew.* Then my stomach growled, and I forgot about everything but my supper. I ate too much and too quickly, and it felt fantastic.

I cleaned my teeth again after I finished a glass of a deep-red wine, then ducked down the hall to the toilets that our room shared with a few others.

When I returned, Aren was taking off his boots. "Careful about leaving the door unlocked," he said.

"Sorry, you didn't leave a key. The maid has one, though." He didn't say anything to that, but leaned back in the chair and rubbed his forehead. "Are you all right?"

I asked. "Have you eaten?" His color was better, but he looked even more tired than I still felt.

"I'm fine, I just need a good sleep." He rested his head against the back of the chair and closed his eyes.

"You're sure you don't want to sleep in the bed? As a person?" He opened one eye, and my face grew warm. "I mean, not with me. It just doesn't seem like you sleep well as an eagle. I could sleep somewhere else."

The corner of his mouth pulled up slightly, and he closed his eye again. "I've never slept well." He pushed himself up and stood, then paced around the room, checking the windows and door. He stopped in the middle of the room and seemed to be listening. Satisfied with what he heard, or perhaps didn't hear, he turned to me. "It's better if I change."

"Fine." My voice came out colder than I'd intended. I turned away, and a moment later heard his clothes dropping to the floor, followed by a flapping noise as he scrambled up to perch on the back of the chair. "But I could be very comfortable on that sofa if you change your mind."

I blew out the trio of candles on the table and climbed into bed without looking at him. I didn't know why I was so irritated. It wasn't like we were going to stay up late and share stories by the fire if he stayed in his human body. After the previous night, I should have been glad to be half-way rid of him. But I was lonely, and being the only person in the room only reminded me of that. I missed my family. I missed my life, even if I hadn't ever appreciated it before. I wondered what my parents, my aunt and uncle, Felicia and Ashe were doing. They had to be worried about me. And what about Callum?

My stomach tightened as I realized that I no longer wanted Callum to find me, whether he knew the truth about magic or not. I was on my own. It was frightening, but good. For the first time in my life I'd chosen to do something unexpected. And there was the magic. It wasn't what I'd imagined it would be, but it was real and fascinating and a part of me. What lay ahead was uncertain and dangerous, but now that I'd decided to keep going, it was exciting, too. And I wasn't completely alone.

I rolled to face the sitting area, where an eagle's silhouette stood outlined against the window. "Aren?"

He snapped his beak to produce a soft clacking noise.

"Have a good sleep."

Clack. *Goodnight.*

Chapter Nineteen

Rowan

"Wake up." I was pulled from my dreams by a hand on my shoulder, shaking me.

My eyes snapped open. The room was still dark, with only a hint of sunrise lighting the window. Aren leaned over me wearing nothing but a blanket he'd wrapped around his waist. I shouldn't have stared, but it was a fantastic view. His body was lean and strong, beautiful. I forced my mouth to close and hoped he hadn't noticed my reaction.

"Get dressed," he said, and stepped back. "We have to get out of here, now."

He'd already set my clean clothes and boots on the end of the bed. I threw off the blankets, grabbed a set of clothes and ran to the other room to get put them on. When I returned, Aren was dressed and pulling his boots on.

"What's going on?" I whispered as I pulled the lavender-scented sachets out of the toes of my boots and tossed them aside. "Is someone coming?"

"Men. Not Severn, but they're his. I've done what I

could to throw them off, but we can't let them find us here. Come on." We took our bags and cloaks, and he pulled me down the hall to a closed door that I'd assumed was another bedroom. Aren turned the cut-glass doorknob slowly, and the door opened onto a steep, enclosed staircase.

"Is this what you were doing when I was in the bath? Scouting escape routes?"

"Among other things." He hesitated, head turned to one side, listening.

We crept down, keeping close to the wall. We'd almost reached the bottom when voices approached the other side of the door.

"Is there another entrance? Another way upstairs? Anything?" A man's voice, accompanied by the sound of several sets of footsteps. It didn't sound like they were right outside the door, but they would be soon.

"Shit," Aren whispered. "We'll have to go back up." He started up, then paused at the top to wait for me.

I moved more slowly, examining the walls as well as I could in the almost non-existent light. *If this building is anything like Stone Ridge... there.*

"Wait." I ran my fingers over a wide groove in the paneling until they slipped into a hidden space. I tugged. Nothing. I tried again. Aren started moving back down toward me, and the narrow door nearly smacked him in the face as it popped open. He ducked around and piled our things on the floor next to a dusty old mop and bucket, then offered me a hand to help me step up into the empty closet. He followed, and I reached past him to pull the door toward us until the latch clicked softly.

The cupboard was tall, but Aren had to hunch over to keep from knocking his head on the top. I was grateful for the vertical space, but it wasn't wide—just enough room to breathe and not step on each other's feet.

The door at the bottom of the stairs slammed open and heavy footsteps clattered toward our hiding spot. I held my breath and pressed my face into Aren's chest, and he wrapped his arms around me. The door to the upper level of the inn opened with a short groan. Someone heavy stepped down onto the top step.

"Henderson!" the top-of-stairs man called. "What have you got?" He continued down, and the two met just a step or two above the cupboard. I couldn't believe they didn't hear my heart pounding, or the blood that rushed through my ears. Aren breathed deeply and quietly, but I felt his heart beating as hard and fast as mine. I had to fight an insane urge to throw open the door and get it over with. I closed my eyes and grabbed on to the back of Aren's jacket, squeezing my hands into tight fists, just to keep myself grounded.

"Nothing, sir," said the man I'd heard downstairs. "They all say the same thing—the only couple they've had pass through here was two nights ago, and they didn't match our description. Some of them don't remember anyone at all. Desk clerk said she thought they'd headed south out of town, but she couldn't be sure."

The other man grunted. "Fine. There's something going on here, though. That clerk had a strange look about her when we came in. I wouldn't be surprised if it was them and he did something nasty to the lot of them. We'll assume it was and go from there. Only lead we've had so far. Send word back to the boss, let him know we're headed south."

"Yes, sir." Henderson's boots scraped the stair as he turned and clomped back down. The other one didn't move.

"Henderson? You take a few men and head north. He might have given them a mixed-up idea about that, too. We're supposed to watch for these things."

"Yes, sir." The sound of Henderson's footsteps grew fainter, but the other one stayed behind. The stair creaked, and the closet door moved in as something pushed on it. Aren tensed, and I held my breath. A scratching noise came from outside, then a sigh. "Damn it," the man muttered, and the door settled back into place. Footsteps descended the stairs, and the door at the bottom slammed shut.

My heart slowed, but I couldn't stop shaking. I don't know how long we stayed like that, not speaking, breathing in the closet's musty air. It seemed like hours, but I felt certain that as soon as we opened the door someone would decide to come storming back up the stairs and spot us. I was fine waiting. There were worse places to be. I felt safe with Aren.

I looked up, but it was too dark to see his face. Was he using magic, sensing the people around us? I never felt anything when he did it, but his eyes sharpened when he focused on his magic. I shivered as I thought of that look. Frightening, but dangerously attractive. I suddenly became more aware of his arms around me.

"They're gone," he whispered, and lowered his hands to his sides. My own fingers seemed frozen, and I had trouble letting go of him. I reached out and felt for the latch.

Aren stepped out, brushed cobwebs from his hair, and then held out a hand to help me. I was glad for that. My legs were like jelly, and I expected to fall out of the cupboard and roll down the stairs.

"Thanks," he whispered, and gave me an uncomfortable smile. "How did you know that door was there?"

"Hide-and-seek. I almost got stuck in a closet like that when I was a kid." I reached behind me for our bags, then pressed the door closed.

Aren took his things and started back up the stairs. I followed cautiously. "Aren't we leaving?"

"I just want to see something. It's safe enough, now."

The doors to the bedrooms were all open. I'd locked ours when we left, and it hung off of its hinges, cracked in the middle. Every room we passed was ripped apart, mattresses overturned and wardrobes emptied. Most had been unoccupied, but I still felt terrible for the people who would have to clean up the mess. I doubted Henderson or Sir would be back to help with that.

Aren leaned against the wall and crouched, resting his forehead in his hands. I sat across from him and waited. He looked up. "That was too close."

I laughed, mostly out of relief. "You think so?"

"Yeah. Sorry about that. It's much more difficult to sense danger when there are other people around, getting in the way."

"That's not your fault. I guess we've been lucky so far."

"Maybe. But I should have known they were coming long before I did. I must have been sleeping more deeply than I realized."

"No harm done."

"For now." He stood and offered a hand to pull me up. "I couldn't have picked a better person to be stuck in a closet with, though." He picked up his bag again and headed toward the dark staircase.

I hoped I wasn't blushing. That would have been stupid.

Chapter Twenty

Aren

What the hell is wrong with me?

I couldn't look at Rowan as we walked to the stable. It wasn't like me to speak on impulse, to say something that revealed so much of myself. But then, I'd been acting out of character too much in the past few days. It was so much easier before. I knew my place, knew what I was supposed to be doing, and who I was supposed to be.

Now that I had thrown that life away, I couldn't seem to remember who I was.

I'd made a plan before I fell asleep. Get her to safety, find someone to break the binding, leave her to make a new life for herself wherever she chose. We'd both be safer once we were apart. Severn would follow me. He didn't need her as much as he needed his revenge. And I would be better able to escape without her. The decision should have pleased me, but it left me feeling empty.

She was becoming more of a distraction as the days passed. In spite of the trouble she caused and the way she always had something to talk about, I found myself enjoying her company, wanting to touch her, to make her smile or to tell her things that would please her. But it was best that I not let her get too close. Every time I caught myself thinking about her, I found that my attention had slipped from my magical defenses.

My reasons for helping her were becoming more clear to me. My feelings toward her were not due to magic—at least, not now. I had to face the fact that I cared for her, wanted to protect her. I would accomplish that task, but the emotions couldn't be allowed to continue. I would acknowledge what had happened, learn from it, but I would not let it make me weak. And she would never know.

Rowan stood talking quietly to her horse while I convinced the groom that he should give us new tack for the horses, plus supplies for ourselves and the animals. She seemed like the sort of person who became attached to people and animals far too quickly. She'd never survive in my family.

She turned to me and smiled nervously after the groom left. *She'll do better somewhere else*, I thought. She could take care of herself. She'd shown that in the dragon cave when she got us both out of that situation, and without any magic to rely on. The hardness she'd revealed in her handling of the dragon was unexpected, and admirable. Finding that cupboard in the inn was a bit of good luck, but still, she'd thought to look, and moved quickly to try and keep us safe. I didn't like hiding, but it hadn't been all bad. It was cramped and uncomfortable, and being trapped in there left us too vulnerable, but even understanding the danger we were in hadn't kept me from enjoying having her body pressed against me for a few minutes.

"Did you really give those people fake memories?" she asked after the groom left to collect our things, pulling me out of thoughts I shouldn't have been thinking.

"In a way."

"And you made that magic hunter kill his brother before we met? That was you, wasn't it?" She looked afraid to hear my answer. No use lying. Better that she know and keep her distance.

"Yes."

"What were you doing to that man who just left? He looked strange. Dazed."

"What I had to do to get what we need. Nothing that will hurt him, so don't worry about it."

She stepped away from me and rubbed her horse's nose. "It seems wrong, though."

With that, my fears of liking her too much disappeared. "I didn't see you jumping in to distract him and keep me from doing it," I whispered back as the groom returned with new saddle bags filled with food and clean bedrolls to attach to our packs. "You're benefiting from this at least as much as I am. If you don't like it, find your own cure." She held my gaze for a moment, then looked away and turned to saddle her horse.

I understood that she was probably confused about everything that was happening, but I was exhausted and in no mood to feel like a villain for trying to help her.

She was silent as we rode away from the inn, through

the still-quiet village and past a faded sign that advised us to "Come Again Soon!"

Not bloody likely, I thought. I'd be lucky to survive the next week if I couldn't keep from being distracted or falling into a deep sleep. Keeping us safe was a far greater challenge than I'd anticipated.

Rowan seemed to be turning things over in her mind for the next while, and it was well into the morning before she said anything. She didn't turn toward me, but watched from the corner of her eye as she spoke. "Have you done that to me at all?"

"No. Not once."

"How can I be sure of that? You could be making me think that I was making my own decisions but really you've been doing it for me, and making me not notice that what I was doing was strange, or—"

Though I was frustrated with her and nearly too tired to think, she almost made me laugh. "Rowan?"

"What?"

"The pleasure of your company isn't worth that much trouble."

A look of shock crossed her face that quickly changed to amusement when she saw that I was smiling. "I'll bet."

"Doing something like that is extremely difficult— not only in knowing how it's done, but in the amount of concentration and energy it takes. I do it when I have to, certainly more than is good for me, but I couldn't have held onto you for this long. That's if I could do it at all. Magic offers protection against it, and I can't even see your thoughts. Like it or not, you're here by your own choice."

"Or you could be lying about all of that, too, and making me believe it." She smiled, but I doubted very much that she trusted me. "Sorry. This is all so strange. I want this to work, but..."

"I know. I don't think I'm actually qualified to act like a hero for anyone."

"I don't know. You're doing a pretty good job so far."

I tried to ignore the warming effect her words had on me. I wasn't supposed to need kindness or praise, but it felt good.

I shook it off.

She squinted up at the sky. "We'd better find shelter soon. Those clouds are coming in fast." The day had started out clear, but the sky was darkening, and gray clouds hovered in the sky ahead. A freezing wind whipped past us, and Rowan pulled her cloak tighter. I stopped to pull mine out from my pack. No sense getting drenched if I could avoid it.

We'd nearly reached the end of the farmland that surrounded the town, and only a few fields remained between us and a return to the uneven, boulder-strewn landscape that surrounded them. A farmer watched us as we passed, but neither of us acknowledged him.

Storm clouds rolled in, shutting out the sunlight until the sky became as dark as night. A light rain quickly changed to a freezing downpour that blew in our faces. Lightning flickered and thunder crashed immediately after, frightening the horses. Then the storm really started.

Sheets of water fell like waterfalls, drenching everything and leaving the road little better than a shallow river. It became impossible to see ahead, but the horses hurried on.

I hoped the rain would be our only concern, but danger loomed at the edge of my awareness. People on the road, following.

Rowan kept pace beside me as the horses raced down the road, their hoofs sending up sprays of muddy water that were lost in the downpour.

I looked back. Lightning flashed, revealing three dark shapes on the road, following hard behind us, close enough that there was no doubt that they were in pursuit.

"Rowan!" I called, unsure whether she'd hear me over the rain. "Rowan!" When she looked, I motioned for her to ride closer. The road swung to the left, but we kept going straight, over the rough ground. The horses slowed.

"What are you doing?" Rowan shouted. She sat hunched over her horse's neck with water streaming off of her hood.

"We're being followed. The road's not safe." She glanced behind her, but it was impossible to see anything. I hoped our pursuers were finding the same.

The rain let up slightly, but the darkness remained. I gave my horse freedom to choose her path, and Rowan's fell behind. I didn't particularly care where we went, as long as it was away from the road, and as quickly as possible. The land sloped upward, and we found ourselves in a tree-filled space between two rocky cliffs. The rain rolled off of the leaves and onto us, but it was some relief from the downpour. The horses grew cautious, slowing they walked against a river of rainwater.

The land opened up, and we were no longer sheltered. A splashing noise behind me indicated that Rowan's horse had stumbled.

"We have to stop!" she called. "They can't keep going like this!"

"We have to!" I pulled back on the reins, though, and waited. When I focused my awareness on the space around us, there was nothing. No one but me and Rowan. Lightning flashed again, silhouetting the crumbling remains of a massive stone building. I turned my horse's head toward the structure. The roof was gone, but it would be better than nothing.

We reached what might once have been a courtyard and found the space occupied by an encampment. A massive tent surrounded by several smaller ones took up much of the space, with several hard-topped wagons parked nearby. I pulled my horse up. I hadn't felt anything. No danger, no human presences at all. If the people here were dead, we'd want nothing to do with this place.

Horses huddled beneath an awning affixed to one of the stone walls, their backs to the wind and rain. A few human faces peered out from the largest tent, letting a sliver of warm light out into the darkness.

That's impossible. And worse than if they'd been dead. I didn't trust it. I was about to turn back when a tall woman in a red cloak stepped out into the rain and waved us down. "Welcome, fellow travelers," she called in a lilting accent. "It's a poor time to be out on the road. Would you honor us by coming in for a meal?"

"Yes, and thank you!" Rowan called. She rode toward where the horses sheltered, and two younger men dressed in heavy rain gear came out of the tent and helped her dismount. I followed reluctantly, and allowed one of the men to take my horse.

"I don't like this," I said in a voice pitched so only she could hear me.

"They're just Wanderers," Rowan said, exasperated. "They're not road bandits."

"I remember. But I can't get a sense of them. It's like they're not here." One of the men handed me my knapsack and bedroll, and they both ran back toward the tent, not waiting to see if we'd follow.

"Maybe you're just tired," she said, and pushed her dripping hair out of her eyes. "And didn't you say you did something to keep Severn from locating you? Maybe they're doing that. Or maybe they're ghosts. Who cares? They're offering a warm place to stop, and we're not getting any drier out here."

She reached under my cloak and threaded her arm through mine, and pulled me toward shelter. A blast of warmth hit us as we stepped between the tent flaps. The inside of the large tent was crowded. Adults sat on cushions scattered in groups around the floor, most of them finishing meals and conversing in low voices. Several ragged-looking children ran around yelling, weaving a path between groups of people who barely seemed to notice them. People turned to look at us, but went back to their conversations a few seconds later. A tall man resumed playing a stringed instrument, and one of the children broke away from the pack to pick up a small drum to play along.

The woman who had greeted us held out a hand. She

was older than most of them, silver-haired and with deep lines around her eyes and mouth, but there was no hint of frailty about her. She radiated calm and confidence, and a hint of low-level magic.

I'd have to watch this one. Her magic didn't seem significant enough to be a threat, but that depended entirely on what she could do with it.

"Jein Hammus," she said. I realized we hadn't come up with identities for ourselves. I'd paid for our room at the inn without giving names.

Rowan reached past me to give the woman's hand a firm shake. "Penelope Jones," she said, then laughed nervously. "I mean, Anderson." She gazed up at me with a sickeningly sweet expression and smiled. "Sometimes I still forget, it's all so new. This is my husband, Doug."

Jein Hammus smiled. "Well, how nice. Terrible time to be traveling, though."

"Autumn?" Rowan asked.

"That, too. Please, sit with my family. Have something to eat."

"That's very kind of you," I said, "but perhaps we should just—"

Rowan interrupted me. "Oh, don't be silly, darling. It would be rude of us to refuse such generous hospitality. Thank you, Missus Hammus."

"Jein, please." She led us toward the rear of the tent, pausing to speak quietly to a few people along the way. The ceiling was high, held up by tall posts. Flaps in the walls indicated either exits or connections to the other tents I'd seen outside. Rowan took my hand. Her skin was icy cold.

We needed the shelter, there was no question about that, and the spiced meat stew smelled wonderful. The horses needed the rest, too. I just hoped we weren't going to become trapped again. Now that we were inside the tent, I could read most of these people better. They seemed curious, but not hostile at all. The Hammus woman remained a mystery.

She introduced us to her husband Johen and their son Frans, who looked to be twelve or thirteen years old.

"Our daughter Patience is here somewhere," Johen said. "Probably with the other children." He offered Rowan his seat, and I took an empty cushion next to her. Frans watched from behind the curtain of dark hair that covered his eyes and said nothing.

"I'm sorry if we've interrupted something," Rowan said. She accepted a plate of stew from Johen.

"Oh, not at all," Jein said, and settled onto another seat. She indicated that we should go ahead and eat. "We accept hospitality where we find it, and we've yet to turn away an honest soul we've met on the road who was hungry or weary." She glanced at our clothes. "Or damp."

"Is this wise, Mother?" Frans asked, glaring at me. "With things the way they've been?"

Jein sighed. "Perhaps not." She turned to us. "Are you trustworthy?"

Rowan looked down at her plate, thinking. She looked up and grinned. "*Bildich rohmnen, pesha,*" she said.

Jein raised her eyebrows. "Not a stranger at all, then!" she said, and returned Rowan's smile. Frans scowled and wandered off.

"I was telling Doug not too long ago that I used to play with a little boy named Romul when his family stopped at my home," Rowan told Jein. "They brought interesting things to sell, and Romul's mother made the most amazing cookies."

They talked for a while, and I tried to act like I'd heard at least some of these stories before.

A thin-faced girl with bright ribbons braided into her white-blond hair stumbled out of the crowd of running children and dropped onto the cushion between me and Jein. "Will we have a show, Mother?"

"I think not tonight, my love. We haven't unpacked here, and our guests are weary from their travels. Another time." The girl pouted, and when the children passed by again she flounced off to join them. Jein sighed. "Sometimes I wonder why we name our children before we know them well. I'm not holding much hope of that one growing into hers."

When Rowan mentioned that there had been other people on the road, following us, Jein excused herself. "Don't worry about anything," she said, and laid a hand on Rowan's shoulder. "We haven't let enemies find us before, and we won't now." She and Johen, along with many of the other adults, bundled into their shawls, capes, or jackets and headed out into the storm. I wanted to follow, but couldn't without being seen. I stayed on-edge, aware, but nothing seemed dangerous. Perhaps these people were what they seemed.

No, I thought. *No one is.*

Two white-haired old women stayed behind, huddled

close to a cluster of burning torches, and half a dozen other adults cleaned up after the meal, occasionally sending curious glances our way. The children continued their game, racing in circles until someone shushed them. Patience gathered the children close and spoke to them, and they all raced outside, yelling. The tent smelled of damp wool and burnt wood, but it was far more pleasant than being outside.

Rowan scooted closer to me. "How was your meal, dear?"

"Just wonderful, Penelope, oh light of my life," I replied dryly, and she stifled a giggle behind her hand. "Nice names. Where did those come from?"

"I once had a goat named Penelope."

"And Doug?"

"I have no idea."

"And Bindig Row—"

"*Bildich rohmnen, pesha.* It means something like 'We are friends, dear one.' Romul's mother taught it to me, said it was a good phrase to know, especially if I needed help from the Wanderers. I had forgotten all about it."

I didn't want to talk too much about what we were doing, not with other people possibly listening, but we couldn't avoid it completely. "We can't stay here. We know nothing about these people."

She rolled her eyes. "Do you think everyone is after us? They're Wanderers. I really doubt they're working for your brother. They obviously don't know who we are, anyway. You're being too suspicious."

"And you're too trusting."

"Well, I guess that evens it out then, doesn't it?"

I didn't know how to answer that. There wasn't time to, anyway. A woman we hadn't met yet was coming toward us with brightly-colored clothing folded over both arms. "Hello, my dears. I'm Alys. Jein thought you might like to borrow some clothes while your own are drying by the fire." I reached into my pack. Everything was damp.

"Thank you," I said, and she nodded.

"If you go through the flap over there you can get changed in the storage space. It's small, but I don't suppose that will be a problem." She winked, then walked toward the old women. Rowan flashed me a smug smile and carried both piles of clothing toward the storage room.

Rowan changed her clothes first, emerging in an orange sweater with a wide neckline and a reddish-brown skirt that fit tight through the hips and fell in loose folds to her ankles. I took my turn, nearly tripping over the piles of boxes and sacks piled on the floor as I struggled to get out of my wet trousers. The smells of onions and spices tickled my nose. Alys had brought me a blue shirt that slipped over my head and laced at the front, far more colorful than I liked, but I wouldn't complain.

I took my dagger from my bag and slipped it into the deep pocket of my borrowed pants. When I returned to the main room, Rowan was waiting nearby. Alys took our wet things and disappeared through another flap in the side of the tent, returning moments later.

"This place must be huge," Rowan said, stretching to try to look through the other doorway.

"I'm sure when you spend most of your time traveling,

you figure these things out. You never saw anything like this in your extensive dealings with the Wanderers?"

She rolled her eyes. "I didn't say extensive. I only met them twice, and not this group. Ours only came out in the summer."

Patience dashed in out of the rain wearing a pink dress that she had to hold up to keep out of the mud, and a floppy red hat that dripped rainwater everywhere. A motley band of seven other children followed her, the youngest just a few years old, all dressed in wild and colorful clothes. "Ladies and gentlemen and extinguished guests!" she bellowed, and Alys chuckled. "Preeeeeesenting the finest show in the entire world!"

"Oh, I love the theater," Rowan said, and joined in the scattered applause that was nearly drowned out by the rain.

Patience's voice had no such problem. She bellowed out a rough program that sounded like it would drag on for hours. When she finished, Rowan clapped again, then stood. "Come on," she said. "We should get better seats."

"You're joking."

She frowned down at me. "Douglas Anderson, are you telling me that you're too important and busy right now to enjoy a show performed by the great actors of the future?"

Once again I didn't know how to argue with her. A few of the adults who had left earlier returned, and though they smiled at the children, none of them took seats with us. I stretched my awareness, but still felt nothing dangerous, and none of these people paid particular attention to us. I decided to stay alert, but went with Rowan to find seats close to the area the children were clearing for their show.

The theater had always seemed like a waste of time to me. I'd seen a few shows, but none like this one, a mixture of made-up play and plenty of opportunities for the performers to show off unrelated talents. I wasn't particularly fond of children, but these ones put on an interesting, if confusing, show. There were several lengthy sword battles, and the littlest troll kept wandering off when he was supposed to be terrorizing a village. Everything was exaggerated and dramatic, and it wouldn't have been hard to laugh at it, but I didn't think it was supposed to be a comedy. I just clapped when everyone else did at the end of the scenes and tried not to jump to my feet every time someone came into the tent.

They surprised me, too. One of the older girls sang a song about a maiden who fell in love with a dragon, and her voice was beautiful enough to have commanded any stage in Tyrea. Rowan was wiping tears from her eyes by the end of that one.

You trust too easily and you cry too often, I thought, *but there are far worse things.* I turned away before she could catch me watching her.

After a tumbling act put on by two brothers who would probably be great performers once they got their timing right—and stopped punching each other when things went wrong—the show concluded with a troll being run through with a collapsing sword and roasted over a fire made from orange and yellow fabrics. Rowan gave them a standing ovation.

By the time the play was over, the smell of another meal was filling the tent. Rowan ran over to the performers to congratulate them and ask about their costumes, and I walked around the inside of the tent, examining the walls and trying to figure out why I hadn't sensed people near the ruins. There were no known or registered sorcerers among any groups of Wanderers, but this protective magic was strong enough that there had to be one here more powerful than Jein.

After supper, during which I stayed quiet and tried to remember everything Rowan was saying about us, we sat with Jein and drank strong, hot tea. The woman was charming and kind, but had a hard edge to her and avoided speaking to me. She had magic in her, and could surely feel mine. Perhaps that made her wary.

Several of the children came to say goodnight to Rowan before their parents bundled them off to bed. "I heard there was a performance this afternoon," Jein said. "The children are always so happy to have a fresh audience. It's good practice for when they're older, but we don't always have time to watch."

"So you travel and perform shows?" Rowan asked. "All of you?"

"We do. We also do a little trading along the way, and yes, we always travel together, though not usually so late in the autumn. People want shows in the summer, when life is easy and fun. Most have no time for them when things are harder, though entertainment would probably do them more good then. It's more difficult to travel in the colder months, too." She glanced toward the tent's roof, where rain was still beating out a steady rhythm. "Obviously. Normally we would be at home now, settling in before the snows come."

I knew what Rowan was going to ask, and I didn't want her to. I thought I could guess the answer. "Why are you traveling now?" she asked, oblivious to my warning look.

Jein sipped from her cup. "Things have been difficult for us, particularly the past two years. The… I don't know whether he calls himself the king yet."

He doesn't, I thought. *Not until our father is declared dead.*

"In any case, our home was a little too close to the capital city, and has been taken over as a military training ground. It's nothing to him to displace a few people who hardly pay taxes and won't swear loyalty to him. There were…" She swallowed hard and shook her head. "It's better for us to be here."

She took us outside into what had become a light drizzle and led the way toward one of the wagons. "No sense you two sleeping on the floor of the hall," she said, and opened the door. The tall, hard-topped structure was cold inside, but they had set up a soft bed in the back with several heavy blankets, and left us a tall candle with twelve hour-markings on it.

"We're not displacing anyone, I hope," Rowan said, and picked up a soft-looking purple blanket to wrap around her shoulders.

"No. Not right now," Jein said. "We'll hope the sun shows his face in the morning. I'm growing tired of lamps and torches."

After she'd gone Rowan asked, "You won't sleep, will you?"

"Probably not. I don't want to change here, and sleeping as a human means I can't be sure of waking quickly if there's a problem." There was more to it, but nothing she needed to know.

"What if we took turns keeping watch? I can stay awake for a few hours while you get some rest."

I wanted the first watch, but she insisted that I needed sleep more than she did. "Can't have you dozing off, can we? Besides, I don't trust you to wake me up to take my turn." She pulled a pillow to a spot beside the door and sat with her legs crossed under her skirt, flipping through a book of plays she found lying on a box of larger volumes. The candlelight picked out the red in her hair, making it glow. I looked away and sat on the edge of the bed.

"I probably won't sleep," I said, but lay down and pulled a blanket up to my shoulders. "If I do, wake me after three hours." She nodded.

I felt myself drifting, and realized that Rowan may have been the only person I would trust while I closed my eyes—not because she couldn't be a threat, but because I believed she wanted to help me as much as I wanted to keep her safe. I yawned. *I won't sleep, though.*

Chapter Twenty-One

Aren

When I opened my eyes again nearly six hours had melted off of the candle. I sat up and looked around, thinking that Rowan must have fallen asleep, but she was standing with the door cracked open, looking out into the courtyard.

"What's going on?" I rolled out of bed and went to her. The floorboards were cold on my bare feet.

"The rain stopped, the stars are out. That's about it. Everything has been quiet." She turned toward me, and the candlelight shadows accentuated the way the orange sweater clung to the curves of her breasts. I wanted to reach out and run my hands over it, to pull her close and feel the heavy wool over the softness of her body. The wide neckline had slipped off of one shoulder. I tried not to stare. *Maybe I do need more sleep*, I thought, and rubbed my eyes.

"Why didn't you wake me?"

She shrugged, sending the knit fabric a little lower down her arm. "You needed sleep. I didn't want to disturb you."

"It's not safe."

Rowan moved toward the bed. Her bare skin grazed my arm as she squeezed past. "Everything is fine. We're safe here for now, and I'm perfectly capable of staying awake to keep watch. But now it's your turn." She handed me the blanket she'd been wearing and crawled into the warmth of the bed. "You try to take everything on yourself, and that's not good for anyone. You're going to have to trust someone some time, you know." She rolled so that she faced away from me, and in a few minutes her breathing became deep and slow.

I pulled the blanket tight around my shoulders and stepped outside. The clouds had cleared, and with all of the lights out in the camp, the stars filled the sky. I closed the door and sat on the wooden steps, gazing up. In spite of everything going on in the world around us, I found myself feeling content for the first time in years, happy that for the moment, Rowan and I seemed to be safe.

A light appeared in the largest tent, moving around with whoever carried it. A lone figure stepped into the courtyard, holding something in each hand, and walked toward me.

"May I?" Jein asked, and I moved over to make room for her on the wide step. Her thin frame didn't take up much space, but I gave her plenty. I also kept one hand near my knife, concealed under the blanket.

She handed me a mug of something warm. "Thought a hot drink might make you more comfortable out here."

"How did you know I was awake?" I lifted the drink and inhaled the steam. Some kind of cinnamon tea.

"Sometimes I know things." Jein took a long sip from her cup. "Doug." She looked sideways at me.

My fingers tightened around the knife's handle. "How long after we arrived did you know who I was?"

"Part-way through supper, though I suspected sooner. There were rumors in a few towns we passed through. Your family may be trying to keep it quiet, but gossip travels so quickly." She quirked a silver eyebrow at me. "Something about you stealing a woman from your brother, and that you may have killed ten men in your escape. Is that right?"

"Not entirely. But that's not how you knew who we were."

"No. It gave context, an idea of why you might be traveling in a rainstorm with a young lady, but I'd have known without that. It's part of our magic."

"'Our'?" As I'd always understood it, magic was a highly individual thing. It couldn't be shared any more than physical strength or intellect could.

"Indeed. None of us are particularly gifted, the way you are, but when we work together, we can protect ourselves." Jein sipped her drink again. "It's something we've picked up out of necessity. Whatever small magic the members of our community possess, we pass on to the leader when the need arises. Me, now."

She didn't offer to explain further, and though I was curious about this idea, I didn't ask. If she didn't trust me with the information, I couldn't blame her.

She turned to me again and gave me an appraising look. "We used it tonight. The men who were following you were gone, but we could have kept them away if they had been nearby."

"I'm sure." I remembered how invisible they'd been to me, and wished I could know how to block Severn as effectively. The trick at the cave had worked in that moment, but I needed practice. "And yet you invited us in." I took a small sip of tea. It was strong and sweet, and the cinnamon burned my throat. I waited, but felt no ill effects.

Jein set her cup down and leaned forward, elbows resting on her knees. "Foolish, I know. You're a dangerous person. You could kill me right now just for knowing who you are."

"I could. I think I won't."

"But I don't imagine your brothers would show us any mercy if they found out you'd been here."

"True." The sky overhead turned from black to deep blue, and the stars began to fade.

"And there's your companion," Jein continued. "She gave me the assurance. We don't teach that to just anyone, but her friend obviously thought she'd need it some day. I could have turned her out, or you, but we take our duty to offer aid where we can quite seriously." I recalled hearing that the Wanderers worshiped several gods, and each band had a particular favorite, but that they all answered to one who rewarded compassion. I wasn't familiar with him, personally.

"A password seems like an easy security measure to overcome," I said.

Jein smiled. "Can you remember it?"

I opened my mouth to speak, and the words wouldn't come. *Incredible.* I had heard of protected words, and thought they were only stories.

"So I had reason enough to think she came by the words honestly, and meant us no harm," she concluded. "If only it were so easy for you to know our intentions, eh? Perhaps you can see now."

As I looked at her, her defenses softened. I didn't probe deep into her mind, certain that she'd shut down and throw us out if I did. But her peace and calm radiated from her, and no ill will. My grip on my knife loosened. "Thank you."

"Hmm."

The ruins became clearer, silhouetted against the lightening sky. Members of Jein's group rose and began their morning tasks, criss-crossing the yard, talking and laughing softly together. Jein closed off my awareness of her again, but not before I felt the pain that flickered through her mind as she watched them.

"When you said your home was taken over for military training, that wasn't everything, was it?"

"No," she whispered. "I didn't think it was appropriate to say anything more, though. Your w—" She smiled. "I almost said your wife. I like her, she lies well. But yes, there was more. It was fortunate that we'd just returned from our summer circuit, and almost everything was still packed. There was no warning. None of our defenses alerted us to danger. There might only have been ten or a dozen of them, but they came down on us like a winter storm. It was all confusion and screaming. Burning. I think the one leading them would have been happy to see us all dead."

"But you got away."

"We were twice this many a month ago."

That would make somewhere around forty dead or lost. My stomach clenched. "The leader of that group. You don't know who he was?"

"Not for certain. But I think you might. Massive fellow, rode a white devil horse. Arms like oaks, laughed as he set fire to our homes." Her voice cracked, but the expression on her face didn't change.

I knew. Wardrel was four years older than me, born to one of our father's secondary wives. His magic wasn't especially powerful for a member of our family, but what he lacked in talent he made up for in physical strength. He was cruel, without reason or purpose. Severn had tried to kill me when I was a child, but it was because he felt threatened. When Wardrel killed my dog, it was because he enjoyed it—both the killing and my reaction. Our father sent him away after the mangled body of a servant's child was found in a cellar room, but Severn brought him back not long after our father disappeared. He thought he could control Wardrel.

It seemed he'd at least found a use for him.

"One of my brothers," I admitted. "I'm sorry. I had no idea anything like this had happened."

Jein's mouth tightened into a thin line. "You had other things to do, didn't you?"

"I suppose I did. I haven't been home much in the past year."

"Doing your brother's work." Jein took a thin, curved pipe and a packet of herbs from her pocket and prepared a smoke, taking her time with lighting it. "It makes me wonder why you're here now, traveling with this girl you took from him. And she seems to be unafraid of you. Have you changed so much?"

"No." I remembered what I'd told Rowan the previous day. "She trusts too easily. And she doesn't know anything about me."

"And yet here you are, guarding the door while she sleeps. Protecting her. Doing what I presume you think is right instead of what your brother wanted."

"It's complicated."

"I'd imagine it is." Jein pulled deeply at the pipe, and sighed a sweet-smelling cloud of smoke. "May I offer you a piece of advice?"

A baby cried somewhere in the camp, and a pair of women walked into the largest tent, talking quietly.

"Of course."

Jein spoke slowly, choosing her words carefully. "Where you come from is nothing. My people, my family, we only look ahead. We'll find a new place, and we'll build a new life. I hope that you will choose to do the same."

She patted me on the arm, then stood and went back to the tent. I sat for a few more minutes, watching the displaced and broken community start their day's work. I finished my tea and went inside to see if Rowan was awake.

#

With the rain over and the Wanderers heading in the direction we'd just come from, there was no reason for us to stay with them any longer. We made ourselves useful while we could. It seemed only fair after all the Wanderers had done for us. Rowan assisted with cleaning up after breakfast and held a few babies for their busy mothers while I helped take down the tents and got our horses ready for our departure. She made the children promise another performance when she met them again, and Alys joked that they were going to steal my wife away and turn her into a true Wanderer.

Rowan laughed. "Maybe when I get tired of him, I'll find you and do just that."

Maybe you will, I thought. It was as good a place for her as any, and Jein was right. Rowan was a convincing liar. She loved a good story, and she'd probably be a great performer. These people wouldn't force her into marriage, or anything else she didn't want. She could have a good life with them.

And then she turned to me and smiled, and I found myself hoping she'd forget all about it.

Chapter Twenty-Two

Rowan

My injuries from the attack had healed, but by mid-afternoon I was more sore than ever from riding. My lessons at Stone Ridge and hours spent on horseback in the woods hadn't prepared me for this. My headache had grown steadily worse since we left the Wanderers, and we hadn't passed a heartleaf tree since the border. Aren seemed deep in thought, and didn't speak unless I did first. I had a lot of time to think, and it wasn't making me any more cheerful. There were still too many questions about my past and my people, and not enough answers that I liked, no matter how I looked at it. I didn't want to think about any of it, so I kept my mind occupied with easier subjects.

"Can you tell me about unicorns?"

"What about them?"

"I don't know. Anything." I wanted to hear him talk. His voice was pleasant, and his accent was even better. At least that was one aspect of life in Tyrea I could easily get used to.

"They look like horses," he said. "But with a horn. And magic."

"That's very helpful, thank you."

"Not a problem."

"Fairies?"

"They're around. Don't see them too often."

"Does that mean you *have* seen a unicorn?"

"No."

Those questions weren't getting me anywhere. I decided to move on to something else. "So, I think I've been pretty good about not asking questions—"

He snorted.

"—*about where we're going.* I'd like to have some idea. Not that the past few days haven't been exciting and interesting, but I think I've reached my geographical limit for traveling blindly away from home with a stranger. All you've told me is that we're going to get some help for me. Maybe."

He seemed amused by my irritation, which only made it worse. *The headache's not his fault*, I reminded myself.

"Sorry," he said. "I suppose I should have said something about that. I've been giving it a lot of thought, and I think I know of some people who might have the information we need, who may be willing to help you."

"Fantastic!"

"But they're hard to locate. They move around a lot, and I'm not sure where they'll be right now."

"Are they Wanderers?"

"No, they just disappear frequently. But they tend to be more intelligent than most people, and they have access to a lot of information. Since I can't go back to the libraries in Luid, they're our best chance at figuring out what exactly happened to you and how we can undo it."

"But you have no idea where to find them?"

He shrugged, and looked toward the sky. "Johen told me that there's some nasty weather coming in from the northwest. There's a lake just north of here where wealthy people from Luid keep summer homes. It should be deserted now, we'll ride out the storm there."

His horse was several paces ahead of mine before he noticed that I'd stopped.

"Wait," I said. "I've been missing from home for what, five days? I haven't been able to tell my family that I'm all right, I don't even know if I *am* all right, my headaches only seem to be getting worse, and you're telling me that we're going to take a few days for a little lakeside vacation? Please tell me you're not serious." I knew I was acting like a petulant child, but had always found it hard to control my mind and mouth when I was in pain.

He didn't say anything until I nudged my horse to move forward and caught up with him. His face was nearly expressionless, but there was a hardness there that I couldn't read. I thought at first that he was trying to keep his temper in check, that I'd crossed some line by questioning him. Then I realized he was trying not to laugh. At least a good night's sleep had improved *someone's* mood.

"I'm sorry," he said. "This is just ridiculous."

"What, me?"

"No, all of it. Everything that's happened in the past few days. If I'm handling this badly, it's because I don't know what I'm doing. I'm usually giving orders or following them, not discussing plans with people. Especially not with someone like you."

"Oh." I didn't know how to take that.

"Did you have another idea about where we should go?"

He knew damned well that I didn't. I scowled at him. "I just want to know what's going on. How exactly are we going to find these mysterious people?"

"There's a good chance they're at the lake."

"You might have mentioned that."

"Might have." He smiled to himself and nudged his horse forward.

I rolled my eyes and followed. *The remorseless killer thinks it's amusing to tease me. Fantastic.*

We turned when we came to a narrow road that cut through rolling, forested land, and I passed the time by observing Aren as he rode slightly ahead of me and to my left. Such a confusing person. Since I'd met him he'd hurt people, done things to their minds, killed them. But while I knew those things were wrong, he'd done them to keep us safe. As I spent more time with him, it all seemed to fade to insignificance. He'd been nicer to me since the incident at the fire, when he'd cut himself. Not friendly, exactly, but more relaxed and less cold. Sometimes it was easy to dislike him, but at other times he seemed like the sort of person I could get used to having around. He was certainly more interesting than anyone I knew back home.

When he said "just north of here" I imagined an hour's ride, maybe two. I was wrong. We stopped to eat and to tend to the horses before we got to the lake, and all Aren could tell me was that it wasn't too much farther. I was beginning to realize that his concept of distance was far different from mine, and resigned myself to another night of being kept awake by my aching butt.

Sunset found us on a bare dirt trail that meandered around a massive lake, weaving in and out of the forest. Dozens of islands dotted the glassy water, and docks jutted out from the shore in small clusters with broad stretches of land between them. Even if they knew we were in the area it would take someone forever to search every house.

I hoped we'd be settling in at one of the closest places. The ones I could see were beautiful. These people's summer homes were bigger and better-built than most of the houses in my hometown. My spirits lifted as I anticipated a hot drink and a soft bed, and soon.

The sun became a sliver of pink light beyond the now-distant mountains, and still we rode. I pointed out a few nice-looking places, but Aren seemed to want to get as far from the road as we could. I gave up and followed, silently cursing him with every step my horse took.

The path grew narrower and rockier, and we dismounted to lead the horses over the uneven ground. I was so close to falling asleep on my feet that I nearly collided with the back of Aren's horse when he stopped in front of me and turned up a dark path.

"Oh, thank goodness," I said, and a loon yodeled back from somewhere across the lake. I pulled my cloak tighter, and followed the horse's rear toward a house, hoping that this place would be even better than the others I'd seen.

It wasn't. It was nice enough, two levels and certainly

more than enough space for two people. The wide-win-dowed, wood-paneled building sat on a broad stone foun-dation, solid but plain. It didn't look nearly as rich or as comfortable as the other houses.

A white chicken burst into the clearing that surrounded the building and dashed back into the forest on the far side. Other than that, the place seemed deserted.

"Trust me," Aren said, and led the way around back, where a stable shared a wall with the house. It was unlocked, and it only took us a few minutes to put the horses' tack away and turn them out to forage.

We searched all around for a key. Aren found one on top of the door frame, but the door remained stuck closed. I remembered the magic Aren had done with the gate lock when we took the horses. "Can you open it?" I asked, hoping he wasn't going to burn himself again.

"I think so." He cracked his knuckles, then backed up a few steps and ran forward to slam his shoulder into the door, which groaned gently and popped open.

"Not exactly what I was thinking."

He grinned and pushed his hair back from his face. "I know. Come on in."

The moonlight from the windows cast eerie shadows on the interior of the cabin, and I hesitated before stepping into the large, open space inside of the door. A group of chairs and a sofa formed a seating area to the right. To my left was a kitchen with only a counter separating it from the rest of the room, and a dining table. Aren pulled a few candles out of his bag and lit them, pressing the bottoms into holders as we found them, making the room far more inviting in spite of the chill that remained in the air.

An open door at the back of the kitchen area led to a room with a large bed. A smaller bed sat in the back, with storage shelves hung on the wall above it. "This will be the best place to sleep for now," Aren said. "If we light the stove, it'll be warmer in here than upstairs." We left our things there and I continued exploring the house.

A hallway behind the sitting area led to a clean toilet room and a back door that opened onto the garden. A good-sized hen house had been left with the door open. Nothing grew in the garden except for a healthy crop of weeds and a few of the summer's leftover vegetable plants, all picked clean. Beyond that, the forest stood silent and shadowed. I pulled the door closed and made sure it was locked before I left it.

The back half of the house had a second level with a wide staircase leading up to an open area flanked by two bedrooms. The beds up there looked more comfortable than the ones downstairs, but the air was freezing. I closed the doors to both rooms and hurried back downstairs.

Aren had both the wood stove and the fireplace lit and was busy looking through the kitchen cupboards. "We should be fine as far as food goes," he said, his voice muffled by the cabinet doors. He stepped back and closed them. "Lots of preserves, and whoever was living here left some fruits and a few vegetables in the freshbox that still look good."

"That's impossible, unless they left this week."

He shook his head, bemused. "I don't know how you people survive, really. There are probably a few of those chickens outside, can you catch them?"

"Not my favorite thing, but I can do it." All I cared about at that moment was sleep. The night at the inn had been helpful, but letting Aren sleep while we were with the Wanderers had left me with only a few hours to rest. I wondered if my body would ever adjust to life at this pace.

I went back to the small room off of the kitchen and sat on the edge of the small bunk to remove my boots. Having my feet free felt incredible. I groaned and wiggled my toes.

Aren followed me and leaned against the door-frame. "What are you doing?"

I looked down at my feet. "Taking off my boots. Sorry."

He pinched the bridge of his nose like he was getting one of my headaches. "No, I mean what are you doing on that bed? The other will be more comfortable."

I gestured toward the large bed. "It's all yours. I got the only bed the other night at the inn. Besides, you're bigger than me. I'm sure this will be fine."

He frowned and looked out the door at the exposed rafters. "Thank you, but it's probably better if I change."

The disappointment that flashed through me caught me by surprise. I tossed my boots into the corner of the room. "Why? Why is it better? Do I make you uncomfortable? Do you find me less irritating when you're not human?"

"I told you, it's easier for me to stay alert that way. Obviously it doesn't always work, but I'd like to avoid repeating the other morning if we can."

I brushed past him and went to the kitchen window. The lake was visible through the trees, glowing in the cloud-diffused moonlight. "So you think they're here now?"

He sighed. "No. There's no one around."

"Why don't you get one more good sleep while you can? You seemed so much better today after you stayed human overnight."

"I'm fine."

I let the curtains fall closed, then sat at the oak table and traced the patterns in the wood with my fingers. "I know it probably seems silly to you, but I also find it's a little less lonely when you're a person. Even when you're not talking to me."

He raised his eyebrows.

That never crossed your mind? Maybe he didn't get lonely the way I did.

"You're right," he said, and rubbed a hand over the stubble that had grown back on his face since we'd left the inn. It looked good. Really good. He didn't seem to notice me studying him, and I enjoyed it while I could. He looked over, and my heart skipped as his eyes met mine. "I should try to sleep, and if we're lucky Severn won't be able to locate us. He might be too busy to focus on that right now. That's not the only thing, though. It's—hang on."

He rolled up his sleeves, pumped water from the faucet into a big kettle and set it on the stove. I suddenly realized that he was familiar with this house. I would have asked, but didn't want to distract him if he was about to tell me something about himself.

As he moved around the kitchen, I caught a glimpse of the inside of his left arm. A clean white scar divided it, all that was left of where he'd cut himself so badly. That bit of insanity was starting to seem like a dream. A nightmare, really, but I could forgive him for it. I certainly wouldn't go so far as to thank him for that pain, but…

"You don't seem like a villain," I said, the words out of my mouth before I could stop them.

He frowned at me as he poured steaming water into a tea pot. "What do you mean?"

Can't you just shut your mouth? I asked myself. I didn't listen. I didn't usually. "Just that you aren't what I expected you to be. Any time I've heard people talk about your family, they were afraid. Sometimes they tried to sound brave when they mentioned how powerful you all are, or horrible things you've done, but I could always tell they were covering up their fear. According to my brother, you're practically the Big Bad Wolf. You know, like from—"

"Fairy stories, I know. I'm familiar with the concept." He set the tea pot and cups on the table.

"I just mean that you've been helping me, even when I thought I didn't want you to. Even when you didn't seem to want to, actually. You're not what I'd call friendly most of the time, but you've been teaching me things…" My words trailed off, and I cleared my throat. "I guess you just don't seem like a bad person, when you let your guard down a little."

He stood frozen in the space between the kitchen and the table, and stared at me. "Don't say that," he said quietly. He sank into the chair across from me and drummed his fingers on the table.

"I'm sorry?"

He flexed his fingers, and the scar on his forearm stood out more clearly. "It's not you. I should have told you a lot of things already, but I was… I don't know. You didn't seem to know much about me, and I didn't want to frighten you off. And then I started to enjoy having you around, and I didn't want you to think badly of me. I mean, you ask too many questions, and it makes things difficult."

"I—"

"But I actually like that you're curious about magic, and everything else your people didn't want you to know about. It was nice feeling like I could help you with some of that. But that's not who I truly am, and you need to understand that. I'm not who you just described. I can't be. Not in the real world."

"I don't think that's true," I said, choosing my words carefully. "If you were really bad or untrustworthy, you'd have shown it by now. You'd have left me to be eaten by that dragon."

"You got out of that yourself."

"You were there, though. You came looking for me. I think it probably took a lot for you to stay with me at the inn when you could have just flown away and saved yourself. If you were such a bad person, you'd be at home in Luid right now. You wouldn't have bothered to save me from your brother. You're tired and under a lot of pressure, and that would bring out the worst in anyone, but you haven't shown that at all. You've been a bit of a jerk sometimes, but underneath that you've been trying to do the right thing."

"You have no idea what you're talking about." He pushed his hair back from his face and squeezed his eyes closed.

"Are you okay?"

"I'm thinking." He took a deep breath, then stood and started pacing. "What have you actually heard about me?"

"Not much. You're sort of a blank to most people I've heard talking about your family. They don't seem to know why, but they're as afraid of you as they are of Severn, or even of your father."

"That sounds about right. How do I explain this?" He continued pacing, and for once I managed to keep my mouth shut while I waited. "I have three brothers, all older. My father was the king, he was always busy while I was growing up. My brothers were able to do work for him before I was, so I was left behind. Like a spare, almost. My father didn't need me, but Severn saw my potential after he tried to kill me."

"What?"

"It happens. I survived, and he eventually realized that instead of getting rid of a rival, he could use me to strengthen his own power. When our father put him in charge of keeping peace in the outer provinces, making sure that no one who opposed him was able to make trouble, Severn took a more aggressive approach than others had in the past. He got rid of those people. Not personally, but he made sure it was taken care of."

"Taken care of by people like the gang that attacked my group on the road to Ardare?" I thought I knew where this was going, but I didn't want to hear it. I didn't want a reason to be afraid of him again.

"He uses people like that for big jobs. Out of control crowds, guarding his own safety. A lot of the time, though, Severn relies on subtler methods of getting things done, methods that are actually more frightening for his enemies because they don't understand what's happening and can't prepare for it. He doesn't want people to be able to prove that he's responsible for these things that happen to them. He can't be openly accused of murder. Or massacre. Or—"

"I get it." I shuddered, remembering the magic hunter my brother told me about. It had been so easy to forget.

Aren crouched in front of me and looked into my eyes. His looked pained. Angry. "I don't think you do. The rest of us all support Severn. There's nothing else for us to do. He won't allow rival sorcerers to live, not if they're any kind of a threat, not even if they're family. I hate him, but I do what he wants. Or I did, until I met you. I had no choice. I've been well-rewarded for my efforts, though. I had a good life in Luid, and often I didn't even feel badly about the things that I did, or the things I'm still doing to keep us safe. I think my brothers enjoy it. Wardrel has killed children while their mothers screamed for mercy and laughed while he was doing it."

My hands gripped hard onto the edge of my chair. "You're not like that."

"No, I'm not him. But you have to understand that while what I do is subtler, it can be just as cruel in its own way."

"The mind-control."

He nodded. "I'm good at it, too. My methods aren't perfect, but I've incited riots by working on a few key people and using their influence to set off a crowd like an explosion. I've turned people against their own brothers, wives, parents. I once made a man kill his best friend, a Sorcerer who had plans to challenge my father. That one drowned himself when he realized what he'd done. I've never killed a child as far as I know, but I've probably made a few orphans."

"Probably? You don't even know?"

He stood again and moved a few paces away. "No. I do my work, and I get out of town before anyone knows I've been there. I don't enjoy what I do as much as Wardrel does, and I don't mastermind plans like Severn does, though I am one of his close advisers. But I've done as much damage as any of my family. Severn made me what I am, and it was his idea that I learn how to do this. As I said, he doesn't know everything I'm capable of, but—"

I stood and pushed past him on my way back to the window, cutting him off. I managed to keep control of my voice, but I didn't want him to see the foolish tears blurring my vision. It shouldn't have mattered. I shouldn't have cared what he was, as long as he helped me.

I'd known that he killed people, but that had somehow disappeared under everything else that had happened. This was bigger than I'd realized, more horrifying. The lack of emotion in his voice as he spoke about it gave me chills.

"I just don't want you to see me as something else and be hurt by it," he added. "I'm not proud of what I am."

I laughed, and the sharp noise that came out was completely unfamiliar to me. "You're not sorry, though, are you?"

His reflection appeared in the window next to mine, then grew smaller as he withdrew to the sofa. "For a long time, I wasn't. It felt good to be appreciated by Severn after years of being ignored by everyone, to have something I was really good at, to be serving my family the way I was brought up to. But I also hated myself for letting Severn use me, though I don't know what I could have done differently. There was no way out. When Dorset Langley shot me, I thought that perhaps dying wasn't the worst thing that could happen to me. Then you came, and I had no choice but to live…"

"And what?"

"I don't know. Your magic reminded me of things I'd tried to forget. Broke me, somehow."

I leaned my head against the window, then stepped back and closed the curtains in case anyone could see the light from outside. I turned back to him. "And then you left me alone. And when you were surprised to see me on the road that day, you decided to help? I don't understand."

"Rowan… No." He leaned forward and pressed his face into his hands. "Yes, I was surprised to see you. But that's only because I thought we'd find you at Stone Ridge. We were on our way to take you in. I'd told Severn about you. I had every intention of letting him have you, because that was the best thing for me, because it would help me get ahead. *That's* who I am."

It felt like I'd had the wind knocked out of me. I couldn't speak. "So up until the last minute…"

"Yes. I'm sorry." There seemed to be genuine remorse in his eyes when he looked up. "It was wrong—"

I didn't care about his remorse. "You're damned right it was wrong!"

"—and I realized that as soon as I saw you. You don't know how difficult it was for me to walk off that ship with you. That was the hardest thing I've ever done, and at the time I didn't even understand why I was doing it." His voice was growing louder. Agitated. Perhaps angry.

"And now I'm what to you?" I demanded. "A suicide mission? An attempt to make you feel better about yourself, or to find some kind of redemption before your brother kills you?"

"No, it's not like that." He looked up, and I turned away.

"I meant what I said earlier," he said. "I like you. I wish my life was like the past few days have been, maybe minus the being chased by people who want to kill us. It's been good to get away from what my life was, and better because you've given me something else to focus on. But it's still there. That's still who I am, and it's not fair to you for me to pretend that I'm something I'm not."

That bitter laugh escaped me again. "Nothing about this is fair," I said, fighting to keep my voice even. My insides churned with anger at his willingness to hurt innocent people, disappointment that he wasn't who I'd come to think he was, and embarrassment for the fact that I'd been stupid enough to care. "Sleep wherever you want, just leave me alone."

I didn't mean to slam the bedroom door. It just happened. And for the first time since the start of the whole adventure, I cried myself to sleep.

#

That night I dreamed that a dragon was chasing me. Not Ruby. This one was much darker than her, and cloaked in shadows. I ran, but its glowing eyes came closer with every step I took. A wooden bridge appeared in front of me, spanning a dark canyon. The boards looked rotten, but the hot breath on the back of my neck forced me forward. The dragon stopped its chase, but the bridge gave out under my weight, and I fell.

And then I was dancing. My dance partner was taller than me, dressed all in black. His hand rested lightly on the waist of my blood-red dress, pulling me close as we moved together. The dance was perfect, but wild, fast and spinning and thrilling. It was nothing like real life, where I had trouble finding the beat of the music and my feet always seemed to get in each other's way. We moved through a crowd of people, all faceless, none of them important, none of them as real as my dance partner. My heart beat wildly, and every inch of my body seemed more alive than it had ever been. The soft fabric of my dress caressed me with every movement, and my skin tingled where my partner's body pressed against me.

I pulled back and lifted my face to see Aren looking down at me, his expression as unreadable as I'd ever seen it. The music stopped, and he walked away.

I tried to follow, but those faceless people kept getting in my way, bumping into me and turning me around. Someone grabbed my arm. It was Callum, smiling and trying to take me back to the dance floor. I knew I was supposed to be relieved to see him again, that I should want to dance with him again, but I kept looking over my shoulder hoping that Aren would come back and cut in.

Callum kissed me. It was sweet. It was nice, and it felt safe. But for some reason I wished I was still being chased by that dragon.

#

Sunrise found me wearing an old pair of coveralls and too-large rain boots, cleaning the chicken coop and searching for fresh eggs. I hadn't slept well after the strange dreams, and I thought that focusing on a simple task might give my mind enough space to sort things out. The conflict in my brain was only making the pain in my head worse. The stink in the coop didn't help, either, but there was only one thing I could do about that.

Three chickens flapped past me and out the door when they woke, but a brown-feathered hen stayed on her nest, eyeing me warily. She gave a warning squawk when I tried to reach under her. Broody. I left her and went back to work.

"It's so stupid, isn't it?" I asked her. "I knew what he was. Is. I saw him control people at the inn. I've heard stories about his family." The hen shifted and fluffed her feathers, but gave me no answer.

I set the rake down and leaned on the handle. "It's just that in the past few days, I forgot about that. I knew it, but it didn't seem to fit him anymore. When I used to wish for adventure, when I wanted to learn about magic and see more of the world, I never imagined it happening with someone like him. He's interesting, sure. And when he has these moments when he seems like a decent person, and like maybe he sees me as more than a problem, or a secret Sorceress. He said he likes me."

"*Brrrrrrk?*"

"Not like that. I don't know what that dream was about." I squeezed my eyes shut to chase away the lingering images. "But I was starting to think of him as a friend, I guess. Or at least someone I could trust. Then he reminds me he's actually a remorseless killer who forces his way into people's minds and turns them into monsters, just in case I forgot that. I mean, even in the past few days he's killed people, and with no more remorse than you'd show for killing a mouse. Oh, and by the way, he was also planning to kidnap me so his brother could do God knows what to me. And this after I saved his life." I sighed. "I don't want to stay with someone like that. Staying is a bad decision. Isn't it?"

He'd help me if I wanted to leave. He'd draw me a map to the nearest town, or maybe help me find the Wanderers again. He'd probably take me there, even knowing how dangerous it would be.

"And that's the problem, isn't it?" I said, and got back to work turning over dirty bedding. "I still don't think he *is* a monster. Or if he is, he's changing. He helped me get away from Severn and whatever was supposed to happen to me in Luid. He gave up everything. I don't know. I believe him when he says he's not a good guy. He's definitely not prince charming. Not that I'd want him to be, mind you."

The hen let out a flurry of clucking noises and stretched her neck toward the window.

"Oh, what do you know? You're a chicken." I set down a fresh layer of straw over the old. The mess below it still didn't smell appetizing, but it would keep the chickens warm. I lowered my voice to a conspiratorial whisper. "Yes, he's very attractive, and sometimes I get this feeling like there's something between us. He can be so charming when he wants to be, but I can't trust that, can I? That's what he does. He manipulates people."

I forced myself to think rationally and tried to forget about those gorgeous brown eyes. "It doesn't matter what he looks like, or that being around him makes me feel good, at least when I'm not mad at him. He's going to help me get this binding thing taken care of, he'll have done what he promised, and then we'll go our separate ways. Nothing else makes sense."

The chicken just watched me with those dark, beady eyes, showing no sign that she cared either way. I sighed. "I miss Aquila. He was a better listener." I didn't feel any better for having talked things out, but I thought I was closer to making a decision. There was one thing I needed to know, that would decide whether I could stay with Aren. I stripped off the coveralls, washed up in the freezing water from the outdoor pump, found a few eggs that were fresh enough to eat, and went back inside.

Aren was still asleep when I passed through the sitting room. I'd been pleased earlier to see that he'd taken my advice and slept as a human after all. He didn't look comfortable sprawled on the sofa with a light blanket pulled over him, but at least he was getting some rest. It was a good thing no one had sneaked up on us during the night. He didn't even seem to hear the door open.

The smell of eggs frying and bread toasting soon woke him, though. He stood and stretched, and the cracking noise from his spine made me wince. *Definitely needs a proper bed tonight,* I thought.

The main room had grown warm overnight with the wood stove and the fireplace burning. Aren wore soft sleep pants, but no shirt. I tried not to stare at the lines of his bare chest and stomach when he stood and folded the blanket onto the sofa. *Not like that, remember?* He pulled a shirt on before he turned to go down the back hallway, and I didn't know whether to feel relieved or disappointed. I couldn't remember ever having so many confused feelings about one person.

Breakfast was ready when he came back and sat at the table. His hair was a mess, there was a faint line across his cheek from the folded blanket he'd used as a pillow... and he looked way too good. I turned away and went back to get the food.

Who cares what he looks like?

He smiled tentatively when I brought his plate over. "Thanks."

"Yeah. I mean, you're welcome." I sat across from him. "I'm going to ask you something, and you need to answer me honestly, even if you think it's not what I want to hear. No tricks, no side-stepping, no vague responses that I can interpret as I choose. Can you do that?"

"You know me too well."

"Can you?"

"I'll try."

"When all of this is over, what are you going to do?"

He raised one eyebrow. Maybe he'd been expecting a different question. "I suppose that depends on what you mean by 'all of this,' and even more on how it actually ends."

"Would you go back to your old life if that were possible?"

"It wouldn't be. But if in some other world Severn were willing to forgive me and let things go back to the way they were, rights and privileges reinstated, all is forgotten?"

I nodded, not wanting to speak and risk saying the wrong thing.

He looked down at his plate, thinking. I sipped my tea.

"No." He looked up. "No, I wouldn't."

"Why? You went back after you left Stone Ridge. You were going to betray me. Why not now?"

He took a sip of his own drink, but his eyes never left mine. "I don't think I could. When I went back, I just wanted to forget about you. That was the plan. But then Severn made me tell him about you, and I'm ashamed to say that I turned you in to protect my own ass." He lowered his gaze. "I think I was trying to prove something to myself, too. That I was strong enough to do what needed to be done, for Severn and Tyrea. And as much as I hated how much control Severn had over me, and the person he was turning me into, I did have a lot to protect. Family obligations aside, I had a good life in Luid."

He reached up to rub the back of his neck. He seemed less certain and confident than I'd ever seen him. I stirred my tea, not wanting to push him to finish even as the waiting tore me apart. "But as I've spent more time away from that life," he continued, "I've realized that it was killing me. I meant everything I said last night. I'm not a good person. But I hate what I've become. I thought the part of me that cared about what happened to you was weak. I've spent years trying to crush it. But I'm starting to think that maybe it's worth hanging on to. If I went home again, the part of me that has appreciated your kindness and tried to keep you safe would die. I would become everything Severn was trying to make me. And I don't want that."

He looked up again and tried to smile, but it fell flat. "I think I've realized that I'd rather have a short life, even if it's spent like this, than live hundreds of years the way I was before."

I realized I'd been holding my breath, and let it out in a long sigh. "Good answer."

He cleared his throat as hint of color touched his cheeks. "Thank you."

We were silent for a minute, eating, and then the corners of his mouth twitched. "What would you have done if I'd said, 'no, I can't go back, because I plan to run away with you to a far-off land and live happily ever after?'"

I nearly choked on my eggs, then stared at him for a few seconds. I smiled sweetly. "Before, or after I ran outside and vomited?"

He leaned back in his chair and gave me that smile that creased the skin beside his eyes and set my heart pounding. "Excellent. You are as wise as you are beautiful." I reached up to touch my pulled back, tangled hair and wondered how exactly I was supposed to take that.

After the food was gone and we took our dishes to the kitchen, Aren asked, "How did you sleep last night?"

"Fine. Strange dreams, but that's normal for me."

"That's good. I didn't think it would be a problem."

"That what would be a problem? My dreams?"

"No, mine. You've never asked how I make people do

things."

I poured a cup of drinking water and went to sit on a soft armchair. "You didn't say much about your magic or how you changed forms. I assumed you didn't want to talk about those things."

He took a seat close to me. "I don't, but you should know. It's something like pulling a person into a dream, but they're not asleep. It's difficult to do it when I'm awake, but when I'm sleeping it sometimes happens on its own, and I find myself in people's dreams. Accidentally. I've never hurt or influenced anyone that way, but most people don't want others to know what they dream about. After Dan found out about it, my brothers all refused to sleep anywhere near me. It's the reason why Severn suggested I learn to control people's minds. He knew I had a gift that could be developed."

"Does that always happen?" Not a pleasant thought, given my dreams last night. I took a long sip of cold water.

"No. I don't know if you'd even be affected. Your magic may protect your dreams, as it does your waking thoughts. I don't think I could get inside of you if I tried to." I choked on my water, nearly spitting it out. Aren held back a smile. "Your mind, I mean."

The silence dragged on for longer than I meant it to. "Well. Good to know you weren't just changing at night because you were sick of me. You didn't dream about dancing last night, did you?"

"Dancing? No." His smile disappeared. "But sometimes it's best if I don't dream, anyway." He stood and went to wash the dishes, and I left him to it. I had more questions, but I also had a lot of answers to digest. It felt like there were mysteries buried in everything he said, and for once I needed a break as much as he did. I decided to do more exploring.

The upstairs wardrobes were filled with clothing, both men's and women's. Mostly summer things, but I found some sweaters, thick pants and a wool skirt on a high shelf, set away for the cold days that must have come to a northern lake even during the hottest months. I didn't find anything in the bedrooms that told me who owned the house, though.

I was about to go back downstairs with my armload of clothes when Aren called, "I'm going down to the lake to check on something. If you want to go for a swim, you should do it soon. It looks like the snow is coming." I imagined how cold the lake must be, and shivered.

"You're crazy!" I called after him.

After he was gone, I dug my dragon scale out of the bottom of my bag. I hadn't thought to look at it since I put it away after we left Ruby's cave. One of the dragon's smaller scales, certainly, but larger than my hand. I balanced the curve of it in my palm and admired the way the light reflected off of it, changing the colors as I turned it over. *Far more beautiful than any treasure.* I set it on the table in the sitting area.

Next I looked over the books on the shelf. There weren't many—a few romance stories that must have been someone's light summer reading, and a "Pictorial Guide to the Flora and Fauna of Glass Lake." The lowest shelf held a dusty toy horse, a miniature wooden boat, and a heavy volume entitled simply, "Child's Tales." I sat in an armchair and rested the book on my crossed legs as I flipped slowly through the stories.

Detailed pictures burst from the pages in brilliant color, bringing the stories to life. The girl trapped in an ogre-guarded castle looked familiar, though the man waiting to climb to her seemed more sinister than any I remembered.

On another page a woman stood on a mountaintop, bathed in light that seemed to pool in her hands, black hair swirling around her, a sword sheathed at her waist. It was an impressive weapon, but it was her magic that she chose to wield against the purple dragon that hovered before her.

I think I could get to like Tyrea, I thought, and flipped the page again.

I was engrossed in a story about a king who made a fateful deal with a sea serpent when Aren returned. Water dripped from his hair, but his clothes were only wet in spots, as though he'd gone swimming without them and put them back on without drying off first.

"Very refreshing," he said. "Should have taken a towel." He wandered off to an upstairs room, leaving a trail of water droplets on the floor behind him.

"You're a strange person," I told him when he came back down.

"You should go out."

"Should I, now? I'm not partial to freezing water. There must be a tub here somewhere that I can use to wash up. In warm water. Indoors."

He shrugged. "Suit yourself, but that seems like a lot of extra work. The water is nice, really. There are hot springs in the lake. Not right here, but they keep things from freezing. I was colder coming back up here than I was in the water. Besides, I left soap down there for you. You're going to have to go get it, anyway." He rocked back on his heels and waited for me to answer.

"Now there's a logical argument if ever I heard one." I snapped the book closed and placed it on the table. "Is it safe? No man or woman-eating monsters? It's a big lake."

"Not as far as I know. I'll come down and keep an eye on things if you want. As an eagle, I mean. Wouldn't want to make you uncomfortable."

"What, because you don't have eyes when you're an eagle?"

He shrugged and leaned against the door-post. "Because I don't care what I see when I'm in a body that's not human. I still have my own thoughts, but that body doesn't seem to have human emotions. Or desires. It can be useful."

The thought of him seeing me naked, whether he cared or not, was terrifying and yet strangely exciting. I grabbed a towel for my body and one for my hair from the closet and picked my way down the rocky path to the lake, with Aren following close behind. I stopped short, and he had to step sideways to keep from running into me. "But when you change back, you'll still remember everything you saw, won't you?"

He grinned. "Yeah, I can't do anything about that. But if it makes you feel any better, I won't look. Not even a little."

"Right. I'm sure you're always a perfect gentleman." His grin widened, and I wondered what he was like with women when he was at home. Powerful, a king's son, deadly attractive, and terribly charming when he wanted to be? *God help the women of Luid.*

I started walking again, and he fell behind as we reached the dock. There was a soft rustling sound behind me, and a feathered body flew past me and up to the top of a high, bare spruce branch near the water's edge. He made himself comfortable, then twisted his neck to study the darkening clouds overhead, making it very clear that he wasn't looking at me.

I'd have liked a few moments to watch him, to appreciate the magic he'd just performed so casually, but I decided I should get into the water before he started to wonder what was taking so long. I stripped my clothes off and set them on one of the wooden crates that were nailed to the dock. He didn't look down once, not so much as a glance.

You are not disappointed in his lack of interest, human or eagle, I told myself as I dipped a toe in the water. It wasn't as cold as I'd expected. The air was freezing, though, and a sharp breeze blew in from across the water. I took my chances and made a shallow dive.

The water under the surface wasn't as cold as a lake should have been in late autumn, but was still cool enough to shock my fire-warmed body. I yelled, sending a flurry of bubbles toward the surface. I arched my back to bring me back to the air and shouted, "It's not exactly warm!"

Aren glanced down, held his wings out to the side in an "I never said it was" gesture, and went back to studying the clouds.

The soap wasn't as fancy as the stuff at the inn, but clean was clean, and it felt wonderful. The water did, too, once I was used to it. I'd been swimming naked more times than I could count when I was a child, but hadn't done so in years, and never with someone like Aren around. I'd forgotten the feeling of cool, silky water slipping over my skin.

I took a deep breath, ducked under the surface, and kicked farther out into the lake, pulling myself along with my arms and relishing the power in my muscles. I'd always loved the water, the way it surrounded me and supported me. It was like flying in a way, suspended between ground and surface. I swam until my lungs burned for air, and came up far from shore. When I looked up, Aren was alert and searching the water for me. I waved to him, and he shook his head and settled back down to preen his feathers, clearly trying to communicate that he wasn't worried. I laughed and started my swim back toward the shore.

I took a deep breath and prepared to dive under again. My breath caught in my throat as something wrapped around my ankle and tugged, pulling me straight down. I barely had time to scream before my head was underwater, the light of the surface moving swiftly away from me.

Chapter Twenty-Three

Aren

She didn't need to scream. I saw her pulled under. I lifted off and plunged toward the water before I thought about what I was doing, and realized that my eagle's body wasn't made for swimming. I would have to change. I'd never done it while I was moving so quickly, and for a second I wondered what would happen if I lost track of where I was and couldn't call my body back to me. There was no time to think. I did it as quickly as I could, and felt the familiar weight of my body rushing back to me before I hit the water. It wasn't a graceful dive, but the fall pushed me deep into the lake.

When the water slowed me, I opened my eyes. The lake water was clear, but with the sun hidden I could hardly see anything. A pale, blurry shape moved below me, struggling as it moved farther away. I kicked my legs, but she was going too quickly. She twisted, and was suddenly pulling herself toward the surface. I continued downward to try to catch a glimpse of whatever had grabbed her, hoping it wasn't what I thought, but it was gone. I turned to follow

Rowan.

She was holding onto the dock when I surfaced, her arms shaking as she struggled to pull herself up. I looked away. Keeping a casual eye on things when I was an eagle was very different from doing it now. Under other circumstances I might have offered to help, but I didn't need things to be any more awkward between us than they already were. I watched the lake for signs of trouble, but there was nothing. It was as calm and flat as it had been when I swam earlier.

"Aren?" I turned back to the dock, where she stood wrapped in a red towel that did a barely-decent job of covering her body, holding another out for me.

"I think it's gone," I said. I took her place holding on to the side of the dock while I caught my breath. Gooseflesh broke out on my skin where it was exposed to the cold air.

"What was that?" she asked.

"I didn't see anything. Just you going under."

"It felt like a hand."

"Did it?"

She held her leg out and turned her ankle from side to side. "No claws, no teeth. Grabbed like fingers."

That's impossible, I thought, trying to ignore her exposed skin. *They wouldn't.*

Without warning, something popped up from the water beside me—or rather, someone. His skin had the same faintly grayish cast to it that I remembered, barely noticeable in the overcast light. His black hair was shaggier than it had been the last time we met, but nothing else had changed.

Rowan jumped back and pulled her towel tighter around her body, but she quickly stepped forward again and held out a hand to help me out of the water.

I spoke more loudly than I meant to. "What the hell are you doing?"

He pushed his wet hair out of his eyes. "I came to ask you the same thing. I was going to be nice about it, though. And I thought there might be a girl here." He looked up at Rowan and gave her a wide, friendly grin. "Hello!"

"Watch it," I muttered, and he looked back to me.

"Aah, I see." He pulled himself up and rested one arm on the splintered wood of the dock.

"Do you welcome everyone to the lake by trying to drown them?" I demanded, gesturing toward Rowan and nearly dunking myself in the lake in the process.

"Is that what the commotion was?" He frowned. "Huh."

"What?"

"Nothing. I'll take care of it." He relaxed and smiled again, as though nothing had happened. "So it's been what, seven years?"

"About that."

"Seven years. Damn. I mean, darn. All that time and I just get a 'what the hell are you doing?' No hug for your best friend?"

"Not wearing any clothes at the moment."

He laughed. "You humans are such prudes."

Rowan knelt on the wooden boards, holding the towel so tightly that her knuckles had turned white. Or perhaps it was the cold. She was still shaking. "Excuse me—'you humans?'"

"Sorry," I said. "Rowan, this is Kel. He's not human."

"And thankful for it," Kel added. He pushed back from the dock and flipped over to dive deep into the lake, showing off a muscular, human-looking torso with gills across his sides that closed in the air. His smooth, iron-gray tail flashed above the water, broad flukes splashing as he disappeared.

Rowan gasped.

Kel turned underwater and surfaced next to her a moment later. "Completely warm-blooded though, I promise." He winked.

He really hadn't changed. I rolled my eyes and pulled myself out of the water. Rowan turned away and held out the second towel, and I dried myself and stepped into my clothes, which still lay in a messy pile where I'd dropped them. I sat at the end of the dock and dipped my feet into the water.

Rowan stood with her arms crossed. "Not to spoil the reunion, but could we please talk about what happened? Someone grabbed me and dragged me under. If it wasn't you, then who was it?"

I winced. She wasn't familiar with mer ways, their discomfort with speculation, gossip, and potential false judgment. Kel offered a reassuring smile. "I have my suspicions. No one you'd know, I'd say. Rest assured, fair lady, you're safe now."

"Thank you." Her eyes passed over what she could see of him again—quick, but not fast enough that he didn't notice. He flashed another flirtatious grin, and got a little smile in return. "Excuse me. I'm going to go over there to get dressed." She went up the path far enough to find some bushes to change behind. Kel watched her until she disappeared.

"Nice," he said. "So you two are…"

"No."

"Huh. So would you mind if I…"

"Yes."

He shook his head. "I'll never understand you people."

"Nor should you want to."

Rowan came back with her towel wrapped around her hair and crouched with her bare feet tucked under her skirt. The shock of her near-drowning seemed to be wearing off. "Am I interrupting?"

"I don't think so," Kel said. "We have a lot of catching up to do, though, and it's getting cold up here. I don't suppose you have any more clothes up at the house?"

"I think so," Rowan said. "I'll go look." She started to walk away, then turned back. "Um, pants?"

Kel laughed. "If you insist. Human magic-users aren't the only ones who can change forms. Want to see? He hauled himself out of the water and laid on the dock, the flukes of his long tail just touching the water.

Rowan's gaze flickered to the end of his tail and back. "That's fine, thanks. I'll just see about those pants."

Kel slipped back into the water, and we didn't speak again until Rowan had disappeared into the house. "How's everyone?" I asked.

"Good. Everyone's good. We heard about your father disappearing. So… Sorry, I suppose." An awkward silence followed.

"It's been too long, hasn't it? "

He looked up and studied me. "Maybe not. Depends. I'm certainly surprised to see you."

"I'm sorry, I know I said I wouldn't come back. I wouldn't have if—"

The door slammed shut up at the house. I excused myself, and went a short way up the path to meet Rowan. She carried a pair of work pants, a heavy flannel shirt, and a pair of clean wool socks.

"Sorry about that," I said. "Kel is a good person. Better than most humans I've met. He has an odd sense of humor, though. Also, he likes human women. A lot."

"Legs are fun!" Kel announced from the other side of the bushes, and Rowan smiled.

"Don't worry about it," she whispered. "He seems nice." She handed the clothes to me. "But I don't need to see him change. I'll go find something to eat."

"I'll help." I tossed the shirt and pants over the bushes onto the dock.

"Hey!" Kel yelled. "That almost landed in the—"

I threw the socks.

"Quit it! There had better not be boots coming!"

Rowan laughed again, and we started walking, taking our time. Kel caught up before we reached the cabin. He looked completely human, the gray in his skin having warmed to brown. If Rowan was surprised by any of it, she hid it. I thought she was handling everything well considering how little experience she had with magic, and felt a completely out-of-place sense of pride.

Rowan went to check on the horses, who had come

back from the woods during the night. I added wood to the fires while Kel poked through every cupboard in the house. He found a belt and was threading it through the loops on his pants when Rowan returned. "You people make your clothes so complicated."

I brought a bowl of fruit over. "You don't usually make any clothes."

"Too right. Only in this form. This sort of body tends to leave sensitive equipment just hanging out in the wind when you're not dressed." He turned to me. "You're an odd lot, you know that?"

"You may have mentioned it before."

Kel declined the food, but was happy to spend time answering Rowan's questions about the merfolk, the myth about them having scaled fish tails, where they lived and how they traveled between inland lakes, whether they could all form legs.

Kel smiled at that question. "Most can, and those who can often do. We have a beautiful place called the Grotto where we dance and cook food, and where we keep our library and beautiful things collected by those of us who choose to brave the human world."

Rowan stared past him. "I would love to see that."

"Maybe you will someday. We do occasionally invite human visitors. Do you have any other questions?"

I snorted at that. "She does, believe me."

Rowan gave me a good-natured glare. "What about the stories of mermaids intentionally making human sailors crash their ships?"

"Absolutely not," he told her. "That story is a common

one, but I've never met a mer who would want to cause that kind of harm to anyone who wasn't an enemy. I know some who might approach lonely sailors, or sing beautiful songs to them to get them through the lonely nights. It's not our fault that human men can't steer straight when they're aroused." He seemed to think this was hilarious.

I soon realized that Rowan had been holding back when she asked me about magic. She wanted to know everything, and Kel was happy to share. I should have been glad to have someone else to do the talking, but I wasn't. I hated how interested she seemed in him, how her eyes shone as she listened, how she laughed when he made a joke. Another out-of-place emotion. It was none of my business what she did.

She decided to go out and catch a chicken for supper. "Aren, can I talk to you for a minute?" she asked, and walked out the back door. She waited for me just around the corner. "These are the people we were looking for, aren't they? The ones who might be able to help me?"

"Yes."

"Why didn't you tell me?"

"I would have," I said, "but they're good at not being found. If they sensed that a stranger was searching for them, they'd have disappeared completely. Sometimes they'll investigate if they're curious, though."

She rested her hands on her hips and glared at me. "So I was *bait*?"

"What? No! Not exactly. But you did make them curious."

"If they know you, why wouldn't they have just come

to see you?"

"I'm supposed to stay away from them. Kel's band of merfolk were friends of mine when I was young, but that changed as I grew up. They know what I am, what I do, and they don't approve of how I've directed my magical gifts." She looked away, perhaps agreeing with them. "It was fine for me to be around them when I was a kid, but when I got older it got complicated. My position in the human world made me a danger to them. I volunteered to stay away, but I think they would have told me to if I hadn't offered. I think they'll help you, though, if it's within their power."

"They're that altruistic?"

"They're that curious. You should get along well with them."

She crossed her arms. "So you were just going to hand me over, and that's it? You were going to send me to this Grotto place and then disappear?"

"I didn't think you'd want to stay with me, anyway, and I didn't know what else to do." The thought that she might not want to leave was appealing, yet worrisome. "You know you'll be safer without me. I can lead Severn away, you can get your answers. They'll know who can help you."

She rubbed her temple, and I wondered if it was a headache or just frustration. I thought headache. Her eyes had a glassy, distant look to them. "I'm not going anywhere without you."

My heart skipped. "You're better off with them."

"But you won't be safe when you're alone. We both know you can't stay half-awake forever, and it's only a matter of time until Severn finds you. At least I can keep watch while you sleep." She pulled a sharp knife off of the wall and started toward the chicken coop before I could say anything else.

I stayed outside for a few minutes before I went back in. Of course I knew I couldn't keep going on my own forever, but it was too dangerous to keep her with me. Possibly pleasant, if things kept going as they were, but dangerous. I turned and went into the house before I could follow that thought any further.

Kel sat on the sofa with his bare feet on the table, wiggling his toes.

"Been a while since you've been on land?" I asked.

"Yes. Everything seems to be working, though." He folded his hands over his stomach and looked at me. I sat in a chair beside him and stared back. He tapped his thumbs together. "So," he said.

"So."

"What is this? You looked like you were going to strangle me when I showed up down there."

"You'll have to excuse that. I thought you'd just tried to drown Rowan."

"Mmm. And she's your… friend?"

"I suppose she might say that."

"And she's important to you."

I understood what he was trying to get from me. "It's not like that. I'm not sure what it is, but it's not that."

"Uh-huh." I could tell he didn't believe me, but at least he let it go. "I didn't think we'd see you again."

"Neither did I. I meant what I said about leaving you alone. I'm not asking you to help me."

"That's good. We've heard what's happening. We can't be involved with Severn." The merfolk had reason to be aware of what humans were doing. They'd seen what we'd done to each other over the years, and they tried to be prepared in case we decided to try to harm them or their home in the same ways.

Before I could ask, he added, "I don't know whether Severn knows you're here, but I haven't heard that anyone's looking for you, if it makes you feel any better."

"It doesn't, but thank you."

He wiggled his toes again. "I can keep my ears open for you as long as you're here. I just hope it doesn't cause problems for us." That was the closest Kel would come to questioning my decision to come back. He didn't have to tell me that the mer elders wouldn't be pleased to hear I'd returned. "I'm assuming it's no coincidence that you stopped here. And I would love to know what you're doing with Rowan."

It wasn't as difficult for me to explain things to Kel as it had been to tell Rowan, either because I was starting to understand the situation better, or because he let me talk without interruptions. When I finished the story and explained why I'd helped her, leaving out any reference to my confused emotions, he smirked.

"That's it? You just felt like you owed her something?"

My back stiffened. "Yes. And I appreciated her kindness. It was more than I'm accustomed to."

"So if she had been an unattractive, smelly old man and had done the same thing, you'd have thrown away your life in Luid, helped him escape from that boat, and nearly killed yourself trying to convince him he was a Sorcerer?" He rolled his eyes. "Sure you would have. It had nothing to do with her being a sweet, intelligent, attractive young woman with a fantastic ass and a need for someone to save her."

"She's quite capable of saving herself, believe me. She just needed to be pointed in the right direction."

"Right. And that's not appealing to you either." He leaned forward and took a sip from the mug on the table in front of him. "I still have so many questions, but we'll stick with Rowan's problems for now. You could be right about her. So why did you bring her here?"

"I couldn't take her to anyone in Luid. Anyone in Tyrea, actually. There's no one I can trust now, and until something is done about the binding, she's in danger. If you can't help, I'm not sure what we'll do. I thought about taking her beyond Tyrea, to Belleisle, but I don't think they'd help."

"Certainly not you. They might take Rowan, if she went alone. That may be what needs to happen. We could get more information for you, but you know that our magic only works in us. We might not be able to fix this."

I'd expected as much, but hearing him say it was disappointing. "Your healers are better than ours," I said. "They might at least help the pain while everything else is being worked out. And you'll be able to find someone who can help her."

"Hmm. But again, I doubt Mariana and Arnav will allow you to come. You think she'd go with me if you stayed here?"

"No," Rowan said. I'd become so accustomed to her

presence that my extended awareness didn't alert me when she'd come back in.

Kel looked from me to Rowan and back. He sighed. "I'll see what I can do. But Rowan, it might come to a decision between finding a way to free your magic, or hanging around with this guy." He swung his feet onto the floor and walked to her, then touched her cheek and looked into her eyes for a few seconds. "Give me a day or two. I'll talk to the elders."

She took a step back as he released her. "You're not staying for supper?"

"No, I have to get home, see what I can find out about your little adventure earlier, talk to the elders. Do you mind if Aren walks me down to the dock?"

"Take him. I have to get the food started anyway."

They exchanged nice-to-meet-yous, and Kel and I stepped out into the cold. I knew better than to ask what he'd seen in her. Merfolk didn't look into people's thoughts the way I did, but in a far less invasive way they were incredibly perceptive. I wanted to know, but prying would be rude.

"Be careful with her," Kel said. "She has a lot on her mind, more than a person should have to deal with all at once. Just give her time, she'll work it out." We reached the dock, and he stepped out of his clothes and handed them to me. I put everything in one of the wooden crates in case he needed it again. He looked out over the dull gray water. "Try to be honest with yourself about what you're feeling for her."

"I don't—"

He held up one hand to stop me. "I know, you don't want to feel anything. It's against your family's religion or something."

"No, I mean I can't let anything like that happen. I told her I'd try to help her. You know as well as I do that staying with me is a bad idea."

Kel looked back at me and raised an eyebrow. "Do you think she'd agree?"

I didn't answer. I had no idea what she thought or wanted.

"I'll see what I can do for her," Kel said, "if you're sure that's what's best. It'll be up to her, though."

"Of course. Thank you." I turned and walked back up the path, and Kel splashed into the water behind me. I took my time walking back toward the welcoming light of the house, trying to sort through my unwelcome emotions as I went.

Thus far, I had managed to ignore it when my body responded to her. I would do the same when I was tempted to let emotion overrule my mind. Even if I wanted her.

Gods, I want her.

I gritted my teeth and walked toward the house, ready to do battle with myself. It wouldn't be for much longer, now.

Chapter Twenty-Four

Aren

I decided to check on the horses before I went in to talk to Rowan. They'd wandered off to forage again, in spite of the more than adequate supply of food we'd left them in the stable. It wasn't snowing yet, but the air had the heavy feel of an approaching storm, and I wasn't prepared to lose the horses if it came during the night. I made the stalls as comfortable as I could, then went searching for them.

I found Rowan's horse in the garden, digging up what root vegetables the summer people had left behind. I clucked my tongue and she came along easily enough. Mine wasn't in the yard, so I took a lead rope and followed the only path into the woods.

I hadn't gone far when a rustling noise from behind a thick stand of pines stopped me. I moved quietly in case it was something other than the horse. The lake was a safe enough place in the summer, but I didn't know what creatures might take advantage of the never-frozen water during the winter.

It was nothing but the black and white horse, standing

in a small clearing and rubbing her hairy side against a tree with a thick, twisted trunk. I clipped the rope to her halter and started to walk away, but turned back. The bright pink leaves blended in with the other autumn colors in the dim light, and I'd almost missed it. The horse had been rubbing her hide on a heartleaf tree.

"Good girl," I whispered, and patted her neck. Rowan would need the bark. It might bring some relief, but it was no cure. She'd have to go with Kel. I just needed to convince her of that.

The first snowflakes fell as I returned to the house. Only a few, but there would be more.

"How did you know?" Rowan asked as I handed her the strands of heartleaf bark. "I was just wishing I had some. Can you give me a hand with the food?"

The meal was delicious, but Rowan hardly ate anything. She was also uncharacteristically quiet, and I wondered whether she'd used up her daily allotment of questions on Kel. More likely she was thinking about one or more of the questions neither he nor I could answer. Wondering whether she'd go with the merfolk if they decided to help her, what she would do after someone fixed her problem, how any of this had happened in the first place.

Instead of talking, we listened to the sounds of the storm building outside, the wind rushing through the trees and the icy snow tapping at the windows.

"I think I'm going to use the bark and go to bed," she said after the table was cleared. "Do you mind washing up?"

"Of course not."

She poured hot water into a teapot, then added some to a jug that looked like it had come from one of the upstairs washbasins. "I'm going to try sleeping upstairs," she explained. "The fires have been burning all day, and I'll take blankets from the other upstairs bed. I'll come down if it's too cold."

She carried the jug upstairs, and returned as I was finishing with the dishes. She wore a blue, pinstriped nightshirt, thick wool socks, and had her hair brushed and pulled forward over one shoulder, her face freshly washed. She looked down and grimaced. "What do you think?"

I thought she could probably make an old grain sack look good if she decided to wear one, but didn't say so. "Your cousin would be horrified."

"No doubt." She smiled, but when she came closer I saw that her eyes had that distant, glassy look again.

She was quiet again while she drank her tea, and seemed troubled. I wanted to reach out to touch her face, to smooth the tension from her brow, to tell her that she was going to get through this and it would all work out. Instead, I sat across from her and watched the snow falling outside the window. Nothing I did would help.

When the medicine was gone, she stood and said, "Well, I'm going to—whoa." She dropped back into the chair. "Are you sure that was heartleaf? I feel like a big fluffy cloud just punched me in the face."

"Oh, I forgot." I tried not to laugh. "The trees here are stronger, remember? You probably should have used a bit less."

"Oh, the thing with the dragons and more magic here,"

she said, and waved a hand through the air in front of her. "I'll get used to it."

"Is it helping the pain?"

She tilted her head to one side. "Not yet, but I don't care about it so much. I'm sleepy, though." She stood and almost fell over again. I pushed my chair away and grabbed her arm to steady her.

"Let me help you upstairs," I said. "You can lie down, but I don't think you should go to sleep until this wears off a little."

"I'm fine. My legs are just a little, you know." She flapped her hands around to demonstrate. They were, too. We were only half-way up the stairs when they went out from under her again. I bent and scooped her up to carry her the rest of the way. She reached up and touched my face. "You're pretty."

"Thanks." It would have hurt her feelings if I'd laughed, but it was difficult not to. She sounded so sincere. I carried her to the bedroom and set her down on the bed, where she wiggled under the heavy quilt.

I lit the glass-chimney oil lamp next to the bed and turned to leave. "Don't fall asleep, I'm just getting more blankets." The house wasn't insulated against winter weather, and even with the door open to the warmth downstairs the air was cold.

She looked slightly more alert when I returned, but I still didn't like the idea of her sleeping right away. I remembered the way she'd looked wearing that red towel by the lake, and my mind was flooded with ideas of ways to keep her awake, none of which were at all appropriate for the situation.

Just stop, I told myself. *You only want her because you can't have her.*

Rowan shifted to make room on the bed. "Come here," she said. "If you want me to stay awake, you need to help."

My heart skipped a beat.

"Tell me a story."

That's probably a better idea.

I sat on top of the blankets she'd pulled up to her chest. "I'm not good at it, but I'll try. What do you want to hear?" I thought I could probably remember a story I'd heard when I was younger, or I'd find something in that children's book downstairs. Or perhaps some Tyrean history. To a person as unaccustomed to magic as she was, this land's past would probably sound like one of her beloved fairy tales.

"Can I have any story?" She yawned, wrinkling her nose.

"Any one I can remember."

"Any one," she mumbled, and closed her eyes. I thought she was falling asleep, but her eyes snapped open again and slowly focused on my face. "I want yours. You never say much about your past. I want to hear your story."

"I don't think that's a good idea. How about something with a dragon, or a princess or something?"

She shook her head, and a section of her hair fell over one eye. "You said any story you could remember. And don't say you don't remember, because I know you do. Besides, the princesses in stories are all useless." She yawned again. "Always need a prince to save them."

"You obviously haven't met any Tyrean princesses."

"Nope. Your story."

It was almost the same trick she'd pulled with the dragon, and I'd fallen for it. "It's not important." I brushed her hair back behind her ear, and she shivered.

"It is to me. Please?"

I wondered whether there was a polite way to ask her to stop saying things that made me feel so warm and pleasant, and decided there wasn't. I almost started with "once upon a time," but remembered that those stories always ended with a "happily ever after." I left it out. No one in my story had one of those. "The first thing you need to understand," I said instead, and Rowan settled deeper under the blankets and rested her head on my arm. "Don't go to sleep."

"I'm not. This is worth staying awake for."

"The first thing you need to understand is that marriages in the ruling family of Tyrea can be more complicated than they are in your country."

She lifted her head. "Oh my God, you're married."

"No. Stop interrupting. Magic is a very good thing, but it causes a few problems. One is that two people who both have strong magic can't have children together. We don't know why, it just doesn't work. It's not usually a problem, because there are very few true Sorceresses. A Potioner could have children with whoever she chooses, but if the father is a Sorcerer, the child will most likely have nothing of either type of magic. If a family is going to stay in power, there needs to be an heir with strong magic, so a king will take several wives, all without magic themselves, but it's somewhere in their family lines. My mother was my father's fourth secondary wife."

"Secondary?"

"There's only one queen. All others are secondaries. Likewise if a Sorceress rules, as my grandmother did. Several husbands, one primary."

"It's all so romantic," she muttered, and settled back down against my arm.

"Love isn't a consideration. In fact, it's discouraged. A ruler has more important things to think about, and love for wives or family is a dangerous distraction. It makes people do stupid things. Makes them weak."

She didn't seem to have anything to say to that, so I continued. "A king takes three secondary wives. It's enough to nearly guarantee at least one child with strong magic, if he's chosen his wives carefully. The selections are complicated, businesslike. My father met my mother when he was traveling in the Eastern provinces, long after he'd married the others. He took her as a fourth secondary wife, and justified it by saying that there was no child from his third marriage."

The wording of that had always bothered me. No one ever said that they'd had no children, only that there weren't any by the time my mother came along. "I'm told she was quite beautiful, and a kinder, more innocent sort of person than should ever have been brought to court. The other wives hated her. She was from too far away, and they were jealous of her."

"Because he loved her."

"I think he did, at least as much as he was capable. I was born a little over a year later, and she died three years after that. But that story can wait for another time. You could probably sleep now."

"It's okay if you can't talk about it."

I sighed. "I can, if you really want to know."

She nodded without looking up.

"Severn is the queen's son, and twenty years older than me. He had—still has—a lot of firm ideas about how things should be, and he's had a burning desire for power for as long as I've known him. He knew that our father favored my mother over his, and hated her for it. He watched her carefully, and managed to intercept letters between her and some enemy of my father's. Instead of exposing her, Severn and his mother went to the king privately with the information. Severn threatened to make my mother's actions public if she didn't do something. The queen and Severn were planning to visit her family—the queen's, not my mother's. When they returned, they wanted to find the last wife not imprisoned, but dead, as proof of the king's strength and as punishment for what she'd done. After all, an extra secondary wife who had already produced a child shouldn't have mattered to him. My father had to choose between losing his throne to Severn, or killing her."

Rowan gasped. "He didn't!"

"I don't know whether he did it himself, but it was done. The queen was angry that he disposed of the body before her return, but he told her that he'd had enough, that even a king's last wife deserved a decent burial, and he wasn't going to have her present to make a mockery of it. She was still the queen after that, but I don't know if he ever spoke to her again except for official business."

"You say all of this like it's nothing to you."

"It was something at the time. No one told me what my father had done, of course. I didn't learn that until just a few years ago, not long before he disappeared. I knew she was gone, though. I barely remember it now, but I was heartbroken. I cried. I behaved badly. I slept little, and when I did, I had nightmares and screamed for her. Things like that aren't allowed to go on for long in my family. It's weakness."

I almost felt something then, almost remembered the pain, but I didn't have any tears left—not for myself, for my dead mother, or for anything that came after.

Someone did, though. I felt wetness soaking into the sleeve of my shirt. "Are you crying for me, or for her?" I asked. "I'm fine."

"For her, a bit. Mostly for that little boy who wasn't allowed to love his own mother." She sniffled, and I put my arm around her shoulders. Her hair smelled like the lake, fresh and clean. I rested my head on hers, just for a moment.

"I was fortunate, really. When my mother was in Luid, she chose loyal servants for herself who became her friends. Most of them left after she died, but her maid Mona stayed, and Mona's husband John, who was a healer. They cared for me, and I'm fortunate that they did. My father wanted nothing to do with me. I think I reminded him too much of her. My mother had a house on this lake, a gift from my father, and they brought me here every summer."

"To this house?"

"No, it's on the other side of the lake. I thought Severn

might think to look there. This house belonged to Mrs. Pritchen, a friend of Mona's. I wanted to stay here because it has smokestone-lined chimneys. So we were here at the lake every summer, and I met Kel and the others when I was eight years old."

"And you came here until you were…"

"Sixteen. That was a good summer."

"And then what?"

"You know, I should go check the fire." I tried to sit up, but Rowan dug her fingers into my arm and held on.

This part was harder. I didn't remember my mother, but I remembered Mona and John. "I wanted to come alone that summer. Mona and John spent some time elsewhere. They were arrested as soon as they returned to the city without me, sentenced to death, and the sentence carried out before I knew anything about it."

Rowan let go of me and sat up. "What? Why?"

"The official documents say they were convicted of abducting a member of the royal family, and that it was suspected they'd killed me. My father wasn't pleased. The charges were obviously false, and it made him look foolish. I believed Severn was responsible, but couldn't prove it. He told me to let it go, that I was too old to need them. He was right about that. I wasn't a child anymore. But they were like family to me, and John was a good teacher. Too good. He helped me develop my magic enough to make Severn realize that he could use me.

"Severn oversaw my training after they died. I hated him, but had no choice but to do what he wanted. In time, I learned to set my resentment aside and forget—Ouch."

Rowan had grabbed onto my wrist, and was gripping so hard that her nails bit into my skin.

"I'm sorry. It's just… is your entire family evil?"

"No. Power-hungry, certainly, and proud, and used to getting what we want. I did come back to the lake once after that, briefly, to tell the merfolk that I would stay away. We were at odds by then over my magic, and I wasn't exactly welcome. The situation with Severn just made that decision easier."

"Why?"

"Because everyone I'd ever cared about got hurt. My mother, Mona and John. There was a little girl I used to play with when I was a child, and she just disappeared around the same time as my mother, no explanation. Even people I didn't care about weren't safe. There was a theologian in Luid who I asked about the things my brothers and I did to people. I wanted to know whether our souls were lost, and I asked whether there was a hell, and if we were going there. He answered me, and when Severn found out, he had the man killed so that no one would learn about my doubts. I think Severn thought he was protecting me. That was long after I stopped coming to the lake, though."

"What did he say?"

"Who?"

"The priest guy. What was his answer?"

It wasn't hard to remember. I heard the words in my mind every time I thought about going against my brother. "He said that my duty in this world was to be loyal to my family, and that I would be rewarded for it. That if it was damnation I sought, I would find it 'surely and quickly' by defying those who had authority over me. I've certainly done that. I guess I'll have to wait and see if he was right."

Rowan was silent for a minute. Her body was still tucked in close to mine, but to me it felt like a chasm had opened between us. Words didn't exist that could make her understand all of it.

I was about to leave when she pushed herself higher on the bed and whispered, "I'm sorry." She kissed me high on my cheekbone.

I drew in a quick breath. It wasn't often that someone surprised me. She pulled away and lay back on her pillow, dark hair spread out behind her, glowing in the lamplight. Wetness still reflected in her eyes, but she was calm, and seemed more at peace than I'd seen her before.

"Sorry for what?" I asked, and looked away. She was too much.

"For everything that happened. For making you talk about it."

I hoped my story wasn't going to give her unpleasant dreams. "I've had good times in my life, too. They were just less significant things. And don't be sorry for asking. Maybe hearing all of that will help you understand why I am what I am."

She closed her eyes. "I think it does, a little. Sleep well."

I went to the door and turned back to say goodnight, but she was already asleep.

Chapter Twenty-Five
Rowan

We were back in the cupboard at the inn, though now there was enough light that I could just see Aren's face when I looked up. I knew it was a dream, but some things seemed clearer than they had when I was awake. The questions that never stopped clamoring for attention in my waking mind became insignificant, and there was nothing outside of that space that mattered.

I stretched up on my toes and clasped my hands behind his neck. "Kiss me," I whispered.

He didn't hesitate. He wrapped his arms around me and pulled me closer, and then his lips were on mine. A bolt of warm energy shot through me, and I was suddenly aware of how our bodies were forced together in that small space. I hadn't noticed before how my breasts were pressed against his ribs, but I felt it now, and tried to pull him closer, to eliminate every bit of space between our bodies. I felt him smile, and he reached up to touch my face, to wind his fingers through my hair as our kiss deepened. His other hand traced the line of my shoulder, then trailed across my collarbone and slipped inside my open jacket, teasing me through the thin fabric of my shirt. His tongue—

A crashing noise jerked me from my dreams, and I found myself sitting up in bed, heart pounding. The room was dark, my headache was gone, and I was alone. I pulled the heavy blankets tight around me, as though they would protect me from danger as they did from the room's frozen air.

There were no more noises. No wind outside, no crashes, no creak of the bed saying that Aren was up to check on things. I leaned out of bed, retrieved the socks that I'd kicked off in my sleep, and left the safety of my room. I paused at the top of the stairs, listening, then crept down and through the sitting room. Nothing seemed out of place.

The door to the little room off of the kitchen creaked when I opened it. Aren shifted in the larger bed. "'S a book," he mumbled. "Knocked over a thing. Don't worry 'bout it."

I would have asked how he knew that, but he seemed to be asleep again, and enjoying a more restful night than I was. He lay on his stomach with the blankets pushed almost down to his waist. Though it was warmer in that room than it had been upstairs, there was still a chill in the air. I reached out to pull the blankets up.

I paused with my hand in mid-air, and squinted. *How did I not see that before?*

A massive scar covered half his back—or at least, I thought that's what it was. The center of it, just beneath his right shoulder blade, looked like the remains of a badly-healed wound, a rippled mess of pale skin. Fainter scars branched out from it, spreading across his shoulder and ribs, silver in the dim moonlight that filtered through the curtains. They reminded me of the patterns that show on a window after a frost, or vines climbing a wall. I felt terrible for prying information from him earlier, but I knew I'd be asking about this in the morning.

I pulled the blankets up, and my cold fingers brushed over the unmarked skin of his arm. He shivered, and I wondered what dreams I might have disturbed.

I climbed into the cot and pulled the quilt over me. It was too cold to go back upstairs. As I drifted off, I hoped my dreams wouldn't pick up where they'd left off. Pleasant as they'd been, I didn't want him to see them.

As it turned out, I worried for nothing. I woke alone in the room with a faint pounding behind my eyes and a vague memory of dreaming about something burning. Though I felt relief that Aren hadn't showed up in my mind, I was disappointed to have not found out where the first dream had been going. But what did that dream say about me?

Maybe I could blame it on the heartleaf.

I stretched and rolled out of bed. Aren was already dressed and sitting at the table. I muttered "good morning" as I passed him on my way upstairs. I shed the nightgown and pulled on a pair of warm pants and a thin sweater from the closet, then raced back to the warmth downstairs. I went to look outside. Snow had drifted halfway up the window overnight, and I couldn't see over it. I supposed being snowed in wasn't the worst thing that could happen to us. The horses were snug in the stable, and we had enough food.

Aren joined me at the window, and I tried not to notice how close he was standing. "Can you see anything?" I asked.

"Yes. Snow."

"Thank you."

"Any time." I held my breath until he turned and went to add wood to the stove. "Were you too cold upstairs?" he asked.

"Yes. I was fine until I woke up, but you were right. It's warmer down here. Um, if you don't mind me asking, I noticed on your back…"

He grimaced. "The scar?"

I nodded.

"I think I mentioned Severn trying to kill me when I was younger. That's what he left me with. He attacked me with pure magic. I would have died if John hadn't been there to heal me, or if Mona hadn't looked after me in the months it took me to recover. No big story for that one."

"So the magic made it all fancy?"

He smiled, and the memory of my dream hit me, the way that smile felt against my lips.

"I suppose," he said.

"Can I see it again?"

He gave me a strange look, but shrugged. He sat facing backward on a dining chair and pulled off his sweater and the shirt beneath. In the bright light of morning the patterns were less visible, white against his already pale skin and showing only a hint of the silver color that the moonlight had brought out. I rested a hand on his shoulder, barely touching him. His skin felt almost feverish in its warmth.

"Do you mind?" I whispered.

"No."

I traced my finger over the scar, brushing over the uneven skin in the center and trailing down to where the curves ended at the bottom of his ribcage, then around and up to his shoulder, over muscles that were hard and tense beneath his skin. The tendrils continued up, and I brushed his hair aside so I could see where they ended on his neck, curled like a fiddlehead fern behind his ear.

A faint tremor ran over his back. I wondered if he could hear my heart pounding, whether he felt what I did.

Aren reached up and wrapped his hand gently around mine. "Rowan, I don't think—"

A knock at the door interrupted him, and a look of panic crossed his face as he turned. I stepped back, and he walked to the window with long, fluid strides, appearing ready for whatever might be out there.

"It's all right," he said, and pulled his sweater back on. He unlocked the door and Kel shuffled in, carrying a large silver-brown fish by the tail. He wore the pants and shirt he'd borrowed the day before, and nothing on his snow-covered feet.

"Thanks," he said. "So, what's happening? Everyone have a good night?"

"Good enough," Aren said, and went to put the kettle on.

Kel flopped into a chair. "Aren, Cassia says hello. She

didn't want to come up, said snow makes her skin itch."

"Who?" I asked.

"Oh, Cassia's my sister. She and Aren used to—" he glanced at Aren. "They were friends."

"I see." I looked at the fish, which now hung from Kel's hand with its face resting on the floor, flat eyes staring at nothing. "So, about that trout?"

Kel seemed to have forgotten about it. "Oh, breakfast, if you haven't eaten yet. I can clean it."

"I've got it." Aren took the fish and grabbed a slim knife from a kitchen drawer. "I was going to let the horses out, anyway. Might as well do this outside."

Kel settled back into his chair and wiped his hands on the leg of his pants. "Decent sort of chap, isn't he?"

"Seems to be, sometimes. Can I ask you something?"

"I assume so."

I sat on the table in front of him and leaned in. "You and Aren haven't seen each other in years, and I'm sure you have some idea of what he's been up to during that time."

"Hmm, I see what you mean. Disappointing, but not surprising given what and where he came from."

"And it doesn't bother you?"

"Bother me? No, it's his life, not mine. I have no say in it. My people and I wished things could have been different, but he did what he thought he had to do, and he had the decency to keep us out of it. But I think what you're wondering is why I'm not more cautious of him now."

"Yes."

"You seem comfortable with what you know about him so far, which is at least enough to make you ask these questions, so…" He spread his hands before him. "I don't know why you're so attached to him, but that's between the two of you. As for me, my people are excellent judges of character, and we don't second-guess our instincts." Kel's brown eyes grew distant. "I remember the last time I saw Aren before this. He was becoming so cold. Not cruel yet, but hard and empty. I was very surprised to see him yesterday, and you with him. He's changed again. Not back to the person he was when he was younger, but he's certainly not who I thought he'd become. I should tell you that I have no way of knowing whether this is permanent. You humans change like the tides. But for now, he's someone I'm happy to call a friend. Good enough?"

I sighed, relieved. I hardly knew Kel, but I still trusted his judgment more than my own where Aren was concerned. "Yes, thank you."

After breakfast, Kel asked if he could have a few minutes alone with Aren. "Of course," I said. "I'm going to make a cup of heartleaf and lie down."

Aren followed me to the kitchen. "Not too strong, though." He looked like he was holding back laughter.

"I know." I thought back to the evening before. I remembered what he'd told be about himself and his family, but what else? I didn't recall much about going to bed, except… *Oh, no.* My face grew warm.

"Did I tell you you were pretty last night?" I whispered.

That damned smile again. "You did."

"Oh." I pinched bark into a cup—about a third of the amount I'd used the night before—and added the water. The strong dose had kept the pain away for longer than I was accustomed to, but I didn't even want to think about what I'd tell him if I tried it again. "I'm sorry."

"It's okay. I bet you're fun when you're drunk."

I took my tea to the little bedroom and closed the door behind me. I drank it as it cooled, and fell asleep to the muffled, comforting sound of their voices.

#

I didn't sleep long, and didn't dream. I did wake thinking about Callum, though. That was over for me. No matter what happened, no matter what he knew about magic and whether I found a cure for my problem or not, I wasn't going back.

But he didn't know any of this. Was he still looking for me? I'd intended to send him a letter when we stopped in a town, but hadn't had a chance to do it. I would have to find a way. I'd tell him I was safe, and tell him what I'd learned about magic. My parents and uncle Ches, too. I wasn't going to be coming home any time soon, and I didn't want them to worry any more than they had to.

Kel and Aren didn't turn when the door opened. Kel was lounging with one leg up on the sofa. A large sheet of paper was rolled up on the table, next to my dragon scale. "An eagle, though?" Kel asked Aren. "Really? You couldn't have gone with something aquatic? It's so much more fun."

"You might be a bit biased," Aren said. "Being stuck underwater isn't convenient for all of the traveling I have to do. It's nothing personal."

I leaned over the back of the sofa and whispered, "It's totally personal."

Kel narrowed his eyes at Aren. "I knew it." He swung his leg down and patted the space next to him, and I sat. The seat of the sofa was high, and my feet barely touched the ground. I crossed them under me, instead.

"I'm not interrupting, am I?"

"Not in the least," Kel said. "We've just been catching up, making some plans. It's been interesting. But I should head home soon." He looked at Aren, then back to me. "I need to know whether you're coming with me."

"Whether we're—" I began.

Aren shook his head. "Rowan, they can't get involved in what's happening with me. Taking you in is different. Severn never needs to know where you went, and he'll find another sorcerer to use. It shouldn't matter to him, as long as he gets me."

"We're happy to have you, Rowan," Kel added. "We have trouble leaving a puzzle unsolved, and your binding could be an interesting challenge. I don't know how much help we'll be, but we'll try. The elders are looking forward to meeting you. But I can't bring Aren back with me."

"How can you both be so calm about this?" I asked, and pushed myself to my feet again. I turned to Aren. "What are you going to do?"

"Get away from here before Severn knows I've been in contact with the merfolk. After that, I don't know." I looked harder into his eyes and saw that the calm was an act. I just couldn't tell what was underneath.

"Then no."

"Rowan," Aren said, but I didn't give him a chance to finish.

"No. I'm sorry, Kel, and I appreciate the offer more than I can say. I would love to meet your people, and having you solve my puzzle would change my life so much…"

"But you're not coming."

"No."

Kel considered for a moment. "Have you thought that it might be easier for Aren on his own? Easier to hide, or to escape if there's trouble?"

I hadn't. "Is that true?" I asked Aren. "Because if you don't want me around, just say you want me to go."

"You should—"

"No, I don't want to hear what you think I *should* do. If you don't want me around, I want you to say it."

Aren opened his mouth to speak, then closed it and looked away. "I can't do this." He stood and walked out the front door, letting it swing shut and latch behind him.

I wanted to run after him and ask what that meant. He didn't want to hurt me? Or did he have feelings for me that were as confusing as mine for him?

I sank back onto the sofa and slumped against the cushions. "It's only a matter of time before they find him, isn't it?"

"Possibly."

"And Severn will kill him when he does."

"If Aren's lucky. But there's nothing you can do about that." His words sounded callous, but there was sadness in Kel's voice.

"So you're just going to let it happen?"

Kel drew in a deep breath and let it out slowly. "It's not up to me. Nor should it be. Our elders make decisions that affect every one of us, and this is what they've decided is best."

"I understand."

"So you'll come with me? I'll take you to the Grotto, you'll meet my people. We can do tests to see what's happened to you, how strong your magic is. Figure out how to help you, maybe who can help you—"

"Thank you so much, but I can't leave him." I tried to smile. "Foolish, right?"

Kel returned a smile that was warmer and more genuine than mine. "Not at all, actually."

I walked him to the door. "I really wish I could come. If the rest of your people are anything like you, I think I'd have liked them very much."

"They'd have liked you, too." He held out his arms, and I hugged him around his waist. We walked together to the dock, where Aren sat on a crate, looking out over the cold, gray lake. He gave Kel a questioning look, and Kel shook his head.

"Can I have a little longer to talk to her about this?" Aren asked.

"Maybe. I'll come back tomorrow if I can, but I shouldn't risk being seen."

"Thank you."

I turned to climb the path back to the house. I knew what Aren was going to say, and I wasn't ready to hear it.

Chapter Twenty-Six

Rowan

Aren closed the door harder coming in than he had going out. I was in the kitchen putting away dishes, trying again to make mindless work do my thinking for me.

"What are you doing?" he asked, nearly yelling as he stalked toward me. "You have to go."

"Do I? I thought I had a choice in this." I managed to keep my voice cool and level, but inside I was trembling. I couldn't look at him.

"You do," he said more quietly, but no less intensely. "But this might be your only chance to make this right. Even if they can't fix this, they can keep you safe until they find someone who can."

"Maybe." I put down the plate I was holding and gripped the edge of the counter. "Do you want me to go? Tell me honestly."

If I was mistaken in thinking that he might feel something for me, that would make my decision simple. I knew that going with Kel was the reasonable thing to do, but I wasn't feeling particularly reasonable. He'd have to say it.

"Honestly?" He stood so close behind me that I felt him on my skin, though he didn't touch me. "It doesn't matter what I want. There's nothing here for you. Nothing good, and no happy ending. You know what you should do."

"I don't think what I should do and what I want to do are the same thing." I turned and nearly bumped into his chest. He'd taken off his sweater, and wore only a shirt that was thin enough that I could see the shape of his body behind it. His pulse beat hard at his throat.

He half-smiled, but his eyes were tired and unhappy. He reached out to touch my hair, then let his hand drop to his side. "Rowan, I think a lot of your problem is that you don't know what you want."

"Don't I?" I followed him as he walked back to the sitting area.

"Not as far as I can tell. When I met you, you were having so much trouble making a decision about getting married that your cousin practically had to decide for you."

"Because I knew that I didn't want—"

He spun to face me. "Then you should have gone and found what you *did* want. Instead you were going to try to convince yourself that whatever you were getting was good enough, even though you knew better."

"You think it would have been easy for me to say no? To pack up and leave?" My muscles tensed as I stepped closer.

"No. But if you go now, if your magic can be unbound, you can do anything. *Anything.* But you don't even know if you want that, do you? You're still afraid of it."

I hesitated for a moment. My anger left me, but my heart

continued to pound as I looked into his eyes. I wanted him. Wanted him to kiss me, to touch me. I swallowed hard, though my mouth had gone dry. "You don't think you can want something and still be afraid of it?"

He sighed. "No, you can. And you should. What you're saying no to is better than you can imagine. This decision should be so easy. You have until tomorrow to decide what you—"

I stepped closer again. "I don't need until tomorrow. I know what I want." I grabbed the front of his shirt, pulled myself up onto my toes, and kissed him. Hard. He froze for just a second, and then his mouth moved against mine. He touched my face, wrapped a hand around the back of my neck and pulled me in. His response was better than anything I'd dreamed, or ever could have. My legs felt like they were melting away. I pulled back, and he sank to the couch, breathing hard. I kissed his forehead. "Can I have that?"

He just looked at me for seconds that seemed to stretch into hours. His gaze left mine and dropped to watch his hand move to my waist. "This is a terrible idea," he murmured as he pulled me onto his lap. "Have you even thought about—"

"I don't need to." I pressed my lips to his again and wrapped my arms around his neck, and let my jaw relax as his did, opening slightly to let him in. Warmth flooded my body as he let me fall back onto the couch. His lips never left mine as he turned to lie over me. For a moment I was afraid—uncertain in spite of my bold actions, lost in my inexperience. But my desire washed away my fear as he ran his hand up my arm and over my throat, over the outside of my shirt. *This is what I've been waiting for.* I arched my back to push against him. His touch sent waves of pleasure through me that settled between my thighs, and I groaned and ground my hips against him.

He drew in a quick breath and grabbed my thigh to hold me still. I pulled his hand back up to my breast. He made me feel dizzier than I had after the strong heartleaf medicine, and I wanted more. So much more. I tried to pull his shirt over his head, but he pulled back, lifting himself to his forearms.

"We can't do this. Not now."

I ran my fingers through his hair, and in my frustration pulled harder than I meant to. "Why? I'm not going, either way."

"And I don't want you to. You can stay as long as you want, but…"

I shifted under him, and he took another sharp breath.

"But what? Do you have some moral objection?" *Because it's pretty obvious that you want to.*

"No. Maybe I should, but I don't. If we knew no one was looking for us, it would be different."

I placed the palm of my hand against his chest to feel the solid contours of his muscles, then trailed my fingers over his stomach. He reached down and threaded his fingers through mine, then moved my hand away.

He leaned down to kiss my jaw just below my ear. "But they are looking for us," he whispered, and pulled away again. "I have to at least try to stay aware of what's happening outside of this house. Every time you're close to me, my focus slips. You saw how easily Kel sneaked up on us this morning when you were touching my scar. I don't ever want to say no to you. But we should think about whether this is really worth dying for."

You tell me, I thought. I wanted so badly to find out. I took a few deep breaths to steady myself.

"Rowan?"

"I'm thinking."

He smiled and kissed me again, more gently than he had before. "I said I was going to keep you safe, and I'd like to spend a bit more time with you before—" The smile vanished, and he rolled off of me and sat up. "I can't let them find you."

I pulled a cushion over my face and screamed into it. "So what are we supposed to do? Just hang around here and I'll try not to touch you, ever? That might kill me, anyway."

"I don't know. Let me think about it." He stood and said something about finding a snowbank to lie down in, and walked out the front door.

Deep breaths, I told myself. I rolled onto my stomach and laid there until my heart slowed and the fire in my skin cooled. When I stepped outside, Aren had changed and was soaring over the lake. *Probably the best thing for now*, I thought, and wished I could set aside my emotions so easily.

He spotted me and swooped down. His landing wasn't perfect, but it was better than his previous attempts. He perched on the fence beside me and nibbled at the sleeve of my shirt.

"Get off," I said, but I leaned over and kissed the side of his beak. He winked at me and took off again.

This is the weirdest thing ever. I went back inside and found a book to try to keep my mind off of him.

It didn't work.

#

I'd been cooking since I was old enough to stand on a chair and help Della measure flour, but that night I found that preparing even a simple meal of vegetables and the previous night's chicken was nearly impossible. I forgot what I was doing every time Aren came close to me. When he touched my waist as he went past, I burned my hand on a pot of boiling water. We sat at the table before we ate, and he rubbed Sara's salve into my skin. I could have done it myself. I didn't want to.

Later, he showed me the map that he and Kel had drawn while I was asleep. It was a beautiful thing, a simple drawing of charcoal on yellowing paper. The eastern part of Darmid filled the left edge of the page, with the mountains, the isthmus that divided our lands, and my home province spilling east from there. To the right, Tyrea spread out like a living thing, arms and legs stretching into the ocean. A large island nearly touched the eastern edge, and smaller ones freckled the shores and bays. They'd sketched in mountains, rivers and lakes, and the country was divided by dash-lines into six territories.

"Where are we?" I asked, and Aren pointed to a lake that seemed far too close to the border with Darmid. He had to lean close to do it, and my heart stumbled over itself as his hair tickled my skin. I took a deep breath. "We can't have only come that far."

"It's not a small country. You can see how flying is most convenient when I need to travel."

"And is all of it like the land here, hills and forests and lakes?"

"No." He pointed to an area in the south of the country, a round bay that cut into the land and was bordered on the east by a protective arm of land.

"That's Luid," he said. "It's warmer there. We still see the seasons, but the winters are much milder. Summer can be unpleasantly warm, which is why wealthy Luidites have these homes to retreat to." His fingers traced a path directly north from Luid. "Here's Cressia. It's not a place I'd recommend you visit. During my great-grandfather's time dragons swept down from the mountains here." He indicated a range bordering the northern sea. "They killed or drove out most of the humans, and for the most part, we've left the land to them."

"Sounds a bit like what my people did to the dragons."

"Perhaps. There are people who still live there in small settlements, and as a population they have stronger magic than people living elsewhere. Severn watches them very carefully."

"What about the rest of the country?"

"You'd like most of it, I think. The silver forest in Tauren is said to be a good place to see unicorns, but that could just be talk to get people to visit and spread their gold around. There's a valley in the east where the trees grow upside down with their roots in a canopy of clouds and their leaves spread out over the ground. There's the Despair bordering Luid in the north, which is better protection from an army than any wall. Something in the middle of that place breaks your heart and your mind the closer you come to it. Most plants won't even grow there.

"Grasslands through the middle here, mountains to the north and west—those would be the Eastern Mountains to you, of course. Gryphons, flying horses and the Ayer in the mountains and foothills, and more creatures you've only read about in other places." He drummed his fingers on the paper. "I grew up with all of this, and it still often surprises me. I wish I could see what you thought of it all."

"Well, we can't stay here forever," I said. "Where will we go next?"

"I don't know. I have a few ideas." He looked more tired than I'd seen him before, so much so that he appeared older than he had the first time I met him.

"Are you all right?" I asked.

"I will be. Constantly using magic takes a toll. Transformations and mind control are difficult, but at least they're fast. This awareness and trying to stay focused is…" He smiled. "It's just draining me a little. I'm going to rest my eyes for a few minutes." He ran a hand over my hair, twirling the ends like I did so often, then went to the sofa and stretched out on his back.

I steeped heartleaf bark again, trying to move quietly so he could rest, then sat at the table and looked over the map again. The terrain was well marked, but Aren hadn't labeled anything. Not natural features, not territories, not cities. He didn't need to. He knew this huge piece of land like I knew the forest around Stone Ridge.

And yet he couldn't think of a single safe place for us to go.

I went up to the bedroom to wash up, and Aren was still asleep when I returned. I thought about waking him up and telling him to go to bed, but I couldn't disturb him. I put out the lamps and opened the window coverings to let the moonlight in, brought a blanket out from the bedroom and went to lay it over him. I'd meant to leave him to rest, but wondered whether he'd object to me staying with him. He'd wanted me earlier, but that was different. He seemed far less comfortable with comfort and affection.

I touched his face. He opened his eyes slightly, and I pulled back. For a moment he did nothing. Then he shifted his body to make space beside him. My stomach fluttered as I sat, then slowly lowered myself to rest my head on his arm.

"It's okay," he whispered.

He wrapped his arms around me, and I fell asleep with his heartbeat drumming in my ear.

#

There were no dreams about being chased by dragons, and no dancing. There was no closet on the stairs. Just a dark, gloomy forest I was very familiar with, though only from my dreams. The ancient trees dripped with moss, and the ground was covered with rocks, fallen trees, and ferns. Nothing seemed to be happening, which suited me well enough. I waited.

Aren walked toward me, seeming to appear out of

nowhere, and sat on a lichen-spotted boulder. I took a hesitant step toward him. "Are you really you?" I asked.

"I think so. I was going to ask you the same thing, but this place definitely isn't mine. Do you come here often?"

"Sometimes."

He looked up into the dark forest canopy. "Such a cheerful spot."

"There are worse places," I said, thinking of the suffocation dreams. The binding dreams, I supposed.

"It's interesting. I really should try to wake up, though. I shouldn't be here."

"Don't." I sat on one of his legs and rested my head on his shoulder. "There's nowhere we'll be safe, is there?"

"No. Not for me, and not for you while you're with me. I've been trying to tell you that. Severn's not going to let this go." He started to stand, but I pressed down on his shoulders, and he gave in easily.

"Did you check to see if he was nearby before you lay down?"

"I did, and there was nothing. That doesn't mean I can relax."

"You can't stay half-awake forever. Just sleep for now, you need it so badly. We can leave tomorrow, as early as you want. They can't possibly get here that quickly, even if you do let your guard slip a little. Right?" I pressed my lips against his throat and breathed in the intoxicating scent of his skin. He felt as warm and as real as anything I'd felt earlier that day, in spite of the dream-like quality of everything around us.

"You might be surprised how quickly Severn can move.

But you're right, I can't keep this up much longer." He held me close, and we sat like that for a few minutes, resting in the peaceful gloom of my forest.

He shrugged his shoulder, and I lifted my head. He cupped my face in his hand and ran his thumb over my lower lip. I shivered.

"Still," he said with a half-smile, "if we're going to risk being caught, it seems a shame to do it for sleep." I was about to agree when he said, "Wait—someone's coming." An instant later we were both awake in the dark house.

"What's—" I whispered, and the door banged open. Kel's dripping silhouette appeared in the doorway. He hadn't taken time to put his clothes on this time. His athletic form would have been distracting if I hadn't been so terrified.

"Get out," he said. "They're coming. Niari was up in town a few hours ago, and she said there were a lot of unfamiliar men there. Severn may have been one of them."

Aren sat for a moment with his eyes closed. "I can't get him." His jaw clenched. "He's been blocking me right back. I had no idea. I'm so sorry, Rowan."

"Don't worry about it. Grab our things, I'll get the horses ready—"

"Don't bother," Kel said. "There's no time, you're coming with me. Both of you."

"What about—"

"You'll never make it out of here over land without getting caught, and Cassia and I decided we can't let that happen. She's waiting in the lake. Take only what you need, and hurry."

"Let's go," I said, before Aren could try to refuse. I shouldn't have worried. He was up and putting his cloak and boots into his bag before I finished speaking. I did the same, and picked up my dragon scale off of the table on my way past. It glowed faintly as we stepped out under the stars, a strangely comforting sight. *You've survived worse*, I reminded myself. I pushed the scale to the bottom of my knapsack.

"We'll go as quickly as we can," Kel said, "but this isn't the best starting place. I hope you can both hold your breath." He didn't stop when we reached the end of the dock, but tipped off the end into a dive that barely rippled the surface of the water.

"Turn your pack around," he said. "Let's go."

I swung the bag around to my chest, pulled the straps over my shoulders, and glanced back toward the house before I jumped into the water. Tiny lights bobbed along the shoreline in both directions, and a few flickered among the trees, all closing in on the cabin. I turned back to the water, took a deep breath, let it out, took another, and jumped in.

Aren splashed into the lake a second later. Strong arms wrapped around my waist and back, pinning my knapsack between my body and Kel's. I wrapped my arms as far as I could around his broad chest, and we shot through the water. I wanted to ask where Aren was, but there was no time.

I needed another deep breath to calm myself, but all I could do was keep my head down against the push of the water and hold on tight as Kel's powerful tail propelled us through darkness that seemed to go on forever as my chest burned and my panic grew.

Chapter Twenty-Seven

Rowan

We surfaced in near-darkness, and I gasped in cool, dank air that tickled my aching lungs. Kel held me up until I caught my breath, then helped me onto a cold stone ledge that seemed to be part of a large cave. My eyes adjusted to the dim light in time to see Aren reach the surface, accompanied by a long-haired woman. He held onto the ledge, as out-of-breath as I had been.

Kel watched him, head tilted to one side. "Aquatic forms aren't looking so bad now, are they?"

Aren stared at him, then burst out in laughter that turned quickly into a coughing fit. Kel laughed, too, and said, "All right, get out of my lake."

"Where are we?" I asked.

"Underwater cave," Kel said. "No one should be able to follow us here." He braced his hands on the ledge as though her were going to follow us onto dry land, then hesitated. "You know, this might be less awkward if you go ahead. Follow the light, see if there's anything for us naked mer-types to cover up with. You two might want to get out of those wet clothes, too."

Aren and I followed what light there was to its source, a small fire that burned hotter than seemed possible, hidden behind a rock outcropping. We found a pile of flat, smooth blankets, and I passed half of the stack to Aren.

"You okay?" he asked.

"I am," I said, in spite of the fact that I was still weak-legged with fear and excitement that were catching up with me now that we were safe. "You know, a month ago I'd have called nearly drowning in an escape from an evil Sorcerer a big deal."

Aren swallowed hard and smiled. "Good. Not that I was afraid that Kel was going to accidentally drown you or anything." I wanted to put my arms around him like I had in our shared dream, but it felt wrong in the real world and far from the cabin. Too familiar. He turned and walked away.

I squeezed most of the water out of my hair, but couldn't get my clothes dry. The things in my bag were wet, too. I hurried to strip down to my underthings and wrap a blanket around me, towel-style. When Aren and the others came back, they were wearing the same. Aren carried his own clothing in a dripping bundle. I tried not to stare at him and Kel as we sat around the fire to warm ourselves.

"We shouldn't stay too long," Kel said. "I'd rather not take chances."

"It'll be fine," the mer woman said, and adjusted top of the blanket she wore, pulling it tighter. "Let them rest for a few minutes, at least."

My first thought when I really looked at her was that

she was the most beautiful woman I'd ever seen. Dark hair hung over her shoulders in wild, damp waves that framed a face built from perfectly balanced features and flawless, cinnamon-colored skin. She'd wrapped her blanket around herself in a way that showed off generous curves and revealed most of her long legs, and when she smiled it was warm and confident. I tried to ignore my jealousy as I realized that Aren had been holding onto that body as she brought him here, and with no blanket to cover her. *She just saved his life. Be happy about that.*

"Hi, I'm Cassia," she said. "You're Rhona, right?"

I remembered what Kel had said. *She and Aren used to be… friends.*

I smiled back. "Actually, it's Rowan, but—"

She clapped her hands over her mouth, then curled them under her chin. "Oh, I'm so sorry! I'm just terrible with names. I tried so hard this time, too. Shoot." She seemed genuinely upset with herself.

"It's okay. You're Kel's sister, right?"

"Half-sister, actually, and I don't admit it unless I have to. I trust he's been behaving himself?"

"Of course," he said. "Don't I always?"

Cassia rolled her eyes.

Aren, Cassia, and I sat by the fire for a few minutes, and I grew drowsy as the flames melted the chill from my bones. Kel paced between the fire and the water, and dunked his head into the water a few times, apparently listening for something.

Cassia shook her head at him. "We'd better get moving before he faints from the pressure," she said. He glared at her, and she added, "It's probably a good idea to get past the first changing before we really relax, anyway."

"Changing?" I asked. Kel and Cassia smiled, and suddenly I saw the resemblance between them. I wondered if all of the mer folk looked that good.

"The tunnels," Kel said.

"Interconnected caves," Cassia added. "Enclosed subterranean pathways. That change."

"I still don't understand. I mean, I understand the caves part," I added, before Cassia could explain that again, "but not the changing."

"They're different every time you go through them," Aren explained. "No one ever sees them change, but it's impossible to remember how you got anywhere because the route is different every time."

"And you can't follow anyone because the caves change behind them?"

"Exactly. It's a brilliant way to keep something hidden, and the fastest way I know of to travel."

"But how?"

"Magic," Kel and Cassia said at the same time, and laughed.

"So you've been in these caves before?" I asked Aren.

"Of course he has," Cassia said, "when he used to visit the Grotto. He *used* to be one of our favorite people." She mock-glared at Aren, but she was still smiling.

When she winked at him, my stomach clenched. I forced myself to relax. She wasn't being any more flirty than Kel had been with me, and that had meant nothing. Maybe it was just a mer thing. "So we're going to the Grotto now?" I asked.

Cassia beamed. "We are. You'll be safe with us, and very comfortable. Our hospitality would be legendary if it wasn't such a well-kept secret. Shall we?"

We gathered our things, and Aren and I slipped our feet back into boots that made wet squishing noises when we walked. I pulled my blanket tighter. Walking around in nothing but what amounted to a large towel would be awkward, but it was better than being wet. I stuffed my wet clothes into my bag and hoisted it onto my shoulders.

Cassia led the way with the rest of us in single file, Cassia before me and Aren behind. He asked Kel what had changed the elders' minds about letting him come.

"Nothing yet," Kel said. "We're bringing you in as a..." He hesitated, and Cassia glanced back at him.

"Seeker of political asylum?"

"That'll do. It will be up to Mariana and Arnav to decide if you can stay. Best we could do."

"I appreciate it," Aren said. "I hope you don't get in too much trouble for this."

"Well, we all do stupid things for people we care about, don't we?"

Aren ignored Kel's question.

The walls seemed to glow with a dim, greenish light that made me think of dragon scales. It wasn't bright enough to be good for much, but it kept us from bumping into the walls or each other. The tunnel soon opened into a wide space with three more corridors branching from it. They all looked the same to me, curving off into darkness.

"Left?" Kel asked, and Cassia shrugged.

"Doesn't matter to me. One's as good as another."

"Wait," I said, "you don't know where we're going?"

"No," Cassia said. "It's always changing, remember? For me and Kel it's a case of all paths eventually leading toward home, but we're not going there, unless you want to end up underwater again. We'll pick a tunnel, find a guide, and see what happens. Left it is!"

She set off down the right-hand tunnel. Kel shook his head. "She's as bad with directions as she is with names," he told me, "but she's actually quite brilliant, and she knows the caves better than I do. Just don't tell her I said so."

Very reassuring, I thought, but followed Cassia. A few turns later we came to a place where orange light flickered against a wall ahead of us. Cassia turned and stepped through a round opening opposite it.

"Perfect!" she called, and leaned back out into the passage. "Come on in."

The room was a rough oval shape with a flat floor and pitted stone walls. Another small fire burned beside the entrance, and a flat ledge with rounded edges protruded into the room, topped with a huge cushion.

"Rest area!" Cassia announced. "There's food here somewhere, but I'm not sure what—" She pushed the lid off of a dusty crate and rummaged through the contents, leaning over so far that I had to look away.

"Someone hasn't been keeping up with replenishing supplies. There's water, though, and this." She pulled out a small vial with a tiny, jeweled stopper, and held in her other hand what appeared to be a small, rock-hard bread bun. A drop of silvery liquid from the vial made the bun blossom into a fluffy, round loaf of bread. She held it out to me. "It's not what I'd hoped for, but it will do."

"It's warm!" It felt like it had just come out of an oven, and the smell was sweet and buttery enough to make my mouth water.

Cassia looked confused. "Of course it is. You didn't think we'd preserve stale food, did you? Anyway, you two can share that, we ate earlier. There's a bed over there, blankets will be underneath. It's warm in here, though, so I don't think you'll need those unless one of you will be sleeping on the floor." That last part was almost a question, but neither of us answered. "Um… there should be another room off here with a hole in the floor for, you know. Oh, there. And I think that's everything."

"It's amazing," I said.

"It'll do," Kel replied. "Cass, we should go find a guide and let these people sleep." Then, to us, "We'll probably be a few hours. Try to get a bit of rest, if you can. I don't know how much farther it's going to be." Cassia waved to us and followed him out.

The bread tasted as good as it smelled, even with nothing to put on it. "This is strange," I said.

"Which part?" Aren lifted the big cushion and pulled out a blanket, which he spread over the top. I watched him, barely ashamed of how much I enjoyed the sight of him wearing nothing but the blanket wrapped around his hips. He spread his wet things out around the fire, and I did the same with mine.

"All of it. Underwater caves, changing tunnels, fresh bread in dusty boxes. Just all of it."

"I suppose it is. There's a lot I haven't told you about. It's good though, right?"

He turned back to me, and I dragged my gaze up to his face. "Very good," I said, and he smiled. "And maybe you can actually sleep now. We're probably as safe as we can get here, right?"

"I'm not tired," he yawned, and lay down in the bed, nearly disappearing behind the edge of the mattress.

"Aren? That dream back at the cabin. Was that real?"

He rested his head on the edge of the bed. "Real as a dream can be, I suppose. Do you mean was I really there?" I nodded. "Then yes, it was real. I can change now, if that makes you uncomfortable."

"No, not at all. I liked it."

"Hmm." He yawned again and moved out of sight.

I was exhausted, but couldn't fight the curiosity that pulled me back to the crate in the corner. There was one set of clothes there, pants and a cream-colored shirt made of a fabric with a loose weave, too large for me or Aren. There was nothing else, no more magical vials or frozen-in-time foodstuffs. I pulled the lid closed and climbed into the bed. The sides were thicker than the middle, like a nest, and I rolled toward the middle when I lay down. I just had time to see that Aren was asleep as the fire shrank down to glowing embers.

He slowly rolled over to face me. The light was just bright enough that I could see his face, and his body above the waist. He'd left the blanket wrapped around him, but the thought of sleeping next to him like that made me warm all over. "I'm still awake," he mumbled, without opening his eyes.

"No, you're not." He wrapped his other arm around my waist and pulled me close. His skin and hair still held the metallic smell of the lake water.

I wanted to remind myself that there was plenty of time, that we were safe now, but there were no guarantees of that. If the mer elders said he couldn't stay, that would be the end of our safety, and then what would I do? I sighed.

His hand moved gently over my hip and rested on my thigh. We fell asleep tangled together, sharing our space and our air.

#

The fire flared to life as Aren climbed over me and sat on the edge of the bed, taking deep, shuddering breaths.

I reached out to touch his arm, and he pulled away. "Did you see that?" he asked. "Were you there?"

"No. Did you have a bad dream?"

He didn't answer, but went through the passage into the toilet area. A minute later, Kel stepped into the room. Without sunlight I couldn't tell how long it had been, or what time it was. It could have been midnight, dawn, or midmorning. It made little difference. I felt rested, and that was enough for me.

"Good morning," he said, and I hurried to tighten my blanket around myself.

Aren stepped back into the room, appearing calmer. "Back already?"

"Actually, I was going to apologize for taking so long," Kel said. "I hope that means you both slept well."

"Surprisingly, yes," Aren said, and stretched as I climbed out of bed.

Cassia appeared in the doorway. She and Kel were dressed in proper clothes, she in a simple, white dress and he in brown pants and shirt similar to what I'd found in the box. Something like a large, gray moth buzzed around Cassia's head, but she didn't seem bothered by it. "Good morning, Aren. Rowan." She hesitated. "It is Rowan?" I nodded, and she seemed pleased. "I knew I'd get it. I found a dress for you, too, if you'd like it."

The dress, like the other clothing, was huge, but the fabric pulled itself tight and fit itself to my body when I slipped it on. "Is everything here like this?" I asked, and Cassia laughed.

"Not all of it," she said, and watched as Aren took his clothes back to the other room to dress. "These clothes are made by a woman in Tyrea. It's an interesting gift, isn't it?"

"It is." I ran my hands over the fabric. It didn't seem special now. Just a dress. "Is all of your clothing like this?"

"No, but we have plenty of options at the Grotto. We just leave these special ones where they might be needed most. We'll send yours back here when you're done with them. If we can find 'here,' right, Jasper?"

The moth thing buzzed closer, and I saw that it wasn't an insect at all, but a tiny man with a round belly and long, thin limbs. The wings that fluttered on his back were the color of dust, and a thin layer of fuzz in the same shade covered his body. His disproportionately large, black eyes studied me, and then he grunted and buzzed back to sit on Cassia's shoulder.

"Jasper's a little ornery at the moment," she explained. "He was sleeping."

"Hibernating, actually," Kel added. "Cave fairies like their sleep. He wouldn't have wakened for anyone but Cassia."

She turned her face toward the creature on her shoulder and smiled. "And we couldn't do it without you, you know." Jasper pinched her ear and turned red under his fuzz.

"The fairies know the caves well, and can find their way anywhere," Cassia said as we stepped back into the tunnels.

Jasper rode most of the way, sitting on Cassia's shoulder and making strange noises into her ear to tell her where to go, or sitting on her head and tugging on her hair to give directions. He didn't seem to like anyone else speaking, so it was very much a silent trip.

The caves were like nothing I'd ever read about or imagined. We passed through one with a thundering waterfall, and later came to a place where massive, glowing crystals hung from the ceiling like chandeliers, and jutted out from the walls so that at times we had to turn sideways to squeeze past them. I was so mesmerized by a spectacular formation overhead that I didn't realize I was walking into danger until Cassia grabbed my arm and pulled me to the side.

"Careful there," she said. "We're underground, but there's still a whole lot more down under us."

I looked down. A wide, black crevasse opened up in the floor next to my feet.

"Thank you," I whispered through the lump in my throat.

"A bit overwhelming, isn't it?" She gave me a reassuring smile and squeezed my arm. "Just be careful. We don't want to lose you." And just like that, she won me over again. Cassia was becoming nearly as confusing to me as Aren was. I gave up trying to figure her out and just followed her deeper underground.

Chapter Twenty-Eight

Rowan

Jasper let us stop to eat in a cave that reminded me of my aunt's garden, but ten times as lush and beautiful. The space was bright, though without an identifiable source of light, and plants covered every surface except for a few paths, climbing the walls and dripping with fruits.

"I love this one!" Cassia exclaimed as she pulled an emerald-green gem of a cherry from a branch overhead and popped it into her mouth. I followed her example and tried several of the fruits that looked at least somewhat familiar. Some were sweet, some rich and savory, but everything was good.

Our stop wasn't long enough for a proper rest, but our guide seemed eager to keep moving, and we had to leave the garden cave all too soon. We walked until we reached a flat, stone wall that stretched so high above our heads that the top was lost in darkness in spite of the glowing crystals surrounding us. Cassia thanked Jasper, who patted her cheek and buzzed away without even a glance at the rest of us.

"He's not usually like that," she said. "They just get really pissy when you wake them up."

She and Kel each pressed a hand to the wall, and a doorway opened in front of us as the stone seemed to melt away.

A bright light hurt my eyes after the dimness of the caves, and I lifted a hand to shield my eyes. The light had a strange, shifting quality, and brighter spots danced across a blue-marble floor. Kel led the way out of the tunnel, stepping into the light.

"Welcome to the Grotto," Cassia said.

"Wow," I whispered. The cavernous room was as different from the caves as it could have been. A high, cream-colored wall stretched out to one side of us, dotted with a row of doors in different colors and shapes, and over them a high balcony with more doors leading off of it. An empty banquet table occupied the far end of the room, and a huge mosaic, the pattern of which I couldn't quite make out, decorated the center of the floor.

It was all beautiful, but it was the wall across from the strange doors that held my attention. It appeared to be made entirely of impossibly large, clear panes of glass. And outside of this enormous window was the bright blue water. Not the surface, as one might see from any other window, but beneath it. This was the source of the mottled light, sunlight that had filtered through the water and been magnified by the glass. As I watched, a school of thousands of small, silver fish swirled past, chased by a few dozen larger fish snapping at the back of the group.

"Is this still the lake?" I whispered to Kel.

"No, my dear. The caves brought us much further than that. This is the sea, though I'm not at liberty to say exactly where."

I stepped closer to the window and looked down. A coral-covered wall dropped away on a slight slope, disappearing into darkness in the depths below. When I looked up, I couldn't tell how far we were from the surface.

"Kel! Cassie!" A child's voice bellowed from an open archway under the balcony, and two children in dirty pink dresses raced across the floor toward us. The little girls jumped into Cassia and Kel's arms.

"We didn't know you were going away," the smaller one said crossly, and squirmed until Kel put her down.

"Kind of a surprise trip, kid," he said, and mussed her curly, brown hair. The girl ducked out from under his hand.

The other girl gave Cassia a kiss on the cheek, then slid down to join her sister. They could have been twins if not for the difference in height, and the fact that the older one had blue eyes and the younger one a warm hazel. Both had clear, olive skin, round cheeks, and the same wild hair. The younger was about five years old, and her sister only a few years older. They stood side by side and stared at me and Aren.

A woman who looked a lot like the girls followed them out more slowly, wiping her hands on her apron. "Girls, I told you they—oh!" She saw that Kel and Cassia weren't alone, and stopped. "I'm sorry, I didn't realize we had guests, I would have cleaned myself up." She gave us a bright smile and came forward again. "Forgive me for not shaking hands. I'm in the middle of baking and I don't want to get you covered in flour."

"Shawn makes the best pies in the world," Kel said, "and she grills an excellent tuna, too, if you like cooked fish. Shawn, this is Rowan and Aren." She nodded to each of us. The taller girl cleared her throat. "Oh, yes. And these delightful young ladies are Sadie and Lisbeth."

The girls looked solemn as they shook our hands. Lisbeth, the younger girl, leaned toward her sister and said, "They're not mer, either." They giggled and raced toward a wide spiral staircase, climbed to the balcony, and disappeared into a room, slamming the blue-and-gold door behind them.

"You're human?" I asked Shawn, and she laughed.

"I'll take it as a compliment that you couldn't tell," she said. "We are, and temporary visitors. Sorry about the girls. I've been busy helping to get ready for the feast and haven't had much time to pay attention to them today. They're going a little crazy." Shawn wiped her hands again, and flakes of pastry fell to the floor. "I really should get back to the kitchen, but it was lovely meeting both of you. Will you be joining us tonight?"

Kel snapped his fingers. "I forgot in all of the excitement. There's going to be a party tonight. Dancing, fancy clothes, music, food. If you're interested."

"Oh, of course!" Cassia's face lit up. "Rowan, you have to let us help you get ready. We'll get a bath ready for you, and I'll see who I can round up while you rest. It'll be fun. Please?"

She seemed so excited that I had to laugh. "Sounds good to me. Aren?"

"Have fun. I'll see you later." There was hesitation in his voice, and he didn't quite accept the invitation for himself. I squeezed his hand, and then Cassia grabbed mine and dragged me toward the stairs.

She's even more enthusiastic about this stuff than Felicia is, I thought, and felt a moment of sadness that she couldn't be with me to see all of this.

Cassia pulled me along the balcony, banging on doors and introducing me to more people than I'd ever be able to remember the names of, all of them merfolk, most wearing soft robes and getting ready for the party.

She found an empty room for me, one with a red door in the shape of a pointed arch. It was a large bedroom, with a wide, wooden bed suspended from the ceiling on thick ropes that attached to the floor beneath. There was a white stone fireplace surrounded by bookshelves, and a large, round tub half-sunk into the floor in the corner. A mismatched dressing table, wardrobe, and wash-basin occupied the space next to it. Cassia ran her fingers over the curved edge of a writing desk. "It's all from shipwrecks. Does that bother you?"

"Not at all."

"Good. Now, make yourself comfortable, get off your feet for a bit. It's going to be a late night."

"Cassia? Are they going to let Aren stay?"

She turned back to where she'd left me standing on the thick, blue carpet in the center of the room. "That will be up to Aren."

I continued to explore the room after she left, but couldn't stop worrying about Aren. Would the elders let him stay? If they didn't, would he come tell me? Cold dread pooled in my stomach. *He wouldn't just disappear. Not now.*

I went to the door to make sure Cassia hadn't locked me in. It was heavy, but pulled open easily. *Silly.*

I took a book from the shelf and lay down to read. The ropes held the bed firmly in place, allowing only a little movement even when I pushed off from the floor.

He'll figure it out, I thought. *He has to.*

I was finishing a story about a young mer-woman who was tricked into falling in love with a land-bound prince when there was a knock at the door. Cassia entered, followed by six of the women I'd met earlier. They brought platters of food and drink, and encouraged me to eat while they went to find dresses.

As they were leaving, another mer woman came in. I guessed she was older than Cassia, but it was difficult to judge any of their ages. She carried herself gracefully, and though her skin was unlined, her black hair was streaked with silver. Her smile was kind and warm.

"Cassia," she said, "I remember your friend Aren, though he's changed much since we last saw him, but I don't believe I've met this young lady."

Cassia took my hand and led me closer. "Mariana, this is Rowan. Kel and I brought Aren and her here because they were in danger and had nowhere else to go." I sensed that Mariana already knew this, that asking was only a formality, but Cassia chewed her lower lip nervously after she spoke.

Mariana smiled. "You are welcome here," she said to

me, "as long as you can make yourself useful and your presence does not cause discord among my people. You are safe here from what would harm you above. Will you be joining us tonight?"

"I look forward to it," I told her. "And thank you."

"You're welcome, my dear. Kel told me about your other problem. We'll want to begin testing in the morning."

"Thank you."

She rested her hand on my arm. "It may be difficult for you, physically and emotionally, but it will be the best way for us to know what to do next."

My stomach dropped, but I nodded. "Whatever will help."

"Good. Try to relax and enjoy yourself tonight. Cassia, I'll send the others in now?"

"Yes, thank you." Mariana left, and Cassia turned to me. "She's lovely isn't she?"

"She's amazing," I said, and tried not to think about what the testing might entail. "She's one of your elders?" I reached for a golden pear and bit into it, and the sweetest juice I'd ever tasted flooded my mouth.

"Yes. If we were human, I suppose she'd be our queen and Arnav our king. They're very wise."

One by one, Cassia's friends came back into the room with arm-loads of dresses and shoes. The colors were like nothing I'd ever seen before in clothing. Rich, sparkling jewel tones layered on top of one another in what should have been an eyeache-inducing clash, but instead seemed warm and exotic and beautiful.

"Don't worry, you don't have to try this all on," said

a red-haired woman when she saw my wide eyes. "We brought things for ourselves, too."

"But there's plenty to choose from!" added a blonde who had the longest eyelashes I'd ever seen.

"All right, bath time!" Cassia called, and led the way to the tub, which was quickly filling with water from a pair of bronze faucets. No one seemed inclined to leave while I undressed, but they weren't watching, either. Some were already busy trying on dresses. A petite young mer who might have been my age sidled over and stood next to me.

"It's okay," she said softly. "It's normal for us to be unclothed around each other, but I can ask everyone to leave, if you'd be more comfortable."

"No, don't worry about it," I said. "I'm in the Grotto, I'll do as you all do."

I stepped out of my dress and into the water. It was cooler than I was used to in a bath, but I didn't take my time easing myself in. After I sank into the water and wet my hair, I sat on a sunken ledge inside of the tub. My new adviser sat on one of the steps on the outside, and smoothed her plain blue dress over her knees.

"Is it too hot?" she asked, and I shook my head. "Things are more different on land than most merfolk realize. We tend to assume that you're comfortable with the same things we are." She brushed her seaweed-green hair away from her face.

Compared to everything else I'd seen since we left the lake house, her hair shouldn't have seemed so strange, but it was. Not the color itself, but how natural it looked against her warm skin and bright blue eyes.

"I'm Niari," she added. "Sorry I missed meeting you earlier."

"Pleased to meet you." I reached for a bar of soap and cleaned myself under the water. "You seem to know a lot about land-dwellers. I thought merfolk didn't spend much time up there."

"Most don't, but some of us enjoy it. If you don't mind me saying so, I find the ways you live simply fascinating." She held up a glass bottle of a thick, clear liquid. "Do you mind?"

"No, please." She poured the soap over my hair and massaged it in, rubbing her fingers in tight circles over my scalp. Having a stranger touch me while I bathed was only uncomfortable for a moment. It felt incredible. "How do you find it different?" I asked.

"Well, compared to what you might be used to, I'd say we're more relaxed. You all have lists of rules longer than I am tall. Rinse."

I ducked my head under the water. When I came up, Niari continued. "It made me afraid at first. I thought that any people who were only a law away from theft and murder must be something like caged monsters, but you're not. At least, most of you don't seem to be."

"Is that the only difference?"

"Not at all!" She leaned closer and grinned. "I have a particular interest in the mating habits of humans."

"Aah."

"You pair for life, or at least hold that up as an ideal. We're much more casual about these things, more fluid. But we're also not as easily damaged by separations as you are. You have fragile spirits, and you become attached to one another so easily. There was a time when I pitied you."

"And now?"

"Not so much as I did." Niari held up a towel for me. I hesitated, and she looked away as I checked to make sure no one was looking, then stepped out of the bath.

"It's just a different world entirely," she continued. "Your people have to procreate like salmon because of your short lifespans and high rates of mortality. We're long-lived and very difficult to kill, so we bring new lives into the world less frequently. When we do, we raise them as a community rather than in the little family groups you keep. We've been accused of emotional detachment, but it's not true. We care very deeply for one another, and are very loyal to our community and even to our human friends. But one adult relationship tends to be like any other. We're not limited like you are."

"Oh." Opposed as I'd been to marrying before I was ready, I'd never thought of being with one person as a limitation. I wondered how Aren felt about that, after spending so much time with the merfolk, and growing up with a father who had five wives. It wasn't the kind of thing I'd have thought to ask.

Niari smiled. "I've met plenty of humans who were willing to accept mer-like terms for a short time. It just doesn't seem to work for most of you on a permanent basis."

I slipped into the dark-blue robe that Niari offered, and accepted a drink with smiled thanks from another mer-girl as she passed by. "When Cassia said that Mariana and Arnav were your elders, I just assumed that they were more permanent than that."

"You're actually correct there," Niari told me. "They're not the only ones, but it's extremely rare. When two mer-folk have that kind of love and devotion to one another, like they're really one spirit in two bodies, we call it a soul-bond. It's absolutely unbreakable. Beautiful to see, but it's not desirable to most of us."

We sat on a firm, curved-backed sofa near the fireplace. A few of Cassia's friends went to the tub and sat on the edge with their feet in the water, chatting and brushing each other's hair like mermaids in a story book. A few more exclaimed over shoes that they'd laid out on the bed. A mer woman who Niari introduced as Dianna sat with us. She and Niari were as interested in my life as I was in theirs, so we had plenty to discuss.

It took me a while to realize that Cassia was missing. I asked if anyone had seen her, but no one had. Perhaps she'd stepped out for some quiet. I decided to do the same, thinking that I might see Aren and ask how things had gone with the elders.

I stepped out the door and away from the sounds of laughter and splashing water, and the sound of music drifted up from the large room. Someone was playing a piano. I'd only ever heard one once before, when my parents took me to meet the youngest son of a wealthy family. His parents had one in the sitting room, and one of their daughters played it for us. I'd been fascinated by the complexity of the music she was able to play, but this was far better. The heavy notes rolled over each other like waves before the music stopped, and then a lighter-sounding song started, something that people might dance to. A woman laughed, and in the silence that followed I heard soft footsteps leaving the room.

I stepped to the edge of the balcony and leaned over the wooden banister to look around. The pattern of the mosaic on the floor was clear from above, still lit by sunlight from the window—a mer woman and man with their tails wrapped around each other. The piano was in the corner beside the window wall, near the banquet table. Aren sat on the bench in front of it, back facing me, shuffling through a thick sheaf of papers. He placed a sheet before him and began playing again. He did it casually, as though there was nothing impressive about it, just something he was doing for a bit of fun. I supposed it was.

I hadn't even known he liked music. Sometimes it felt like I was getting to know him so well, and then these things happened and reminded me that I really knew nothing at all.

Cassia came out from the balcony carrying more papers. She perched beside Aren, and they looked through the music together. She leaned in and said something as she pointed to one page, and Aren placed it and the few that followed onto the piano and began playing without any false starts or misplaced notes that I could pick out. It sounded familiar, some old song I'd heard back home, but I couldn't think of the name. Aren said something to Cassia and she laughed, then rested her head on his shoulder.

I turned and went back to my room.

Felicia once told me that she could never be bothered to compare herself to other girls. She was so sure of herself, so certain that she was good enough that anyone would have to be crazy not to like her. I wished I had some of her confidence. True, Aren had wanted me before, but our bond wasn't as permanent as what Niari had described. He was probably used to having whoever he wanted, and whenever.

It was hard to look at beautiful Cassia, with her alluring curves, her glowing skin and her shiny, perfect hair, and not feel unbearably plain. What was worse, Cassia was interesting and seemed like a gracious and genuinely kind person. I didn't think I could blame Aren if he wanted to be with her again, now that he had the chance.

You don't know that's what's happening, I scolded myself, and realized that was just the problem. I didn't know what was happening between him and me, either. He hadn't given me any reason to think he was mine, had he? He'd said I could stay. He'd kissed me, and more might have happened under other circumstances. Maybe I was reading too much into that.

The mer women were calling for me to come back and find a dress and have my hair done, and to admire a beautiful mother-of-pearl necklace that Niari wore. I'd never enjoyed dressing up and going to parties because I always felt like I had to impress someone, but no one here seemed particularly concerned about that. They were excited to have an excuse to wear beautiful clothes and to make themselves look good, but there was no sense that they were competing.

It seemed impossible. In my world there was always a competition, always someone judging who you were good enough to marry. I decided to go along with it, to try to set my uncertainty about Aren aside for a while and have fun with my new friends.

I joined in the excitement, admiring what everyone else was wearing. When Dianna said a dress looked beautiful on me I said "thank you" instead of deflecting the compliment like I normally would have.

When I looked in the full-length mirror, I saw that she wasn't wrong. The strapless dress was an incredible peacock-blue that flashed green when I moved. It ignited the red undertones in my hair, and made my gray eyes look almost blue. The fabric wrapped tight at my waist and fell straight from my hips to the floor in folds of rich color. Even before Niari found me a pair of gold shoes that matched the stitching in the dress, and swept my hair back in a sapphire and emerald comb, I felt more beautiful than I ever had before. The girl in the mirror looked like some princess I'd never met, until I smiled and recognized myself.

Cassia came in and dressed in a sleeveless, turquoise dress that came up high in the front and plunged provocatively low in the back. She told me I looked lovely, and she didn't sound like there was any reason I should think she wasn't my friend. I told her she looked stunning, and she hugged me.

"Fun, right?" she whispered, and I nodded. I realized that whatever was going on, Cassia had no intention of hurting me. If there was something happening with her and Aren, in her world there was nothing wrong with it. I wanted to ask, but I couldn't.

Everyone chose a different style and color to wear, and by the time we were all ready, it looked like a rainbow had settled underwater for the evening.

"We find it so interesting that humans allow the females to be the more colorful ones," Niari said as she slipped on her silver shoes and turned her ankles to admire the reflections from the lamplight. "In most species the male takes that role. It's certainly fun for us!"

I had to agree. In spite of everything, for this one night it really could be fun to dress up and dance. Trouble still waited on the surface.

The morning might bring pain, or difficult decisions. But tonight I was going to enjoy myself no matter what. Hard as it would be, all of the other questions would just have to wait.

Chapter Twenty-Nine

Aren

After we entered the Grotto and Cassia dragged Rowan away, Kel showed me to a room beneath the balcony. I was drained, emotionally, physically, and mentally. Though I knew I was as safe in the Grotto as I could be, I couldn't escape the feeling that I had to stay aware of my surroundings. Perhaps if I hadn't been so distracted at the lake house, Severn wouldn't have been able to find us. I couldn't let go of my awareness as I washed up, and knew Kel was coming before he knocked at the door.

"The elders will see you now."

Mariana and Arnav waited for me in a small room with an ornate blue carpet and a fire crackling in the marble fireplace. The air was warm, and the chairs comfortable, but the silence that followed their invitation to sit was anything but. I took a seat, but found it impossible to relax.

When I was a child and a guest at the Grotto, the adult merfolk smiled and welcomed me, and they never failed to offer a drink of fresh spring water as soon as I arrived. When I was older they offered wine, but the ritual was the same. It's a habit for them, essential good manners if one wants a guest to feel welcome.

There were no such offers from the elders this time, though a decanter of blood-red wine and three glasses sat on a table in the corner. That simple omission told me exactly how they saw me: a guest, perhaps, but not a welcome one.

"We didn't expect to see you here again," Arnav said at last. He reached up and rubbed his fingers over his gray-streaked beard. He and Mariana looked the same as I remembered them the first time I met them, so many years before.

"I didn't think I'd be back," I replied. "I never intended to cause trouble for you or for your people."

Arnav leaned back in his chair, one ankle crossed over the opposite knee, but Mariana sat straight-backed and tight-lipped. "And yet you came to the lake," she said.

"I didn't know where else to find help. Kel told you about Rowan's situation?"

Mariana nodded. "I've just met her. She's not what I expected, but I agree with Kel's assessment of her."

"And me?" I asked.

Neither of the elders answered until they'd exchanged a long glance that would have communicated volumes if I'd reached out to take it in. They'd have felt it if I did, though, and that would be the end of our meeting and any chance I had of staying.

"You're aware of our thoughts on what you are," Mariana said, speaking slowly.

Of course I was. It had taken me years to understand

that I was a monster to them, an unnatural creation born of generations of careful breeding designed to create the strongest magical gifts possible. Merfolk revere magic, but they fear the way humans use it, our recklessness and greed. If they cared for me when I was a child, it was the way one might love a bear cub. I was a dangerous pet that they knew would show its teeth eventually.

"I've never used magic against any of you."

"You have used it against others of your own kind," Arnav said. He leaned forward. "This is not something easily overlooked by our people. To reach into a man's innermost thoughts, to manipulate his emotions and desires, to make him into a puppet..."

"It's unnatural," Mariana concluded.

She didn't use the word lightly. *Unnatural* means to merfolk what *unholy* means to humans. Abominable. Unthinkable. Unforgivable.

"Your very existence is unnatural, to an extent, but that is not something that you chose. You did, however, choose how you've directed your abilities." She stood and walked toward the table in the corner.

I glanced at Arnav. He was watching me, frowning slightly, but not showing the anger that burned like poison in Mariana's voice.

My own anger responded to hers, stoked by my pride. *You know nothing about me*, I thought. *You have no right to insult me.* I wanted to answer her, to make her understand exactly who she was speaking to, to remind her of everything I could have done to her people but hadn't. I wondered what she and Arnav would think of me if I told them secrets they'd never heard from my childhood. About how I'd brought my dog's body back to life after my brother killed it, and how I sent it after him, fueled by my magic and my pain.

If they were going to hate me and fear me, they might as well have a good reason. I wasn't raised to bear insults without pushing back.

Perhaps I would have said something if I'd been alone, with nothing to lose. Instead I looked toward the fire, and I pushed the rage back down. I forced my jaw to unclench before I spoke, and reminded myself that these people might help Rowan.

They were waiting, both of them. Mariana poured two glasses of wine, then stood motionless beside the spindle-legged table. I realized that they were testing me. That meant there was a chance I could stay, if I could respond correctly.

"I don't know whether an apology is appropriate," I began, "as I haven't caused you any harm. I can tell you that I have no desire to continue using my magic to hurt people, though I have no plans to give up using it entirely. I can promise again that I will never use magic to harm one of your people. Or I can leave, if that's what you want. I don't know whether Rowan will stay. That will be her choice. I hope she will, if you think you might help her."

Another long glance between them, and a nod from Mariana. She poured the third glass of wine, and the tension in her posture eased. "That won't be necessary," she said. "You may stay, for now. It would be a shame for us to lose Rowan. We might gain valuable knowledge by studying her situation. And we wish to help her, of course."

I accepted the wine, and we drank together.

"We believe you when you say that you desire change," Arnav said after Mariana sat again. "We wonder whether you understand how difficult it will be."

"I don't think I'll have to worry about that for long. Severn's already found me once."

"Nevertheless, it bears consideration," Mariana continued. Her expression had softened. "You are giving up everything you've been taught was important, the things you take pride in. You will have to learn again who you are, decide for yourself what it is that you value, what you live for when your family isn't all that you have and are. These choices will be tested. You will be tempted to return to your old ways. Have you thought about any of this?"

"No," I admitted. "Right now my concern is finishing what I've started with Rowan. Getting her the help she needs. Making sure she'll be okay later."

Mariana tapped a long fingernail on the side of her glass. "We will help as we can with that," she said, "and we wish you well with what comes after, though you understand we can't remain involved. You may stay here with Rowan for the time being. You should go and rest now, before the party."

I stood to leave. "Thank you." I sensed that things were not entirely settled, that I would still be watched carefully, but it was enough.

"One other thing," Arnav said as I turned away. "Do you still play?"

#

I wandered past the humans and merfolk who were setting up for the banquet and down one of the winding, downward-sloping hallways that led to the saltwater pools. Each pool connected to open water, a doorway to the merfolk's ocean world. I settled onto a comfortable stone bench and closed my eyes.

"Do you want to be alone?" Kel's voice. I shook my head without opening my eyes, and he sat beside me. "They found out what happened to Rowan in the lake."

It took me a moment to think of what he was talking about. Those moments of panic seemed insignificant compared with everything that had followed. "Did they, now?"

"Nobody you know, not from this community. He didn't intend to kill her, just to frighten you off. He had no right to be there, anyway. We took care of it."

"Thank you." I didn't ask for details. Though the merfolk were kind and generous to their friends, they dealt with enemies as coldly and efficiently as my own family did.

"Did they ask you about Rowan?"

"They already knew what you told them." I opened my eyes to watch the light dancing on the ceiling.

Kel slouched lower in the seat and stretched out his legs. "There were things I *couldn't* tell them, though. Like why she wasn't going to come here without you."

"Your curiosity is going to get you hurt some day."

He just shrugged and waited for me to go on.

"I don't know," I said. "I told her to come and not to worry about me, and she said no, and I said she could stay."

"She cares for you."

"She seems to." I tried not to be happy about that. "It doesn't make much sense, does it? She knows enough about me that she shouldn't."

"And what about you? What are your feelings for her?"

That word made me uncomfortable, and Kel knew it. I remembered what my father told me not long after my mother died, and what Severn repeated after Mona and John were executed. *We don't feel. We think, we do. We have, we are.* It was a lie, of course. We felt pride, and pleasure, and disgust, and a thousand other things. But never what Kel was suggesting. Even now, I wouldn't let myself think about her in those terms. Wouldn't give in.

"If I cared for her very much I suppose I'd have made her leave with you to keep her safe, wouldn't I? I could have lied, could have told her she was more trouble than she was worth, that I'd be better off without her."

"You could have said that you didn't want her."

"Exactly."

"But you didn't want to hurt her."

"No. I could have, though. She'd have been better off. Wanting her to stay with me was selfish."

Kel was silent for several minutes, but I was done talking.

"Do you think she's stupid?" he asked.

"No. She's got more brains in her head than I gave her credit for when she agreed to marry that muscle-headed magic hunter."

Kel laughed. "I wouldn't judge that decision too harshly. She hadn't met you yet."

"Kel…"

"You told her the truth, or as much of it as you were capable of, and you let her do what she judged was best. You didn't do anything wrong. It's probably better than her own people ever offered her."

"Good. So I respect her as an intelligent person. I like her. I enjoy her company. Is that good enough for you?"

"You find her attractive."

"Who wouldn't?"

Kel turned to me. "If you had moved on from the lake together instead of coming here, you would have done whatever you could to keep her safe and find help for her."

"Yes."

"And you could walk away from this right now?"

"If I had to."

"Really?" He didn't seem surprised by my answer, but it was clear that he didn't believe me.

"Could and will if it comes to that. Kel, I know what you want this to be, and it can't. I just want to see this through, whatever it takes."

He stood. "I have to say that this is rather disappointing. You humans have no idea how fortunate you are. I know it makes me unusual among my people, but I would give almost anything to have what I see when she looks at you, and you at her. I can't have that, but I want it. You can, and you push it away because you're afraid."

"I'm not afraid."

"No, you're not allowed to be, are you?"

A small girl in a pink dress raced into the room and tripped over her own feet as she passed Kel. He scooped her up before she could hit the floor.

"Slow down, speedy," he said. "New legs are hard to work, and they're no good around water." He set the child down and pointed her toward the door she'd come in, and she raced off like a re-directed wind-up toy. He turned back to me. "Aren, you can have your family's stupid pride, or you can have Rowan. Don't expect to have both. She deserves better than that."

He followed the little girl out of the room. I gave him a few minutes' head start, then went back to the main hall. Cassia stood near a seating area by the window, looking up toward the sunlight that cut through the water in hazy beams. She turned and smiled as I stopped beside her.

"If you're going to ask me anything about my meeting with the elders, or anything else that's happened in the past few months," I said, "I'd rather not."

"Bad day?"

"Could be worse. I'm not dead and didn't get kicked out. Yet. I'd rather not talk about it, though."

She raised an eyebrow, and gestured toward the piano that someone had rolled in and placed near the window. "Not to reference the meeting that shall not be discussed, but were you asked to play?"

"It's the price of my admission to the banquet."

"Excellent." She grinned. "Better get practicing. You're probably terribly rusty."

It was strange to sit at an instrument again after so many years. Luid was a city of culture, of learning and art, famous theaters and music pouring from the houses, but not for my family. Let the masses be distracted, let those with lesser magic live their lives as they wished. We had a greater purpose. I would never have had anything to do with music if not for the merfolk.

The tension that had built up during my conversations with the elders and Kel slipped slowly away as my fingers remembered their places, as I laughed with Cassia over mistakes and old memories while we selected music for my small part of the evening. It was strange to be back in that place, with friends and music and laughter. I had no reason to expect it to last, but I'd enjoy it while I could.

Getting dressed took longer than I'd expected. The style the mer men were wearing was a structured suit, simple enough in the jacket and pants once I found something to fit, but the shirts seemed unnecessarily complicated, requiring added equipment to close the cuffs and a tight tie about the neck. I liked the dark, muted colors though.

In spite of the difficulties our clothing caused, we were all ready before the women came downstairs. They were as colorful as we were plain, and were obviously enjoying themselves. It took me a minute to find Rowan in the group. A young mer woman with green hair had her by the hand and was pulling her along, and Rowan laughed as she stumbled slightly in her heeled shoes. The world seemed to slow as I watched her.

Kel chuckled. "You poor bastard," he said, and stepped forward to show Rowan to her seat.

The dress she wore hugged her body in all the right places and made her skin glow. She turned back to me and smiled. In that moment she wasn't cute, or pretty. She was perfect.

So that's that, I thought, and followed her. I wouldn't give Kel the satisfaction of telling him he was right, but there it was.

Someone had set out cards with a guest's name on each, one at every place setting. Rowan and I weren't seated close to each other, but I stopped behind her chair to lean in and whisper, "You look incredible."

"Oh," she said, and turned as far as her dress would allow. Something about the curve of her neck as she looked up at me was nearly overwhelming. "You are... I mean, you look fantastic."

Arnav clapped his hands to signal that everyone should find their seats, and I reluctantly left her. When I looked back, she was still watching me.

I was seated between the green-haired mer, Niari, and a human man. When I looked down the table I saw Shawn and her daughters, along with a few other humans. It was unusual for the merfolk to have so many "land-bound" guests at one time.

Over supper, the man next to me, who introduced himself as Jeck, told me their story. They were from a town in the North, in dragon country. It was a small town, but many of the people had strong magic. Orders had come from Luid for those with significant gifts to report immediately to the capital. They'd ignored the orders, and learned quickly how serious Severn could be when he wanted something. Some had escaped, but had been lost and freezing when they set up camp on a lakeside beach. The merfolk found them, and the humans had been stay-ing at the Grotto ever since, acting as caretakers, cooking for the merfolk when they came up, making occasional trips to the surface, and trying to figure out what they were going to do next. He didn't seem to know who I was, and I hoped no one would tell him.

I had Jeck talking to me on one side and Niari on the other asking me about life in Luid as we dined on fish, shellfish, fresh bread and roasted root vegetables. I think I answered and at least acted like I was listening, but Rowan kept distracting me. Before the meal was over she had the youngest mer child sitting on her lap, eating from her plate. She seemed to be making plenty of friends.

After much of the food and most of the wine were gone, a few volunteers cleared the tables. They brought out silver plates piled with desserts—my signal that it was time. I went to the piano and played a few of the songs that Cassia had helped me choose earlier. Music wasn't a gift that my magic helped me with. I did a good enough job, but had to concentrate on the papers in front of me. I didn't notice until after the fifth piece that Rowan was watching me. She looked melancholy, though her expression became animated again whenever someone spoke to her.

When the band finished their dessert and stepped up to replace me, people started pairing off and heading toward the dance floor. I offered my hand to Rowan before anyone else could. "Care to dance, my lady?"

She stood and gave me a strained smile as she took my hand. "I'm not very good at dancing," she whispered.

"Doesn't matter," I told her. "It's not very difficult. Is your head all right?"

"How did you—oh, never mind. It's normal, I guess.

Nothing to worry about."

"Do you need anything?"

"No."

I pulled her closer as we moved across the floor. "See?" I said. "You're not even stepping on my toes."

She smiled and rested her head against the front of my shoulder. "No, it's good. Just like a dream."

When the song ended, Kel came and asked if he could have a dance with Rowan. "No offense," he told me. "She's just a lot prettier than you are."

"Probably looks better in a dress, too," I added.

I turned to walk away and heard Kel say, "I hope we never have to find out."

Rowan laughed.

I sat at the table to watch the dancers go by. "Hey," Cassia said, and sat next to me. "Everything good?"

"Excellent," I said, and she rolled her eyes at the undisguised lie. "Thank you for your help earlier."

"Not a problem," she said, and pulled her chair closer to mine. She leaned back and crossed her legs, revealing a slit in her skirt that reached almost as high as the dress dipped low in the back. She watched me, appearing deep in thought.

"What?"

"You've grown up a lot since the last time you were here."

"I should hope so. You've hardly changed, though."

"Mmm. Walk with me a minute?" I looked back at the dance floor. Rowan was still with Kel, and seemed to be enjoying herself. I followed Cassia back to the empty pool room I'd been in earlier. She sat on the bench and patted the spot next to her. "Sit."

"Cassia I—"

"Just for a minute."

A trio of children ran in after us and sat at the edge of the pool, splashing their toes in the water. The oldest boy stripped off his clothes and jumped in, changing to his tail before he resurfaced. I sat next to Cassia, and we watched them play for a few minutes. Cassia laughed when the boy in the water slapped his tail on the surface and sent up a fountain of water that missed his friends but soaked the messy pile of his own clothes.

"Are any of them yours?" I asked. "Biologically speaking, I mean."

"Oh, heavens no," she said. "I mean, I adore them, but I'd rather be auntie to all of my little darlings than go through all of that. I already have enough to deal with." A little girl waved, and Cassia wiggled her fingers back at her.

Kel came in a few minutes later. "Rowan's gone to lie down," he said. "Her head was getting worse, I told her to go."

"Where is she?"

"I took her up to her room. She said not to bother you, but I thought you'd want to know. Una's up there with her, one of our healers." Kel narrowed his eyes at Cassia. "What are you doing?"

"Just catching up," she said. The mer boy pulled himself from the pool and changed back to legs, then chased the other children out of the room, dripping and yelling. Kel gave Cassia another suspicious look, then turned and followed them. Cassia placed her hand on my thigh.

"Cassia, please don't."

"Just listen. It doesn't matter much to me either way, really. But you look fantastic, and it's been a long time for us. If you're lonely tonight, or bored, or if you've missed me, or whatever other excuses you people need..."

"I thought you and Rowan were friends now."

She seemed surprised. "Oh, we are. I like her a lot. But she didn't say you were hers."

"No, I suppose she wouldn't have."

Cassia bit her lower lip and looked at me from under her dark eyelashes. She really hadn't changed at all. She was still flawless. "Are you? Hers, I mean."

"I think I am."

She patted my leg, stood, and smoothed her dress over her hips. "Good to know. It's too bad, but I know how it is with you humans." She leaned down and kissed my cheek. "Still friends?"

"Always."

"Good. I'm going to see if Niles is still around." She walked away, and I leaned forward and rested my head in my hands.

"Hey, mister, you okay?"

Dear gods, how many children do they have around here? I didn't remember so many when I was at the Grotto before. "I'm fine, thanks."

It was the younger of the two girls we'd met earlier. I couldn't remember her name. "Are you guys living here, too?" she asked.

"I don't think so."

"Oh."

"Shouldn't you be in bed by now?"

She plopped herself on the seat next to me. "Yeah, but Kel said he'd dance with me, and I can't find him anywhere."

"I'll let you know if I see him." She followed me back to the dance floor and rejoined her family, and I went to find Rowan.

Niari told me that Rowan's room had a red door, of which there were two. I knocked at the first, and Kel opened the door.

"Your little lady friend is looking for you," I told him.

"Lisbeth?"

"Could be."

He glanced behind him into the dimly-lit room. "She's awake, but groggy," he said. "Una gave her something that should let her sleep. I didn't want to leave her alone."

"You're a good person, Kel."

"I know," he said. "Don't say it too loud, though. People will think I've gone soft. I have a reputation to consider. Wait… no, that's you."

I laughed. "You're such an ass. I've missed you."

He grinned. "I know that, too." We switched places, and I closed the door behind him, shutting out the music, laughter, and clinking of glasses from below.

A single lamp flickered on the fireplace mantel, its light reflecting off of the blue dress laid over the back of the sofa. Rowan rested under a heavy blanket on the bed. She opened her eyes slowly. "You didn't have to come."

"No, I did. You said it wasn't too bad." I kicked off my shoes and sat down on the edge of the bed.

"It wasn't at first. And I didn't want to leave. That was the best party I've ever been to."

"Maybe because there were no terribly dull people trying to marry you."

She gave me a groggy smile. "Maybe that's it. Anyway, you can go back. I'm not even awake. She gave me something that tasted like seaweed."

"It probably was. You sure you don't want me to stay? I think I'm finished down there."

"No, go on. I heard the music, there's still plenty of party left. Have fun." She paused. "Is Cassia still there?" She sounded slightly clearer-headed than she had the night she took the strong heartleaf, but she could barely keep her eyes open.

"I don't know. Why?"

"No reason," she said. But it didn't sound like no reason.

Rowan's hand rested on the pillow near her face, and I reached out to touch her fingers. "Cass is a good friend. What I had with her before… that kind of thing never lasts longer than a summer with a mer. It was perfect for both of us at the time. It was what it was, and I didn't have to worry about losing her as a friend when it was over."

"And now?" Her eyes had closed again, and I wondered whether she'd remember any of this in the morning.

"Now I'm glad I have friends down here. It's good to be back with them and to hear what they've been doing since I left, even if sharing my side of the story isn't so pleasant. And it's good to be able to relax a bit, knowing that we're safe and that these people will take care of you. I'm sorry if you thought there was anything else."

"Okay." She pulled the blankets up over her cheeks, which had become flushed. "But if I wasn't here?"

"If you weren't here, I wouldn't be here. And even if I were, it wouldn't be anything like what you and I have... Rowan?"

She was asleep, her breathing deep and regular. I stayed for a few more minutes, and then went back to the party. I was pleased to have that much of the discussion out of the way, but more than happy to leave any more of it for another time.

Chapter Thirty

Aren

All was quiet in the Grotto the next morning when I left my room to go up to Rowan's. The food and dirty plates had been removed from the table, but a few wine glasses still sparkled in the sunlight, and dirty linens littered the surface of the table. By the end of the day it would all be cleared away, but for now everyone seemed to be sleeping.

Well, almost everyone.

Niari was in Rowan's room clearing away a few dishes and collecting Rowan's dress and shoes. "Good morning," she said, her voice huskier than it had sounded the night before.

"Is everyone still at home?" I asked. They all would have returned to the water for the night. Being on land could be fun for a while, but most mers found that it became uncomfortable if they stayed up for too long.

"Mostly. Their homes, or each other's." She grinned wickedly. "You're looking for Rowan? Una came and took her to the healer's room for tests. If you help me get this stuff to the kitchen, I'll take you there. You probably won't be able to see Rowan, though."

I frowned. If Rowan had known about the tests, she hadn't mentioned anything about it to me. "What are they doing?"

"Darned if I know." She tossed the blue-green dress over one shoulder and stacked five delicate teacups into a teetering stack that she carried in one hand. "Some kind of testing of what she can or can't do, I suppose. Trying to figure out what's got her blocked up. I don't understand it. I'm going to the library to help with research. The elders are already there, and a few others. Everyone else is probably in bed."

Niari gestured toward a small stack of papers that sat folded and sealed on the table next to the bed. "Letters," she explained. "To her parents, a friend, some guy. My hands are full, can you get them? I said we'd have the humans send them back. Just telling folks she's safe, I think, but not saying where she is."

I wondered what the letters said, especially the one addressed to Callum Langley. Did she tell him what she was, or only that she wasn't coming back? Whatever it was, she probably said it more kindly than he deserved.

I handed the letters to Shawn when we reached the kitchen, and she promised to do her best to make sure they crossed the border and made it safely to Lowdell.

I'd never been to the healer's room before. Niari led me down a long, dim hallway to a closed door made from solid oak. She knocked softly, and Mariana opened the door just enough to step out. A pained moan came from inside the room.

Rowan.

I tried to see in, but Mariana pulled the door closed behind her and gave me a sharp look that made me take a step back.

"What are you doing in there?" I asked, and Mariana grabbed my arm to steer me away from the door. She watched to make sure I wasn't going to cause trouble, then nodded to Niari to indicate that it was all right for her to leave us.

"Only what we have to do. This is what Rowan wanted. She said she'd rather we learn what we could and be done with it. She's handling it quite admirably, all things considered."

My stomach clenched. "There's nothing I can do?"

"Not now, no." She released my arm, but her voice remained cold. "We'll be through soon, but she'll need time to rest here before she goes anywhere. I know this must be frustrating for you, but you've done all you can for her."

It was more than frustrating, it was infuriating. I wasn't accustomed to being useless, but Mariana was right. There was nothing I could do. "I'll go help with clean-up," I told her. It wouldn't take my mind off of Rowan, but at least it would accomplish something.

"Excellent idea. I'll have someone let you know as soon as she's ready to see you." She opened the door, releasing a cry from within the room. I wanted to break the door down, to make them stop whatever they were doing to her.

It's what she wants, I reminded myself. *She could stop it herself, any time.*

Mariana closed the door behind her.

I stood for a few minutes in the silent hallway, fighting the urge to break my promise to the elders, blast the door in, and make them stop. But then Rowan would never find her cure.

I ignored the ache in my chest, and hurried back to the main hall.

#

It was many hours before I heard anything else, and each dragged on longer than the one before. It's hard to tell what time it is when there are no clocks and you can't see the sun clearly. The other clean-up volunteers avoided me, seeming to sense that I wasn't interested in speaking, and then left me alone to pick at the piano when the cleaning was finished.

I didn't know what else to do with myself. Had it been only a week before that I'd thought Rowan talked too much, that her company was irritating and that I might have made a mistake in helping her? All I wanted now was to have her in my arms again, and to hear her laugh.

The light was fading from the water outside the window when Kel found me. "We're in the library," he said. "Arnav wanted to talk to her alone first, but she said she'd rather have you there."

"Why? What's going on?"

"Just come with me. It'll be… she needs you, okay?" He wouldn't say anything else.

The library was a huge room. Even so, papers and

books overflowed from every shelf. The merfolk's curiosity extended to many subjects, but their watery cities were no place for the materials they collected on land. Someone once told me that the Grotto's library held a more complete history of my own land than our universities did. I had no doubt that it was at least a more objective one.

We entered the round room near the painted ceiling. Three balconies separated us from the floor, with doors leading off of each level. Glass cases set into the walls between shelves featured collections of gems and stones, dragon scales, insects, plants, maps, and anything else that could be kept and preserved.

Rowan should have been wandering around looking at everything. Instead, she sat curled up in a soft chair on the bottom level near a table that was covered in books and loose papers. Mariana sat at the other side of the table, and Arnav paced behind her, paging through books he pulled off of the shelves seemingly at random, then shaking his head and returning them. I greeted them, then took the chair next to Rowan's.

"I'm sorry I had to leave the party so early last night," she whispered. Sitting as she was with her hair damp and pulled back into a pair of plaits, she looked as though the morning's trials had erased five years from her age. "I hope no one thought badly of me."

"No," I told her. "You're the mystery woman, now. When I went back, everyone was asking about you." I hoped that would please her, but she seemed too distracted.

Kel came over and gave Rowan's hand a squeeze, and Niari offered an encouraging smile as they followed a few others out of the room through a lower-level door, leaving me and Rowan alone with the elders.

Mariana reached for several flat, cream-colored pages covered in fresh ink. "Aren, you thought that someone may have placed a binding on Rowan when she was young in order to keep her magic a secret."

"It made sense to me."

"It seems you were correct."

I'd never been less pleased about being right, but at least we knew.

Mariana turned to Rowan. "There's no way for us to know who did this, or exactly how, but what's happening here is consistent with the bindings that were once performed on Sorcerers in Tyrea as precautions or punishments. According to our records, it was done by Potioners, using a formula we haven't tracked down."

I winced. Potioners. No wonder I hadn't found records in the old Sorcerers' records. They'd have had nothing to do with each other.

Mariana caught my expression, but said nothing about it. "The methods used in your case seem to have been somewhat..." She looked to Arnav.

"Sloppy?" he suggested, and Mariana nodded.

"That will do. Not surprising, given where you come from."

"Does that mean it will be easier to get rid of?" Rowan asked, not sounding hopeful.

"I'm afraid not," Arnav said. "Now, most records are not complete. People who had this done to them were able to disappear quite effectively because there was no trace magic to track them by. It was hidden, completely useless."

Rowan didn't say anything, so I did. "Why has she been able to use it, then?"

"This interested us," Arnav said, "these instances of her healing you, but never herself. It's happened twice now?" Rowan nodded, but didn't look up from studying her hands as they rested against her thighs. "When we say the methods were sloppy, we mean that while the binding is rigid, it's not without flaws. This may be one of them. A certain amount of stress on the mind or emotions plus a build-up of magic, perhaps aided by proximity to a magic-user, caused some sort of leak."

Rowan lifted her head. "If it's relieving pressure, why did it hurt so much?"

Mariana stood and set the papers down in front of her. "We don't know. It may be some sort of punishment for using magic, a failsafe of sorts. Or it may just be your body's reaction to that unfamiliar power. We can't know without speaking to whoever did this. So much depends on the individual magic-user. Do you know of anyone in your country who might have been able to do this? Perhaps someone who worked with potions or herbal remedies?"

"No. But my mother would."

Mariana and Arnav glanced at each other. "Are you sure?" Arnav asked.

"I'm sure. My grandmother once told me that my father wanted to name me Holly, but my mother convinced him to change it before my naming day. Rowanwood is supposed to protect against..." She stopped and took a shaky breath. When she spoke again, her voice cracked.

"Against witches. She knew what I was."

I knew what she was thinking. "You're not a monster," I told her.

"I know." She didn't sound convinced.

"So what do we do?" I asked. "If we find the person who did this, can it be undone?"

"No. I'm so sorry, Rowan."

I couldn't sit still anymore. I stood and paced behind the chairs. Mariana kept her gaze trained on me as Arnav spoke. "We won't say that there's no way to fix this, only that no one has ever found one before. We found two documented cases of Sorcerers attempting to use the magic trapped within them to break their bindings."

"And?" I asked, growing impatient.

"In both cases the toll of attempting such a massive and unfamiliar use of magic destroyed them completely," Mariana said. "One physically ruptured at every one of his joints, and died in great pain. The other vanished completely."

Rowan shuddered. "So what happens if we just leave it? If I keep the binding and try to manage the pain?" Arnav hesitated, and she patted his hand. "It's okay, I think I know. You can say it."

He looked away. "In a case like this, according to what records we've found, the people all had pain much like you have, which became worse as time went on. You seem to be at a very late stage of this."

"Then what?"

Rowan was watching Arnav, and didn't see Mariana reach up to wipe a tear from her own eye. "They died, my dear," she said. "Many went mad from it first, but it ended the same for all of them."

"Oh," Rowan said. "Okay."

"What?" I spoke more loudly than I'd intended, and Mariana gave me a sharp look. "There is nothing okay about it. This isn't how this ends!" Rowan turned toward me, then stood and walked over. She wrapped her arms around me, and I squeezed her harder than I probably should have. "There has to be something. How long does she have?"

Arnav sat in the chair that Rowan had just vacated, and Mariana walked over to stand beside him. "We don't know, exactly. Weeks. Months, perhaps. No more."

Rowan didn't react to the news.

"There's not much we can do," Mariana said, speaking to Rowan. "After this morning's testing, we can only offer advice. Don't try to use magic again. You're lucky that the past two times didn't kill you outright. They certainly weakened you. Don't expect to be so fortunate a third time."

My blood turned cold. *I almost killed her.*

"Other than that," Mariana continued, "all we can offer is a safe place to stay, and help with the pain."

"That's not good enough," I said. "What if she went to Belleisle? They might know how to help. They wouldn't turn her away, would they?"

Mariana tilted her head slightly to one side. "I don't know. We haven't had anything to do with that land in years. They have their own problems to deal with there, but Ernis Albion is a compassionate man, and I understand he's now married to a gifted Potioner. It's possible they'd take her in for a time." She emphasized the word 'her,' and Rowan lifted her head.

"What does that mean?"

"I'll tell you later," I said. "But there's a chance?"

"There's always a chance," Mariana said softly. "I'd suggest going the other way to see what you could find out from your parents, Rowan, but it would be too far to go in your condition, and for such a slim chance of learning anything useful."

"I'll go." Kel stepped back into the room. "Rowan needs to be where she'll get help, not answers. But I can go."

Arnav closed his eyes and sighed. "Very well. If you three are agreed on this—"

"Four." Cassia appeared behind her brother. "I'm going, too."

Mariana narrowed her eyes at the pair of them. "We'll have to discuss this. Rowan, I'm sorry we can't do more. Please let us know your plans after you've had some time to think about things." She and Arnav excused themselves, and went out into the corridor with Kel and Cassia.

Rowan pressed her face against my chest, muffling her words. "Did she say I'm going to die?"

"She did, but they're wrong. You're going to get better. We'll find a way."

She looked up at me. "Do you believe that?"

"I do," I said. "I have to."

#

The Grotto was dark and quiet when we left the library. The merfolk had gone back to their homes, and there was no sign of the humans.

"They were going to town today," I said. "They took your letters."

"Oh, right." We stopped in front of the kitchen. "You hungry?" she asked, and I shook my head. "No, me either."

I extinguished all but one of the lamps, and carried the light over to the sitting area near the window. Rowan followed. She seemed completely drained. Not sad, not afraid, certainly not ready to go find anyone else to help her. Just flat and defeated, and she looked as worn out as I'd been feeling the past few weeks. I sat on the sofa, and she curled up beside me.

The water was a wall of black outside of the window, sprinkled with tiny, softly glowing, blue lights. I turned the lamp's flame higher and set it on the table. Maybe seeing something new would make her happy for a few minutes.

"Can I ask what you told them?"

"Who?" she asked. "Oh, in the letters? I don't remember exactly. I told Callum and Felicia what had happened—not about you being an eagle and all of that, but about you helping me. Not a lot of details. I explained what I could about what magic really is to Callum." Her continued belief that he couldn't be a part of the plan to kill off people like her touched me in a surprising way. It was more loyalty than he deserved, but I wouldn't be the one to disillusion her. Not now. "I told him I'm not coming back, and not to look for me. Maybe he's not, anyway. I hope not. I told Felicia I'm sorry I won't be at her wedding."

"And your parents?"

"I sent my love to Ashe and my sisters. I told my parents

that I know what I am, and that whatever happened to me when I was little to keep my magic inside is what's causing my pain. Maybe my mother knew that already, I don't know. I don't think I was very nice about it."

They don't deserve nice, I thought, but kept my mouth shut. I didn't want her to defend them.

"I should have waited to send the letters," she said after a minute of silence. "Maybe I would have said nicer things if I'd known I wasn't going to see them again."

I didn't know what to say. I wanted to tell her that of course she'd see them again, that after we found someone to help her, she could send them a message to meet us near the border. I wanted to say that she had a long life ahead of her, as much time as she wanted for that sort of thing, more than she ever could have expected in her old life. But I couldn't.

All of the learning I've done, the lengths I've pushed my magic to so that it would grow, the secrets I've kept so that I could accomplish it… and I can't do anything when it really matters.

Well, that wasn't entirely true. There was one thing I could do, though she might not like it.

I didn't realize how hard I was gripping the arm of the seat until Rowan reached over and pried my fingers open and twined hers into them.

"It's okay," she said. "None of this is your fault. You've done more to help me than anyone has. Ever."

She gasped as a face materialized from the darkness beyond the window. Huge and hideous, it seemed to be all blank, white eyes and a gaping mouth filled with teeth like mismatched swords and knives. It filled the window and stared into the room for a few minutes, flexing its massive jaw, and then turned and swam away, its long body weaving its way back into the darkness.

"What was that?" She didn't sound afraid. Maybe once you've touched a dragon and come out alive, a monster behind a glass wall isn't so frightening.

"Kel called it Fangface. I don't know what it is," I said. "It was here last night after you went to bed and almost everyone was gone. It stays in the depths during the day and comes up at night. It likes the lights."

She shivered. "I hope the merfolk are all safe in their homes."

"They know how to handle these things."

We waited for a while longer, but Fangface didn't reappear. "I didn't realize you were up so late last night," Rowan said. "You should be getting more sleep while you can. While it's safe." She stood, still holding onto my hand. "It's been a really long day. I need to go to bed, but I don't want to be alone. Will you stay with me?"

As if I could say no.

Chapter Thirty-One

Rowan

The fog began to lift from my mind as Aren followed me up the smooth curve of the staircase and back to my room, but everything still felt wrong. I knew I should be feeling something. Sadness, perhaps, or a sense of loss. I should have been grieving the end of the life I'd hoped for, even if I'd never managed to pin down exactly what I wanted that life to be. Instead, I felt nothing but exhaustion after the morning's trials and the emotional upheaval of what the elders had told me—or rather, had told us. Aren had actually taken the news worse than I had. He seemed to want to find a solution, to keep searching until we'd exhausted every possibility.

All I wanted to do was rest.

I stepped behind a screen to change out of my clothes and into the pale blue sleep pants the merfolk had left for me. The fabric was thin, and softer than anything I'd ever felt before, like wearing a cloud. The top was made of the same, and looked more like underwear than a proper thing to wear in front of people, just loose fabric and thin straps.

I slipped it on, then shook the braids from my hair, leaving loose, clean, still-damp waves hanging over my shoulders. Not suitable for visitors, but the thought of Aren seeing me in it pulled me out of my emotionless stupor and sent pleasurable shivers over my skin.

I stepped back into the room and found Aren standing near the fireplace, which burned with a smokeless fire. He seemed distracted and troubled.

A week ago I wouldn't have noticed that, I thought. He kept his thoughts and emotions buried far below the surface, but I was learning to recognize when he was trying to hide something.

"What's wrong?" I asked. He turned toward me and stared for a few seconds, not trying to hide the way his gaze traveled over my body, drinking me in. My skin prickled in spite of the fire's warmth, and I realized that the only thing I wanted, the only thing that might make me feel alive, was to be close to him.

"Nothing," he said at last, and turned away to sit on the edge of the bed. "Everything, really, but there's nothing you can do about that. I'm just trying to think about what we should do next."

"Are we going to go to that island place?" I climbed across the bed and sat behind him.

"I don't see what other choice we have. Ernis Albion is a powerful Sorcerer with no ties to Severn, and his current wife is a Potioner. If someone like her did this to you, maybe she'll know how to fix it. It's just a lot to think about, and traveling there won't be easy, especially if your pain gets worse."

"I'm sorry." I reached out a hand and laid it on his back, over the center of his scar. "If this is too much, you don't have to do it."

He looked back over his shoulder and smiled sadly. "I want to. It's just… this isn't what I expected it to be. I wanted to help you, but I didn't think I'd actually care so much if things didn't work out."

"Well, if it makes you feel any better, this isn't exactly what I expected when I stopped to help that eagle in the forest."

His attempt at a laugh caught in his throat. "Who knew an act of compassion could muck things up so horribly, right?"

I pulled myself closer, so that my knees rested on either side of his hips. "I don't regret any of it," I whispered, and brushed his hair aside to kiss the back of his neck. "There's still a chance for me. This hasn't exactly been the fairy-tale adventure I always dreamed of, but it's brought me here with you. I wouldn't change anything."

He sighed, and reached up to take my hand and press it against his lips. A warm ache spread through my chest, a mixture of sadness and a strange sort of gratitude. I sat back so I could run my fingers lightly over his shoulders, and he leaned forward to rest his elbows on his knees.

This wasn't like it had been at the lake house. Here, there was no reason for me to stop touching him. The heat of pure desire washed over me, and this time, I relaxed into it.

I pressed my fingers harder into him. The muscles under my hands were hard and knotted. I once heard someone talk about a person having the weight of the world on his shoulders, and I thought it would feel something like this. I reached under his arms to unbutton his shirt.

"Shouldn't you be the one getting special treatment?" he asked, but held his arms back as I pulled his shirt off.

"Just tell me what you're thinking. I want to hear your voice." The beautiful part of his scar was almost invisible in the firelight, but I could see it well enough to trace it again with my fingers before I went back to kneading his shoulders with both hands. His skin burned under my fingers, and under my lips when I brushed them against his back. He tensed, then relaxed slightly.

"I was hoping we wouldn't have to go to Belleisle," he said. "It's not part of Tyrea, and they've never had particularly good relations with my family. That might actually make you safer there, but… well, if Ernis Albion might be able to help you, we can't stay here. Especially not if you're running out of time."

"No, I suppose not." The prospect of having very little time left didn't bother me. At that moment, there didn't seem to be any reason to worry about anything outside of that room. What would be would be. Such a strange way to think after years of making plans or fighting against them.

I let my hands slip down Aren's back and around his chest, and he drew in a quick breath as my breasts pressed against his back, only a wisp of delicate fabric sliding between us. He reached back and moved his hand over the outside of my thigh. A tremor ran through me, a feeling like the air after lightning has struck close-by. My body hummed with an energy I couldn't control, and all I wanted was for him to touch me more.

I moved sideways off of the bed to stand in front of him, and he put his hands on my hips, pulling me closer. I leaned in and pressed my lips to his, then pulled back just enough to look into his eyes, those deep brown-and-green pools that made my knees so weak.

I took a shaky breath. "This wasn't supposed to happen, was it?"

"Not at all." He reached up to run his fingers over my jaw, and I turned to kiss his fingers.

"No," I agreed. "We never should have met each other, really. And I'm pretty sure I should still hate you, but I don't. I did though, you know."

"I know."

"I shouldn't... I shouldn't love you." Why was it so hard to say that? Perhaps because we'd been together for such a short time. Maybe I'd given up on finding what I was feeling now, thinking that it was only true in stories, and I didn't trust it. I was past denying it, though, past trying to protect myself. "But I think I do."

His gaze flicked away from mine. "In spite of what I am?"

"Because of who you are."

He pulled me closer again and kissed me, long and deep. I forgot about my pain, about dying, about home. I pushed him back on the bed, my lips never leaving his as my knees pressed into the bed on either side of him, and he pulled my hips down onto him. His hands slipped under the loose fabric of my shirt, and I groaned into his mouth. He pulled the shirt off over my head. We rolled so that I was on my back and he lay beside me, kissing me and touching me until I thought that the feeling would kill me before anything else had a chance to.

"Rowan," he whispered, "Are you sure this is what you want?"

"Yes."

He looked like he was going to say something else, but hesitated. I slipped my thumbs into the waistband of my pants and pulled them low, wiggling my way out of them, then reached for his.

He seemed to forget what he was going to say.

#

I woke to the feeling of Aren placing a gentle kiss between my eyebrows. "Mmm," I said. "Can I wake up like that every morning?"

The darkness under his eyes and much of the tension that had always been in his face were gone. He looked younger and more relaxed, if not as untroubled as I felt. Though he wore a faint smile, there was something in his eyes that didn't match it. My own problems were still there, but it felt like they'd drifted farther away during the night.

"I'll see what I can do," he said. "I don't think it's still morning, though."

My stomach growled as if in agreement. "Feels like about half-past morning."

I rolled out of bed with a strange combination of self-consciousness at my nakedness and a sense of confidence, of all being right with the world.

The fire had burned out while we slept, and the room was cold. I reached for my sleep clothes and pulled a long sweater over my head on top of them, then leaned back to kiss Aren. He smiled then, a real smile, as he closed his eyes. I had to fight the urge to lie down and touch him again. I had more urgent needs to think about.

In the kitchen, I found a cold box filled with left-over food from the banquet, and piled a plate with everything that would travel well back to the room and could be eaten without forks or knives. Pastries, fruits, a few sweets.

"Good morning," sang a soft voice behind me. Niari sat at the long table, holding a cup with steam rising from it. "Did we have a good night?" She sipped her drink, and her eyes grinned at me over the top of the mug.

"We did. Were you looking for us?"

"Not me, no. I came up with Kel and Cassia. They wanted to look over some maps. There was no one in Aren's room when Kel knocked, so we decided not to check yours."

I laughed. "Thanks."

Niari tilted her head to one side, and her high pony-tail fell over one shoulder. "You look better than you did yesterday," she said. "We were worried about you. You looked half—" She stopped herself. "Well, just flat after your testing. You seem better now. Have you decided what you're going to do?"

"No. We didn't really talk about it last night."

"I'm sure. Care for a cup?"

I didn't want to be rude. I sat, and Niari poured me a cup of something that smelled like a field full of berries. I drank it quickly. "Thanks," I said. "I should be getting back. I'll see you later?"

"Of course."

Kel and Cassia were in my room talking to Aren when I returned. I set the plate on the table, next to the maps they had spread out there. "I'll just go get some more clothes on," I mumbled. Aren was already dressed and looking at something Kel was showing him on a large map, but he looked up and gave me a slow smile that made me think I might melt into a puddle on the floor.

Cassia snapped her fingers. "You," she said to Aren, and pointed back at the map. "Brain. Here."

Kel laughed.

"Rowan, come with me," she said. "We'll find you something nice." She led me down the balcony to a room that was filled with clothes. I reached for a pair of dark green pants with pockets on the legs, but Cassia took them and set them aside.

"Save those for when you're traveling," she said, and reached past me for a light-blue dress with a wide neckline and a shorter skirt than I was accustomed to. "Try that. And really, take whatever you want when you go. We have too much of this stuff here."

"Thank you." I pulled the sweater off and put on the undergarments she handed to me, then the dress. I turned so Cassia could close the back for me. She had judged the fit perfectly. "So what's going on?"

She shrugged, and pulled at the waistband of her own ankle-length skirt, which she wore with a sleeveless top that showed the lower portion of her flat belly. It was casual and plain, but something about the way she held herself made her look like a warrior ready for battle. "Mariana and Arnav are going to let us go. Someone needed to visit the

South shore on a diplomatic issue anyway. We might as well do it, and if we go over land we can stop in to pay your parents a visit. Think they'll like me?"

"My brother will."

Cassia raised an eyebrow. "Oh, I hope so. But really, I need to get away for a while and do something different. I'm getting bored here."

"Well, I appreciate it. I don't imagine going to Darmid is an appealing prospect for you. Are you sure it's safe?" I didn't think most people would recognize them for what they were, but a magic hunter would.

"Safe as we are anywhere these days."

"So you'll be careful?"

"We always are." She smiled and found a brush to run through my hair, just as Felicia used to do. I closed my eyes, and for a moment I was in two places and times at once. I remembered another person, frightened and trying to do as she was told, relatively normal and absolutely safe. Was that really me?

"You just worry about getting yourself better," Cassia continued, and I opened my eyes. "Aren would never admit it, maybe not even to himself, but he needs you." She shook her head. "You poor creatures are so vulnerable that way."

Kel and Aren hadn't moved in the time we were gone. "If you put the maps in a waterproof bag, though," Aren was saying, "you could swim around the mountains instead of crossing overland."

"We could. We'd still have to cut down the other side at the isthmus, but that could work." They both looked up as we walked in.

"Are we making any progress?" Cassia asked.

"Not really," Kel told her. "It's too bad the caves don't go farther west." He turned to me. "But you can take them almost all the way east. If you're going that way, I mean. Cassia can arrange to have the fairies take you." He looked at Aren, who didn't say anything.

"Of course," Cassia said. "Much faster than over land, if we find you a good guide."

Kel was still looking from Aren to me and back. "Have you talked about what you're doing?"

"Only a little. We'll be going east."

"When?" Kel asked.

"Soon," I said. "It's lovely here, and you've all been so wonderful to me. But I miss the sky. I think I'll go crazy if I stay underground much longer."

Kel exchanged another glance with Aren. "Sounds good," Aren said. "I don't think I'll be welcome here for much longer, anyway."

"Tomorrow morning, then," Kel said. "Early. We'll have a guide meet you at the doors we came in, and someone to do introductions. I'll ask Arnav to send a message to Belleisle to let them know you're coming. Cass, we should go."

I hugged Kel. "I'm going to miss you."

"Take care, okay?" he whispered. "Whatever happens. We'll see you again soon."

Cassia forced a smile and kissed me on the cheek, and then they left us.

"What's going on?" I asked Aren.

"It's nothing," he said, and picked up a bright-red apple. He carried it with him to the bed, tossing it from hand to hand, then stretched out with his head on a pillow. "I don't want anything to happen to you."

"I'll be fine as long as you're around," I said.

He turned toward me, and for a brief, frightening moment I was reminded of the way he looked the first time I saw him. Cold. Hard. Calculating. It passed quickly, but left me unsettled.

"Do you think you could have come here without me, if you knew you would have done well on your own?" he asked.

"No, I'm glad I didn't leave you. This worked out better for both of us, right?"

He flexed his left hand, making the rapidly-disappearing scar stand out. "It did. This time."

"Aren, what's wrong?"

He sighed and rubbed a hand over his eyes. "It's nothing. Ernis Albion, the Sorcerer you're going to see, doesn't like my family. I'm not excited about the reception I'll get, but Arnav will send that letter explaining what I'm doing with you." He smiled. "It will be fine. I can only imagine what you'll do with your magic when it's freed."

There was something in his expression I didn't quite trust. "Aren, is there something you're not telling me? They will let you stay, right? You don't have to protect me from anything. I can handle it."

He frowned. "I said they would."

"You did, I'm sorry. Will you tell me more about Belleisle now?"

"We'll have plenty of time to discuss that as we travel. Let's just enjoy the peace here while we can."

I released the breath I'd been holding and laid down beside him with my head resting on his shoulder.

He offered me the first bite of the apple, then took one himself. "Rowan, I—" he hesitated, then pulled me closer. "You know I'd do anything for you, right?"

"I know." I smiled and kissed the underside of his jaw. I knew too much about his family and his history to expect him to say he loved me. That was close enough, for now.

"Good. I know they'll be able to help you. I should have taken you to Belleisle first."

"I don't think this part of the trip was a complete waste of time."

He kissed me. "Not a complete waste, no."

The peace and happiness flooded back. Maybe this would work out, after all.

Chapter Thirty-Two

Rowan

The Grotto was beautiful and the caves and tunnels fascinating, but after another two days of walking, nights spent in less-comfortable caves than we'd found before, and several more hours of travel in a tunnel that became smaller as it ascended, I was ready to see the sun.

Stepping out onto the snow and into the cool, fresh air was like being reborn. I laughed as the brisk breeze lifted by hair and twisted it around my face, and I raised my arms as though I could fly up into that beautiful, blue sky. I was too happy to feel embarrassed by the childish gesture.

We had emerged from a small opening in rocky earth surrounded by trees, a forest that fell silent at our appearance. One by one the winter songbirds resumed their twittering and their flitting between the trees. Thin afternoon sunlight blanketed the snow-spotted ground, broken only by the shadows of naked trees. I turned back to see Aren climbing out of the cave, followed by the two buzzing shapes that had been our guides and unintentional chaperones during our journey. They lingered at the cave mouth, reluctant to fly into the wind and the light.

I knelt close to them, and the fairies flew over to hover near my face. I couldn't understand their language, but they knew enough human speech for me to speak to them. "Thank you," I said. "You've been most helpful. Is there anything we can do for you in return?"

The wild-haired female who had been introduced to us as Beryl whispered something in Jasper's ear and he shook his head. That made her laugh, a high-pitched sound like sleigh-bells. She buzzed back into the cave followed by Jasper, who waved us off over his shoulder before he disappeared into the shadows. Strange little creatures. I hoped we'd see them again.

My boots crunched over the snow as I caught up with Aren, who stood with his hand pressed against a massive tree trunk, apparently trying to get his bearings. Without an interpreter, there had been no way for the fairies to tell us where we had ended up.

"This has to be the stone forest," he said. "They've brought us all the way to Artisland."

I laid my own hand on the tree, and was surprised to find that the rough bark felt like it was carved from rock. "That's in the far east, isn't it?"

He nodded. His jaw was clenched tight, and I recognized the tension returning to his face. He closed his eyes, checking our protections. I didn't know how the shifting of the tunnels had helped us travel so quickly, but I was grateful for it. My own pain wasn't too bad at that moment, but we needed to get out of Tyrea and to safety as soon as we could. Aren seemed less pleased, though.

He turned his head, listening. "Water flowing that way," he said. "Lots of it. That will be the Sisswinn River, which will take us to the bridge to Belleisle if we follow it downstream. Less than a day's journey, if we keep moving." He pressed his lips into a hard line, clenched his fists and flexed his fingers, then set off toward the river.

I followed, but the uncertainty I'd felt back at the Grotto returned. Aren had seemed fine as we journeyed through the caves, answering all of my questions, explaining that his father and this Ernis Albion had had a falling out years ago, and that differences in approaches to magic had caused a rift between Tyrea and Belleisle long before that. But he said they were known as kind and generous people, and that if anyone could help me without risk of turning me in to Severn, it was this Albion. He'd seemed confident. Happy, even, though he'd retreated to his more familiar moodiness at times. I'd believed him, not wanting to question him again after we'd been through so much. But now I wondered. "It's safe there, right?"

He reached up to rub the back of his neck. "Safe enough." He stopped and turned to me, arms out, and I slipped into his embrace, enjoying even the rough feel of his clothing against my face. "We should go," he whispered, and turned away before I could read his expression.

"Aren, just tell me what's wrong. We'll figure it out."

He didn't answer. We moved as quietly as we could with our feet crunching over the snow. The landscape and season seemed to be to our advantage. We would see anyone approaching from a great distance between the trees.

Then again, I thought, *that means we can't hide, either.*

We certainly left enough of a trail for anyone following us, but that couldn't be helped. The snow wasn't much trouble most of the time, but in a few lower spots it was nearly waist-deep. I followed in the path that Aren broke ahead of me, but there was no way to go back and erase those tracks.

Aren was on high alert, looking around and watching the sky above us. I did the same, but didn't see anything other than high clouds gathering, and the tiny birds that continued about their business in the trees. A few squirrels had strong words for us, but otherwise we seemed to be passing unnoticed. Still, Aren seemed distant and uncomfortable. The sun wasn't yet touching the tops of the trees when he suggested that we make camp for the night near a large windfall of trees piled in a messy tangle some distance from the river.

"Why?" I asked. "We've got plenty of light left. Wouldn't it be wiser to get as close to the bridge as we can?"

"Perhaps. But I don't think we'll get across tonight, and this is a good spot to camp. No snow, sheltered from the wind." He sat on a log and rested his elbows on his knees, hands dangling between his legs. "Would you rather keep going?"

I set my backpack on a bare, dry patch of ground. "I don't know. I was hoping for a bed, but if you don't think we can make it tonight, this is perfect." I smiled, but he didn't return it. The damp chill of the surrounding air crept into my stomach.

He stared at his hands for a few more seconds, then

stood and rooted through his pack, pulling out food and unrolling bedding. I didn't know what else to do, so I went to pick up kindling and firewood from around our campsite and piled it nearby.

Things didn't get better as the afternoon moved toward evening. Aren was even more reticent than usual, nearly silent as we cooked the oats and dried fruit that Niari had sent with us. He reached out to touch me once in a while, but looked away every time I caught him watching me.

Halfway through the meal I couldn't take any more. "I'm going to go crazy if you don't tell me why you're acting so strangely. Whatever it is, it's—"

"We could have been there tonight." His hair had fallen forward to cover his eyes, but he didn't bother to brush it away. "I'm sorry. I just… I wanted a little more time with you." He set his bowl down and pressed his fingertips to his eyes.

My heart skipped. Not for the first time, I didn't want to hear what I thought he was saying. "Please tell me you mean time alone. Do you think we won't be allowed to see each other when we're in Belleisle? Because you said—"

"I can't go to Belleisle. At all."

My hands shook, and I set my own things on the ground. "You said we'd be safe there."

"I said *you* would be safe there." He stood and paced around the fire. I wished he'd stop. My head was spinning anyway, and starting to hurt. "Maybe if it was just the problems between Albion and my father, there would be a chance. But it's more personal with me. There was a riot a few years ago in the town where Albion's wife grew up, here in Tyrea. It got out of control, people got hurt who shouldn't have, and her sister was killed."

"And you did that." A spark of anger ignited inside of me. I stood and crossed my arms over my chest.

"On my father's behalf and my brother's orders, but yes. I didn't mean for it to happen that way."

"Why didn't you tell me?" My voice cracked.

"Because it was the only way to save you. Gods, Rowan. You…" He winced. "You always seem to let your heart get in the way of your head. You said you loved me. I didn't think you'd come without me, so yes, I lied."

"You had no right!"

He took a step back. "I'm trying to do the right thing."

"The right thing?" I breathed deeply, but it didn't calm the hurt. "Aren, I've spent my whole life with people lying to me and trying to control me because they thought it was the right thing. You know how that hurt me, but you're doing exactly the same thing."

His mouth dropped open. "It's not like that. I care about you. I want you to be safe."

"That's what they said." I crouched in the snow and rested my face in my hands, blocking out the light. My emotions were making the headache worse, and I couldn't think straight. "I thought you respected me more than that. I'm not a child, Aren. This wasn't your decision to make."

"And what would your decision have been?"

"We would have figured something out!" I glared up at him, but he refused to meet my eyes. "I don't know what. You haven't given me many options. Maybe I'd have surprised you. Maybe I'd have gone alone, left you to be hunted down and… and I'd be fine never knowing what happened to you." I brushed away the tears that blurred my vision, not willing to let them fall. "I guess we'll never know."

"I guess not." His lips narrowed as he studied the ground at his feet.

No apology. I was beginning to think he didn't know how to do it.

"I never meant to hurt you," he said, and knelt beside me. "I also never meant to…" His voice caught in his throat.

"What?"

He swallowed hard, and closed his eyes. "I didn't mean to love you."

My heart leapt at his words. I wanted to believe it. But it was wrong. "You wouldn't use that word before," I whispered, fighting the lump that held my voice back in my throat. "Please don't use it now. Not after you've lied to me." I wanted to forgive him, to see only his good intentions, but his manipulation stung like a slap in the face. "I trusted you."

He stood and stepped back, eyes narrowed. "Maybe that was your mistake, then. How many times did I warn you, explain how I've used people, tell you how I've hurt and manipulated them to get what I want?" His face hardened, closed off. "Why would it be any different if what I want is for you to be safe? Because that's all I have left to want."

"Damn it, Aren! That's not love!" Anger flashed again, and pain. "I don't even know whether you're being honest now, or lying to push me away."

"Which would you prefer?" His voice was cold. "You're

going to have to tell me what I'm supposed to do now, because damned if I know what you want."

"I want you to leave me alone. How far is it to the bridge?" I knew I was being irrational. He wasn't going to hurt me any worse than he already had, and I'd be safer if he took me to the bridge in the morning. But reason was drowned out by emotion and the physical pain that clawed at my head and my heart. I rolled up my bedding.

"A few hours' walk, straight down the river." His voice softened, but I didn't know whether that was genuine, either. "I know you're angry, but you can't leave."

"No?" I slung my pack onto my back. "Tell me more about what I'm allowed to do. You know best." *Calm down, Rowan.*

His lip curled in a snarl, and he raised one hand. I winced, and the anger dropped from his face. He ran his hands through his hair. "I don't know what I'm doing. I don't… Damn it. I don't understand any of this." He looked down at his hands, held open before him.

"I want you to be safe and find a way out of this binding," he said, "and I want you to get there before Severn finds us. I want you to go, but I don't want to let you go." When he looked up, his eyes seemed wet. Maybe it was just the firelight. He shrugged, and his shoulders slumped forward.

My hands were freezing in spite of the fire, and I tucked them under my arms to warm them. I wanted to forgive Aren and figure out a way to move on, but to what? And could I forgive so easily? There was a time when I would have, because I'd have been afraid to do otherwise. But I'd changed since I met him. Toughened up. Learned more about the world.

I sighed. "I need time to think. Just let me go for a while, okay?"

"I'll go. Stay by the fire." He reached out to take my hand, and all I wanted was to fall back into his arms.

"Thank you, but I need to walk. You value rational decisions over emotional ones, and that's what I'm trying to do. I just can't do it when you're looking at me like that."

He nodded toward my bag. "Will you come back? Or are you going to keep walking until you get there?"

"I don't know." I sighed. "Yes. I'll come back."

He didn't look like he trusted that answer. "I'm going to change and scout the area. I don't sense Severn, but something doesn't feel right. Come back if you get cold."

"Yeah. We'll talk when I get back."

After he walked away into the darkness, I slipped my bag off and left it. *You can't run away from this. Come back and end it, one way or another.*

The sun had set while we were fighting, and there was little moonlight to guide my way even when I reached the wide river. I stayed close to the banks where the trees were thin.

The tears I'd been holding back came, and froze my cheeks even after I wiped them away.

The pain in my head began to fade, as did my anger. *He didn't know any better,* I thought.

"He should have," I muttered. He'd meant well, but he'd hurt me. That seemed to be the pattern of our relationship, from the day we'd met to the night he proved my magic, until now. I trusted him, he betrayed me, I got hurt and felt naïve and stupid about it until he was charming and I forgave him. I kicked a rock out of the way, and it splashed into the river. "That's not a relationship."

If I'd stayed with him, perhaps he would have changed. Or maybe I was the fool for thinking he would.

Something snapped deep in the forest. I stopped and listened, but didn't hear any footsteps in the snow behind me. No wings in the trees, either. "Aren?" I called. I slowed, but kept walking.

It couldn't have lasted anyway, I told myself. *It was this, or being on the run forever. Is that what you wanted?*

"It hasn't been all bad," I whispered. We both had a lot of learning to do. Maybe—

A gust of freezing air blew into my face from downstream, and I gasped as it cut through my cloak. When it didn't let up, I moved into the shelter of the trees.

I thought I heard something again, and froze. But the woods were silent, save for the river and the wind in the trees. I decided to go back, anyway. The darkness and silence gave me chills on top of what the cold was providing.

I stepped into a large clearing and paused. It seemed too dark, even compared to the rest of the forest, and it felt wrong. Like someone was watching me, though I didn't see anything. I backed away.

A searing light blazed up from the ground in the center of the clearing and I ducked, throwing my arm across my eyes. When I opened them I was blind, my vision eaten up by white spots. Something moved in front of me and I turned to run, but a pair of strong hands grabbed each of my arms and hauled me back. The light remained, now a flickering orange column of fire burning high as the tree-tops, against which I could only see shadows.

I blinked hard to make my eyes adjust. Another hand gripped my arm, and something rammed into my stomach. Pain exploded through my abdomen. I tried to gasp, but my breath wouldn't come. I doubled over, but the arms holding me wouldn't let me fall.

My breath came back in a ragged gasp. I let my legs drop out from under me, and when the men didn't let go of my arms I pushed back and shook myself as hard as I could. A woman laughed. I tried to kick, but only managed to catch one of them in the shin.

Someone stepped in front of me, blocking the light, and wrapped a hand tight around my throat. He squeezed until I stopped fighting. My vision cleared, and I struggled to keep my feet under me as I recognized the white-haired figure as one I'd seen before, though never clearly.

He released me and bent closer. One of the men pulled my hair, twisting my neck so that I looked up. "Do you know who I am?" His voice sent chills through me.

"Severn," I whispered, and fought the urge to scream. If Aren heard, he'd come find me, and I didn't want him to. Maybe Severn couldn't find Aren, and he'd settled for me instead. Maybe Aren could still get away.

"Such a little thing to be wandering the woods at night," he said, and sneered. "You really should have someone watching over you."

Though he didn't look like Aren, his expression was

familiar. That, and the shape of his eyes. The small similarities made me shudder. I stayed silent. "No mind," he said. "I'm sure he'll be along shortly. But what to do with you in the meantime, hmm? You're not as important to me as you once might have been. It turns out that your people were all too happy to get rid of a mid-level magic-user that they had in custody. And you're not much use as leverage, either. Did you know that your betrothed refused to negotiate for your safe return?"

When I didn't react, he smiled. "That doesn't matter to you, does it?"

He seemed to be enjoying my discomfort, and didn't order his men to loosen their crushing grip on my arms or to let go of my hair. "Perhaps if you offered a small demonstration of the powers my brother is so convinced you have, I might be persuaded to keep you around. Take you back to Luid. See what happens."

"You don't know anything about me," I whispered, and he laughed.

"My dear, I know everything I need to about you. Aren told me so much. But what to do with you while we wait for my dear brother?" He glanced at the men who held me. "Maybe these fellows have some ideas."

He leaned back, and I saw a group of five more uniformed soldiers, two women among them, watching us closely.

Severn leaned in again to whisper in my ear, and the hand that had been holding my hair dropped to my shoulder. "Call for Aren, bring him here, and I'll let you die peacefully."

The cruelty in his voice sent tremors through my body, and fear wrapped its cold hands around my heart. I felt myself growing weak, and then something else. My limbs tingled, my heart raced, and claws of pain dug into my skull. The firelight at the edge of my vision shimmered.

The magic. Not now, please. I'm not ready to die.

I whipped my head forward. Severn was quick, but I hit his cheekbone with my forehead as he pulled away. It strained my neck and sent me nearly to my knees, but at least it was something.

He glared at me. "Take her away," he said. "I don't want to see her again. Tell Grissom and Delain to come back and wait. He'll be here soon enough when he hears her scream."

The men wrestled me back to my feet and pulled me toward the fire. I twisted and fought as hard as I could, but the headache was getting worse. It was as though the insides of my skull were expanding, and the pressure was causing so much pain that I couldn't think.

Sweat stung my eyes as we passed the fire, which burned hotter than any I'd ever felt before, but my body shook as though it was warmed by fever instead of flames. Jumbled, terrified thoughts screamed through my mind. One of the men whacked me on the back of the head, sending star-bursts of pain forward. I bit my tongue and held back a cry.

Suddenly the man on my left let go and screamed. The one on the right pulled me away, but I felt a strong, cool breeze, and the tips of long feathers brushing against my face.

I tried to yell for him to go back, but couldn't make any

sound. The guard spun me around and pinned my arms behind me, using me as a shield. He held me up even as my knees weakened and I slumped against him.

I lifted my head and watched a scene that seemed like a dream unfolding at half-speed before me. An eagle was attacking a dark-haired man. I'd once doubted Aren's choice of forms for use in battle, but now saw how wrong I'd been. His long talons ripped at the man's face while his massive wings beat around the head, confusing him. The guard's face quickly became slick with blood from wounds in his cheeks and scalp, and one of his eyes hung limp against his cheek.

It would have been terrifying if anything had mattered to me at that point, but I felt completely separate from all of it.

The screaming man stumbled backward into the fire and almost pulled his foe in with him, but Aquila—*no, Aren,* I thought—shrieked and slashed down with his beak into the hand that held him, and the man flung him off. The smell of burnt feathers filled the clearing, but Aren flapped away as the guard fell into the flames and disappeared.

Aren flapped down to land on the bare ground at the edge of the clearing, then pushed upward again, lifting off a moment before a net hit the ground. He landed on a tree branch on the other side of the clearing, panting. The rest of Severn's guards had frozen in place, but someone yelled and they moved forward together. The first to reach Aren was a large man wearing elbow-length dragonhide gloves. Aren shrieked and took off, climbing high, hovering, then dropping toward the man. He put his hands up, but Aren got his talons around the man's thin neck, and they fell to the ground together, rolling toward one of the women.

I found my voice and yelled. The guard holding me clamped a hand over my mouth, but Aren had heard. When he pulled free, leaving the man lying still in the dirt, he was ready for her. She wasn't wearing gloves, and pulled back when he slashed with his beak. He backed under a tree and disappeared into the shadows.

I looked to Severn, who stood in the flickering light, face devoid of expression, taking in what was unfolding before him. If he cared that his people were being sacrificed, he didn't show it.

The woman screamed. Aren lunged from the trees at face height. His talons caught her throat as he passed. He fell to the ground, one wing held out to the side, bent.

The guard pressed both hands to her wound and stumbled toward Severn, crying, "Help me, please!"

Severn only watched her for a moment, then waved his hand at her. The blood flowing between her fingers turned into flames that consumed her almost instantly.

Aren fought hard. When I looked back, the remaining soldiers were splattered with blood. But he was tangled in their net, and a man wearing heavy gloves that looked like thick dragonhide held him tight. Aren's blood-streaked head was pinned against his breast, and he shrieked as the man crushed his injured wing.

Severn smiled as he stepped forward. Aren glared fiercely up at him.

Severn removed his gloves and reached out to touch the

golden feathers that stuck out through the netting. "Pretty," he said. "It's a shame, really. We could have accomplished so much together if only you'd been honest about your abilities and let me guide your power better. Seems like such a waste. Now change back. I want to look you in the eyes—your human eyes—before you die." Aren struggled against the net. "And if you try to harm me, I'll have them kill her. Drummond, put him down and step away. All of you, step away."

Aren looked at me.

Fight and live, I thought. *I'm done.*

Aren nodded as well as he could bound in that net, and Severn stepped forward and reached for the strings, which dissolved under his touch. He stepped back—too quickly, I thought. Aren glanced at me again, shook his feathers out, and changed.

One moment he was there, and then not. He reappeared so quickly that if I'd have blinked, I would have missed it. He crouched on the ground, still glaring up at his brother. He stood, and I wondered how it was possible for someone to look completely self-assured and calm standing naked before the one person he'd been afraid of for so long. Severn wore boots with low heels, but Aren stood tall enough to look straight into his eyes. His injured arm hung limp at his side, the forearm twisted awkwardly inward.

Severn drew a twisted knife from beneath his cloak. Dark-bladed, like the one Aren used.

"A bit old-fashioned, don't you think?" Aren asked.

Severn shrugged. "Unlike you, I enjoy getting my hands

dirty, but I suspect that things may be rather complicated with you and my magic. Besides, if I do it right, this will be more fun." He pressed the tip of the knife into the front of Aren's shoulder, the exact spot where I'd rested my head when we danced. Blood blossomed around the knife and flowed freely toward the ground as Severn pushed harder.

Aren gasped and tried to pull back, but the guard behind him wrapped his hands around his arms. Light flashed, the fire dimmed briefly, and the guard fell away.

Aren leaned forward, bracing his good arm against his knee. "Did that hurt you?" Severn asked. "Drain you? You never were as good at that as I was. And I don't imagine it's easy while your magic is busy trying to heal you." He placed the tip of the knife under Aren's chin and flicked it upward, cutting him again. His other hand shot forward and grabbed Aren's broken arm, twisting it. Aren gasped and fell forward.

I twisted out from behind the guard's hand. "Stop it!" I yelled. Severn grinned.

Aren's back heaved as he took in deep breaths of the smoky air. He looked up at Severn, then slowly stood, holding his arm against his side. Blood poured from his shoulder in a river that flowed over the hard curves of his tensed muscles, and when he raised his chin a tiny stream dripped from his face. "I'll survive."

"I doubt it."

Someone groaned. When they both turned to look at me, I realized that the sound had come from my own throat.

"Oh," Severn said. "I did say that if you showed up I'd let

her die quickly. Shall we take care of that now?"

Aren's jaw muscles flexed. "I'd rather you didn't," he said through clenched teeth, and lunged forward to grab the knife. Orange flame flashed between them, and Aren pulled back, hissing.

"Then stop fighting," Severn growled. He motioned toward me, and the guard dragged me toward them.

"Aren, fight. Run. I don't—"

The guard twisted my hand up between my shoulder blades, cutting off my words as I sobbed. Aren lunged at him, but halted as Severn turned his knife on me. I sank to my knees and Aren dropped beside me. He put one arm around my shoulders and pulled me close. I leaned in, pressing my face to his blood- and sweat-slick skin.

Severn laughed, a low, cold chuckle, and I looked up. "Gods, Aren, look at you. Pathetic. I always knew you had your mother's weakness in you, but I never thought I'd see this day."

I felt Aren tense.

Severn inhaled sharply, air hissing through his teeth. "Don't." The guard who'd been holding me fell to the ground, then climbed to his feet in a daze and began backing away. When I turned to look at Aren, he had his gaze locked on the guard. The man disappeared into the darkness and returned with a black horse that tried to shy away from the fire.

Severn kicked out, and his heavy boot caught Aren in the side of the head. I tried to catch him, but my body was too weak, my limbs uncoordinated. We both fell to the dirt, and my stomach muscles seized in a spasm of pain.

Aren pushed himself up on his good arm.

Aren wiped the blood from his chin. "I'm not going to stop fighting until you let her go."

Severn tilted his head to one side. "You know you can't win."

"I'll try."

"Hmm." Severn looked at his guard. "Take her to the horse. Aren, make this easy and she can go. I want to be done with you. Now."

Aren narrowed his eyes at his brother. "I don't believe you."

"We'll give her a head start while I deal with you, then."

"She makes it to the bridge. And I won't fight you. No magic. Nothing."

Severn rolled his eyes. "Fine. But I make no promises after. If she returns to Tyrea, she's fair game."

Aren turned to me. "I think that's the best I can do for you."

"No," I groaned as the guard pulled me away, dragging me over the dirt.

"It's all right," Aren said. "Just go quickly. I have no doubt that they'll be after you as soon as I'm dead."

The guard pushed me against the horse's broad, sweaty side. The saddle leather scraped my face. I turned back. "I can't. You go." I remembered his objection when Arnav said I was going to die. "This isn't how it ends."

He tried to smile, but looked so sad. "I think it is. I've done many things wrong in my time, but this isn't one of them. You're going to live and be safe."

Severn rolled his eyes. "Dear gods, you're disgusting,"

he said. "You should thank me for putting you out of your misery." He grabbed Aren by his injured arm and lifted him, then spat in Aren's face. Aren didn't seem to notice.

Severn checked the blade of his knife and tested it by slashing at Aren's arm, several shallow cuts that painted his skin with blood. Aren twitched and his lips pulled back in a snarl, but he didn't resist. Severn touched the blade to Aren's throat, just hard enough to hurt, to draw blood. Taking his time. Enjoying it.

Aren's face relaxed. He'd known this end was coming since he decided to help me.

And that's love.

Silence descended over me, blocking out the sounds of the fire, the river, and the wind. That power that I now recognized as my own magic roiled inside of me, ready. I sensed that I could hold it back, perhaps for long enough to make it to Belleisle.

I wondered what a place called "beautiful island" would be like, and decided I would never know. *One more time.*

A rushing noise filled the silence, as though a mighty dam had been opened, and everything inside of me was tossed in the power of the force that gripped me. Light bright enough to wash out even the pain in my head burst around me, and I fell to my knees. My arms swung out in front of me, and the magic tightened every muscle in my body in excruciating spasms as it swept out of me and toward the people who stood near the fire.

The horse behind me screamed and bolted.

Aren's eyes widened, and Severn turned toward me, startled. The remaining guards yelled, but all fell silent at the same instant. I tried to hold on, to watch what happened, but the white light ripped through me and stole my sight, leaving me blind and falling into a darkness I welcomed with everything that was in me. I was ready for the end, and went hoping that Aren would be spared from whatever it was that I'd unleashed.

Chapter Thirty-Three

Aren

I had only a moment to react, to realize that she had released her magic and to shield myself from that flood of raw, destructive power. I began to change and halted the transformation in the instant when I was without a body. Everything in me screamed for physical form, and trying to hold it at bay was like drowning, like trying not to take the breath that would kill me. It was the most dangerous magic I'd attempted since my first transformation, but there was nothing else I could do.

Even without a body I felt the blast pass through me, though it felt more like a hot breeze than the punishing wave that crashed over the others. I had no eyes to watch what was happening, but I was aware of lights being extinguished all around me. Severn's burned red, and didn't disappear like the others. Instead it seemed to rush away, growing smaller and more distant in the instant before the others were destroyed.

I felt myself slipping away, being pulled in a thousand directions, scattered. I fought to call my physical self back to me. For a moment is seemed that it wasn't going to happen, that I was as dead as any of the others. Then it came rushing back, blessed weight and form, blood and bone and muscle, as though grateful not to have been forgotten. The world took shape around me and I gasped in air that now burned with cold. Severn had taken his fire with him.

Piles of cloth littered the moonlit clearing. I crawled toward one, but there was nothing there. No bones, no ashes, nothing to indicate that someone hadn't just stepped out of his clothing and gone about his business elsewhere.

I was fortunate that the first items of clothing I found were large. I struggled into them as quickly as I could, but my muscles refused to work together properly. When I tried to stand, my legs bucked under me. Perhaps this was the price I was to pay for my experimentation.

At least I was alive.

I pulled a dirty cloak around my shoulders and dragged myself to where I last remembered seeing Rowan.

She seemed to have disappeared, too. The pile of cloak and boots seemed far too small to hold a body.

"Rowan," I called, my voice a hoarse whisper. No answer.

I dragged myself closer and found her curled on her side. The faint moonlight played off of her pallid skin, giving her a ghostly appearance. I collapsed beside her and pulled her close. Her body was limp, and she didn't respond to my voice or my touch. I shook her gently, and her head rolled from side to side. She wasn't breathing.

"No," I groaned. "What did you do?" She could have got away. I wanted to be angry with her for releasing the power she knew would kill her, but I couldn't. Hadn't I been willing to do the same for her?

I tried to push myself up, but my arms gave out, and I lay with my head resting against her chest. I closed my eyes.

Thump.

I reached out and pressed my fingers to her throat. There was movement. Barely a tremor, but her heart was beating. I put my face near her mouth, and felt a slight warmth as she exhaled. It was enough. I didn't know how, but she was alive.

We needed to get away from that place as quickly as possible. I didn't know what she'd done to Severn, but he was still alive somewhere, and certainly furious. It seemed we both knew tricks that the other was unaware of.

Or maybe he knows all of mine, after all, I thought. He'd been prepared for my eagle form. I cursed myself for underestimating him again. No, he would be back sooner or later, and I didn't have the strength to protect us. I couldn't stand, let alone carry or even drag Rowan anywhere. Some connection between my mind and my body had been broken when they were separated. All I could do was try to keep her warm and hope that both of our conditions were temporary—and that she'd done enough damage to Severn to keep him away for a while.

I tried to imagine all of the magic I had ever used coming out of me at once, and thought it might have looked something like what had just happened. I didn't doubt that the binding had been broken, but there was no magic in her that I could feel, and when I tried to reach out to her mind there was nothing. It wasn't like before, when she'd been there but inaccessible. Now she was completely absent, her body an empty shell. She wasn't sleeping, not dreaming, not drifting nearby. As long as her body was alive, though, it was possible that she could be brought back.

I'd exhausted my own supply of magic in finishing my transformation, and anything that came to me went straight to healing my body. But that didn't leave me completely helpless. I curled my body around hers, laid my mending arm over her waist, and wrapped my cloak around both of us. Still the cold night air pressed in around us, greedy, stealing every bit of warmth.

My people know a number of deities, the great unnamed Goddess and a seemingly limitless pantheon of lesser gods. They'd shown little concern for me over the course of my life, and for the most part I'd done them the same courtesy. Now, though, I closed my eyes, and I begged.

Get us through this night. Let me get her to safety. Keep Severn away, and I'll do anything. I'll change. If you demand it, I'll go back and face whatever I now owe to my family. Just let her come back, let her live. I didn't even know who I was praying to, only that I needed to hold onto those thoughts to keep me from going mad.

No sense of peace or assurance washed over me, only exhaustion that threatened to pull me away. I would have to rest, and try to get Rowan away in the morning. I dozed a few times, but my sleep was fitful and interrupted by noises and disturbing dreams. By the time the sky began to fade to gray, and the stars disappeared, I could control my body better, but still lacked the strength to carry Rowan.

As I saw it, there were three options. One was to change again, fly as quickly as I could, and try to bring someone back to the clearing to help. That was no good. It would be too much of a risk to try another transformation before my magic and my body recovered fully. Or I could try to get Rowan back to the caves. But the fairies would be gone, and we'd be lost.

The last option was to follow through on my original plan to take her to Belleisle, and leave her there in the hopes that Ernis Albion and his wife would take care of her.

My chest tightened. The thought of leaving her there had been wrenching enough before, when she would have been able to take care of herself. She'd have hated me for lying to get her there, but she was resilient and clever. She would have moved on. She was far stronger than she realized.

Was.

Now she was helpless, at least until she woke, and leaving her with strangers seemed unthinkable. But there was nothing else I could do, and the longer I waited the more likely it was I would lose her completely. It was time to go.

As I searched the clearing for anything that might be of use to us, I found that the destruction was more shocking than it had seemed in the dark. Not only were there piles of clothing scattered about (from which I picked the warmest and cleanest items I could find, as well as a few weapons), but branches had fallen from trees, and in a space just outside of the fire circle I found bridles, saddles, and assorted horse gear in jumbled piles. It would break

Rowan's heart if she ever found out she'd done that.

Something crashed in the trees behind me, and I lurched back toward Rowan. A black horse appeared, wide eyed and snorting. His reins had become tangled in a branch, and it dragged behind, frightening him.

"Shh, it's all right," I murmured. He shuffled sideways, and I followed. He pulled back, and I stayed close. We continued the dance for a few minutes, until he allowed me to remove the branch.

I scratched behind one of his ears. He had thick legs, a wide face, ridiculous mule-ears, and his left flank was covered in ugly scars. In that moment, though, he was the finest horse I'd ever seen.

"Never in my life have I been so happy to see an animal," I told him.

Getting Rowan onto the horse was awkward. I nearly dropped her once, and something fell from one of the big pockets on her pants. I set her gently on the ground again and picked it up. It was the dragon scale she'd taken from Ruby and kept with her all this time, nearly unrecognizable now that its hard surface was cracked in a dozen places. A few pieces snapped off when I touched it. I gathered up the pieces and tucked them back in Rowan's pocket.

It was a strange way to ride, trying to hold Rowan, wondering if she could feel anything and whether I should be worried for her comfort, stopping occasionally to make sure she was still breathing.

The air grew misty as dawn approached. We reached a place where the river moved more quickly, gaining momentum as it neared its end. It plunged over a cliff and into the ocean in a great waterfall.

We followed the coast along the edge of the cliff until an island emerged from the fog, and then a bridge. I'd never seen the bridge before, and now understood why Belleisle was so often described as being nearly inaccessible. Sheer gray cliffs defined the strait on both sides. A long, arching bridge seemed to grow directly from the land, tapering toward the middle into an invisible junction. The curve was high and steep, the wind and waves hard. I turned the horse back toward the forest and kept riding south.

The rest of the ride seemed impossibly long when I thought about the need to get Rowan to safety, and terribly short when I thought about what would happen when we arrived. In truth, it took perhaps twenty minutes to reach the bridge that had seemed so distant in the haze. It looked even more treacherous from where we stood at the point where the solid stone structure melded into the mainland. There were no hand-holds or railings to offer support or protect from the elements, and the smooth stone arch seemed to narrow toward the middle, making every step more dangerous than the one before.

I left the black gelding at the edge of the forest and carried Rowan onto the bridge, holding her close, supporting her with my arms under her knees and shoulders. She felt so much heavier than she had when she was awake and aware and full of life. My muscles began to ache as we started across the bridge, and the place where my left arm had broken the night before felt the strain in a sharp line of pain. But I kept walking. The wind whipped our hair and clothing, and high waves crashed far below.

No more hesitation, I told myself. *You owe her this.*

A man started toward us from the island side of the bridge, an unburdened mirror of my own journey. We would meet in the middle, and I supposed that was the closest I'd ever come to seeing the mysterious land of Belleisle.

Apprehension clawed at my stomach, and I wanted to turn back. Crossing the bridge might have been the best thing for Rowan, but it felt like I was abandoning her to an unknown fate, and each step I took was the most difficult thing I'd ever done. I reminded myself that part of the reason we so despised the people of Belleisle was that they were weak—kind and compassionate. That could only help Rowan now.

The man who met us wasn't Albion. He was my age or slightly younger, blond and strong and capable-looking. I hated him immediately.

We met in the middle. He slowly removed his gloves and folded his arms across his chest while mine shook with the weight I carried.

"You know why we're here?" I asked, my voice not nearly as strong as I'd have liked it.

"We do," the stranger said, sounding as though "we" encompassed all of the people who really mattered. "My father received a letter from the merfolk yesterday, and we've been expecting you. Expecting her, I should say. I don't suppose I need to tell you that you won't be going any farther."

My jaw tightened. "I thought as much."

The man held out his arms, and after a moment's hesitation in which I almost dropped her, I let him take Rowan. By then my muscles were so tight that I could barely straighten them, but I'd have taken her back in a second if he'd offered her. He didn't.

"How convenient for you," he observed as he studied Rowan's face. "You get to leave her here and forget about her, and no one would think poorly of you for it, because you can't come anyway." He gave me a cold look. "That is, if they were inclined to think of you at all. She'll be well cared-for here. Not that it matters to you, I'm sure."

If he hadn't been holding the only thing in the world that mattered to me, I'd have pushed him off of the bridge right then. Instead I held my tongue, took a step back, and asked, "Will he be able to help her?"

He shrugged, causing Rowan's head to rock to the side. Her hair danced in the sea air, appearing bright red in the hazy sunrise light. "I don't know. Perhaps if you'd brought her here sooner it would have been easier. Still, my father is a powerful man."

You're not though, are you? I thought. There was no magic in him. *I hope that hurts. I hope it burns you.*

"There may still be hope," he added. Not to encourage me, certainly, only to remind me that Albion would do what I obviously couldn't.

I decided that when I died I'd come back and haunt this man's nightmares until the end of his life, and I'd enjoy every moment of it. He turned and walked confidently back over the narrow bridge as though it spanned a garden stream instead of a wild and windy stretch of ocean. I could barely see Rowan, save for the top of her head and her boots. I realized I hadn't said goodbye to her.

I considered falling off of the bridge then and letting the waves consume me, but a lifetime of fighting for self-preservation had left me with an aversion to suicide.

Severn and his people will be here soon enough, I thought. *Maybe I'll even welcome them.*

I turned and made my way back to the forest, and turned the horse in the direction we'd just come from, back to the place where it had all ended.

#

We passed by the clearing without stopping. There was nothing there for me. We followed the path Rowan had left through the snow back to our campsite, and I gathered the things I'd left scattered when I went after her. I changed into my own clothes when I found them behind a tree, and packed up bedding that was now damp and frozen.

"What now?" I asked the horse.

He flicked a massive ear at me and went back to excavating a hole under a tree.

There was nowhere for me to go, and nothing to do. For the first time in my life I was completely without purpose or direction. True, I'd thought I was lost when I first betrayed Severn and took Rowan away from him, but then I'd decided to help her find the answer to her problem. It had been difficult and only somewhat successful, and had led me far from the course I'd expected, but it had been a direction.

Now what did I have? I couldn't go home to Luid, to my rooms in the palace, to the university libraries that were my second home, or to any of the places I was familiar with. Mariana and Arnav weren't going to take me in again, and I had no way of finding Kel and Cassia, wherever they'd gone. I could try to leave the country, but Severn would have people watching for that. Even if I could have slipped away somehow, the thought of being that far from Rowan made me feel ill.

No, there was only one place I wanted to be. I had to at least try to see her again, to make sure she was with the right people.

And what if I could help, and I'd given up too easily?

But I couldn't just cross over the way I was. I'd have to fly again.

The horse carried me back to the cave entrance, and I left my things there. We wandered westward for the rest of the day, and in the evening I found a farm where a young family agreed to let me spend the night in their barn in exchange for the horse. They seemed suspicious of my generosity. In fact, I was just glad to have found a good home for him. Rowan would have been pleased.

I slept in the hay loft on an itchy blanket that kept me alert, but I didn't use magic to protect myself. Instead, I let my reserves recover in anticipation of what was to come.

The next morning, the thought of transforming again made my stomach churn, and memories of nearly losing myself crowded my mind.

This is Tyrea, I reminded myself. *There's more than enough magic here. I've done this a hundred times before, this is no different.* I laughed at myself. Hadn't I just been thinking that I had nothing left to live for, no purpose to speak of? If I truly didn't care whether I lived or died, I wouldn't have been so nervous.

So stop whining and live.

A moment later I had done it, and was climbing toward the sky on wings that felt as weak as my human arms had.

The clarity and detachment that always came with my eagle's body were missing. My thoughts stayed with Rowan, and my concern for her and the need to see her again only grew as I flew closer to the island.

By the time the island came into view, I felt as though the turmoil within would tear me apart. In my desperation I ignored my mind's warnings that there would be protections around the island. I flew on, not caring what happened to me. If I went to her, I could be killed. If I didn't, I'd surely go mad. For the first time I truly understood why my father was so afraid of love.

There was nothing, not even a whisper of protective magic as I passed over the water to the forested lands beyond. The road from the bridge ran through a tiny community, but no one so much as looked up as I passed over. I soared high, hidden in the clouds, descending occasionally to check my course, gliding as often as I could to save my strength. I had seen a few old maps of Belleisle, and thought I could find the capital city if I followed the road.

Forests passed under me, bare branches and pines, small lakes and ponds, swamps and towns, grasslands, hills, like a miniature version of my own country.

The sun was setting behind me when a city appeared beyond a high, grassy hill, surrounded by a low wall that appeared to be more for definition than for defense. In a trick of the light the buildings seemed to shine, bright and clean. Green-copper roofs contrasted with red and white stone walls, and the cobblestone streets flowed in a rough pattern of concentric circles near the center of town, breaking formation as they spread toward the ocean on one side and the hills on the other.

I settled in an old oak tree next to the outer edge of the wall to wait for morning.

Chapter Thirty-Four

Aren

Dawn lit the city. Horse-drawn carts entered by the gates nearest me, and their occupants set up booths in a street market that quickly filled with customers, many of them laughing as they bartered with the vendors. I wondered whether life here was always so pleasant. It wasn't unlike the life of people in Luid. Not my life, of course, but I'd seen it. Not at all what I'd expected from people who were supposed to be so different from my own.

The largest building visible from my perch was wide and white, with a tall clock tower rising from one end. The governor's home and offices, if I recalled correctly. Not Ernis Albion's home, though. If this had truly been a smaller version of Tyrea, he would have ruled, and I would have found Rowan there. Albion had never taken that office, though no one could have stopped him if he'd wanted to. It was one of many things my father had never understood. Power was a game to him, and anyone who refused to play wasn't to be trusted.

I flew around the outside of the city walls, past a busy

and well-guarded harbor and several more gates, over farms and a smaller village that sat apart from the city proper. I caught sight of a building that looked like a hospital, and a school with children rushing to the doors as a young woman rang an over-sized bell to call them to class, but nothing that I could identify as the home of the island's most powerful sorcerer.

A flash of light-colored hair caught my eye as I passed by a small gate, and I dropped closer to investigate. There was no doubt, even from a distance, that this was the man who had taken Rowan from me on the bridge. Even had I not been able to recognize his features, the haughty tilt of his chin would have given him away. He attached a full burlap sack to the back of his horse's saddle, mounted, and rode west on the road out of the city.

I followed, staying well back and out of sight. He turned north and continued toward the shore until he passed through the iron gates of a well-kept property at the end of the road. He stopped to close the gates behind him, then disappeared around the back of a red-brick house, larger than any I'd seen in the city.

I kept to the cover of the trees, gliding just over their tops, and made my way around to the back. I settled into an orange-leafed elm with a wooden bench encircling the base. The position gave me an excellent view of the property, and the leaves would shelter me from the wind.

Their lack of security troubled me. There should have been something to keep intruders away, some warning of approaching danger, even if most people wouldn't recognize me as such. Perhaps they didn't usually need such precautions here, but I was proof that that could change very quickly. I began to worry that I'd made a terrible mistake, that this Albion wasn't as powerful as everyone thought he was. Elegant and well-kept as this place was, it was hardly extraordinary.

The sounds of mid-day meal preparation coming from a door below me were nothing special, though the odors that wafted up reminded me of how long it had been since I'd eaten.

The young woman who walked toward the white-washed barn didn't see me. Neither did the middle-aged woman who went to the low-walled vegetable garden and picked slugs off of the plants, tossing them to a small flock of brown hens that followed her up and down the rows.

The next hours were among the most tedious of my life as I waited for some hint that I'd come to the right place. I saw no sign of Rowan, heard no one speak of her. Every time the door opened I hoped it was Rowan coming out, or someone carrying her clothes out to the wash-line, or a few people discussing a new addition to the household, but there was nothing. Around mid-afternoon an older man appeared. He looked like the descriptions I'd heard of Ernis Albion. He was tall and slim, with short, graying hair and a neatly trimmed beard, wearing glasses that someone as powerful as him shouldn't have needed. He passed near, spoke quietly to a pair of young girls who were returning from a horseback ride in the woods, and returned to the house without so much as looking up.

This is wrong, I thought again. *He should know by now.*

The older woman was back in the garden, and Albion

seemed to be following her instructions as they picked vegetables.

Where are their servants? I shifted on my branch, lifting my feet and stretching my stiff toes. The woman started toward a bench inside the garden, but Albion gestured toward the bench beneath my tree. I froze.

"I just thought we might get out of the wind for a few minutes," he said as he eased himself down onto the bench.

"Whatever pleases you." The woman sat and began snapping the ends off of beans.

"How's our patient today?" he asked, and took a handful of beans to work on.

The woman gave him a sidelong glance. "No change. I thought Bernard would have told you."

"I suppose he must have. Perhaps I'm becoming forgetful in my old age."

She picked up a gardening glove from between them and slapped his arm with it. "Not if I can help it. Maybe I should put you on the regimen she's on, eh?" She sighed. "Not that it's doing much good so far."

That would make her Albion's wife, Emalda.

Albion patted her knee. "Give it time. I have complete faith in you." He looked upward and spent a minute studying the back of the building. "Have you thought about moving her to this side? The morning sun might do her some good. I believe there's a guest room available." I followed his gaze to one of the small balconies that jutted out from the building at regular intervals on the second and third levels.

"Hmm," Emalda said, not looking up. "If you think it

would be better, I'll have Marie put fresh linens on while supper's cooking, and we'll move the girl after. It'll free the infirmary up for students, and she'll be closer to my rooms that way. Yes, that will do nicely. Excellent plan." They sat in silence as they finished their work, then stood together to go back to the house. Emalda stopped and looked up at the window. "Ern?"

"Hmm?"

"How long will we keep her? She's certainly no trouble, but how long do we keep trying?"

He took her arm. "I don't know." He turned back and looked straight up at me. My heart jumped. "I suppose we'll just wait, and pray that something happens to change the situation." He turned away before Emalda saw him looking at me, and they went into the kitchen.

I waited for my feathers to lie flat and my heart to slow, then stretched my wings and flew toward the forest. I passed over the trees and came to the coast, where a white lighthouse perched precariously at the top of a steep cliff. A fat brown rabbit sat near the base. I killed and ate it. I doubted I'd find a better meal any time soon.

If Albion knew what I was, surely he knew *who* I was. He didn't seem eager to be rid of me, though, or alarmed at my presence. Perhaps he was so confident in his own power that he wasn't concerned. His attitude toward Rowan seemed appropriate. She was getting help. But apparently they couldn't cure her.

What to do, then? I had to see her. Perhaps then I would know better.

He had been very clear about where and when she was

to be moved, and it would make for an effective trap if that was his intention. I told myself that I'd need to carefully weigh the risks of going back, but I already knew what I was going to do.

#

The sounds of clanking dishes and animated conversation flowed from the kitchen windows when I returned to the house. Something broke, and several young voices laughed. I searched for a different hiding place, but the other trees were all too far from the house. I settled back into the elm on a high branch that reached toward the balcony, nearly touching it, but I stayed well back, hidden.

A tall window swung open with a soft creak.

"She'll need fresh air, Ernis," said Emalda, leaning out over the tiny balcony and breathing deeply. "We should leave this open, unless it gets too cold. Bernard, get some more quilts from downstairs, will you?"

The blond man passed close to the window a few minutes later and spread blankets over a lump in the bed, which was mostly hidden in shadows.

Don't you touch her. I supposed I should be grateful to him for bringing Rowan here safely and for leading me back to his home, but it was all I could do to keep myself from flying in through the window and ripping his eyes out.

I shook my head to clear my thoughts. This was so unlike me as an eagle.

Albion came to the window, and looked past me at something in the fields. He smiled to himself, with an expression I didn't understand. I found reading emotions difficult when I wasn't human. It didn't look like a dangerous smile, but I had no idea what the man was thinking.

A clinking noise drifted from the room, metal striking glass. When I edged along the branch to get closer to the window I smelled peppermint and a few other herbs. I risked moving closer to the window to try to see Rowan, but the angle was all wrong. I shuffled back toward the trunk and dug my claws into the branch so I wouldn't soar through the open window to her. *Patience*, I told myself. *They'll have to leave some time.* The door opened again, then closed, and finally the room was silent.

I waited and listened for a few more minutes. I heard voices and sensed presences in other parts of the house, but not in that room. I pushed off, landing on the wide stone railing on the balcony. My wings made too much noise as I flapped to catch my balance, but no one came to the window.

And there she was. Not in trouble, certainly. She looked clean and comfortable, resting under several warm quilts that lay flat over her body, pulled up to her shoulders. It meant she wasn't moving at all. Any time I'd seen her sleeping before, the blankets had ended up twisted around her legs and the bed sheets creased from her tossing and turning. I couldn't see her face, hidden as it was in the shadows. I had to get closer.

She didn't stir when I flapped into the room, or when the bed's footboard creaked as I settled onto it.

"So," said a voice behind me.

My head snapped around. Ernis Albion rested in a chair in the corner of the room closest to the window.

"What are we going to do about this?"

Chapter Thirty-Five

Aren

My talons scratched the hard wood of the bed as I turned to face him.

Albion made no sudden movements, did not speak. My skin prickled, fluffing my feathers, and I lifted my wings slightly. I had no real idea what he was capable of, or what he was thinking. He had been waiting for me, and I'd let my need to see Rowan make me careless. I deserved whatever I got for it.

His hand twitched, and I spread my wings farther to the sides, ready to fly out the window, or straight at him if I had to. That strange smile came to him again and he moved his hand more slowly, lifting a tea cup from the table beside him.

"Calm down, boy," he said. "I think I know why you're here, and I'm not going to hurt you for it." He took a sip from the cup and grimaced. "I thought I might try what my wife has been giving to your friend, to see if it might wake me up a little. Probably a good thing she can't taste this." He set the cup down and stood slowly, keeping his arms spread and his hands open, non-threatening. I settled my wings, but every muscle in my body remained tense, ready to fly or to fight.

Albion moved toward the bed, moving in a wide arc around the end where I perched. He took a handful of Rowan's hair and let it fall through his fingers. "Was it like this before? I don't imagine it would have been easy for her to hide this at home."

I hopped onto the mattress and side-stepped into the shadows at the head of the bed. I narrowed my eyes, and moved closer again. The strange tint I'd seen in her hair on the bridge hadn't been an illusion. What I saw now was a complex color built from shades my human eyes would never pick up. To them, it would all be an unnatural, deep red. I shook my head from side to side.

Albion walked back to his chair and sat again. I stayed where I was, but never let him out of my sight. He reached for his tea again, then seemed to decide against it and folded his hands in his lap. "I'm curious about what caused her current condition. It seems Bernard didn't get many details from you when you met."

I shrugged as well as I could.

"So you don't speak in animal form." It wasn't a question, so I didn't try to answer. "I don't, either. I need to ask you some questions that might help me decide what to do here, but I suppose you'll need to change first. Will you need clothes?"

I nodded.

"I'll find you something suitable, and see if I can keep everyone else from disturbing us for a while. I won't be lying if I say I'm working on something to help her, will I?"

When he was gone, I used one foot to pull the blankets down a little and rested my head on Rowan's chest just above her heart. She felt colder than she had the last time I touched her, but other than that, her hair, and the thin white nightgown she now wore, nothing seemed to have changed.

Albion returned and set a pile of clothes on the bed. Pants, a belt, a shirt. He also brought a plate of sandwiches. When he left again I changed and dressed quickly, and examined Rowan's hair. Definitely a magical change. A minor thing compared to the rest of her troubles, but I wondered what she'd think of that when she woke. My human eyes picked up things I hadn't noticed before. Hollows under her eyes, the paleness of her skin, the shine of whatever Emalda had put on her lips to keep them from drying out. These people were doing what they could for her, but I doubted Rowan could stay like this for much longer. I brushed my fingers over one oddly-colored eyebrow. She didn't move. Her face was a perfect mask.

Albion returned a few minutes later, lit a few lamps, and sat on a sofa across the room from the window. He appeared far more relaxed than I felt.

"Sandwich?" he asked.

"Thank you." I was too hungry to refuse.

We ate in silence, and I watched him, trying to figure him out. He was more intimidating now than he had been when I was an eagle. It wasn't physical. He was shorter than me, and looked like a strong wind would send him flying. Part of it was how relaxed he seemed. If he wasn't threatened by me, he had to think he was more powerful than I was. He could have been right. I felt the magic in him, familiar and yet not, ready for when he needed it. I didn't trust him.

He poured two glasses of a yellow drink. "Now, questions. I imagine you have some as well?"

"I do, but I think yours are more likely to help Rowan. What do you need to know?"

"Quite a lot. I received a letter from Arnav telling me about her situation, but there are many details missing. A few weeks ago I heard about this... turmoil, I suppose, in your family. You disappearing for the second time in a month, and this time with something that belonged to your brother."

"She never belonged to him."

"No, of course. This is just what I heard. Very confusing reports."

I set my drink down on the low table. "You have people watching us?"

He smiled, and leaned back in his chair. "Not exactly. That would be dangerous, wouldn't it? But I do have people who live in your land and keep their ears open, and tell me when something interesting happens. And *this* was interesting. From what I'd heard before, you were one of your brother's top advisers."

"He has others. But I would have been his Second one day."

"It's a lot to walk away from, isn't it? Did you know that Severn has had twenty-seven people hanged since you disappeared with her?"

"No."

"A few who were supposed to be watching you the day you left, but most were people who were already in the jails or prison for crimes that deserved rather less than execution. Your brother has quite a temper."

A quick flash of pain shot through my shoulder as I remembered my own experiences with it. "Rowan learned that, too."

I told him about the night Severn appeared—catching her, the deal I'd made with him, the destruction that followed. Albion's brow furrowed. He was beginning to look familiar to me, but I couldn't think why.

He shifted in the chair and crossed his legs. "Do you have any thoughts on why this happened? Why she let that magic go when she knew it would kill her? Or how she did it?"

"I don't know how. These bindings are supposed to be unbreakable. As to why, she must have been terrified and didn't know what else to do." I squeezed my eyes closed. "She did it for me. She shouldn't have, but she did. Does that tell you anything helpful about the situation?"

"No, but it is interesting. As is the fact that while you were talking…" he nodded toward Rowan.

Her head had turned slightly toward us. It could just have been her muscles relaxing. There was still no expression on her face, and no other movement.

Someone called to Albion from somewhere else in the house. "Can you come back tomorrow?" he asked. "The old lighthouse is well-stocked, if you'd like to sleep there. Slightly dusty and drafty, perhaps, but better than the woods. I have evening lessons now. Did you know we took in students?"

"I did. My father never trusted it. He thought you were raising an army."

Albion chuckled. "Not exactly, but I—"

Footsteps approached in the hallway. I stood and ran to the window, changed without stopping, and threw myself out the window and into the air as the door opened. I flew hard toward the forest, and no one followed me.

#

It wasn't the most comfortable night, but I wasn't about to complain. I needed to spend time in my own body. One of the great dangers of transformation is becoming too comfortable in another form, until eventually it becomes impossible to become fully human again. I slept on a lumpy cot under a pile of blankets, and in spite of the cold I woke several times covered in sweat, shaken by nightmares.

I was awake to welcome the sun when it rose, and I changed again so that I could perch on the railing outside of the lamp tower, warming my feathers as the gulls took flight below me.

After a quick pre-flight preening I plummeted from the lighthouse, spreading my wings at the last moment to cut through the salty spray of the waves before turning back toward the house and Rowan.

I found my clothes from the previous day neatly folded and waiting at the end of the bed, and a breakfast of fruit and cold meats waiting on the table. I ate quickly, then sat on the bed and talked to Rowan while I waited for Albion.

I held her hands, touched her face. Anything to get her attention.

"Please come back," I whispered. "The world needs you. I need you."

There was still no one there in that cold, beautiful body.

The door creaked behind me, and an orange fox nosed its way into the room and stood waving its tail back and forth. A moment later Albion stood in its place, fully clothed in the loose brown robes he'd worn the day before. *Interesting.*

"Good morning," he said, with a respectful nod that made me uncomfortable. He should have displayed his power and kept the advantage, not treated me as an equal.

"No change overnight?" I asked.

"No. Emalda is taking care of her body as well as she can, but hasn't been able to reach her mind yet. Have you had any ideas?"

"Not yet. But if you think she can hear me, maybe I'll just stay here."

"By all means. I'd like to stay. I do have some more questions, and you said you did, as well. Perhaps I could explain how I change into clothes when I change forms, if you're having trouble with that."

I narrowed my eyes. "Sure."

He explained a theory about "essences" that made little sense at first, but that I thought I might be able to sort through later. Magic is very much an individual phenomenon, and he couldn't give me instructions on how to do anything, only tell me how he shaped his own thoughts to make it happen for himself.

He answered my questions as well as he could, and we discussed magic theory for a while. I expected him to ask me about my own experiences, perhaps to gain information about my power or about my family, but he didn't. He seemed to have no agenda other than to offer help, and to keep me there until Rowan showed some sign of hearing my voice.

He had to go for lessons before lunch, leaving me alone to talk to Rowan again, and he brought food and drink with him when he returned. While we ate, we talked about dragons and the scale that Rowan had destroyed.

I found myself growing comfortable with him, but suspicious of his motives. It made no sense that he should be so open and trusting. When the meal was over I asked, "Why are you being so kind to me?"

He paused with a glass of cold tea halfway to his mouth. "I'm sorry?"

"You shouldn't want me here. I'm glad you want to help Rowan, but this isn't at all what I expected. My father is no friend of yours, and I think your family has reason to hate me. I assume that your wife doesn't know I'm here. I was surprised when I was able to get onto the island, and then into your home, and now you're feeding me, talking to me like a friend or a student. I'd like to know why."

He leaned back in his seat and scratched at his beard. "No, Emalda doesn't know. She won't be pleased when I tell her, which I should do soon. It's unfair of me to keep secrets, but I thought it was worth the risk. Perhaps she'll see it that way. I knew you were coming before you crossed the water. If you'd come with ill-will, you wouldn't have made it. I allowed it because you came for her, and I was at a loss when I tried to think of anything else that might help her. As to why I'm being kind to you..." He shrugged, and his lip twisted up at one corner. "Perhaps I'm just a nice person."

"I appreciate you taking Rowan in more than I can say. But letting an enemy into your home for a purpose is one thing. Treating him as a guest is another."

He sighed. "Did you know that your mother was from Belleisle?"

"Was she?" That was news to me. Another reason for Severn to mistrust her, I supposed.

"Oh, yes. Lovely girl. Somewhat rebellious, of course, as one must be to run off with a man like your father. Still, a part of you belongs here. Not that it changes anything about what or who you are."

"No."

"But thus far you've behaved respectfully and given me no cause to treat you badly. And I would very much like for this girl to wake and tell me her story. There's much I'd like to know about what she's experienced. I don't want to chase you off if you're the key to bringing her back."

"Do you think that I am?" I wanted to be. I wanted her to need me.

"It's possible. My son, Bernard, mentioned something yesterday, some old stories where a princess was somehow cursed into a long sleep. Do you know any of those?"

"I'm familiar with the concept. Why? Does your son consider himself a heroic prince? Does he want to kiss her and break the spell?" I couldn't keep the disdain from creeping into my voice.

Albion looked away and smiled sadly. "Not precisely, but in the absence of any other options, he thought it might be worth a go. He hasn't tried, but you can see why he'd want to. Bernard has no magic. Perhaps he thought that if he woke her she would fall in love with him and they'd be married, just like in the stories."

"How terribly romantic." The thought of him touching her made me ill.

Albion shrugged. "There are practical considerations, as you well know. He has no magic himself, but if Rowan's magic returned to her, their children could be quite amazing, given his family background."

That was something I could never give her, along with safety, an end to her pain, and the kind of love she'd grown up waiting for. As she'd said herself, I didn't even know what that word meant.

I turned to look at her again. *This was never going to work*, I thought. *I was never what she needed.* I'd wanted to help, and had done nothing but hurt her. I'd thought things could be different this time.

The room seemed to be becoming smaller, the air thicker. It was time to leave, at least for the day. "I'm sure you have other things to do today," I said.

"I do, in fact. Is something wrong?"

"No." I needed to get outdoors so I could breathe. "Please tell your wife that I mean no harm to you or your family. I just want Rowan to come back, and then I'll leave." Though I felt uncomfortable doing it with a near-stranger in the room, I stopped on my way to the window, leaned down, and kissed Rowan on the forehead.

Albion gasped. "Do that again," he said. "Her finger twitched." I did, but nothing happened. "Try again. Kiss her on the lips."

"This is rather awkward, I'd rather not—"

"It's important."

He was actually suggesting that it might work like in the old fairy tales, just like his idiot son.

This is ridiculous, I thought. I took a deep breath, leaned in, cupped her face in my hand, and kissed her cold lips.

Albion waited a moment, then sighed. "Nothing I could see," he said. "I'll have Emalda check her over, anyway. It was probably a silly idea."

I looked down at Rowan. She looked so peaceful. A real-life fairy-tale princess if ever there had been one. "Maybe not," I said. "Maybe I'm just not the prince she's waiting for."

I changed and flew out the window. Albion said something, but I wasn't listening. I was too busy trying to decide whether it would be better if I didn't come back.

Chapter Thirty-Six

Rowan

It was so peaceful there.

Time didn't seem to exist. There was no night or day, and the light filtering down through the forest canopy never seemed to change. I drifted off to sleep sometimes, but couldn't have counted how many times it happened, even if I'd thought to try. It wouldn't have meant anything to me, anyway.

I was curious about the place when I first arrived. I had no idea how I'd gotten to the forest, or what might have happened before I was there. But once I'd taken in the details of what was around me—the shimmering surface of a narrow river, the damp, earthy scent of its banks, the delicate ferns and the ancient, mossy trees that surrounded me—I completely lost track of the idea that there had been a "before." There was only the forest.

A path ran through the clearing where I rested. In one direction it curved between the trees, leading toward a place that seemed brighter. In the other direction it seemed to lead deeper into the woods. It was much darker that way, and there were bare branches and brambles choking the path, and arching tree roots waiting to trip unwary travelers. It seemed like I'd eventually have to choose to go one way or the other, but there was no hurry. I wasn't hungry or thirsty. I wasn't bored, though nothing ever happened except for an occasional breeze ruffling the highest leaves in the canopy.

The voice came so gradually that at first I didn't notice it as being something apart from the forest. It was nothing more than a whisper in the breeze that sounded like words in a language I didn't understand, and I forgot about it as soon as it stopped. When it happened again, it was clearer and more familiar. I lifted my head from where it had been resting on my arms, trying to find where the sound was coming from, and trying to figure out why it seemed to mean something. And then it was gone, but not quite forgotten, a lingering whisper clinging to a back corner of my mind.

The voice was clearer the next time I heard it, and for the first time since I'd settled in the forest, I remembered that there was something beyond that sheltered spot by the river, that there had been a *before*, and that there had once been other people.

I wandered around the edges of the clearing and up and down the river bank as far as I could, trying to tell where the voice was coming from, but it was no use. The sound was everywhere and nowhere at the same time.

The wind began to blow stronger, and for the first time, the light around me grew dimmer. The wind whispered my name. I'd forgotten that I had one.

A warm gale swept through the clearing. It twisted around me, blowing my hair into my face and sending a strange energy through my body, and then it disappeared completely. The voice disappeared, too, but it had done what I thought it came to do. I remembered that there was somewhere else I was supposed to be.

I sensed that my time in the forest was over, and I needed to choose a path. I just didn't know which way I was supposed to go.

Chapter Thirty-Seven

Aren

Emalda was waiting when I flew in through Rowan's window early that evening. She wore a black dress and a scowl, and the way she had her graying hair pulled back into a tight knot at her neck only emphasized the severity of her expression. Her pale blue eyes could have been cut from a mountain glacier.

I perched on the end of the bed and she watched me for a few minutes, then frowned and looked away while I changed and dressed.

When Emalda turned back, she waited for me to speak. I didn't try to read her thoughts. I didn't need to. The hate was obvious, the disgust and the pain. She poured three cups of whatever she'd prepared for Rowan and passed one to me, careful to not let our fingers touch.

"My father was a beekeeper," she said, finally breaking the silence. "He always told us that what's good for the queen is good for the hive. I've been hoping this would do something for Rowan, but it certainly won't hurt us. Drink." She took a sip from her cup, and I did the same.

The tea stung my mouth and made my eyes water, but the taste wasn't terrible. "What do you think?"

I cleared my throat. "I think it could probably wake the dead."

"Wouldn't that be something?" She finished her drink in a single gulp. "Would that I could have brought my sister back. Did you know she was a low-level Sorceress?"

"No."

"No, you wouldn't, would you? She had a special talent for reading people's bodies and determining what their troubles were, so her abilities complimented mine perfectly. We did good work in our town when we were younger. Long after I married and moved here, someone back at home irritated your father, and you were sent out to take care of the problem."

"I'm—"

"I'm not finished." Tears shone in her eyes, but her voice was steady. "I've waited five years to have you in front of me, and you're going to listen. Dorin was a peacemaker. I was visiting her when you stopped by our town. I told her not to go, but when she heard there was trouble in the square, she had to try to make people stop fighting. When I found her she was unconscious, bleeding from her head, bruised everywhere. There was nothing I could do except try to ease the pain. She suffered for two full days before she let go."

"I don't suppose it would help if I apologized."

"No," she snapped. "I don't want anything from you. I don't think you *can* be sorry. There's too much of your father in you." She stepped closer, fists clenched. "I don't

- 424 -

want you here. Nothing would make me happier than to turn you out and let you and your brother destroy each other. But my husband thinks that this poor, misguided girl needs you, and he seems to think he can accomplish something with you, as well. He's wrong. It's too late. But if it satisfies his curiosity or eases his guilt, perhaps that alone is worth something."

"His guilt?"

"About what happened to your mother. He still wonders what might have happened if she had brought you back here instead of staying with that monster. He would have let her come back. They sent letters, talked about it before she died. She refused. He loved her, though, even after what she did to him."

My mouth went dry as I realized why Albion looked so familiar. "She was his daughter."

"You didn't know?" That seemed to please her. "By his third wife, before me. He has the decency to take his wives one at a time, but he's been around for a long time. He sees your mother in you, and it blinds him to what you really are."

Someone knocked at the door, and it creaked open. "May I join you now?" Albion asked Emalda, and she nodded.

"Of course," she said. She took the third cup to Rowan and poured a few drops at a time into her mouth, then checked her pulse and pinched the skin on the back of one hand. She turned back to Albion. "He can stay until she wakes, or until we decide his presence is doing nothing to help her." She looked at me. "After that, you are no longer welcome in my home or on this island. Do you understand?"

"Yes." It was hard not to say anything else. I knew she was right to be angry, but I wasn't accustomed to being spoken to so disrespectfully by someone like her. It had been bad enough to be insulted by Mariana, who had earned my respect and who had once cared for me. To take such abuse from a stranger was much more difficult.

Emalda left us and closed the door behind her, and Albion let out a long breath. "She'll be back."

"I do hope so," I said, and immediately regretted it.

Albion frowned. "I'm sure she's not easy for you to get along with, but she has good reasons for feeling the way she does about you. I'm surprised she's willing to let this happen at all. Emalda is a better woman than you know. Not everyone would make these compromises."

"But she's not making them for me."

He had turned to check on Rowan, and spoke without looking back. "She told you."

"Why didn't you say something when I asked yesterday?"

"I thought you had enough on your mind without all of that." He stood straight and crossed his arms. "Perhaps I was concerned that you'd hold me responsible in part for what happened to Magdalena, because of the letters."

"No. Learning that she wasn't a traitor is the best news I've had in years." The letters that got her killed had been nothing more threatening than correspondence with her father. One more thing Severn would answer for if I ever saw him again.

Albion sank into the chair nearest the bed. "There's so much I'd like to tell you, and to ask you, but there's not time. Rowan is holding up for now, but we don't know how long her body can go on like this. Emalda had an idea last night, though. You can get into people's minds?"

"In a sense, but—"

"Were you ever able to do it with Rowan?"

And then I understood what he was suggesting. "Not while she was awake."

Albion nodded. "I wondered. Would you be willing to try it now?"

"You mean sleep here?"

"It would be easier than moving her to the lighthouse."

I sat down to think. It was probably impossible. Rowan wasn't sleeping. If she was dreaming or thinking anything at all, it was at a far deeper level than I'd ever tried to reach. It would be dangerous. I could lose myself completely, and even attempting it would leave me vulnerable to attack.

But if there's a chance…

"I'll need to be alone with her. I can't have anyone else in the room." Albion didn't say anything. "Emalda wants someone watching, doesn't she?"

"She suggested supervision, yes. She may be concerned for the girl's safety—"

"Rowan has been with me for quite some time. I'm not going to hurt her now."

"Indeed. But there may be a concern of what could happen in a circumstance like this. Also, there's the possibility of the students finding out. We have strict rules about propriety, and Emalda wouldn't want to make an exception for someone like... well, for you." He sounded apologetic. It didn't help. "Let me speak to her. Perhaps if I slept in there?" He gestured toward an open door that led to a smaller bedroom. "I think that's the best I can offer. I'll close the door, if it helps."

"Not really. Better you than her or someone else, I suppose." A headache was brewing behind my eyes. "I'll do what I can. That's all I can promise."

#

I returned long after dark, having spent the hours between visits flying, trying to tire myself and make it more likely that I'd sleep.

And I planned.

Albion seemed trustworthy, but then, so did I when I needed to. Even if he meant no harm to me or Rowan, there were still other people in the building. There was that window that would be so easy for someone to get in through. I would have to leave a significant part of my awareness in the room, ready to pull me back if there was trouble. To do otherwise might let me deeper into Rowan's mind, but the risks were too great. It would have to be enough.

Emalda offered to make me something to help me sleep, but I declined. I needed to be able to wake quickly, and I didn't trust her. The woman looked like she'd just swallowed something bitter every time she looked at me, and it seemed an unnecessary risk.

After she left and Albion retired to the adjacent bedroom, I focused on leaving a portion of my awareness in the room. I lay down beside Rowan and tried to clear my thoughts so I could drift off.

Jumbled and confusing images of the past few months filled my mind. After some time, dreams began to crowd in. Rowan was running away from me, and when I looked down, my hands were massive, scaly things with dangerous claws. I dreamed I was consumed by fire, and then that I woke with Rowan safe beside me, back at the Grotto. There was a dream where Rowan was asleep in a tower like a story-book princess, guarded by a red dragon and missing for a hundred years. But none of those versions of Rowan were real or reachable.

I reluctantly relaxed my hold on reality, and slipped deeper into something that was like a dream, and yet not. The world expanded around me and lost the surreal, slippery quality that always gave my dreams away. This was a different state, one I'd never experienced before.

I flew over a large expanse of water in my eagle body. There was land in the distance, but the wind was pushing me back as fast as I could fly forward. The colors of the clouds and the water were muted, and the sound of the waves and wind seemed to not quite reach me, but this place felt far more real than any of my previous dreams. If I was going to find Rowan, it would be here.

I tried diving down to get under the wind, but huge waves threatened to soak me. There was no getting above the storm, either. Lightning flashed through the clouds each time I tried. The wind pushed me back again and again, and each time it did, the bedroom flashed into my mind—the window with moonlight shining through, shadows of the elm tree on the floor, the wind whistling at the corner of the building. Two doors fought for my attention, one I would never be invited through, and another that sat open just enough that I couldn't be sure no one was going to come through. Albion was awake on the other side.

The more I focused on the real world, the harder the winds pushed me back in the dream. A sudden gust sent me tumbling toward the water, and I barely managed to climb back into the air before a massive wave could soak my feathers. I was growing tired, and knew I couldn't keep flying for much longer. Staying would be far too dangerous. I sensed that an accident in this strange world would have very real consequences. There was also a chance that if I went any deeper I would lose myself completely in her mind. I decided to pull back and try again after I'd had a chance to wake and come up with a better plan.

The bedroom began to solidify in my mind, and one more thing caught my attention. *Rowan.* There was the tiniest hint of a frown on her brow, and her hand twitched—the one I could see myself holding. She was responding to my presence, but it wasn't enough yet. I knew then what I had to do.

I gave up.

I let go of the consciousness that held me to the room and to my body, not knowing whether I would be back. It didn't matter. What mattered lay beyond the storm. I let myself fall completely into the dream, and the colors and sounds of that place blazed to brilliant life.

I found a channel of calm over the water, between the

howling winds that still grabbed at my wings if I drifted to one side or the other. I flew forward, and rushed toward the land ahead me.

Towering stone cliffs rose from the water, and storm waves pounded on the jagged rocks at their base. A warm breeze pushed me from behind, and I rose over the edge of the cliff. Dark trees formed a line just past a rocky, barren field next to the cliffs. Strange vines wound their way through the trees, and mosses blanketed the rocky ground. Some unfamiliar bird trilled in the distance, and I realized that this place reminded me of the dreary woods in Rowan's dream.

I flew over the trees, searching for a path, a clearing, any indication that I'd find what I was looking for.

"Rowan!" I'd expected to have nothing but bird noises come out, but my own voice echoed out over the endless forest. How long had I been flying? Every muscle in my body burned from the effort, but I couldn't rest. I was running out of time. If I woke, I might not get another chance to come back.

"Rowan!" I called again, desperately listening for the response I wanted more than anything I'd ever wanted in my life.

There was nothing. My hope faltered. Perhaps I'd been wrong, and this was nothing but an empty dreamscape.

Then, from somewhere near a river that was just barely visible, sparkling beneath a break in the trees…

"Aren!"

I turned and forced my aching wings to beat harder, pushing toward the river, my heart pounding. *Please don't let this be just a dream*, I thought. I dropped toward the treetops.

Chapter Thirty-Eight

Rowan

Nothing had changed, except that now I was waiting. I couldn't quite wrap my mind around what it was that I was waiting for, but I held desperately to the idea that there was *something*. When I felt myself drifting back into the haziness that had held me before, I brought the voice back to mind. If I could remember it speaking my name, I could remember myself, if only in a vague way. Layers of fog in my mind kept me from remembering exactly what my name was, but I knew the voice had said it.

I heard it again, once. It was distant and muffled, not speaking any words that I could understand, but hearing it again filled me with relief and longing. "Don't forget me," I whispered.

I paced the edges of the clearing, counting my footsteps and finding it impossible to keep track of the numbers. The dark path was still dull and shadowy and vaguely frightening, while the other path remained bright and inviting. It smelled good, too, like there might be a meadow just around that bend in the path, filled with warm sunlight and sweet peas and clover. Maybe strawberries. I stepped onto the path, intending to go just far enough to see, when a sound froze me where I stood.

"Rowan!"

The voice again. So close and so clear, coming from somewhere above me. I noticed my heartbeat. Had that been there before? Certainly not so loud or so fast. I knew that this was important. Rowan was my name, I was sure of that, but who did the voice belong to? I felt the memory becoming clearer, but still just out of reach.

"Rowan!" the voice called again, and everything came flooding back—the world I'd grown up in, my family, my past, magic, and pain, and a long journey. And…

"Aren!" My voice was far too quiet. I cleared my throat, took a deep breath, and shouted again. "Aren!"

I kept yelling, not really aware of what I was saying, desperate to be heard. A shadow passed over the clearing, and I looked up in time to see a winged shape gliding overhead, gone before I could wave my arms to attract attention.

Which way had he gone? Suddenly I couldn't keep any of it straight in my mind. I ran to the river and shielded my eyes against the sun, searching the sky, seeing nothing.

"Rowan?" His voice was behind me now. I spun around to see him standing at the place where the dark path met the clearing. Almost. I almost saw him. He didn't seem real, and I could make out the shapes of the trees behind him. I stepped slowly toward him and halted a few steps away. I was in shadow there, and I could see him better without the sun in my eyes.

"I can hardly see you," he said.

"I'm here." My voice cracked again.

He held out a hand and I tried to take it. There was nothing there but warmth. Nothing I could hold on to. An empty pit opened inside of me. "Are you alive?" I asked. He certainly looked like a ghost.

He smiled. "Yes."

Another thought occurred to me. "Am I?"

"So far," he said. "I don't know for how long, though. You've been gone for too long."

"I thought so." I took a long look around the clearing. "I want to go back with you."

He looked behind him, listening for something. "This way," he said. As I watched, he flickered out, then returned. "I don't think I can stay here."

"You've been in my dreams before."

"I don't think this is really a dream," he said. "Not for you. Maybe that's why I can't see you properly."

"Guess we'd better go then." I wanted desperately to take his hand, but all we could do was walk beside one another, occasionally overlapping when we climbed over a fallen branch or dodged a boulder. He kept disappearing, and appeared less substantial every time he returned. A crashing noise grew louder as we stepped out of the forest onto unfamiliar, stony ground. I could barely see Aren in the bright sunlight.

He pointed out over the water. "That's how I flew in."

I stepped closer to the cliff. There was no way down. No path, no handholds, no boat at the bottom to carry me home, just rocks and crashing waves a terrifying distance below me. I stepped back. I'd always been afraid of heights.

When I turned toward Aren again, he was gone. I waited, but he didn't reappear. I wondered whether he could still see or hear me, or if he was awake now, waiting for me to follow. I walked along the cliff, but everything around me stayed the same.

Ahead of me and behind me, the edge of the land stretched out in a straight line as far as I could see. Below me, that horrible drop to the rocks, the water, and waves that crashed so hard that the spray wet my skin. The path into the forest was still there, ready and waiting. I knew that I could go back, that the sweet-smelling path to the meadow would be there for me. But I also understood that while going that way would lead me to a beautiful place, maybe a better place, it would never lead me home. My body would die. I would never see Aren again.

I turned back toward the cliff. My heart slammed, and my stomach tried to climb into my throat.

I hope this is a dream.

I closed my eyes, leaned forward, and dived off of the edge.

At first it didn't feel like falling, aside from the wind rushing into my face. The sound of the waves quickly grew louder, though, and nothing happened. I didn't transform into a bird or a fish, the waves and the rocks didn't disappear. The roaring beneath me only grew louder. I forced my eyes open and was faced with the unforgiving surface of a huge rock, so close that I could see the barnacles clinging to its cratered surface. I threw my arms around my head, knowing that it wouldn't do any good.

The impact knocked the wind out of me, but was considerably softer than I'd expected. It didn't even hurt, once I managed to draw a breath. The air didn't smell like salt, but like air-dried laundry, and I felt warm again. My body was heavy, though, and it was a struggle to pull my arms away from my face, to drag them down over the soft, smooth surface my body rested on.

When I manage to force my eyelids open, I found myself in an unfamiliar room. Moonlight flooded in through a large window near the end of the bed. My neck was stiff, but I managed to turn my head to the left. Furniture—a sitting area with sofa and chair. A glass vase of flowers and a teapot on a low table in the middle. A bookshelf, too far away for me to be able to see what kind of books it held. Interesting, but not at all what I was looking for.

I took a deep breath and forced my head to turn the other way.

Aren lay beside me, still asleep. His breath was heavy, but uneven. Dreaming. Was he trying to get back to me? Or perhaps he'd made it back, and found that I had disappeared.

I only enjoyed the sight for a moment while I worked up a bit more strength, enough to try moving my fingers, to lift my hand to his face. His cheek felt rough under my fingers.

I lifted my head and slowly shifted my body toward his, every movement a little easier than the one before it. I thought I might cry. Instead, I leaned in and kissed him, brushing my lips gently over his, then pressing harder, not wanting to let go.

His eyes snapped open.

"Hey, sleeping beauty," I whispered. "What took you so long?"

Chapter Thirty-Nine

Aren

"Rowan?"

She kissed me again, and laughed. She was back, no question—bright eyes, mischievous grin, and looking like she'd just wakened from nothing more than an incredibly restful nap.

I looked past her at the door that separated her room from Albion's, waiting for it to open, but nothing happened. He didn't know she was awake, or he was giving us a little more time. Either way, I would take it.

Rowan laid her head back down on the pillow, and I ran my fingers through her hair. She sighed and closed her eyes. I pulled my hand back, and her eyes blinked open. "Why did you stop?"

"I didn't want you falling asleep again."

She smiled. "For the first time in a long time, sleep is the last thing on my mind." She touched my face again, brushing her thumb over my eyebrows, smoothing away the tension. "You look like you could use a little more, though."

"Probably. But not now." Her hands were still cold, but felt so good touching me.

"You can sleep," she said. "I'm not going anywhere."

I'd always thought heartache was a sentimental concept imagined by someone with no understanding of the human body and even less sense, but I was learning I'd been wrong. This hurt.

"I want to ask where we are, and what happened," she said, and traced her fingers over my face, pausing over the faint scar on my chin that magic had yet to heal completely. "But I need to say something first. Back at our camp—"

"I'm sorry for all of that. For lying, for not trusting you to decide for yourself, trying to push you away. I—" I hesitated, searching for an excuse or a way to gloss it over, but there was none. "I was wrong."

Her face broke into a warm smile. Perhaps she understood how difficult those words were for me. "I'm sorry, too," she whispered. "I said some horrible things. I was just so angry. But I do love you. And I was coming back."

"It's okay to be angry." I took her hand, and her fingers curled between mine. "Maybe not as often as I am, but sometimes. And I promise, no more lies. No more keeping information from you for your own good."

"And maybe we'll try to be more understanding of each other when we get it wrong." She turned to look around the room, taking in everything that the moonlight revealed.

"Don't let your curiosity kill you," I said, and she laughed quietly.

"Is this Belleisle?" she asked, and I nodded. "And they're letting you stay?" She sounded cautious, as though she knew she wasn't going to get what she wanted this time.

"Well, for now. Just don't talk too loudly. It's temporary." The door to Albion's room opened wide enough to allow his fox face to peer into the room. "Never mind."

"What?" Rowan turned toward the door, still moving slowly, and gasped. She pushed herself up to sit with her back against the pillows and watched the fox slink into the room. He leaped onto the bed, landing so lightly that he seemed to be made of air, and sat with his enormous tail wrapped around his black-gloved paws, head tilted to one side, watching Rowan.

He looked at me next. "Not yet, please," I said, and he gave a little nod before turning back to Rowan.

"Rowan," I said, "may I introduce Ernis Albion. My grandfather." She looked from him to me in surprise, then back. "He and his wife have been caring for you. If I'm not mistaken, you're to stay here while you recover. Perhaps longer, if your magic returns." The fox nodded again. "They'll teach you how to use it properly."

"Oh," she said, and held out one hand. The fox stepped closer and sniffed it. They looked into each other's eyes, and I wondered whether he could read something in her that I couldn't. He spun and bounced to the end of the bed, made a playful bow to us, and trotted out of the room.

"What was that all about?" Rowan asked.

"I was just about to tell you. I'm still not welcome here. I was able to stay as long as I might help bring you back, but no longer. You're here now, which means my time is up."

Anger flashed across her features. "But that's so unfair!" she whispered. "I wouldn't be here without you. You saved my life." She pulled herself closer to me and curled up with her face pressed to my chest.

I traced circles on her back with my fingers, unsure how else to make her feel better. She didn't move or speak, but I felt my shirt growing damp. I wondered whether she cried so much when I wasn't around.

"We make a good team, you know," I said.

"We do. So what am I supposed to do without you? I don't even know these people."

"I might point out that you didn't know me a few weeks ago, either. They're good people, Rowan. This is my fault, not theirs. They have students here, and they don't want my kind of influence around them. Or around you, I suppose."

I could tell she wanted to say something to that, but she seemed to change her mind and instead sat up and wiped her eyes on the sleeve of her nightgown. "Is there no chance you can stay? Like with the merfolk?"

I remembered the hate in Emalda's eyes when she looked at me. "No. If there's any way I can come back to see you, I will, but it's better for everyone if Severn knows I'm not here. Especially for you. These past few weeks, though... they've been amazing, in spite of the crazy parts."

"The best."

It wasn't long before the day's first light glowed in the window, followed all too quickly by a bright, clear sunrise, and a knock at the door. Albion entered, followed by Emalda, who carried a tray loaded with breakfast foods, a towel-wrapped teapot, and several labeled glass jars filled with dried leaves, berries, roots, and scraps of bark.

I stood and moved out of the way, and Emalda took

over the space around the bed.

She smiled at Rowan, a warm, kind expression I hadn't seen on her before. "Hello, my dear," she said. "Welcome back."

Rowan returned the smile, but she looked wary as her eyes searched Emalda's. "Thank you. Aren tells me you've been taking excellent care of me."

Emalda's smile tightened at the sound of my name, then relaxed. "Well, it seems he's done well too, hasn't he?"

"I never would have found my way back without him."

"Is that so?" Emalda glanced back at me. "I'm very glad. We were beginning to think you were lost forever. Are you hungry?"

Rowan's stomach growled loud enough for everyone to hear, and she grimaced. "I think I might be," she said, and Albion carried the tray of food over to the bed.

Emalda came toward me, her lips pressed together in a hard line.

"She's out of danger now," she said quietly. "I'll do some tests after she's eaten, see what she needs to get her strength back. It seems to me that she's empty of magic right now. It might not come back, you know." She looked up and stared straight into my eyes, challenging me. "Does that change your feelings or intentions toward her?"

"No. But it might change your son's."

She raised an eyebrow, then glanced over her shoulder and saw Rowan watching us. "Might we speak in private?"

Emalda started toward the other room, pausing at the bed to test the temperature of Rowan's forehead. "Please eat. We'll be back."

The room Albion had slept in was much smaller and more plainly decorated than Rowan's, with a desk beside the narrow bed and a door opening into the hall. "Extra student room," Emalda said, and gestured for me to sit in a hard-backed chair. She stood looking out the window. "We have a problem."

"I know, you need me to go. If I could just stay until she's comfortable here—"

"Please don't interrupt me." She waved her hand toward the door. "The problem is this. Not her. She seems like a sweet girl, and we're happy to help her. If what you've told Ernis about her is true, she's the sort we'd take as a student under normal circumstances, though she would have started at a much younger age. She can work to pay her tuition, and I know Ernis will be interested to learn from her experiences. But she seems quite attached to you."

She drummed her fingers on the window sill. "Ernis and I spoke this morning when he came to tell me she was awake. He thinks that for now it would be best if you stayed. He says it's for her, but I know he has a personal interest in your situation. He's left the decision entirely to me." She turned to face me straight-on. "Tell me, are you sorry for the things you've done?"

It's none of your business. "Yes."

"Were you sorry when these things happened, or only now that it matters to me, someone who has every intention of separating you from the only person who seems to be important to you? Though I doubt you care as much for her as she thinks you do." Contempt dripped from her voice.

I wasn't going to open up to her or beg for forgiveness, and I certainly didn't owe it to her to explain what Rowan meant to me. Still, I pushed my pride aside and answered as I had to.

"I wasn't sorry at the time, but I am now. For all of it."

Her lips tightened. "If only I could believe it. I can't know for certain, can I? I lack your gifts." She sighed. "It doesn't matter. Nothing you say will bring my sister back, or any of the others."

She went to the door and looked in on Albion and Rowan, and her expression softened. "I'm doing this for him, not for you," she said softly, and looked back over her shoulder at me. "You can stay. Not in this house, and not for long. If you want to be here, you're going to work. Goodness knows there's enough to be done around here, especially once the rest of the students return. You will have no unauthorized contact with the students, you will follow the rules as I give them, and you will not use any form of magic on any living creature on this island. I expect that if your presence becomes a threat to any of us—"

"I'll leave before that happens." It took a moment for my mind to process her words. Had she really just said that I could stay? The strict conditions troubled me—not because I couldn't follow them, but because they were obviously a way for Emalda to try to control me. I didn't know how much of her contempt and disrespect I'd be able to take. I was already feeling the pressure of it. But still, I'd be with Rowan. My heart leapt at the thought.

"I'll accept your conditions."

She nodded and turned back to the other room. "I

think it's best for her that you be here for now, until she's more comfortable and we know what her situation will be. I hope you understand that she'll have some decisions to make that may be difficult for both of you."

I had already considered the fact that we'd been pushed together by extraordinary circumstances. It was possible that she wouldn't see me the same way when our surroundings changed, that she'd see who I was more clearly, that she would realize that she didn't need me. "I'll stay for as long as she wants me, and as long as I'm permitted."

"I suppose that's settled, then."

I followed Emalda back into Rowan's room, lightheaded with relief. Rowan sat in one of the soft chairs laughing at something Albion was saying. She stopped when she saw us.

Emalda pursed her lips and busied herself with organizing the herbs on her tray. Rowan watched her, then turned to me. "Are you... I mean, can you..."

"Yes. For now." Rowan gasped and jumped up from her chair, almost falling over as she tried to run to me. She laughed when I caught her in my arms and pulled her close.

"And none of that, miss," Emalda said over her shoulder. "I'll have no bad example set for the students, especially if you become one."

Rowan just grinned and held me tighter.

#

Albion and Rowan exchanged a seemingly endless stream of questions as Emalda carried out her tests, which involved checking Rowan's strength while she held different plants under her tongue, then having her taste different mixtures from the kitchen. Though the teas probably tasted terrible, I thought that this testing was vastly preferable to the merfolk's experiments.

I sat in the corner beside the window, joining in the conversation when invited, but staying silent most of the time. Emalda's fists clenched every time I spoke, and it annoyed me.

I felt as though I hadn't slept at all. My eyes kept drifting closed, and my muscles ached as though they'd actually pulled me through a storm. My mind raced, though. The realization that we'd never be safe as long as Severn was alive began to overshadow my elation at being allowed to stay, and I started planning again.

I wanted nothing more than for Albion and Emalda to leave so that I could be alone with Rowan and talk through my ideas with her—an exciting notion, now that I'd accepted it. But there was no chance. They held her attention all afternoon.

In spite of her insistence that she'd never want to sleep again, Rowan grew tired and began yawning well before sunset. Emalda hurried through the last few tests and said she'd send someone up with enough supper for both of us. "But just for tonight," she added as she hoisted her tray and left the room. "Then he's out."

I moved to the sofa, and Rowan lay down and rested her head on my lap. Birds twittered in the branches outside of the open window, and a few younger students yelled as they played outdoors. Otherwise, all was quiet. I thought

Rowan had fallen asleep, but she opened her eyes and took my hand, winding her fingers between mine and resting them on her stomach.

"So what happens now?" she asked.

"Hmm?"

"After the handsome prince wakes the girl. Isn't that the end of the story? The happily ever after part?"

It hardly seemed like it. She still had a lot of work ahead of her to get her magic back and learn how to use it. As for me...

"I think life just goes on," I said. "Severn is going to come for us. You might be his worst enemy, now."

"So what do we do?"

"I'll stay while you get settled, but then I leave." She winced, but had obviously been expecting this. "But I'm not going to run away from Severn this time. I'm going to destroy him."

"I'll help you."

"I think you'll have work to do here. If your magic comes back, you'll have to work hard to learn to use it. Ernis and Emalda will help you, but it's not going to be easy."

"No, I suppose not. But if you're going to need me to save your ass again some day, I might as well be prepared." She smiled, but worry creased her brow.

"Not the happy ending you were hoping for?"

She shrugged. "There's always more to the story, right?" She struggled to sit up, then pressed her lips to mine. I tangled my fingers in her wild hair and pulled her closer still, and for a brief moment felt the tiniest spark of her magic. She pulled back, rested her forehead against mine, and sighed. "We can have happily ever after later."

"Of course," I said.

I didn't believe it, but I wanted to.

The End

Dear Reader

Thank you for taking this journey with me! I hope you've enjoyed reading this story as much as I enjoyed writing it. If you had a good time, please consider leaving a review on e-book purchasing sites and/or on Goodreads—they're so important. Tell your friends, if you think they'd like it. Tell your family. Tell your dog's previous owner's girlfriend's little sister. Word of mouth is life for a new book, and your support helps me continue producing stories for you to enjoy.

For information on upcoming releases, deleted scenes, bonus stories, cover reveals, news, release parties, and a chance at free advance copies, join my mailing list! Never spammy, always fun.

And on that note…

Watch for the story to continue in Torn, coming Winter 2015.

Much love,
Kate

About the Author

Kate Sparkes was born in Hamilton, Ontario, but now resides in Newfoundland, where she tries not to talk too much about the dragons she sees in the fog. She lives with a Mountie, two kids who take turns playing Jeckyll and Hyde, three cats with more personality than most people she meets, and the saddest-looking dog on the planet. She'll keep writing and sharing stories as long as her imagination lets her, and assuming the dragons don't eat her.

Facebook: www.facebook.com/katesparkesauthor
Twitter: @kate_sparkes
Blog: disregardtheprologue.com
Mailing list: http://mad.ly/signups/96420/join

Special Thanks

To my early readers— Shannon Andrews, Hayley Morgan, Mike Lowden, Katelyn Lowden, Kat Armstrong Nicholson, and Scott Holley: your encouragement has been the difference between this book going up for sale or going in the trash. Thanks for the support and love, guys. And to Jennifer Cousteils and Alana Terry, thanks for the last-minute typo spotting in early ARCs.

To my critique partners— KL Schwengel and Linda Washington: your tact and honesty pushed me farther than I knew I was capable of going, and your faith that I could pull this off encouraged me to throw my whole ass into it (not just half, which was so tempting, so often).

To my editor, Joshua Essoe— You are the master of the shit sandwich. Thanks for the encouragement, the kind words, and the tough love when the manuscript needed it. You made this book better than I ever hoped it would be.

To my cover designer, Ravven— Thank you for your patience in the face of my indecisiveness, and for the beautiful artwork you've created for this book.

To my family, Andre, Simon and Ike— I know this process hasn't been easy for any of you. Living with a person with her mind in another world 78% of the time is a challenge, but you all rose to it. I love you so much.

To God— Thanks for getting me through the tough times and blessing me with an imagination that just won't behave.

And to my parents— None of this would have been possible without you. I mean, literally… I wouldn't be here. But also for your love and support. Mom, if you ever get through this book and read this page, I'll give you a medal.

33916665R00276

Made in the USA
Lexington, KY
17 July 2014